INTO THE WINDS OF FEAR

by
W. J. Brown

PublishAmerica
Baltimore

© 2005 by W.J. Brown.
All rights reserved. No part of this book may be reproduced, stored in a retrieval system or transmitted in any form or by any means without the prior written permission of the publishers, except by a reviewer who may quote brief passages in a review to be printed in a newspaper, magazine or journal.

First printing

ISBN: 1-4137-6060-0
PUBLISHED BY PUBLISHAMERICA, LLLP
www.publishamerica.com
Baltimore

Printed in the United States of America

*To my wife Nancy, who nourishes in me
a joyful disposition, a love of adventure,
an appreciation for family, and a playful imagination.*

Epigraph Page

No passion so effectually robs the mind of all its powers of acting and reasoning as fear.

-Edmond Burke
On the Sublime and Beautiful, II, ii

For God hath not given us the spirit of fear, but of love, power, and a sound mind.

-St. Paul to Timothy
II Timothy 1:7

Preface

In response to the terrorist attacks on September 11, 2001, the United States established the Department of Homeland Security and launched a military campaign to destroy terrorist networks threatening its citizens. As a result, thousands of terrorists who declared war on the U.S. have been killed or captured and dozens of terrorist plots have been quietly disrupted.

Unknown to most Americans, other plots in progress are hotly being pursued by unpublicized heroes who risk their lives daily to make sure the horrific intentions of terrorists never come to fruition. *Into the Winds of Fear* is a story of one such battle, fictional but reflecting the reality of today's worldwide conflict. We can be thankful that a great many of those who guard our safety do so with vigilance, divine guidance, and unselfish commitment to the ideals by which our forefathers founded this nation.

Introduction

Since the terrorist attacks against the United States on September 11, 2001 until January of 2005, the U.S. spent an estimated 150 billion dollars fighting terrorists in Afghanistan and Iraq and ousting the regimes that provided havens for them. In 2005, the U.S. was spending about 6 billion dollars per month stabilizing Afghanistan and Iraq and protecting their citizens against continued terrorist attacks. The Department of Homeland Security has spent more than 100 billion dollars since 9-11 overseeing 22 agencies protecting the U.S., and President Bush has allotted more than 41 billion dollars for the Department of Homeland Security for the 2006 annual budget. Fighting terrorism around the world and homeland security to prevent further terrorist attacks in the U.S. will likely cost U.S. tax payers more than 10 billion dollars a month in the foreseeable future. This number is approaching 1,000 dollars per person annually for those paying federal income taxes.

Yet, despite these enormous sums of money, Americans are still extremely vulnerable to terrorist attacks both abroad and at home. The cost of truly securing our borders against all forms of security breaches would be astronomical. There are more than 6,000 miles of contiguous coastline to defend on the east and west coasts of the U.S., excluding Alaska and Hawaii.

Although much attention has been given to deliberating how to protect the 2000-mile span along the U.S.-Mexico border, the 5,000 mile U.S.-Canada border is even a greater challenge. Much of this border can be breached by boat. The coastline of the Great Lakes is 10,900 miles, more than half of it bordering nine U.S. states. Probably the least amount of attention has been given to this security threat.

Likewise, the metropolitan areas of New York City and Los Angeles have received the most critical attention to preparing for terrorist attacks, while the nation's heartland has received much less attention. Yet it is in the nation's heartland where terrorists would love to score a victory.

A simple analysis of homeland defense shows that it is not the amount of money we spend that will provide the protection needed, but it will be the continued heroic acts of ordinary people who will risk their lives to protect their fellow citizens who will stop the terrorists from being successful.

Acknowledgments

I wish to thank Dr. Dennis Hensley of Taylor University and Dr. Gillette Elvgren of Regent University, two accomplished authors and colleagues who provided substantial encouragement and very helpful feedback on multiple drafts of this work. I also thank my colleagues at Regent University for creating an atmosphere of creativity and achievement and for a university administration that values research, scholarship, writing and publication, both academic and professional.

The idea for the great cover design is contributed by my colleague, Markus Pfeiffer, who continually helps me to make my computer do what I want it to do. I greatly appreciate the tireless efforts of my administrative assistant, Suzanne Morton, who knows a good novel when she sees one and whose Master's degree in English has always enhanced my written work that invariably ends up on her desk.

I especially thank my wife and two daughters, Natalie and Heidi who provided inspiration for my characters and gave me time to write. Finally, I thank my mother and father for their constant encouragement and confidence in me, and I thank Nancy's parents, who love and accept me as one of their own. May you all enjoy this great adventure and overcome every fear you face.

W. Joseph Brown
February 17, 2005
Chesapeake, Virginia

About the Author

W. Joseph Brown is Professor and Research Fellow in the School of Communication and the Arts at Regent University. He held the position as Dean of the College of Communication and the Arts at Regent University for ten years before becoming a Research Fellow. He received his Bachelor of Science Degree in Environmental Science from Purdue University, his Masters Degree in Communication Management from the Annenberg School of Communication at USC in Los Angeles, and his Masters and Doctorate in Communication from the University of Southern California. His academic research interests include media effects, terrorism, social influence, and celebrity influence. He has published numerous academic journal articles and book chapters in the field of communication during the past 15 years, and writes both fiction and non-fiction. His most recent work is on biological terrorism.

Dr. Brown has taught classes at the University of Southern California, the University of Hawaii, the University of the Nations, and Regent University. He travels extensively to conduct research and to write. During the past four years he has been working in Africa each summer with funding from the U.S. Department of Defense to produce HIV/AIDS prevention films. Dr. Brown has conducted research and lectured in more than thirty nations.

CHAPTER 1
Kailua-Kona, Hawaii

Niloa's parents waved good-bye as she slowly propelled her 42-foot sailboat away from the Kona shore.

"Tell me we're not crazy, letting her go alone during the typhoon season," complained her mother with a sigh.

"We didn't let her. This is her choice." Chris replied.

"She's 21, Chris. We have to let go sometime. At least she knows how to sail the Pacific as well as anyone, thanks to you."

"Hey – she chose to sail solo against my counsel. I told her it was not safe for a young single woman."

"But you taught her well, Chris."

"I know. I just wish she had inherited your caution rather than my recklessness," Chris replied, wrapping his strong arms tightly around his wife.

Nanci leaned forward and kissed him. "Don't worry honey," she whispered, "God's with her in spite of herself."

Chris, though he disliked having to bring God into everything, knew Nanci was right. He had been holding his daughter to a different standard than he had lived by. In retrospect, he regretted allowing himself to get into a big argument with his only daughter. He had given her such a hard time when she said she planned to sail alone from Hawaii to the Solomon Islands.

"Remember her first solo race?" Chris asked.

"Yeah," Nanci recalled, "We were crazy then—letting her race at age 12."

"It was only the teen novice program!" Chris defended.

"We should have gotten a clue after she won the Big Island to Maui race that she would never settle for a normal life," Chris continued.

"She was just 16 then and it seems like yesterday," Nanci said sadly. "I'm going to miss her. I still wish she had not quit school."

"She'll eventually finish – only needs 16 more credit hours," Chris replied.

"If she lives long enough," Nanci chided. "I don't think she knows the meaning of the phrase "too risky."

"No, she does," Chris answered. "I remember saying once, 'Niloa, is there any danger you're not attracted to?'"

"What did she say?"

She said. "Yeah, Dad. Illegal drugs, drunken parties, and casual sex. After that I decided to be content that she had finally developed a moral backbone."

"Are you sure she just didn't get sick of drinking and sleeping around?" Nanci asked sarcastically.

"We've been through this discussion before," Chris answered in frustration with a tinge of anger. "I'm sure she has changed. She isn't stupid or irresponsible, just fearless.

Remember, she did just win the Rolex Yachtswoman of the Year."

"I'm sorry, honey." Nanci replied. "I still hurt from the six months of hell she put us through. I do believe she has changed. It's taking a long time to rebuild my trust."

As Niloa stood on deck gazing at her parents, tears filled her eyes. She wondered if they would ever understand her internal struggles, the pressure she felt to perform, to become something great, to measure up to their expectations.

She thought about her three new sponsors: Compaq, Pepsi, and American Airlines, who would help fund her competition in the *Around Alone* yacht race, the longest solo race in the world. She knew the 27,000 nautical mile course spanned some of the most dangerous and remote oceans on earth. She looked forward to racing against world-class sailors like Isabelle Autissier of France, Giovanni Soldini of Italy, and Mike Golding of the United Kingdom, sailors she both admired and emulated. Yet, deep inside she still felt an empty place in her heart.

She remembered one of the conversations she had with Mike before a race. He had asked her, "Niloa, do you like training alone?"

"I love it—like a long distance runner. Me and the *Dawn Treader II* on the open ocean. Nothing like it!"

She realized that she loved to train alone. Practice sailing trips were her most favorite times, especially when she was just sailing for the pleasure of it. She had always wanted to sail alone to the Solomon Islands, but not in a race, just by herself at leisure.

I have one more summer to prepare for the Around Alone race, she thought. *This was the right decision, despite my parents' misgivings. Dad made his first trans-Pacific solo trip when he was only 19. I'm two years older.*

Although Niloa's life was full of excitement externally, she was becoming more dissatisfied internally. Sailing consumed most of her time. She had few opportunities to develop deep friendships and wasn't interested in meeting people at the drinking parties that were a part of the sailing culture, a culture that almost ruined her life and strained her relationship with her parents. She was bright, attractive, physically fit, kind, and courageous; but also shy, insecure, and melancholic. She went through deep bouts of depression and self-doubt. She had a room full of trophies but felt she had made very little difference in the world.

It's ironic, she thought, that people who work in office buildings, or who drive taxis, or who collect tolls on freeways, or who clean schools at night, or who do any one of thousands of jobs they consider to be mundane, have more influence on other people than I have had as a solo yacht racer. Niloa wanted her life to count for something more.

"Mom and Dad," she had argued, "what could be more therapeutic than sailing from Hawaii to the Solomon Islands alone? I need some time alone. I could meditate during the day without interruption and talk to God every night. I'll be free from time deadlines. Nothing to worry about, no other racers to beat, and no schedule to keep. I can set my own pace sailing through the pearls of the Pacific."

Despite all her achievements, Niloa's parents still worried about her. When she was a young teenager, she struggled with eating disorders. She went to counseling, which eventually helped, but still experienced bouts of depression. She turned to alcohol and sex as a means to cope with self-doubt and despair. She struggled with self-worth.

I'm over all that now, she said to herself. *It's time to move on to a new phase.*

Niloa felt a strange sense of relief as she watched the shoreline of Kona fade into the ocean. She kept her gaze on the island until the ocean covered the peak of Mona Loa. She could finally relax. The first three days at sea couldn't have been better. The strong westerly trade winds carried the 42-foot *Dawn Treader II* across the South Pacific at a comfortable 12 knots. The September air temperature stayed a comfortable 82°-85° F in the daytime hours under mostly sunny skies and cooled down to a balmy 75° F at night. Niloa was able to keep the rudder on autopilot most of the time with the steady winds, taking the helm occasionally to break the monotony.

The first and second days were uneventful. She established a daily routine. After two night watches with intermittent sleep, she arose at 6:00 a.m., exercised on deck for 45 minutes, and did stretches, push-ups, sit-ups, tai chi, and light aerobics. She then made a light breakfast of instant coffee, a hard-boiled egg, one half a bagel, and a piece of fruit. After reading, praying, and meditating for an hour, she then sailed hard for a seven to eight hour stretch before breaking for a short 15 to 20 minute nap. She also fished between 5 and 7 in the evenings. At night she made exquisite Poisson dishes. She adjusted her sails as needed for the evening and put the boat on autopilot through the night.

Just before sunset on day three, Niloa snagged a large 20-pound mahi. She also had caught four medium-sized Tilapia, providing her with enough fish for two weeks of protein. Just before pulling her line in for the evening, a large Marlin grabbed the bait on her line. She knew she didn't have the line strength to bring it in, nor did she have the storage capacity for several hundred pounds of fish. After struggling with it for a long time she wisely cut it loose.

She wrote in her journal that evening:

> *At 5:45 p.m. my fishing line hooked something big. I soon realized I had a 300-400 pound Marlin in my grasp. I knew it was too strong for my line and would be too difficult to fillet and store on board. I thought I'd play with it a while; but in retrospect, perhaps it was playing with me. I had the feeling it could break free anytime it wanted. I cut it loose before it had a chance and declared victory. The Marlin had the last word though. Ten minutes after I let it loose, it resurfaced beside the boat, reminding me who was in control of the situation. Certainly not me. As for my seafood cuisine? 'Ono! 'Ono!*

Day number three ended with Niloa writing fish stories in a journal while eating delicious Mahi Mahi barbecued on a small grill with a glass of California white Zinfandel, a present from her uncle for special occasions.

Niloa awoke much earlier than she had planned, sensing a change in the ocean movement. The waves were choppier and large swells were building. Before she could assess the situation, her satellite phone rang.

"Aloha nui loa, Dad," Niloa answered before the caller could say a word.

"Hey, I didn't even get to say hello. I might have been the President wishing you well on your trip, and he probably doesn't know nui Loa," Chris replied.

"Well, I send much love and fondest regards to the President too," Niloa replied.

"Why were you so certain it was me?"

"Just knew, Dad. I could always hear you comin'. It's not like I gave my phone number out to a bunch of people."

"You mean you didn't give McKenzie your number?"

"He's over, Dad. Why'd you always pick on Michael? He was a good *haole* boy and good to me."

"Sorry, honey. I just didn't see you married to an Irishman the rest of your life."

"Did you hear the latest weather report?"

"I checked the satellite this morning, Dad. I can also feel the ocean, and the swells are buildin'. It's still dark, so I can't see any evidence of the storm but I sense it's out there and a threat to me."

"I heard there may be a tropical depression forming," Chris explained with a deep concern in his voice. "If it intensifies, it could be a typhoon in another 24-48 hours. You're going to need to take evasive action."

"Dad, you just sounded like you're in the army again."

"Niloa, just take the best evasive action you can immediately!"

"I'll check the weather conditions on my short wave and let you know my plan. Hope to talk to ya soon. Dad, one more thing, this dukine phone isn't always predictable. Sometimes a call gets through and sometimes it doesn't. Same for making calls—I can't always connect. It depends on the time of day, as they told us when we bought it."

"It also depends on the weather conditions," Niloa's father added. "Call me before it gets too stormy. I'll also try and call you again."

Niloa put away her phone and tuned in to the weather information on her short wave radio. The report confirmed her intuition; a tropical depression had formed 180 miles to the south and was intensifying as it moved northwest at 6 knots.

Encountering storms in the open ocean was not a new experience for Niloa. She had sailed through four major storms during her nine years of sailing. She knew that no matter how hard a sailor prepared for an ocean storm, he or she could never avoid the terrorizing thoughts of breaking up at sea. It had happened to her once while on a friend's boat caught in the winds of hurricane Iniki that devastated the island of Kauai. Fortunately the Coast Guard was nearby to rescue them.

Her best course of action to stay out of the way of the storm was to change her intended southwesterly course to a northwesterly course, and then turning west to stay on its northern edges. There was always a danger that the storm could pick up speed as it intensified, or that it could turn north instead of maintaining a northwesterly path, putting the *Dawn Treader II* in its path. Despite the sophisticated weather technology, outrunning a tropical storm in the open ocean was more of an art than a science; and Niloa was a gifted artist. Yet she knew that sometimes you had no choice but to sail into the wind, even the winds you most feared. The satellite phone rang again.

"Hi, Dad," Niloa said before her mother could say hello.

"Hi, honey, I'm just calling to say hi and tell you I am praying for you. I know you'll be able to sail around the storm, just get moving quickly."

"Mom, you're home! I thought you were gone."

"I got back this morning."

"I'm going to be fine, Mom," Niloa reassured.

"Dad wants to hear your plan now," Nanci said. The line went quiet then Chris voice came on the phone.

"Got you that time," Chris said with glee.

"Dad, you fooled me."

"I told you the President might call some time. Now what's your plan?"

"Tropical storm Erika is south of me by about 175 miles and is moving northwest at 7 knots. Its sustained winds are now 60 miles per hour and its tropical force winds extend 75 miles out from the center. So I have a good cushion. If I turn south I'll sail into the tropical winds; and I don't want to sail southeast toward South America."

"I thought it was moving at a lethargic 6 knots," Chris responded.

"The updated reconnaissance information just came in a few minutes ago, and it's picking up speed," replied Niloa. "Forecasters expect it to continue moving northwest, increasing its speed to 8-10 knots in the next few hours. At the same time, the sustained winds are expected to increase to hurricane force and extend further from the center. I have a 100-mile cushion, Dad, so I'm going to sail northwest, get ahead of it before it speeds up, and then sail west to cut across its path to its north."

Chris thought for a moment. The *Dawn Treader II* could sail 18-20 knots or more in those strong winds on the outer edge of the storm. Even if the storm speed doubled, Niloa should still be able to flank it and cut across to its northwestern edge, and then sail southwest away from it back toward the Solomons. She would have to sail into the Marshall Islands, and if the storm changed direction and threatened her, she could always hunker down in the Marshalls before the sea became too turbulent.

"*Oia ho'i*," Chris said after a long pause.

"*Oia ho'i*," Niloa replied, indicating that's it, that's her plan.

"Dad, you are thinking so loud I can hear your brain churning all the way here," Niloa interjected into the long conversational pause.

"It's a good plan honey. You need to head for the Marshalls, keeping ahead of the storm. If it turns toward you or dramatically speeds up, you need to hunker down there."

"Dad, if I remember my geography, those islands are as flat as Kansas. I'd hate to face a hurricane there."

"It's better than the open sea, honey. Remember Iniki?"

"As I was saying, I love those flat islands, Dad, but I'm gonna outrun this devil Erika."

Erika intensified as expected and almost doubled its speed. However, it unexpectedly turned west northwest, an unusual ocurrence, and headed toward the Caroline Islands. The storm plowed into the southern Philippines as a category 4 typhoon with 140 mph sustained winds. It thrashed the islands of Leyte and Cebu with winds gusts of up to 160 mph, 22 inches of rain, and a 15-foot tidal surge, washing coastal villages into the sea. Niloa had escaped a very deadly storm.

She settled down in the evening to record the day's events in her journal. She would not be writing about her fifth major storm at sea. Instead, she would be writing about her only shark attack. She recorded the following account:

> While sailing fast to keep ahead of the storm, I had
> to manage some large swells and shifting wind gusts.

It was very difficult. I wasn't surprised when I ended up in the water. An unpredictable wind shift and strong gust moved the main sail to the port side. Leaning back to avoid the boom that swung toward me, I lost my balance and fell backward into the treacherous swells. My storm experience had prepared me for this. Not only was I wearing my harness and life vest, I also had another long life line that I had clipped to my nylon waistband, which was anchored to metal rings on deck. There was no way I would risk being separated from the *Dawn Treader II*.

A large swell pushed me away from the boat. Instinctively, I began swimming toward the portable ladder I use for diving, which was about 10 yards away, grabbing my life-line as I pulled myself toward the boat. After making headway, I saw movement under the water and knew something menacing was moving toward me. I did not question for a moment their identity, which helped save my life. Within seconds of assessing the danger I was in and adjusting my harness so I could swim underwater while my life jacket floated on the surface, one of the sharks moved aggressively toward me. I moved quickly to the right of its path, recognizing it would seek to bump me first before biting me. The shark did not anticipate my movement. I reached for my knife in a sheath attached to my lower right leg.

The second shark then moved menacingly toward me. I could not completely elude its attack. It caught my right leg between the knee and the ankle, biting into my flesh and the heavy leather sheath for my knife. Fortunately, it was a small shark, less than 7 feet in length. I felt the excruciating pain of the shark's teeth rip into my leg. The shark then felt my fury as I plunged my knife into its head. Using all my strength, I stabbed it twice, and was thankful I had the six-inch knife rather than the other 4-inch one I often carry. Blood filled the water as it let go of my right leg. I continued a stabbing motion, inflicting five deep wounds, including one stab wound through the left eye and eye socket of the attacker. I knew I had mortally wounded it when I gauged the amount of blood oozing from its head.

The other shark circled around, setting up for another attack. I swam behind the wounded shark, placing it between the second attacker and me. As expected, the second attacker was indiscriminate. It unmercifully began devouring the wounded creature, forgetting about me. I swam vigorously toward the *Dawn Treader II* and climbed on board. I cleared the water just as four other sharks arrived to feast on one of their own. My wounded leg required 27 self-administered stitches, but the punctures were not life threatening. I thanked God that I had narrowly escaped death.

I am still under the influence of the morphine I took to dull the pain. I felt so elated that I remember shouting to the ocean in defiance, 'Go tell your shark friends *ahahana*! Shame on all of you! You should never try and take me on again! *Aikola*

Niloa ended her journal entry, grateful that she was alright, by quoting her Uncle Jarvis.

"I always wondered if I might become paralyzed with fear meeting a shark in the water, and might not be able to think or act in self-defense. Now I know. As Uncle Jarvis had told me, 'sometimes you have to sail into the winds of fear to propel you through the storms of life.'"

After the shark attack, navigating the storm seemed easy. She had sailed on the northern edge of the Marshall Islands, several hundred miles off course. Checking her position with the satellite navigational technology on her laptop computer, Niloa determined she was more than 1300 miles east and a little bit south of Guam, less than 120 miles southeast of Enewetak and about 130 miles southeast of Bikini. She recalled that there were several medical facilities in the Marshalls, but did not want to stop there with a storm in nearby. She grabbed her cell phone and tried calling home, but there was too much interference from the storm clouds. She had to make this decision on her own. She could either turn south back toward the Solomons, or sail into Guam to have her leg checked by a doctor, just in case any infection set in. Although she had penicillin and antibiotics on board, she still had a couple weeks of sailing to do.

In Guam, she could call her parents and take a short rest. Also, she had always wanted to explore the Mariana Islands where her grandfather had fought during World War II. On the other hand, the Mariana Islands were a long way out of her way. She could always explore them if she wanted to after she reached the Solomon Islands. Niloa decided to stick to her original plan, but only after sailing through the Marshall Islands to make sure the storm was well past her. She would then turn due south toward the Solomon Islands. Niloa thanked God that she felt little pain in her leg the rest of the day and through the evening. Tomorrow would be different.

CHAPTER 2
San Gregorio, California

Melinda sipped her luke-warm coffee and watched the sunset as she sat on the second floor lanai of her remodeled San Gregorio beach house. Her emotions were churning again. The children were with her parents for the weekend, but she decided to come alone to keep the family tradition. Every last weekend of the month Jack and Melinda would spend at the beach house. They made sure no other family, work or church commitments were scheduled. Jack even tried to schedule all his travel to the Pacific anytime but the end of the month, but this last trip could not be avoided. Melinda had dreaded Jack's trips to the Pacific. She knew his work was important, but she hated the secrecy, the spur-of-the-moment excursions, and the classified experiments that he could not talk about with her.

"Jack," she had asked him recently, "couldn't you be a normal scientist working at a private company lab with a five-day a week work schedule?"

He just smiled and said, "Maybe after this project, my love."

At other times she told herself that was a selfish request to ask him. Jack's work for the U.S. Department of Defense was more than a job; it was his service to his country, the country that had saved both sets of grandparents and the country for which he would give his life, if required.

Melinda poured another cup of coffee, adding a spoonful of

Nestlé's Quik. She thought about the endurance of Jack's grandparents during Hitler's reign of terror. His father's parents had been taken captive by the Nazis first, arrested in Italy in June of 1944 for helping Jews escape the SS troops that were sent to round them up. On his mother's side, Jack's other set of grandparents had been arrested in Hungary three months later, also for aiding the Jews. Both of Jack's grandfathers had been university professors and both grandmothers had run small businesses. All four had been taken to Flossenbuerg, a Bavarian concentration camp where some of Germany's most famous political prisoners were held. Fortunately, both young married couples had no children. Very few children survived Flossenbuerg.

Jack's two grandfathers had first met in the Messerschmitt plant where they helped build fighter planes for the German military. They rose at 5:00 a.m. to wash up, eat a meager breakfast, and stand through the grueling 5:30 a.m. roll call. Those who had died during the evening were removed and buried in a mass grave. Those too sick to make roll call were marked with a tag and given one week to recover. If they didn't get better, they were taken away and never seen again. Work assignments were given out at 6:00 a.m. Work in the plant ended at 6:30 p.m.

Both of Jack's grandmothers had worked in the camp's kitchen, preparing boiled turnips, peas, and potatoes for the 16,000-prisoner population housed there in 1944 and 1945. Their grandparents built a close friendship based on their mutual faith and desire to help save Jewish people from the onslaught of death and annihilation.

During the long nightmare in Flossenbuerg, Jack's grandparents were able to meet and befriend four of the seven brave Germans who attempted to assassinate Hitler: Admiral Wilhelm Canaras, General Friedrich von Rabebau, Reserve Captain Dr. Theodore Struenck, and Pastor Dietrich Bonhoeffer. Jack's mother's parents from Hungary, had befriended two other Hungarian prisoners at Flossenberg: Hungarian Home Secretary Franz Keresztes-Fischer, and his brother Ludwig, a Hungarian General. They all had been executed between April 9 and 12 of 1945, less than two weeks before the camp had been liberated by Allied troops on the morning of April 23rd. Miraculously, all four of Jack's grandparents survived. They stayed close friends after they were freed and met several times after the war, which is how their children met, Anthony and Krisztina, and eventually became best friends and were married after both finishing their university studies in Europe.

Melinda caught sight of a small sailboat coming to shore, reminder her of Jack's love for sailing, passed down from his father. She remembered her first encounter with her father-in-law in Italy.

"My precious Melinda," he had said before she could even say hello, "I'm a so happy my son has found a special woman as you."

He had hugged her, complimented her, and praised her within the first two minutes they had met. Melinda's mother-in-law, Krisztina, was just as warm and loving.

Jacks' parents had hoped that Jack would find someone to balance his intellectual proclivities. They had not been surprised that Jack was an extremely precocious child given the fact that both his grandfathers were professors at prestigious European universities. The University of Milan offered tuition benefits to the children and grandchildren of its professors, so Jack entered the university as a student at age 17 while his grandfather was still on the Faculty of Psychology. He completed the pre-med program by age 20 and completed his graduate medical education there at age 23, earning a medical degree and a Ph.D. in biochemistry. Jack then moved to the U.S. in 1992, accepting a post-doctoral research fellowship at Harvard University Medical School in Cambridge, Massachusetts. Melinda was very proud of him. He quickly distinguished himself as a brilliant biochemist and began a career of applied research in pathological medicine.

Melinda poured her third and last cup of decaffeinated coffee. As she peered out into the ocean again, she thought about the first time she had met Jack during his post-doctoral work at St. Elizabeth's hospital in Boston. A dark, handsome Italian man had walked into her office suite.

"Excuse me," he asked politely, "would you direct me to the pathology lab?"

I remember the warmth and sparkle in his dark brown eyes; the same beautiful eyes as his mother Krisztina.

"I can take you there," Melinda had responded, instantly deciding that she wanted to spend some time with this man.

The short conversation down the hallway sparked enough interest in Jack to move him to ask Melinda out for coffee the next day. Like Jack's mother, Melinda was a nurse. During their courtship they grew to love each other's company, especially at Red Sox games. Krisztina was always asking Jack, like any good mother of an eligible bachelor consumed with his work, whether he had met any attractive women in Boston.

At the end of one letter that Jack had sent home, he had written, "Mother, if I ever meet anyone as brilliant and beautiful as you I will ask her to marry me, and you'll be the first to know."

Krisztina was shocked six weeks later when she had received a postcard from Jack saying, "Mom, I met her. Her name is Melinda and she's just like you. You and Dad pack your bags and get ready to come to America."

Melinda continued reminiscing.

I loved our wedding in Cambridge. It was a completely beautiful day – May 10, 1993, at the First Congregational Church in Cambridge. My parents and Jack's parents liked each other from their very first conversation, just as I had hoped.

Jack's parents had been amazed by the standard of living and work opportunities in America. I'm so glad they had encouraged Jack to stay in America and become an American citizen. My parents had been so grateful and overjoyed when Anthony and Krisztina encouraged them to settle in America. That was such a sacrifice they had made, knowing their grandchildren would be living so far away from them.

Melinda had hated to move from Boston in 1995, but Jack was offered a research position to study pathology at Johns Hopkins University. Two years later he was given a prestigious research fellowship at Stanford to study the pathology of dangerous biological and chemical agents that Iraq and several other countries had been manufacturing during the 1980s and 1990s. Melinda had been very happy to leave Baltimore for the rolling hills of Los Altos, California, where they built a beautiful home 12 miles southwest of Stanford.

Then there is this dilapidated beach house, Melinda thought. San Gregorio, "A quaint community of intellectuals and aspiring creative artists," as Jack liked to say.

Their beach house was about 20 miles from their Los Altos home. It had become their weekend project, their special place of solace and peace, and the site of many warm memories with their young children.

Jack loved his work at Stanford, where he befriended several scientists working with the U.S. Department of Defense. He was deeply grateful to the U.S. military for defeating the Nazis during World War II and freeing his grandparents from Flossenbuerg. His happiest day after his wedding day and the days when their two children were born was the day he was sworn in as a U.S. citizen.

Melinda had worried about the new friendships Jack had made. She just didn't know the people very well whom Jack had befriended. Eventually, these friends led him to accept an offer from the U.S. government to work at a biological research laboratory on a small island in the Pacific.

Melinda remembered the day he told her, July 4.

"The project is funded for three years. I'll be spending about half my working hours at Stanford and the other half on an island in the Pacific."

"Where in the Pacific?" she had asked.

"I can't say, honey, that is classified information," he had answered.

Those three painful words, "I can't say," hurt deeply. Melinda and Jack always shared everything. They did not keep secrets from each other.

Melinda immediately had suspected that he was traveling to a remote island controlled by the U.S. military. After Jack had made six round trips during the first year of the project, she was able to estimate that it took him nearly a day to travel by plane from San Francisco to his destination. She knew that he enjoyed the challenge and surmised that the research was very exciting.

Jack must have hated that he could not tell anyone, especially her, she anguished.

She also concluded that his work must have been dangerous since it had to be conducted in the middle of the Pacific.

Melinda was not be surprised when she later found out that Jack was working in the islands of Micronesia. Not satisfied with not knowing the general area where Jack was working, she began tracking the times of his satellite phone calls. Since he would regularly call her after his safe arrival, she deduced that he was probably flying to a site somewhere near Guam. She just didn't know which island he was on. Jack had inadvertently gushed excitedly about snorkeling in the deepest part of the ocean after one of his trips. Thanks to her proclivity on the Internet, it didn't take long for Melinda to learn that the deepest ocean in the world was the famed Marianas Trench, which lay 35,500 feet below the ocean's surface. Jack often said to Melinda that she would cherish a visit to the area where he worked and that one day they would go there together.

She always wondered why Jack used the word "cherish" rather than "like" or "enjoy." Then one day it occurred to her, *perhaps Jack's on Tinian.* Melinda had seen pictures of Tinian taken by her grandfather when he was a pilot during World War II. Tinian had a military airstrip and had played a strategic role in the Pacific arena of America's war with Japan. It was from Tinian that the two atomic bomb attacks on Hiroshima and Nagasaki were launched.

Tinian would make perfect sense for a research laboratory. It lay fewer than 120 miles north of Guam, had a well developed infrastructure, and the U.S. military still leased much of the island. Melinda had always wanted to visit Guam and Tinian. After Jack's tenth trip, Melinda was 90 percent sure she knew where Jack was going, which gave her much more peace of mind. She was very close to guessing the exact location.

Despite her concerns, Melinda never feared for Jack's life. She knew the biological research he conducted posed dangerous risks, but she also knew Jack was meticulously careful. What never entered her mind were the extraordinary efforts that terrorists would make to acquire biological agents and their antidotes. U.S. intelligence agencies and the Department of Defense never imagined that terrorists could find this isolated lab on a speck of land in the middle of the Pacific. The possibility of an attack was so remote that the U.S. military forces providing security on Farallon de Medinilla considered their work a paid tropical vacation. Melinda never even entertained the thought that she'd one day have to rear her two young children without Jack, who'd never been harmed or threatened in his work.

"Enough reminiscing," Linda said out loud to herself. "And enough coffee."

It was now 9:00 p.m. She had been sitting on the lanai sipping coffee for two hours. She said her prayers for Jack, as she always did, read a little, and went to sleep.

Melinda woke up suddenly in a cold sweat. She looked at her alarm clock: 1:15 a.m. She could feel her heart pounding and a strong emotion of panic overwhelmed her. She tried to pray but felt paralyzed by fear. She calculated in her mind that it was 6:15 p.m. in Tinian. She felt something was not right. She sensed that Jack was somehow in trouble. Her fear was then replaced by a peace followed by a deep sadness. She began weeping softly, not sure exactly why. She reasoned that she was just missing Jack terribly.

She rose out of bed, put on a white robe, and opened the double windows of their second bedroom. She looked out across the calm Pacific toward the Marianas. The moon was full and the night clear and bright. With tears streaking down her face, she whispered, as if her words would be carried by the soft tropical breezes across the ocean to Jack's ears, "I love you."

She could almost hear Jack respond to her. She looked upward into the starlit sky, and whispered one more time, "God, I miss him." She then collapsed on her bed and cried herself to sleep. She couldn't wait for Jack to return home.

Chapter 3
Ewenetak, Marshall Islands

Niloa woke up with throbbing pain at 4:00 a.m. Her leg felt like it was on fire; the effects of the morphine had worn off. She had stayed at the helm until 1:00 a.m., navigating west, before setting the *Dawn Treader II* on automatic pilot. The storm threat was over but she was hundreds of miles off course. She had managed just three hours of sleep.

Not bad, she said to herself, three good hours. No more *maka hiamoe*.

Looking down at her leg, she noticed the wound was not completely closed.

"Oh, *pupuka!*" she said in disgust as she saw the unseemly stitches.

She grabbed the syringe, placed another plastic tube of morphine in it, and reluctantly gave herself another six hours of freedom from pain. She then self-administered another seven stitches in her right leg.

Niloa strongly disliked the lost sense of control she felt while under the effects of the morphine. Things seemed to move more slowly than normal. She felt like she was in a daze. She could not effectively feel the ocean currents or sense the subtle changes in wind direction. It was frustrating not being able to navigate with 100 percent of her faculties. Checking her laptop computer's navigational positioning system, Niloa calculated her position as ten miles southeast of Ewenetak Island, a small island in the Marshalls and the site of nuclear testing by the United States in the late 1940s and 1950s. Niloa remembered from her history studies that dozens of nuclear bombs, both atomic and hydrogen, had been exploded on or near the island, contaminating almost half of the Marshall Islands and thousands of islanders with harmful radioactive fallout. She cringed at the thought of sailing through one of the most abused areas on earth.

Niloa departed the Marshall Islands as fast as possible, sailing in a northwesterly direction between the islands of Ewenetak and Bikini. She was now heading toward the southern tip of the Mariana Islands. The weather seemed to have returned to normal, although there were still dark clouds on the horizon. Niloa began to think about her grandfather, William Opukaihea, her mother's father, who had fought under General Douglas MacArthur in the Philippines. She remembered the stories her grandfather told about his good friends who fought in Saipan, two who were among the nearly 3000 Americans and 28,000 Japanese soldiers who died during the Battle of Saipan in June and July of 1944.

Her grandfather had been a senior at Punaho High School when the Japanese attacked Pearl Harbor on December 7, 1941. After graduating from high school, William had joined the U.S. Navy in June of 1942 and had became a fighter pilot. He had been shot down twice by the Japanese but rescued both times, once at Guadalcanal and once at Leyte. At Guadalcanal he was able to land his damaged plane in a sugar cane field away from the fighting.

Local islanders helped him out of his burning plane before it exploded on the ground. William's second brush with death was when he was shot down in the Philippines on the first day of the Battle for Leyte Gulf. After downing three Japanese zeros and taking several hits from enemy fire, William was wounded in the left arm and was unable to return his severely damaged plane to his ship in the U.S. Third Fleet. He had to ditch his plane in the shark-infested waters of the Philippine Sea.

Fortunately, he had been well-equipped with a life jacket, two waterproof flares, two handguns and several clips of ammunition.

During his three hours in the water waiting for rescue, William fought off two sharks, wounding one of them and killing the other. He was eventually rescued by a patrol boat and returned to his ship. His arm wound would keep him out of an airplane but not out of harms way. Recounting this incident, he later told Niloa how fortunate he had been to have been rescued after learning about the gruesome fate of the men of the *USS Indianapolis*, who spent three days in the Philippine Sea. Niloa would never forget that story. It had come back to her when she first saw the shark fins circling after falling off the *Dawn Treader II*, but she had quickly put the story out of her mind.

Neither of her grandfather's two harrowing experiences of being shot down put him out of the war. His third brush with death did, and had occurred also during the Battle for Leyte Gulf. Niloa remembered hearing her grandfather tell the story when she was just ten years old.

"My ship was the *USS Princeton,* and we were part of Task Group Three under the Admiral Frederick C. Sherman's command. In the morning of October 24, just a day after I had been shot down and rescued, we sent planes from our ship against Japanese airfields on the Philippine Island of Luzon. While our planes were gone, Japanese planes came upon us from Clark and Nichols airfields. A 500-pound bomb hit us and exploded after crashing through the flight deck and hangar. The explosion knocked out our ship's fire-fighting system. I was in the hospital ward when the attack occurred. A chain reaction of explosions soon followed.

Admiral Sherman sent two ships to help our crew put out the fire. Just as they were able to get it under control, we spotted more Japanese planes. The two rescue ships that were helping us had to back off. I left the hospital ward and helped to put out the fires with the one good shoulder I had, but we couldn't contain them. At 3:23 p.m., the reserve bomb and torpedo stowage blew up. Shrapnel was blasted across the deck of the *USS Birmingham,* which was right beside us. It was horrible; 229 men on deck were killed. My left leg was pierced with shrapnel but I managed to get off the ship before it sunk in the Sibuyan Sea. Ninety-eight of my comrades and ten officers went down with my ship."

Niloa recalled every detail of the riveting story. Her grandfather said he had told the doctor on the *USS Reno,* the ship that had rescued him, "I would rather have been shot down a third time than face the fiery inferno of the *USS Princeton.* The ocean is unforgiving but not as hellish as fire." Niloa could see in her mind's eye the flash of the explosion of the *Princeton.*

A crack of thunder interrupted her reminiscing and Niloa instinctively turned around to gaze at the growing thunderhead to the southwest. She had not even seen the lightning, or perhaps she did as she imagined the fire on the *Princeton.* She glanced at her watch—9:30 a.m. She had sailed for 36 hours since first encountering the outskirts of tropical storm Erika.

Two storms must be moving close together, she wondered.

Niloa struggled to find her position on her laptop as another flash of light filled the sky. She looked at the second hand of her watch and waited for the thunderclaps. "Ten miles away," she said to no one in particular. Since thunderstorms could travel 20 to 30 miles per hour, Niloa had little time to take an evasive course of action. She could sail west and try and outrun the storm; or she could sail north and get out of its path, letting it pass to the south. If it was another tropical depression, she preferred to sail through it.

Niloa timed another flash of lighting — nine miles away. The storm was moving slowly. Moving carefully to the front of the boat, Niloa hoisted a storm jib. She then trimmed the main sail and decided to take a course due west. The brisk winds quickly filled the main sail, lurching the boat forward with great force. Within a few minutes Niloa had found the rhythm of the wind and brought the *Dawn Treader II* under control while maintaining a speed of 12-13 knots. The *Dawn Treader II* was a stable boat at high speeds but a mistake at that speed she could get knocked down. The brunt of the storm seemed to be heading more west than north, but the lightning kept coming closer. Niloa had encountered dangerous lightning before, but an electrical storm in the open ocean was very frightening. The lightning rods on the mast were designed to protect both her and the boat. However, in severe storms several bolts could strike the boat simultaneously, making it dangerous to be out in the open.

While pondering her safety, a weak bolt of lighting struck the mast. The lightning rods were working properly; but there was some damage to the instruments. Niloa could not risk riding this one out on deck. She saw a couple of bolts of lightning strike the water but no closer than 100 yards from the *Dawn Treader II*. She set her course and went below deck for safety. Her instincts were correct. She was sailing away from the center of the storm, keeping far enough north but still unable to sail out of reach of its dangerous lightning. Through the heavy rains Niloa could see the dangerous lightning strikes moving away from her.

Just as Niloa breathed a sigh of relief, a large lightning bolt struck the boat, knocking her to the floor. Niloa could not see and a high-pitched ringing stung her ears. The cabin also had a lightning rod so there was no fire damage. After a minute Niloa blinked her eyes several times and was able to regain her sight. Her hearing was still impaired but the pain in her ears had subsided. With much apprehension she placed her fingers in her ears and took them out. "*Laki*," she said, greatly relieved, "no blood, no perforated eardrums."

"Oh, *dukine!*" she yelled, looking at her smoking satellite phone and laptop computer. She had been charging them when the storm struck.

How could I be so stupid? she thought. She hoped her hard drive was not wiped out.

The lightning passed through the electrical circuits in the cabin and fried everything plugged in. Now she was cut off from communicating except for her short wave radio.

Her hearing eventually came back as she continued sailing due west. No more lighting bolts struck the *Dawn Treader II* after that. The storm was a dangerous one, even on the outskirts. She was glad she decided not to try to outrun it.

After traveling another hour due west, Niloa found herself east of the Mariana Islands. She checked her position: she was now 800 miles off course 1200 miles directly east of Saipan. Niloa decided it would be best to sail to the Mariana Islands, as she had considered before. Instead of sailing first to Guam, however, she would sail to Saipan, a well-developed island and seat of the government of the Federated

States of Micronesia. From there she could call her parents, check the *Dawn Treader II* for damage, have a doctor check her leg, and explore the Mariana Islands before sailing southeast to the Solomon Islands. Her parents were obviously anxious to hear from her and were undoubtedly following the tropical storms on the Internet. She had been out of contact with them for several days because of the storm.

Niloa's westward trip to Saipan was one of the most beautiful stretches of sailing she had ever experienced. The skies were relatively clear during the mornings with some cloud build-up in the late afternoons and an occasional brief shower. After the gentle rains dissipated the low-lying clouds on the western horizon provided the raw ingredients for some of the most beautiful sunsets she had ever had the pleasure to enjoy.

They were spectacular displays of dark gray clouds with purple underbellies that turned to broad brush strokes of green, with streaks of burnt orange underneath and sometimes hints of light green and dark yellow. The streaks of color would emanate from the point where the sun dropped into the ocean, and then darken and change as the light rays and cloud formations interacted. Niloa realized they were not static or predictable, but paintings in the making as if witnessing the master painter creating on a canvas of water and sky. Even the beautiful sunsets in Kona were not as brilliant as these masterpieces.

For six days she sailed west into six beautiful sunsets, capturing all of them with her digital camera. Once she reached shore, she could try and recover the hard drive on her laptop, retrieve the digital pictures she had taken, and send them to her parents via the Internet. For six days she had fair weather, and time to think and meditate.

I'll be 22 soon, Niloa thought. *My life has been a series of adventures and sailing. I have had no time to develop close relationships. I have hardly dated; for that matter, I have rarely been asked out. Perhaps I'm too much of a tomboy, like my older brothers have said. Perhaps guys are afraid to ask me out; or, worse yet, perhaps I am not very attractive to guys—too muscular and not very feminine.*

Niloa caught herself drifting toward self-doubt and those horrible destructive thoughts she had struggled with as a teenager. She promised herself and her parents she would never allow herself to succumb to Bulimia again as she did when she was 13 and 14. In fact, Niloa had a gorgeous figure; she was 5'8" and weighed between 125 to 127 pounds on average. She was muscular yet very feminine; she just didn't fit the model of the popular girls in high school or young women in college that men seem to flock to, or so it seemed to her.

I'm sure I'm too opinionated, she thought again. *On the other hand, I'm beginning to accept myself more and more. I just wish to God I could do something worthwhile, like be a missionary or Peace Corps worker. Maybe I should go to Bhutan and teach; or help the Maasai in Tanzania. But then how would I sail? How can my sailing help anyone? Am I just trying to escape the world?*

Niloa contemplated these issues for days. Yet even as she did, she felt less self-doubt and less self-condemnation as in the past. She thought extensively about her life, her vision for the future, her goals, and her purpose. As the days went by, she began to feel more comfortable about leaving all these big questions about her future and her purpose to God. She didn't need to figure it all out; but just trust that He had it all figured out. By the time she spotted the shores of Saipan, Niloa felt as good about herself as she ever had in her life. That is what she had hoped would happen on this trip: to spend time alone, make peace with herself and cherish the person God had made her. She wrote into her journal that evening, *God, you gave me this love for sailing and love for adventure; so I'm going to enjoy it and not feel guilty about it any more.*

The next morning Niloa arose early, before sunrise. She was excited about exploring the Marianas Islands. The pain in her leg had completely subsided. She had heard much about Guam, Saipan, and Tinian from her grandfather, but didn't know much about the smaller islands in the island chain. Niloa decided to sail into Magicienne Bay, anchor there, and wade ashore at Laulau Beach. She dropped the anchor at about 5:00 p.m. There were only a few people on the beach. She spotted a young couple who had been sun-bathing gathering their beach belongings. The couple did not even see Niloa sail into the bay until she introduced herself.

"Hi, I'm Niloa Stephenson."

The couple both sat up and gave Niloa a smile.

"Hi, I'm Jason and this is my wife, Tanya. Can we help you?"

"Yes, I'm looking for a ride into town so I can get some supplies. I've been out at sea a long time."

"No problem," Jason replied. "We're staying in the Hyatt Regency on the west side of the island. There's a town on the way called Garapan where you can pick up supplies."

"Did you say you've been sailing a long time?" Tanya asked.

"Yes, I left Hawaii a couple of weeks ago. I'd wanted to go to the Solomons but somehow ended up here."

Niloa saw the surprised looks on their faces. They didn't quite know how to respond. She smiled at the thought, *They must think me lolo.*

"I ran into big storm. Had to come here first."

"For a moment I thought you'd set the rudder wrong," Jason said, finally catching Niloa's humor.

"Oh, I get the drift of it now," Tanya added.

"Our conversation's sinking fast," Jason countered.

They all began laughing.

"Excuse us for the bad puns, Niloa," Tanya said. We were both English majors."

"You know, I still can't believe I married an English major," Jason said.

Niloa quickly realized they were on their honeymoon. That's the kind of relationship she wanted some day – one with witty and fun-loving conversations. She'd even take the bad puns.

The honeymooners drove Niloa to Garapan. Before they dropped her off, they did something totally unexpected.

"Niloa, after you're finished," Tanya said, "Get a taxi or ride from someone to the Hyatt Regency where we're staying. We're booking you a room there for two nights— it's our treat. It's an awesome place and you need a good couple of nights of rest."

"No need to fuss about me," Niloa replied. "I have money to stay here."

"No, we want to do this," Jason replied. "We already decided. Save your money for the rest of your trip. If you want to stay longer than two days, then use your money. But two days are on us. We were given lots of wedding money – so please accept our hospitality."

"You guys are the best," Niloa said, deeply emotional. "You have aloha spirit. Your marriage is gonna be awesome. Keep that aloha spirit alive and you'll have a great life together."

Jason and Tanya both gave Niloa a warm embrace.

"Don't forget about the doctor I told you about," Tanya said as Niloa got out of their rented convertible.

"I'm going there as soon as I get my phone in for repairs. Thank you both so much. I'll see you before I leave the island."

Niloa found everything she needed in Garapan. Her satellite phone was beyond repair, so she bought a new one with her credit card. Fortunately, her computer's hard drive had survived the storm and its damage was repaired. The shops in Garapan provided her with bread, salted beef, butter, fresh fruits and vegetables, and dried fruit. At a drug store she resupplied her medical necessities, including a new suture kit and plenty of antibiotics. The twin masthead VHS antennas that were damaged by the storm were harder to find, but she finally found an electronics shop that had one in stock. She then bought 20 gallons of fresh water to refill one of her two forty gallon tanks and arranged to have all the supplies delivered in a pick-up truck to Laulau Beach the next morning.

Niloa took a taxi to the Hyatt and checked into her room on the top floor. The room, like all 325 rooms in the hotel, had a beautiful balcony facing the ocean. Niloa opened the sliding glass door to the balcony, plopped down on the bed, and called her parents. They were more than anxious to hear from her after they had lost contact for several days. They put Niloa on speaker phone when she finally called.

"You'll never guess where I'm at now," Niloa challenged her parents, humming the music to *Jeopardy* in the background.

"You're in Guam!" her father guessed.

"Close, Dad, but not Guam."

"You're in Tinian!" her mom said excitedly. "Where your grandpa was stationed."

"Not yet, Mom. But I will go there soon"

"Saipan!" her dad said, confident that he was right.

"But you'll never guess where in Saipan," Niloa egged them on.

"I'm laying down on a most comfortable bed, looking at this awesome sunset over the ocean, on the top floor of the Hyatt Regency Hotel at Micro Beach."

"We want to come too," her mom said.

"I see you didn't lose your credit card," her dad goaded.

"No, Dad, I used the card for my new cell phone and laptop repair. I'm staying here for free."

Niloa went on to explain the generosity of the couple she had met and the new supplies she had purchased that day. She hoped her refurbished Motorola 9500-Iridium phone would work better than the old one. Her parents thought she had bargained well, getting it for $450.

Niloa told them of her plans to rest for two days on Saipan, and then visit Tinian nearby and some of the other small islands to the north Saipan during the next several days. She would then chart a course to the Solomon Islands.

While sitting on the balcony facing the ocean, Niloa wrote in her diary.

> *Tomorrow, after the doctor's appointment, I'll meet the delivery truck at Laulau Beach and load the supplies on the Dawn Treader II. Then I'm vegging out on the beach the rest of the morning. I'll hang out at the pool all afternoon. Maybe I'll run into Jason and Tanya. I forgot to ask him if he has a brother.*

It was a very beautiful cloudless night. The stars were very bright that evening. Niloa felt good. She felt content. She realized she had not been depressed during the whole trip. Things were working out well. Niloa slept soundly.

The next two days went by quickly. Niloa's wound was healing well. The doctor gave her a B+ on her stitching work and an A on her ongoing care. She was able to see Jason and Tanya at the pool her last evening at the Hyatt. They sipped some cool drinks and talked about Niloa's sailing adventures. Tanya had always wanted to sail but had never had the chance. Niloa invited them to join her on a short day-trip to Tinian. They were thrilled.

The next morning the three of them took a taxi to Laulau Beach and swam out to the *Dawn Treader II*. Niloa took them to Tinian to explore the island. They went to the site where the atomic bombs that destroyed Hiroshima and Nagasaki were loaded onto American planes. Niloa was glad to visit the place where her grandfather had been during the war but also was glad he was not on those bombing missions to Japan. She had always felt uneasy, growing up with many Japanese friends in Hawaii, about the awful destruction the U.S. had brought about in Japan, not on the military, but on the civilian population. She understood all the arguments about saving American lives, but still wished that the war at been won differently. She concluded while on Tinian, *I know we'd do it differently now. Our military is smarter and I hope we're more compassionate.*

Niloa learned while there that the U.S. had several military installations in the islands. The Mariana Islands had become more important because of the military base closings in the Philippines. The islands were now a very important line of defense in the Pacific region.

Niloa took Jason and Tanya back to Saipan at about sunset so they could watch the sun go down while on the water. They thoroughly enjoyed themselves. Their short sailing trip was one of the highlights of their honeymoon. Their mutual generosity initiated a friendship that would grow over the years. Jason and Tanya promised to stay in touch and wanted to hear about the rest of Niloa's adventure once she returned to Hawaii. Niloa would have much to tell them.

CHAPTER 4
Farallon de Medinilla, Mariana Islands

The 45-foot sailboat took down its mainsail as it slowly eased its way into the waters just off shore of Farallon de Medinilla. Three men tightly gripped deep sea fishing poles with their lines cast aft in the sparkling warm waters of the Marianas Islands. They were dressed in baggy long pants and brightly colored short-sleeved shirts with typical hats worn by local fisherman. A U.S. marine patrol boat quickly approached the vessel.

"Good aye! One of the fishermen shouted to the marines, who were carefully surveying *The Sulu Breeze*.

Strange accent, thought Lance corporal Jesse Phipps. He sounds Aussie but looks Filipino or Indonesian. *Definitely not locals.*

"You need to move your boat half a mile away from shore!" replied Phipps.

"This is a restricted area patrolled by the U.S. military."

"Sorry mate," the fisherman responded with a broad smile. "Ahl the good fish are ere! Weel take er out."

Phipps relaxed when he sensed the friendly disposition of the man. He turned around toward the second marine in his patrol to signal their return to shore, but before he could say a word, three bullets passed through his back, exploding into his internal organs.

He slumped over the side of the boat and fell into the ocean. The second marine, hearing the muffled pops, knew what was coming but did not have enough time to react. A hail of SS190 bullets penetrated his protective vest. The three men on deck lowered their FN P-90s with silencers and navigated their sailboat into the island's small harbor.

The dozen terrorists were well trained and meticulously followed a plan. They had studied the activities of the marines and scientists for several days, learning that they were not at full strength. Eight marines had traveled to Guam early in the morning for a training exercise. Methodically and quietly, ten terrorists killed ten marines on the beach and moved quickly up the trail leading from the beach to the military compound near the center of the island. Two terrorists stayed with the boat. With the element of complete surprise, six of the terrorists surrounded the largest building, which contained a small dinning room, large kitchen, eight bedrooms, and four bathrooms. It was lunchtime and a dozen marines were eating together at two round tables. A well-built dark-skinned man of medium height with a deep scar on the right side of his face motioned for the attack to begin. He was the only one who didn't wear a hood. Two terrorists entered through the back door and two came through the front door, while two others guarded these exits, the only two escape routes other than the windows. They burst into the dining area and fully utilized the 50-round capacity of their weapons, killing the marines in their seats. Again, there was no time to react. Those with weapons by their sides could not even fire a single shot in defense.

Four other marines were in the recreation room of another building watching the early 12:00 p.m. news. The P-90 silencers suppressed the sound enough so they could not hear the shots that were fired next door. Two terrorists killed them easily with their fully automatic weapons.

The terrorists planned to kill the scientists last. Two terrorists quickly identified their living quarters, a pre-fabricated 1200 square foot four bedroom home. Only two scientists were in the house. Dr. Jack Costellona had gone for a short walk for lunch, as was his custom on Fridays; and Dr. John Parker and Dr. Greg Staunton were still working in the lab.

The terrorists entered through the unlocked front door into the living room. To their right, a colorful display of framed family pictures filled the glass surfaces of the wicker end tables on each side of a long couch. Opposite the couch was a matching wicker sofa chair where one of the scientists was seated. He rose to defend himself as soon as the intruders entered. His blood spattered across the Hawaiian print of the large sofa pillows. The other scientist at home was in the kitchen pouring himself a glass of diet Dr. Pepper when he heard the muffled pops in the living room. He had a couple seconds to find a way of escape. Before he could dive through the kitchen window, he was shot in the back. He fell backward and collapsed onto the kitchen floor, staring up at the black-hooded demon who had suddenly snuffed out his life.

The terrorists rendezvoused in the center of the compound. One of the scientists they could not locate. They knew four of them were working in the lab. Frantically, they organized a quick 15-minute search across the tiny island.

When they reconvened, the scar-faced man emerged from the lab holding two metal cases, each about 3ft x 2ft x 2ft is size, with a satisfied look on his face. He shouted to the other terrorist in the center of the military compound in the language of Cebuano, "We've got all the samples. Get the men now! We're leaving!"

"What about the other scientist?" a man named Paulo asked.

"Since you let him get away – you stay here and kill him!"

"I agreed to be your navigator!" shouted Paulo in anger. "I didn't agree to do this. You said this was scouting trip and that there would be no killing!"

"You want to rot in an American prison Paulo?" the terrorist replied with a look of disdain. "Then find him and kill him – and your reward will be waiting for you back home!"

Paulo glared at the man and raised his weapon in anger. Suddenly, from behind, he received a strong blow to the back of his head and fell unconscious.

Eleven terrorists left the island just before 2:00 p.m. having fulfilled their mission.

Jack Costellona, on the north side of the island opposite the harbor, lay on the beach watching the sunset. He had finally accepted that, for him, tomorrow would never come. Although he was not afraid to die, he feared dying alone. Death was manageable, but the loneliness of a slow death was unbearable. He wondered how he found himself dying on less than half a square mile of limestone isolated in the middle of the Pacific Ocean. He could not comprehend how God could allow such a tragic fate. He contemplated in soliloquy, lying on his back on the coarse sand while venom of the deadly Stonefish slowly crept through his body. Its tortuous movement was unmistakable. It entered through his left foot, where eight of the stinging fish's thirteen dorsal spines had pierced deeply into his flesh. Then it moved up through his calf, into his thigh, meticulously destroying tissues and cells. Jack felt the horrible onset of muscle weakness and paralysis, which he knew would soon incapacitate him. The venom of the Stonefish would kill him in a few hours without an antidote. Soon his breathing would be affected and eventually suffocate him.

Jack was perplexed by the irony of his demise. Alerted by gunfire that had occurred when one of the terrorists removed the silencer from his weapon, which he could clearly identify on the small island, he was fortunate to have spotted the terrorists first when they came looking for him. Having found refuge behind a boulder in shallow water near the beach, he sought safer haven by wading out further into the inlet to hide behind a larger boulder, just in case the terrorists came out onto the beach near the shoreline and saw his footprints. He remembered warning Mike, a fellow scientist, just a few days earlier about the dangers lurking just offshore. Mike had been snorkeling near the wreckage of a Japanese aircraft in shallow water.

"Careful around the wreck Mike!" he had warned.

"I had a Kiwi friend that stepped on a Stonefish in Saipan, near one of the tanks. We used to play 'king of the tank' near Susupe. One of my friends pushed another friend off the tank a couple years ago. He fell kinda awkward and stepped smack on top of one. He was instantly paralyzed, screamin' in pain. Had to pull him out of the water to keep em from drowning. We got him to the hospital in Saipan, but the nearest antitoxin was in Australia. We just kept sneakin' rum into the hospital to keep him half drunk until the pain subsided. The doctor said he barely made it. Just two spines in the left toe; but he still feels the pain today."

Of all people, Jack knew the danger, but couldn't avoid it. He simply stepped in the wrong place. After having survived three years of experimenting with all sorts of deadly venoms and toxins in Australia, to die by accident was incomprehensible. He lay there on the beach, overwhelmed more by confusion than by the pain. He was so focused on the enemy he could see, he had forgotten about the unseen *Synanceia sp.*, its scientific name, which camouflaged itself both in shape and color to resemble a rock in the sand. The initial pain had been so excruciating Jack could not remember how he'd managed to get back onto the shore after the terrorists left.

Jack agonized with the thought that he might die on Farallon de Medinilla, a place Melinda didn't even know existed. The isolated island, only 0.4 square miles of uninhabitable land, lay 45 miles from Saipan and just 16 degrees north of the equator. The U.S. military leased the island from the Commonwealth of Northern Mariana Islands for military exercises. It was far enough away from any population centers that a catastrophic accident would pose little danger to the people who lived on the other islands in the Marianas chain. More importantly, the island was only accessible by boat and, thus, was deemed a low security risk.

We underestimated the terrorists again, Jack reflected in anger.

He made up his mind that he would not die like this. He would not let terrorists win.

The quiet ocean waves broke gently across the white sands. The beach was peaceful; the sun glistened serenely over the turquoise waters, sinking on the horizon. As Jack stared up through the swaying palm trees, the setting for his death acquired a surreal quality. No spot on earth appeared more beautiful to him as he contemplated the last hour of his life. No spot on earth seemed so lonely. How could he die in such a beautiful place, a place meant for sunny days on the beach and joyful relaxation?

"Oh, God, not now, not like this," he uttered with little breath heavenward. "No one knows what I've discovered. No one knows what these people now have. I must warn them. Help me warn them."

Mustering the remaining strength in his paralyzed body, he rolled over, gasping for air as the neurotoxin began to shut down his breathing system. He crawled to his knapsack ten yards away, resisting the debilitating pain that threatened to throw him into unconsciousness. Frantically, he thrust his hand inside and pulled out a plastic water bottle one-third full. He carefully unscrewed the top, took a drink, and emptied the remaining fresh water into the sand.

With his left hand he then began pulling out the contents of his knapsack: a well-marked map of the Mariana Islands, a peanut butter and strawberry jelly sandwich that he had made for lunch, a malfunctioning cell phone that could only receive calls, and a white t-shirt with a large blue U.S. navy emblem. Reaching to the bottom, he found what he needed — a three inch by five inch yellow pad and a ballpoint pen that he always carried so he could jot down ideas during his walks on the island. He pulled the pad close to his chest, now gasping for air, struggling to make his diaphragm work. Fighting to stay alive with all the strength he had, he printed the number "919-628-3346" on the yellow pad. He then wrote with broken lines, "Melinda, I had to try. One day you will understand. It was worth giving my life—giving our lives together, our future. Stay true. I love you forever."

He then printed what looked like "www.intothewindsoffear.com" and "code 777-NL-45S" or code "SSS." Last, he printed, "Ken, we did it. It's out. You must help stop them. Take care of Melinda and children. Remember, be a good godfather. Say good-byes for me. God with you. Love, Jack."

After he scribbled those last words, hoping they were legible, he tore the sheet of paper off the pad, rolled it up tightly, and placed it in the empty water bottle. He reasoned that if he left the note on the beach, the terrorists might find it while looking for him. He tightly closed the bottle with the aluminum cap and crawled back toward the water. His timing could not have been better. The tide was coming in and a strong rip current was developing to a distance of 30 yards off shore, flowing out through a narrow opening in the coral reef. The warm ocean water set his body at ease as he entered the surf, slowing the convulsions that were occurring more frequently and with increasing intensity. The waves were gentle that day.

Using the power left in his arms, he managed a strong enough breaststroke to ease his way through the surf and into the current that would carry him out to sea. He was almost clear of the reef when his right leg, which he no longer had control of, dragged across the sharp coral rock, deeply cutting his calf and foot. He could see the blood but could not feel the 3-inch long gashes. Within a short time he was past the reef, and rolled onto his back, still clutching tightly to the bottle with his last words inside.

Jack thought he could see the rescue helicopter, even though he couldn't seem to hear it. He saw the two men descending down the rope ladders. His pain was so great, he could barely remember them pulling him into the chopper. He heard many voices as he drifted in and out of consciousness.

"Pull him up slowly. We gotcha now. You'll be alright—you'll be alright. His eyes are dilated. Antitoxin shots now. Keep em steady. His body's shutting down."

What seemed like hours later, but while still in the helicopter, after the pain had subsided, Jack heard a medic say, "He's stabilized sir. We got him in time. He's gonna make it."

Then everything became crystal clear. He was walking up his long driveway in crutches. Melinda came running to meet him in a long flowing beige satin nightgown, her long dark wavy hair blowing in the early morning breeze. He could hear the birds singing in the tall Sycamore trees that lined their driveway. He could hear his children yell "Daddy, Daddy!" as he embraced his wife. The overwhelming feeling of peace enveloped him, as he knew he was home and would never have to leave again. His scientific work for the military was over. He could now spend his time the way he had always wanted to, at home with his family.

His last memory he recalled saying, "I'm home, honey, I'm home for good."

Jack let go of the bottle 50 yards offshore as he lost consciousness for the final time. The sharks of the famed Marianas Trench quickly found his lifeless body, attracted by the blood oozing from his deep coral wounds. Jack did not die, as he had feared, with no human warmth or comfort. He died with memories of home, wrapped in his wife's arms, with his children, knowing the deep love of his family. The waves rolled gently across the shores of Farallon de Medinilla. Once again it was a peaceful place. The sharks ignored the floating water bottle. It bobbled along with the drift of the current with small pieces of Jack's shredded clothing.

CHAPTER 5

Annandale, Virginia

Colonel Matthew Kelvin Siefer quickly reached for the telephone, trying to keep it from waking his wife Kathy. He managed to pick it up after only one ring. Kathy still slept. He glanced at his digital clock. *Must be a serious,* he thought. *It's only 4:30.*

"Siefer here," he answered softly, walking into the bathroom with the cordless phone.

"Colonel Siefer, this is McGwire. We have a military emergency in the Pacific region. There has been a security breach at one of our research laboratories. I need you here right away."

"Yes, General," Matt replied. "In your office?"

"Yes. I'll be there in 30 minutes."

The line was momentarily quiet. Then McGwire added with personal concern and sensitivity, "And Matt, you should wake up Kathy and tell her you may need to go on a highly classified trip overseas. I don't know yet for sure, but pack a suitcase and bring your travel necessities with you."

"Understood, I'll let her know and I'll be at your office as soon as I can."

Siefer eased himself back into the bedroom.

"Let me know?" Kathy interjected sleepily with a laugh. "When do I ever know where you are going on these secret missions?"

"Hi, love. Sorry to wake you so early. We've got a military emergency at one of our Pacific bases. They may need to send me there. I'm sorry, but I have to go right away."

Kathy was used to these kinds of situations. At least once a month Matt had to travel somewhere overseas to attend to some kind of emergency. Due to security measures Matt could not always disclose exactly where he was going, and often he didn't even know the destination until he was in the air.

"You sound like a John Denver song," Kathy replied.

"And you're not sorry," she said sarcastically but playfully. "You get to go to some exotic tropical paradise in the South Pacific to meet friends in the sun-filled cafes and talk about who-knows-what around glistening swimming pools."

"It sounds so romantic, Kathy. I only wish it was half that much fun. Okay, sometimes it's a little exciting, but without you there it isn't much fun. And for that I'm truly sorry."

"Just remember, Matthew Kelvin, you promised not to get sucked into those silly emotional pits."

Matt learned to pay attention when Kathy used his full name.

"I know—never say I'm sorry when I'm doing my job," Matt recited.

Matt used to beat himself up verbally and emotionally when he had to leave his family on military mission trips. Kathy finally put an end to it, reminding him that this was the life they had chosen together. They had a military life of risk and uncertainty, but also a life of excitement and great fulfillment.

Kathy was very proud of Matt's advancement in the National Security Council and his work on matters of great importance to the security of the United States. He had made real progress in rebuilding his self-confidence after his department's failure to prevent the terrorist attacks on the U.S. embassies in Kenya and Tanzania. Matt almost opted out of the intelligence business after those tragedies, but decided to stay on after he and his colleagues began to recognize the growing threat of terrorism within the U.S., a concern fully realized on 9-11.

After grabbing the bag he kept packed for such occasions, Matt kissed Kathy good-bye and she went back to bed to enjoy another couple of hours of sleep. Unlike many military wives, Kathy never feared for Matt's life. He was extremely careful and was always well prepared for multiple contingencies. He had a great knack for anticipating the many things that could go wrong on any mission, and planned in such a way as if he was expecting things to go wrong. As a result, nothing seemed to take Matt by surprise. He had an amazing ability to anticipate danger and strategically think through how to escape threatening situations. Kathy was not unrealistic about the dangers he faced; she just had great confidence in him.

Immediately after Matt sped from his quiet Annandale neighborhood to make his way to the Pentagon, he began contemplating what group might attack a research facility. Lt. Gen. McGwire could tell him few details on the phone of the attack, but perhaps that was a security precaution. There were numerous terrorist groups seeking weapons of mass destruction: the Islamic Jihad, the Hamas, al Qaeda, and the Shining Path were a few he thought of immediately. The number of groups that could acquire the raw materials for chemical, biological, and nuclear weapons was great, but very few of them had access to the technical knowledge to know how to create controlled weapons.

While thinking about each potential threat, Matt developed an uneasy feeling that gripped his stomach. His friend Jack Costellona was working at a biological weapons research laboratory at Stanford but also was making trips to the Pacific.

"God I hope he wasn't involved," Matt said under his breath. *I need to call him right after the briefing with McGwire.*

Lt. Gen. Sharon McGwire was the highest ranking female officer in the Army. She was in charge of the U.S. military's research facilities throughout the world. A brilliant biologist, McGwire had earned a Ph.D. in microbiology at Johns Hopkins University in Baltimore while on a military scholarship. She had served two tours of duty in Viet Nam, where she had studied the effects of Agent Orange on both the environment and on civilians and military personnel. McGwire was among the most intellectually gifted and calculating military officers in the army, having risen through the ranks rapidly. She had fourteen years of experience working in the National Security Council. McGwire seemed to always maintain her composure even in the most dire circumstances. She had also mentored Colonel Siefer. Lt. General McGwire and her husband, a doctor at Johns Hopkins Medical Center, were very good friends with Col. Siefer and his wife Kathy.

Knowing Sharon's high level of emotional control when under stress, Matt became greatly perturbed by the concern he had discerned in her voice. He knew biological experiments were being conducted at U.S. research laboratories in different parts of the world. American intelligence sources and information from allies indicated an increased threat of biological terrorism.

Matt put a cassette tape into his car's audio system to listen to highlights of the last briefing on biological and chemical weapons by Major Joseph Corpi.

"So let me summarize my major points," Corpi lectured. "First, our primary chemical threats are sarin, mustard gas, soman, hydrogen cyanide, VX and phosgene. Both mustard gas and phosgene were used during World War I but are difficult to manufacture. It is unlikely that terrorists would gain access to these chemicals.

"Sarin was developed during World War II and was the agent used in the Tokyo subway attack that killed 12 people and injured more than 5500 others in March of 1995. Sarin can be manufactured and released by terrorists, as the Aum Shinrikyo cult demonstrated. They had their biological weapons research lab hidden in a shrine. Sarin is colorless, odorless, volatile, and highly lethal. The terrorists concealed the gas in lunch boxes and soft drink containers, which they then punctured with umbrellas at a train station during morning rush-hour."

"A month later," Corpi continued, "these terrorists launched another gas attack in a subway station in Yokohama, sending 400 people to the hospital who suffered dizziness and respiratory problems. In July of the same year, they struck several more train stations, this time with a deadly form of cyanide gas. The terrorists used a timer that mixed together cyanide soda and sulfuric acid."

"When the Aum Shinrikyo terrorists were finally captured, Japanese police discovered they were growing the deadly botulinum toxin, owned a truck capable of pumping chemical and biological agents, and were planning more devastating attacks on innocent civilians."

Cold sweat poured down Matt's back. He could imagine a sarin gas attack in Washington's subway system. No one would ever believe it could happen in America. *That is why we are so vulnerable. No one believes the threat is real.*

"Now, let me summarize the biological terrorism threats, which primarily are anthrax, smallpox, cholera, botulinum, plague, and brucellosis. Among these, anthrax and smallpox are the most likely bioweapons to be used against the U.S. Anthrax is an infectious disease that causes fever, respiratory failure, and death. Antibiotics can halt the disease, but we don't have enough stockpiled to stem a major attack, and infected people need six treatments for an 18-month period. Anthrax is easy to grow; you can get Anthrax spores in the environment and grow them in a Petri dish. The spores can be spread by aerosol. Fortunately, it is hard to weaponize and is not contagious."

"Smallpox, in contrast, is highly contagious and deadly. Americans have not been vaccinated against smallpox since the 1970s and there is no drug treatment once infected. Last year we only had 12 million dozes of smallpox vaccine stockpiled, but we've tripled that amount in the last six months and are still making more. Only Russia and the U.S. have large quantities of smallpox, but some samples are believed to have fallen into the hands of dangerous nations that have sponsored terrorism."

"However, we cannot rule out other biological agents. Al Qaeda operatives have tried to obtain anthrax and botulinum in Czechoslovakia. Members of the Islamic Jihad in Egypt have tried to obtain samples of the deadly Ebola virus in Uganda. Even a common bacteria like salmonella was used by followers of the Bhagwan Shree Rajneesh cult in 1984 to contaminate drinking glasses and salad bars, during the second documented biological attack in the U.S. Remember the first biological attack in America occurred when early settlers purposefully gave blankets and clothing infected with smallpox to North American Indians. Hundreds of thousands of Indians were killed as a result. Smallpox is still a relevant threat because we have not vaccinated children against the disease since the early 1970s."

Matt stopped the tape as he pulled into his parking spot in the Pentagon. He was eager to find out what was taking place. His sickening feeling had grown worse. He was not ready emotionally to grapple with fighting a biological or chemical attack on U.S. soil. The thought of it was repulsive. He walked into Lt. Gen. McGwire's office at 5:20 a.m. There were seven others present. McGwire had a somber look on her face as did the others.

"Thank you all for coming at such an early hour on such short notice," McGwire began. "Without further delay, let me begin my briefing."

Matt Siefer opened his notebook and grabbed his pen. He didn't want to miss one detail. A new journey was, indeed, beginning.

Chapter 6
Los Altos, California

When the phone rang, Melinda hoped that it was Jack, calling to say he was fine. It was 3:30 a.m. She also hoped her vivid premonition during the night had been a bad dream.

"Hello," she answered softly, "this is Melinda. Can I help you?"

Through considerable static a female voice responded, "Hello, Melinda, I'm Niloa Stephenson, and I'm calling from just north of Saipan, an island in the Marianas Islands, a trust territory of the U.S. just north of Guam. I'm sorry to call you in the early morning hours."

"I'm glad to talk with you, Niloa. I am familiar with Guam and Saipan. My husband works in the Pacific region."

Perhaps Jack was all right, Linda thought for a moment. Perhaps he injured himself and this woman is a nurse calling me from the hospital to let me know he is there. Jack must have given the hospital our home phone number.

"Is my husband Jack there with you?" Melinda asked through the static. She then realized that was a stupid question to ask a stranger.

"I'm sorry," Niloa said, "I can't hear you clearly."

"Are you calling about my husband Jack?" Melinda asked.

"Yes," Niloa answered clearly. "I have not seen your husband, but I found a note in a water bottle that your husband had written for you. Your phone number was on the note. I just found it a short time ago."

"Niloa, can you give me your number so I can call you back and get a better connection?" Melinda asked. "I can't hear you well. I thought you said you found a note from Jack in a water bottle."

"Ok," Niloa answered. "My number is 818-254-1816."

"Isn't that a Hawaii number?" Melinda asked.

"Yes," Niloa confirmed. "I'm on my mobile satellite phone but I live in Hawaii."

Melinda put down the phone. *A note in a water bottle?* she wondered. She dialed the number. Niloa answered.

"Hello, Niloa."

"Hi, Melinda. I can hear you very clearly now. Thanks."

"Me too."

"Melinda," Niloa continued, "I was sailing through the Mariana Islands and came near the lagoon of a small island called Farallon de Medinilla, about 45 nautical miles north of Saipan. The island is used by the United States military."

Melinda's heart began to succumb to a deepening dread.

"While sailing past the barrier reef I noticed what looked like a part of a shirt floating in the water. I also saw a water bottle that seemed to have paper inside of it. I picked the bottle out of the water and found a note that I believe your husband Jack must have written."

There seemed to be an eternity of silence on the other end of the line, so much so that Niloa wondered if they had been disconnected. Niloa waited in apprehension for Melinda's response. She thought about repeating her report but held her tongue.

Melinda was preparing for the worst. She had felt in her heart that Jack was in trouble. She had difficulty accepting that her emotional turmoil was not just a nightmare.

"Please, go ahead and read the note, Niloa," she said.

Niloa hesitated. "Melinda," she said with obvious sadness in her voice, "the note is…it is…." She struggled with her words; she could not say *it*.

It's a farewell note, Melinda thought in despair. "I know this is hard, Niloa, but it is important for you to read the note to me. I'm ready."

"Here's what the note says," Niloa replied, gathering her composure.

"'Melinda, I had to try. One day you will understand. It was worth giving my life—giving our lives together, our future. Stay true. I love you forever.'"

Tears streaked down Melinda's face as she realized the man she had loved for 27 years, her best friend, might be gone. Her heart ached with a pain that took her strength away. She could barely sit up. She struggled to breathe, to respond in any way other than succumb to an overpowering grief. Even though she had sensed that Jack was in danger, and that he might have been injured, she had been hoping against hope that he was alright. They had too many years yet to live together. But she knew Jack would not have written those last beautiful words unless he had known he was close to death. The words were obviously Jack's words: passionate, purposeful, poignant, and full of love and encouragement.

Niloa began to cry softly as she sensed the agony of Melinda's loss. Both women fought to regain their composure.

"There's more to the note," Niloa said gently. "There is a website: www.intothewindsoffear.com and code 777-NL-45S. Then there's a message for Ken. It says, 'Ken, we did it. It's out. You must help stop them. Take care of Melinda and children. Remember, be a good godfather. Say good-byes for me. God with you. Love, Jack.'"

"Niloa," Melinda asked with great solemnity, "where did you find the water bottle with the note and when did you find it?"

"I found it just outside the coral reef of Farallon de Medinilla about ten minutes ago. I called you immediately. I'm still in my boat and haven't been on the island."

"Niloa," Melinda spoke again, "thank you for finding the note from Jack and for calling me immediately. Jack was working on a very important military research project. He may still be on that island. If you think it is safe, can you search the island to see if there are any signs of Jack? Do you have any protection? Are you by yourself?"

"Yes, I can search the island," Niloa responded. "It's very small—less than a square mile in size. And yes, I'm alone but well protected."

"I'll call Jack's commander and let him know what you've told me," Melinda replied. "Thanks for looking for Jack."

"Melinda, I'm happy to help you. I know the note sounds bad, but perhaps your husband is injured and still alive. I'll start looking for him on shore immediately."

"Thanks so much, Niloa. You're a very special person. I'll always be grateful for your help."

Tears welled up again in Niloa's eyes.

"I'll try and call you again, Melinda, as soon as I find out what's going on."

"In the mean time," Melinda added, "I'll also contact Jack's friend Ken and I'll give him the message you told me Jack had written for him. Take care of yourself, Niloa."

"I will. Bye," responded Niloa as she turned the *Dawn Treader II* toward the small beach on Farallon de Medillina.

Niloa sailed over the reef and entered the small bay. She could sense something was wrong. There was a strange quiet. She anchored the *Dawn Treader II* in shallow water, grabbed a loaded semiautomatic rifle on board, and waded to shore. A smell of smoke and an eerie deadness was in the air. She spotted two people lying on the beach face down. She drew closer and stared in horror. Two Marines lay dead in the sand, their bodies riddled with bullet wounds. She walked cautiously up a path leading to the center of the island. There were no signs of living people.

Just before entering a clearing in the tropical jungle, Niloa suddenly dropped to the ground. She heard something, or somebody. She scrambled off the trail into the savanna grass nearby and crawled slowly and quietly toward the clearing. Through the grass and coconut palms she saw several structures in a u-shaped compound. Several more dead Marines lay in the center of the compound. It seemed that nobody was alive. Whoever had done these killings was already gone.

Niloa rose and walked quietly to the buildings, holding her assault rifle with two hands in an defensive position. Although she had no particular attraction to guns, Niloa had learned to use one after a harrowing experience with a small group of inebriated gang members in San Diego. Fortunately, the men were too drunk to harm her, but the weapons they had carried frightened her enough to sign up for a weapons training course a week after the incident.

Niloa surveyed the area. There were three small concrete buildings, each powered by solar panels and auxiliary diesel generators. None of the generators were on. Air conditioning units lay outside the buildings. Cabins surrounded the buildings for sleeping quarters and a large outdoor eating area in a gazebo-like structure with a thatched roof was situated at the opening of the u-shaped compound. Two cooking areas with large kilns were adjacent to the eating area. After inspecting the two cooking fires, both that had warm embers, Niloa thought about entering the one-story buildings. Remembering what Melinda had said to her on the phone, she concluded it was too dangerous to enter them. She decided instead to look inside the buildings through windows and open doors. She was careful not to touch anything. Through windows she could see that more bodies were inside the structures. They were obviously some type of laboratories. Niloa had a strong sense that Jack Costellona was not inside.

She knew she needed to make a quick search of the island, although she dreaded what she might find. There were only two additional paths from the compound besides the path she entered on. She followed one to a small strip of sand on the northeast corner of the island, just a quarter mile north of the main beach were she had entered. Cautiously, she approached the beach. She took a deep breath and sigh of relief she saw there were no dead bodies on it. She had seen enough bodies in pools of blood. Walking toward the shore, she spotted a knapsack close to the water and several items in the sand, including a well-marked map of the Mariana Islands, a broken cell phone, a waterproof jacket, a compass, and some clothes. She picked up the knapsack, which was wet on the outside, and looked inside. There was a passport holder and a wallet inside, which was still dry. She reluctantly opened the passport, hoping it was not Jack Costellona's. His warm brown eyes, sandy brown hair, and handsome square jaw gleamed off the page of his glossy passport photo. It was him. She then flipped through Jack's wallet and paused, transfixing her gaze on a family picture of Jack, Melinda, and their two children. It was at that moment that she realized what Melinda might have lost. *He looks like a wonderful man, a loving man*, she concluded.

    She swallowed hard, again caught by strong emotion. There was no sign of Jack, but clear evidence he had been there lying in the sand. She could see the markings in the sand where he had crawled into the water. Floating in the surf, Niloa spotted a yellow pad of paper. It was the same color and size as the three inch by five-inch note she had found in the bottle. Then she knew. Jack had written the note right there on the beach. She looked around. *Such a beautiful place*, she thought, *and such a lonely place to die.* Looking out into the ocean, she noticed the shoreline was treacherous with many large rocks, but there was a small opening about 30 yards wide out to the coral reef and to the open ocean.

    Why would Jack come here? she wondered. Perhaps to hide from the killers behind these large stones. Niloa searched the surf for a body but found none. There were no signs of blood and no signs of a body. Perhaps he is dead inside the buildings. No, he can't be. He wrote the note on this pad. Perhaps he tried to swim away from the terror and drown. Niloa labored to make sense of it. If he was wounded, she reasoned, he could have written the note, swum into the surf with the bottle, and sought to swim away from the island until they left. But then there should be blood on the path or in the sand.

    Niloa ran back to the compound and explored the other trail to the south. The trail made a steep ascent to a clearing. While running through the clearing she saw an outline of a man in her peripheral vision. She stopped, jerked her head to the left, and was aghast by the site. A dark-skinned man was tied spread eagle to the ground, baking in the hot sun. He was either dead or unconscious. Niloa slung her weapon on her back and pulled her 6-inch hunting knife from its sheath. She cut the ropes from his hands and feet, which were tied to the base of nearby trees. She then dragged him into the shade. He was extremely dehydrated and sunburned, but still alive. Cupping her hand gently under his head, she slowly poured some fresh water from her canteen on his face, wetting his lips. She then helped him to drink, although he had great difficulty due to his swollen tongue and semi-conscious state. She continued pouring water over his head, intermittently helping him drink more and more water. He finally returned to full consciousness and whispered, *"Salamat, salamat. Tagasaan ka?"*

Niloa tried to remember the few Tagalog phrases she had learned growing up in Hawaii.

"Kumusta. I'm Niloa, " she replied softly. "Tagasaan ka?"

"Philippines," he answered. "I speak English."

"Who did this to you?"

"*Abu Sayyaf,*" he whispered. "They left me to die. They couldn't shoot me—I'm a believer. They shot everyone else. I told them to stop, but they kept shooting."

"What's your name?" Niloa asked.

"Paulo," he replied. "I'm Paulo Rizaldi Browning, from Mindanao."

"I'm Niloa Stephenson, from Hawaii."

"Niloa," Paulo said in delirium, almost weeping, "I tried to stop them. They killed everyone but me. I saw one scientist ran away. Maybe he made it. I wanted no part of this. They deceived me and used me."

Paulo then explained to Niloa his skill as a navigator and how the *Abu Sayyaf* had told him they would attack the American lab only to acquire antidotes to biological weapons that would be used against their group by the government of the Philippines. Once the shooting began, Paulo unsuccessfully tried to stop them, threatening to shoot the mission leader if he did not stop the carnage. Paulo didn't go through with his threat. The *Abu Sayyaf* would not spill his blood because he was considered a faithful Muslim brother. They left that up to God. If he died in the sun, God would then have performed the execution. If he escaped, God would then have been merciful to him.

"Where'd they go?" Niloa inquired.

"Back to Basilan. They've got all the vials," Paulo explained. "They can kill many more people now."

"What vials?" Niloa asked.

"Deadly viruses," Paulo replied in a chilling emotionless voice. The *Abu Sayyaf* now has them. This is a weapons lab here."

Niloa had read about the *Abu Sayyaf* when researching a sailing expedition in the Philippines. The group was a splinter group from the Moro National Liberation Front (MNLF). The MNLF eventually signed a peace agreement with the Philippine government in 1996, but the *Abu Sayyaf* was not interested in making peace. Instead of seeking redress for its grievances within the rule of law, it launched a wave of terror in 1991, including bombings, assassinations, extortion schemes, and kidnapings, often victimizing innocent civilians. The group's goal was to create a Islamic state, similar to the way the Taliban created an Islamic state in Afghanistan. Their name, which means "Bearer of the Sword" or "Father of the Sword" in Arabic, reflects this philosophy. Several years after founding the *Abu Sayyaf*, Abduragak Abubakar Janjalani, its leader, was killed in a gun battle with Filipino police on Lamitan Island.

Niloa told Paulo to rest while she searched at the end of the trail. She found more dead bodies in American military uniforms. When she returned to Paulo, he was standing upright. He had regained some of his strength. Niloa was disturbed to see a handgun under his belt and an automatic weapon on his shoulder. She was mixed with fear and intrigue. He was tall for a Filipino, she thought, judging him to be just over six feet. He had a lean, muscular body and lighter than expected sandy brown hair with hazel eyes. Most Filipinos had black hair and dark brown to black eyes.

"Niloa," Paulo announced, speaking with a strong voice and good English, "I'm going to have to take your boat. I'm sorry, but I'll be arrested and imprisoned by the Americans for being aligned with the *Abu Sayyaf* if I stay here."

"So, you're one of them," Niloa said in disgust.

"No, I'm not part of their group. But no one will believe that I tried to stop the killing. Who could I convince that I did not know this was going to happen, that I was only a navigator to take them here?"

"Paulo, the *Dawn Treader II* isn't going without me," she responded without intimidation, raising her automatic weapon. "Just because you claim to be a navigator doesn't mean you can sail my boat; and my boat doesn't go anywhere without me."

"How do you think I got here?" Paulo asked.

"Power boat," Niloa answered.

"That's what everyone will think," Paulo said. "The *Abu Sayyaf* aren't as stupid as many Americans think. They know that Navy submarines can track motorboats from great distances with their equipment. But they can't track sailboats. Patrolling pilots don't expect guerrillas to be sailing leisurely across the ocean. I'm a very good sailor."

"Sounds like you're defending the *Abu Sayyaf*," Niloa responded. "I think terrorists like these men are cowards."

"They're not cowards," Paulo shot back. "They're brutal sometimes, and deceived, but not cowards. I know them well. All too well. Niloa, please believe me, I'm not a terrorist. I didn't do this. I have a family to support in the Philippines. I can't live my life in an American prison cell."

"Okay," Niloa assented, lowering her weapon. "I'll sail you to the Philippines on my boat. Just tell me what island and I'll take you there."

"It's treacherous where I am goin'," Paulo replied.

"I know," Niloa replied, "I've sailed around Mindanao alone."

"So, how good are you at sailing? Niloa inquired with a tone of skepticism."

"I know the Philippine Sea, Sulu Sea, and South China Sea as good as any."

"So, you helu 'ekuahi?"

"Yeah, number one. I know some pidgin too," Paulo answered.

"With two of us who know how to sail, we'll have much greater safety," Niloa assured. And like I said before, I'm not going anywhere without *Dawn Treader II*."

"Dawn Treader II — what's that mean?"

"Haven't you ever read C.S. Lewis?" Niloa asked.

"I'm afraid not."

"Well—just know that she's a hell of a good yacht. We say *'helu ekuahi'* in Hawaii — second to none!"

Collecting as many supplies as they could, including several extra weapons and rounds of ammunition that the *Abu Sayyaf* had left in haste, Niloa and Paulo immediately set sail. They were losing valuable time.

   They sailed due west toward the islands of the Philippines. They disappeared in the vast Pacific less than an hour before the first military helicopters landed at the compound. The military recovered the bodies of 16 dead Marines and four dead scientists. Jack Costellona's body was not found. He was officially declared missing. A massive search for him ensued. A few pieces of clothing were found in the water offshore, but it would take many days of DNA testing to try to establish the owner's identity. The bloody attack was the worst attack on a military installation in the U.S. since the Pentagon attack on September 11. U.S. military leaders had not expected this – not on such an isolated island that very few people even knew existed.

CHAPTER 7
The Pentagon

"Good morning, ladies and gentlemen," Lt. Gen. McGwire began. "I realize it's very early and I appreciate your haste in getting here for this briefing. As you have probably surmised we have an emergency situation. About four hours ago there was a security breach in the Mariana Islands. I want you to listen carefully to a telephone call from Niloa Stephenson to her parents, which they received on their answering machine at 4:15 this morning." Lt. Gen. McGwire played the message.

"Hi, Dad and Mom, I realize you're still sleeping and that it's way too early to be calling. I was sailing around the island of Farallon de Medinilla just north of Saipan when I saw a part of a shirt and a water bottle floating outside the reef. The bottle had a note in it from a man named Jack. He thought he was about to die. The note was to his wife so I called her in California and told her about it. I heard that the military was using the island but didn't see anyone, so I decided to go on shore."

Niloa began to cry and her voice quivered. "Mom and Dad, I saw dead Marines on the beach. There are no signs of life. I'm on the beach now and am going to look for survivors. Please call the military and get help here. I'll call again soon."

McGwire turned off the recorder, then turned to his overhead projector.

"Now let me read an email that was sent at about 8:10 last night, Eastern Standard Time. The message was not read until 4:40 a.m." McGwire displayed the message on an overhead slide.

This is Swordfish 2. We're being attacked. We don't know who they are but they have automatic weapons. Must have arrived by boat—we had no warning. Cannot provide visual description. I'm locked in my office but they will be here soon. Have to begin destroying data. Send Hel—

The message was sent by Dr. Greg Staunton," McGwire continued, "and that's not a typo. The message was never finished. Two Marine rescue helicopters were dispatched to the island from Saipan and arrived on Farallon de Medinilla just a little while ago. They have confirmed 20 dead.

McGwire paused to allow everyone to sense the severity of the situation.

"We also received a phone call from Melinda Costellona, the wife of Dr. Jack Costellona, one of the scientists on the island. Ms. Stephenson called Mrs. Costellona after she called her parents and read the note she had found to her. She told both her parents and Mrs. Costellona that she was going to search the island to look for Dr. Costellona. Her parents have not heard from her since. Neither has Mrs. Costellona. This is all the information we have now on this attack," McGwire concluded.

"I'll be directing Colonel Siefer to fly to Guam at as soon as he can. In Guam he will rendezvous with one of our biological terrorist experts on the president's advisory board for terrorism. They will make a connecting flight to Saipan and travel to Farallon de Medinilla to survey the situation. The initial reports indicate this is probably an attack by a terrorist group seeking biological weapons. We don't know yet what they might have taken from the lab, but there is a stark probability we are dealing with terrorists who now have biological weapons capabilities. Are there any questions?"

"Yes General," replied Captain Connie Parker, a senior weapons analyst, "Can you tell us the nature of the biological samples in the lab?"

"We had multiple projects in progress at the lab," answered McGwire. "We were developing new antigens to combat anthrax in response to last year's anthrax attacks. But our main work was with botulinum, which scientists had found naturally occurring in the sand sediments around the island. The hot and humid climate was conducive to growing bacteria cultures, and the isolation of the island away from any populated areas made it a good area for experimentation, just in case of any accidents. The nearest inhabited island to Farallon de Medinilla is 45 miles away."

"Have the dead been identified?" asked Major Whitmore.

"Not by name," answered McGwire, "But we know there were five scientists, two lab technicians, one communication specialist, one cook, and 12 military personnel on the island at the time of the attack."

Colonel Siefer hated asking the next question, but he knew he needed to ask it. "Lt. Gen. McGwire," he said reluctantly, "was Dr. Costellona on the island at the time and do we know which scientist is missing?"

McGwire had as much difficulty answering the question as Colonel Siefer had asking it. Costellona was a personal friend of both of them. Their three families had enjoyed camping trips, barbecues, and fishing expeditions together.

"I'm sorry, Matt," McGwire replied, barely controlling her emotions. "The note found was clearly a farewell. Jack arrived on the island a day before for a series of tests on an antidote he had developed for botulinum. However, he could be the one person who is still unaccounted for. We should know soon who the missing person is once all the bodies are identified."

"Does Kent know yet?" Siefer asked.

"I don't know, but I'm going to call him right after this briefing," McGwire responded. "Dr. Costellona's wife Melinda may have already called Kent."

McGwire took Col. Siefer aside after the briefing for a private conversation.

"I'm going to call Melinda as soon as I can," Sharon said softly. "She and the kids are going to need us."

"I'm here to help," Matt responded. "Thanks, Sharon, for putting me on this. We'll catch these guys."

"Be careful, Matt. These terrorists are ruthless. They rarely take prisoners."

After the short conversation, Colonel Siefer's military attaché sped him to Andrews Air Forces base a few miles southeast of Washington, D.C. There, he would board a military flight to Hickam Air Force Base in Hawaii. Then he planned to take another military transport plane to Guam. On the way to Andrews he called Kent Mariuchi.

"Hi Matt," Kent answered, I've been anxious to talk with you. Melinda called me earlier this morning.

"Then you know Kent?" Siefer asked in a shocked voice.

"Yes. Melinda told me everything and relayed the note to me."

"What did Jack say?"

"It was a farewell note as if he were certain he would die. Jack also wrote a web address on the note and said that 'it's out' and "I must help stop them.' I haven't yet had time to check out the site but will later this morning."

"Do you understand what he meant?" Siefer asked. "What's out?"

"Colonel, I believe those who attacked our lab now possess the weaponized botulinum that Jack and I were working on, as well a the botulinum antidote. They also might have a new strain of anthrax that Jack was working on."

"Does anyone else know how to make this stuff?" Siefer asked.

"Only the two of us," Kent replied. "But I still don't know how to make the antidote. Jack was testing various samples of botulinum and must have had a breakthrough. I'm sure, if he had the time, that he left the testing information for me on the secured website he had set up."

"I'm on my way to the Marianas now," Siefer explained. "I wish I could talk with Niloa Stephenson."

"I anticipate she'll try to call her parents again soon," Ken replied.

"Well, when you get into the website where Jack directed you to go, please contact me," Siefer requested. "Also, if you hear anything else about Stephenson, let me know."

Immediately after Siefer concluded their conversation, Kent turned on his computer at home and connected to the Internet. He then found the secure website Jack had set up: www.intothewindsoffear.com. He typed in the security code Jack had left: 777-NL-45S. The first web page that appeared offered a warm welcome message from Jack that was streamed with a web cam and stored on the site. Jack's picture appeared to the right of the screen in a three square inch box.

"Hi, Kent," Jack said. "I know the bandwidth is not great, but I should look pretty good. This is an emergency website I set up for you and Melinda just in case something went wrong. If you read through the 127 pages of material here, you will be able to fully comprehend the seriousness of the situation you face. On the anthrax project, I was able to develop an aerosol spray that will attach tiny antigens to the smallest anthrax spores that have been weaponized to date, and kill the spores on contact. The spray consists of a natural biological agent that kills the harmful bacteria but poses no threat to people or animals. It is also inexpensive to produce. You can see the chemical formulas on this site with specific directions on how to manufacture the antigen agent. The most important advantage is that the spray can be used as a preventative agent that will kill weapons grade anthrax before it can infect anyone. I've sent a copy of this information to you and Dr. Switzler at Stanford so you could test it also."

Kent was humbled by the discovery Jack had made. They had worked together for 16 months on developing an effective protection against anthrax. The anthrax attacks in September and October of 2001 only strengthened their resolve to find a preventative solution.

"That's the good news Kent. The bad news is the discovery we made on the botulinum toxin and botulinum antitoxin we were developing. It's dangerous, Kent—a bigger threat than anthrax."

Kent stopped playing the audio-video file to contemplate what Jack had said. He recalled the many long ethical debates that he and his colleagues had had with the military community. The debates were similar to the ones scientists had engaged in while working on the Manhattan Project. Many of them wondered if this was the right thing to do, to even experiment with biological weapons. They anguished over the risk that they might unleash biological agents that could not be controlled. Just as physicists struggled with the need to achieve certainty in knowing that they could manage nuclear fission and fusion, Kent, Jack and their colleagues had wanted the certainty that they could control biological agents that might be released into the population by accident or by terrorists.

The botulinum-F toxin they had developed had the potential for destruction on the scale of devastation brought about by the bubonic plague outbreak in China in the early 1330s. That outbreak eventually spread to western Asian and Europe, killing 25 million Europeans, one-third of the continent's population, in a five-year period. In a cruel twist of history, the Chinese were again victims of the plague in modern times when the Japanese weaponized the bacteria during World War II. They first tested the effectiveness of the plague with prisoners of war and then unsuspecting civilians, achieving a 50 to 60 percent mortality rate when released through infected fleas.

The full horror of the Japanese biological attacks on China occurred in Manchuria, where Japanese planes bombed villages and cities with munitions shells containing large numbers of plague-infested fleas. No one knows exactly how many Chinese died in these terrifying attacks on civilians.

Although botulinum-F toxin could not be spread by fleas and rodents like the plague, it could be weaponized, inhaled as a fine powder like anthrax or ingested through tainted food supplies as basic as coffee creamers and sugar packets.

Kent and Jack were keenly aware of the potential for small radical terrorist groups to obtain biological agents for acts of terror, demonstrated by the Japanese cult group *Aum Shinrikyo's* anthrax attacks in Japan in the mid-1990s. Scientists from the cult had managed to weaponize and test a non-virulent liquid form of anthrax that they sprayed into a neighborhood for 24 hours. Cult members had also tried to smuggle samples of the deadly Ebola virus out of Uganda. They feared that a strain of the botulinum toxin could also be weaponized into both powdered and liquid forms and used in terrorist attacks.

An outbreak of the Ebola virus in a city like Los Angeles or New York could kill more than a million people before adequate measures could be taken to protect people. Likewise, a new strain of botulinum toxin could be released in major cities through the air, food, and water supplies, killing millions before antitoxins could be distributed.

Kent clicked on the audio-visual file again.

"Kent, I know you are aware of the risks. The botulinum F toxin we developed and are still testing is extremely deadly. It can be transmitted both in a fine powder and also dissolved in water. It is odorless and tasteless. In the solid form, not only can it be inhaled, but in can be ingested through contaminated food. The good news is that the antitoxin prototype we developed to kill botulinum F is extraordinarily effective in killing this bacteria. It will kill all six forms of botulinum discovered to this point in time, types A through F. We also think it will kill any new strains of botulinum developed in many years to come. We suspect other scientists in Iran, North Korea, Syria, China, and Russia are also working on new strains of botulinum. However, they are very difficult to weaponize; and except for Russia, these countries are many years away from successfully turning botulinum into a weapon of mass destruction. Kent, only you know fully about the breakthrough I made to develop a virulent weaponized form of botulinum F and its effective antidote.

"If by any chance, rogue nations or terrorists were able to acquire this botulinum toxin, you would need to stop them from using these agents at all costs. You must warn the President and other leaders and immediately begin manufacturing the antitoxin in large quantities. Hopefully, that won't be the case now, and my incapacitation or death will simply be a result from some sort of minor accident. I hope and pray you never see this video, but if you do, please know I look forward to talking with you again, if not in this life, then in the next. Remember, Kent, how Jarvis used to encourage us to 'not be afraid to sail into the winds of fear'? You'll need that kind of courage. Good-bye for now."

Kent sat there for a couple of minutes staring at the computer screen. He couldn't believe that Jack might have been killed. *They had to have kidnaped him,* he thought. *He would be much more valuable to a terrorist group alive than he would dead.* Kent thought how journalist Terry Anderson had been kidnaped and kept alive in Lebanon for many years before eventually being released.

The second audio-video file Jack had made was for Melinda. Kent emailed it to her with a supportive message letting her know of the biological agents Jack had developed before his disappearance.

Kent called Colonel Siefer and relayed to him what he had discovered on the website.

Siefer decided to contact Winnifield Jarvis, a close confidant. Jarvis was a former National Security Council member who was an expert on biological terrorism. He retired from active service and was now living in Sete, France, a southern port on the Mediterranean. Recently the President had asked him to join his advisory board on terrorism. Jarvis (he never used the name Winnifield) loved sailing and had built a restaurant and hotel in Sete to cater to the yacht racing teams that trained there during the summers. Although Siefer was very careful who he discussed the security breach in the Mariana Islands with, the State Department provided him clearance to consult with Jarvis.

Jarvis was an occasional consultant to the CIA, FBI, and State Department, whom he assisted as an advisory board member without compensation. He lived comfortably in France on the retirement package the U.S. government had provided and on the 30 years of wise international investments he had made that had generated millions of dollars.

Siefer was not eager to call Jarvis. He would certainly be depressed and deeply saddened by the news that Jack was either kidnaped or murdered. Jack was one of the best friends of Dennis Treyberg, a fellow research scientist who was like a son to Jarvis.

Treyberg's father, who was under Jarvis' command, had been tragically killed during a helicopter crash on a military mission in the cocaine fields of Columbia. Jarvis virtually adopted Dennis into his own family. Jarvis also invited Dennis's mother, Gina, to come live with him and his wife in their suburban home in northern Virginia. Gina eventually remarried, but their families maintained their strong friendships, and Jarvis continued to relate to Dennis like a son. Jarvis knew Dennis would be devastated by the news about Jack.

Siefer was unable to reach Jarvis by telephone because Jarvis was out at sea and did not have a satellite phone with him. He decided to send Jarvis an email. Within 15 seconds of sending a message, the instant messenger chime rang on Siefer's computer. He was surprised — Jarvis was on-line and was using instant messenger. Jarvis's pen name was Sea Breeze.

His first message stated:

Hi Matt. It has been a long time. I was just checking my messages and was pleasantly surprised to hear from you. I was eagerly waiting to hear an update about Jack's disappearance. Jim Stephenson told me about the attack.

Do you know the Stephensons? Siefer typed.

Chris Stephenson is my mother's half-brother. Although Chris and I are almost the same age, I am actually his uncle. However, I am much more of an uncle to Chris' children. Niloa Stephenson is very close to me. She calls me Uncle Jarvis.

You mean the young woman who found the note is your niece? Siefer typed incredulously.

I am actually Niloa's great uncle.

You did hear about the note?

Her father told me about the note. Chris Stephenson contacted me to tell me that Jack was officially considered missing. He also said that the note that Jack had written to Melinda sounded like a farewell message as if he knew he were dying.

I am so sorry Jarvis. Jack was my friend too. I am struggling with the possibility he may be gone.

You know Matt, Jack was a good friend of Dennis. I always knew this day might come for both Jack and Dennis because of the danger of their work. I was always prepared to die when I worked for the NSC on covert missions, but I was never prepared for one of my close friends to die. When I lost Dennis's father in Colombia, I wish I had died in his place. Let's pray Jack is still alive.

INTO THE WINDS OF FEAR

I am hoping against hope that he is, Siefer typed.
Can we meet? Jarvis asked.
Yes, where are you now? Siefer inquired.
I'm in my boat anchored off the coast of Corsica. I have friends in Rome that can help us. Can we meet there?
No, I've been ordered to go to the Marianas to inspect the site of the attack as soon as I can. Can you meet me in Guam?
Yes, that will work, replied Jarvis. *Where and when?*
Let's plan to meet at 1:00 pm in the Naru Hotel in Agana on Thursday.
Have a safe trip, Chris, it will be good to see you.
Siefer and Jarvis both signed off Instant Messenger.

Jarvis finished off the bottle of fine Bordeaux wine he had opened and sailed his yacht to Milan. After anchoring his boat at a local yacht club, he caught the train to Rome. Col. Siefer traveled to Guam on military flights. Their travels seemed much longer than usual. They both felt great anguish over the probable loss of Jack. Neither one of them believed deep down that Jack was still alive.

CHAPTER 8
Mindanao, Philippines

Stephano Pelagong knew his fourteenth birthday would be a special one. His older cousin, Manny, had bought him a book that would change his life.

"A book on Che!" Stephano had exclaimed after unwrapping the gift from his cousin. "How did ya know I wanted this, Manny?"

"Something about a poster of Che in your bedroom," Manny replied.

Stephano was fascinated by what he had heard about the Argentinean revolutionary who fought with Fidel Castro during the communist revolution in Cuba. He idolized the life of Guevara, a rebel to some but hero to others. Stephano was raised in a culture that regarded the Muslim fighters for independence as heroes. Zamboanga City, Stephano's home, became a center of activity for the Moro National Liberation Front, or MNLF. Every weekend he used to travel into town from the plantation ten kilometers away where his father worked. Every Saturday afternoon they would buy some ice cream, his father would drink a few beers, and they would listen to the stories of the latest heroic exploits of the MNLF.

In the beginning their activities seemed fairly restrained to Stephano's family, friends and relatives. The MNLF would conduct raids on large copra plantations at night and take food, money and supplies from wealthy landowners. Most of the families of Mindanao, like Stephano's family, worked many long hard hours for the wealthy class just to keep themselves from slipping into poverty. Stealing from the corrupt landowners, who reinforced an inequitable system of wealth, power, bribes, and corruption, was not seen as criminal or even wrong. The dictatorship of President Ferdinand Marcos was considered to be criminal, not the Robin Hood exploits of the MNLF.

Stephano's father never became too concerned about his son's infatuation with the MNLF, since Stephano was a gifted learner who excelled in school and never talked about wanting to be like the MNLF. Stephano's mother Gloria, however, disliked the way her sons seemed to look up to the MNLF fighters as role models. Nevertheless, it was not until Stephano's fourteenth year, after he had read the biography on Che Guevara, that Stephano decided he wanted to become a Muslim freedom fighter. It was a peculiar decision since he was raised as a devoted Catholic and knew little about Islam.

By the time Stephano reached age 16, Marcos had dispatched the army into Mindanao to capture or kill MNLF fighters. Many MNLF leaders disappeared, as well as many men whom the Philippine military believed to have been supporters of the MNLF. Stephano and his family learned that year about two prominent newspaper reporters from Zamboanga City who were found dead in the harbor. They were officially called victims of drowning, but everyone knew Marcos' secret police had silenced their voices. The articles they were writing revealed too much of the corruption of the Marcos regime.

One week short of Stephano's seventeenth birthday, an unthinkable tragedy radically altered Stephano's life. He had begun to become disillusioned with the MNLF, who had begun assassinating political leaders, setting ambushes for military patrols, and planting bombs in popular eating establishments frequented by wealthy landowners. Stephano's father had strongly encouraged him to think about attending the University of the Philippines in Manila to study agriculture and business. His father had saved enough money to buy Stephano and his two brothers a small farm to work into a profitable business. Stephano was at the top of his class academically and had a very good chance of receiving a scholarship to the university, one of the best in the country.

All of these prospects suddenly vanished with the disappearance of Stephano's father. He was last seen at a bar in Zamboanga City frequented by MNLF supporters. The bar was bombed on a Friday at about 10:30 p.m. Stephano's father, Renaldo, had only one indulgence away from his family. After a 60-hour workweek, he would visit with his friends every Friday night at one of their favorite restaurants and taverns in town. He would promptly leave the establishment at 11:30 p.m. every Friday, his commitment to Gloria not to abuse his one night out each week. In 24 years of marriage, Renaldo had never come home drunk. Then one night, Renaldo never came home at all.

A powerful bomb had blown apart the Blue Pelican so violently that it was difficult to find survivors. Many bodies were literally blown to pieces and others were incinerated in the ensuing fire. Marcos' secret police were believed to have planted the bomb. Renaldo's body was never found. He could have been kidnaped, tortured and killed later, as was the fate of some, but no one knew for sure. Gloria had hoped and prayed that he was sitting near the bomb and had suffered no pain. Stephano was inconsolable when he learned of his father's death.

"Tatay was completely honest," he shouted in anguish to his mother, sobbing. "He never hurt anyone! He loved everyone! Why did they kill him? Why? Why?"

Renaldo was well respected. Everyone knew how much he loved his family. His death was a shock to everyone. He had never spoken any public criticism against the Filipino government.

The day after Stephano's seventeenth birthday, he told his mother, two older brothers and two younger sisters, that he was joining the MNLF.

His parting words to his mother were, "They're evil, Mom. Marcos is a murderer. They must be driven from power. I have no choice but to fight. I'm fighting because I love my family. I'll uphold the honor of my father."

Stephano could not overcome the burning hatred in his heart for Marcos, his corrupt regime, and his evil security forces that he believed were responsible for his father's death. Stephano vowed to fight them to the bitter end. He would either help overthrow the wicked regime, as Che Guevara and Fidel Castro had done in Cuba, or he would die trying. He would avenge the death of his father and the torture and death of many innocent civilians murdered by Marcos and his henchmen.

During the time that Stephano had been an active member of the MNLF, from 1978 to 1990, he prided himself in never having killed an innocent person or committing what he considered to be a terrorist act. His MNLF unit was assigned strictly to counter-intelligence. The MNLF leaders astutely recognized Stephano's intellectual abilities and put him in charge of documenting the activities of Marcos' security forces, particularly their payments of bribes to corrupt leaders and blood money—direct payments for assassinations. Stephano would collect this information through an intricate network of people within local communities who were sympathetic to the MNLF.

Within a few years, Stephano developed a reputation as an honest freedom fighter who would never break his loyalty to his family, friends, or MNLF comrades. By the time the Philippine people's revolution climaxed in 1986, Stephano was respected by both the MNLF hierarchy and local community leaders who fought against the MNLF. Despite his many years with the MNLF, Stephano never did abandon his Christian beliefs for Islam, although he did manage to read the Koran. Like many of his comrades in the MNLF, he simply wanted political and economic freedom—freedom from government dictatorship, freedom from dominance by wealthy landowners, and freedom from the Catholic Church. They were corrupt institutions in Stephano's eyes.

When Corazon Aquino was elected President of the Philippines in February of 1986, two and one-half years after her husband Benigno's assassination by Marcos's security forces, Marcos and his wife Imelda were exiled to Hawaii. President Aquino immediately began implementing democratic reforms and dismantling the Marcos dynasty. The MNLF continued its activities in quest for a separate Islamic state, but Stephano lost the object of his intense hatred once

Marcos was dethroned. Some of the corrupt military leaders were tried for their crimes and imprisoned, although most were never brought to justice. The men believed to have planted the bomb that killed Stephano's father were never found or heard from again.

Stephano, without a Muslim faith to motivate him, left the MNLF in 1990, two years before it entered serious peace negotiations with the new government. By that time he was 29 years old and had spent almost half his life at war with a corrupt government. One of Stephano's young colleagues, Abdul Ashmad, became frustrated with the compromises the MNLF was making with the government. He urged Stephano to leave the MNLF with him and others and to join a new Islamic group founded by Abdurajack Janjalini, the *Abu Sayyaf*.

Trying to convince Stephano to join them, Abdul declared to him, "This will be much more exciting, Stephano! Abdurajack fought the Russians in Afghanistan with the Mujahideen. He knows how to fight and how to win. We will free the southern Philippines and create our own country."

"You mean your own Islamic state like Iran?" Stephano asked. "I don't want to live under any particular religious domination. I just want to live in country where we are free to believe whatever we want to believe. Besides, Marcos is gone now. Why should I keep fighting Abdul? I've spent almost half my life fighting. I want to become educated, find a wife, and have a family. I'm not getting any younger or any more desirable to a potential wife."

"I told you, Stephano," Abdul replied, "if you became a Muslim you could have many wives. That is not a problem. The women love brave freedom fighters like us."

Stephano laughed. "Abdul, I'm 29 and you're 30. We have fought together for many years. I have never seen any women flocking to meet us. I don't see any now. They all are afraid of us."

"You'll see, Stephano. By the time I am 35 I'll have three wives. Just watch me. It's going to happen," Abdul said confidently.

"Stephano, I'm going to miss you. I really wish you would reconsider. The *Abu Sayyaf* is going to make history."

Stephano had an eerie feeling his friend was right. He had known Abdul for many years. He was intelligent, charismatic, and a good fighter. He also had one major flaw—he was hungry for power and wanted to make the southern Philippines into a strict Islamic state like the one in Afghanistan when the Taliban ruled.

The *Abu Sayyaf* also tried to recruit Paulo, one of Stephano's best friends. He warned Paulo to stay away from them. Paulo also had no interest in forcing Mindanao to become an Islamic State.

Within a short period of time, the *Abu Sayyaf* gathered a sizable military force and began waging a campaign of terror. It carried out kidnapings for ransom, using the funds to purchase modern weapons, boats, and other military equipment. By the mid-1990s the Abu Sayyaf was better equipped than the Philippine army troops sent to oppose it.

Stephano kept his eyes on the group's activities while he pursued his educational goals. His big break came when he met Kel Steider, a missionary doctor from New Zealand who had come to Mindanao to establish a medical mission and Bible school. Kel had first moved to the Philippines with his young family in 1984. When he began his work in Mindanao after several years in Manila, the Muslim leaders threatened to harm him. After Steider helped several Muslim families with medical needs, including the son of an influential Muslim leader, they changed their minds and allowed Steider to stay in Mindanao and do his work unhindered.

Stephano first met Kel at Canopy Bar and Restaurant in Zamboanga City. Stephano was still trying to deal with his bitterness about the loss of his father and close friends through frequent visits to various bars. Kel went to the Canopy about once a week to build friendships with young fathers who needed help to overcome their drinking problems. He would then provide treatment and family counseling as part of his medical practice. Kel instantly liked Stephano, and during the next several months, they became good friends. Something Kel said one evening changed Stephano's life.

"Stephano, when I was eight years old a neighbor got drunk one day and killed my older brother with his pick-up truck while my brother was riding his bike home from the store. My father became very bitter. I watched that bitterness destroy his life for five years. The man went to jail for five years, but my father suffered more than he did, because of unforgiveness. When that neighbor was finally released from jail, I saw something I thought I'd never see if I lived a million years. My father made a beautiful desk for him and brought it to him as a gift the day he returned to his family. I could not believe it. I did not understand what was happening. I saw my father put that desk, the one he had worked on for four months, in his pick-up truck, and I saw my mother crying as he rode away. I didn't realize until later my mother's tears were tears of joy."

Kel then had looked straight into Stephano's eyes as if looking into his soul.

"My father took that desk over to our neighbor and said to him, 'Jake, you have wasted five years of your life in prison and I have wasted five years of my life being bitter. It's time for both of us to have a new beginning. I forgive you for killing my son. We cannot change what happened that day. Now you must forgive yourself and start anew. I made this desk for you. Every time you see this desk, I want you to remember the forgiveness you have received. May bitterness never touch our lives again.'"

"You must have been in shock," Stephano said.

"I didn't learn this until after my father had come home. I had asked him in disbelief why he had given this awful man who killed my brother that beautiful desk. My father then told me what he had said, and added,

'There is one thing worse than the pain of injustice, son. That is, the anguish of never forgiving. I will never make that mistake again.'

My father experienced a remarkable change in his life after that day. I heard him laugh again. My mother was profoundly happy too. My father had been in a bad mood for five years, like one caught in a bad dream. Then he woke up."

Stephano was mesmerized by the story Kel had shared. He felt just like Kel's father in the story, caught in a bad dream. During the next couple of weeks Kel helped Stephano to forgive those who had killed his father and close friends. Stephano felt like heavy weights had been lifted from his body. He felt like a new person.

With a strong letter of recommendation from Kel to one of the administrators he knew at the University of the Philippines, Stephano received a scholarship and went to the main campus of UP in Manila for two years. He returned to Mindanao in 1992 to finish his last two years at the UP campus in Davao. In 1994, he completed his college education with a double bachelor's degree in business and agriculture. He returned to his home in Zamboanga, still single, but determined to begin a new life. The Philippine government had granted him full amnesty as a former MNLF fighter. Unfortunately, Stephano could never completely escape his past. The *Abu Sayyaf* became more radical, reckless and dangerous. Stephano would eventually have to face his former comrades again, but not as an ally.

CHAPTER 9
Philippine Sea

Niloa and Paulo sailed due west through the Philippine Sea toward the Philippines. Once inside the safety of the island nation's coastline, they turned south and followed the string of islands to Mindanao. In addition to keeping alert for Pacific storms, their most urgent concern was ruthless pirates from China, Indonesia, Malaysia, Thailand, and Borneo, who roamed the Philippine Sea, the Sulu Sea, and the Celebes Sea, looking for ships to hijack and cargo to steal. Often these pirates would kill the entire crew or leave them stranded without food, fuel, or water.

Paulo had heard recently that a Chinese gang out of Hong Kong had hijacked an oil tanker traveling from Singapore to Japan. The crew of eleven men had no chance against the seven heavily armed pirates who would not hesitate to kill if provoked. The pirates had paid off the port authorities in the former Portuguese colony of Macao, a port south of Hong Kong, where they could unload the stolen cargo onto smaller vessels and make several millions of dollars in profit, even after paying half a million in bribes. The tanker's crew was found locked in the ship's refrigerator unit, very cold but unharmed. They were fortunate to have lived.

Niloa looked toward Paulo as he carefully scanned the seas.

"You're worried about pirates, Paulo?" she asked, already knowing his thoughts.

"Have you ever faced pirates, Niloa?" he asked in return.

"I've been fortunate, Paulo, but a good friend of mine, Peter Blake, was killed by pirates on the Amazon River. It was one of the saddest days of my life. He won the America's Cup for New Zealand in 1995, only the second non-American to win it in its 144 year history."

"You knew Sir Peter Blake?" Paulo asked with surprise.

"I knew him before he was knighted by the Queen in 1991. My father introduced me to him at a major yachting event in the U.K. He was *aiwaiwa* adventurer, fearless but very kind. I was just thinking about him."

"What happened?" Paulo asked with marked sadness in his eyes.

"He was on board the *Seamaster*, his boat, resting quietly while it moored at the mouth of the Amazon, when several men with automatic weapons boarded from a small dingy. Peter had a gun and managed to shoot off the finger of one attacker, but his gun then jammed and he was shot to death. He was truly a great man who loved the seas."

"You know Paulo, we can't outrun pirates who come in speed boats," Niloa remarked.

"I know. We need to avoid them."

Paulo was very familiar with the pirates who operated in the popular shipping lanes near the Philippines. The pirates avoided tangling with the MNLF and feared the *Abu Sayyaf*, but did not hesitate to take on Filipino military patrols. Paulo had on board an AK-47 assault rifle, 500 rounds of ammunition, one Colt-45 semi-automatic handgun, and five close range percussion grenades.

Niloa had one Berretta semi-automatic 9mm pistol, a semi-automatic rifle, and the M203 40mm grenade launcher in the locked cabinet, a weapon attached to an M16A2 5.56mm rifle used by the U.S. Marine Corps that her Uncle Jarvis had acquired. They concluded that together they could defend themselves against several pirates, but not a larger group, especially in a surprise attack.

Niloa and Paulo sailed to the coast of Samar without incident, encountering no storms, no pirates, no government officials wanting bribes, and no common thieves wanting the *DawnTreader II*. They then turned south toward Leyte Gulf, weaving through the many small islands on the way to the Bohol Sea north of Mindanao. The more than 7000 islands in the Philippines archipelago provided safe havens for pirates, terrorists, and various clandestine groups in thousands of obscure coves and inlets.

They traveled mostly at night when the skies were clear, purchasing supplies in small villages during the day. Fewer ships traveled in the evenings and it was easier to avoid the scouts of the various armed groups and government security forces who were tracking illegal activities and collecting bribes. Neither Niloa or Paulo had much cash on board to pay off authorities or local militias for safe passage.

During their travels they talked for many hours about how they could locate the *Abu Sayyaf* and biological weapons they had stolen. They first considered contacting Filipino authorities. Paulo had a cousin who worked for the government intercepting contraband, mostly illegal drugs, from a central office in Cebu City, a major commercial center. However, his cousin had told him that several military officers were accepting payments from the New People's Army (NPA), MNLF, and other rebel groups. Paulo's cousin was honest, as was his superior officer, but he did not know who to trust.

They then considered contacting the U.S. military through the American Embassy in Manila, but Paulo was very hesitant. Niloa was able to contact her parents and ask for their advice. The U.S. had placed several military officers in the Philippines to assist with strategic defense and internal threats.

After the September 11th attacks, President Bush sent counter-terrorism military advisors to specifically deal with the *Abu Sayyaf*. This option seemed the best one, since Niloa was an American and the U.S. Embassy and U.S. military could be trusted. Paulo, however, feared he would be arrested and be held responsible for the murders in the Mariana Islands. Niloa's father agreed that this was not the time to try to clear Paulo's name. No one was alive to testify that Paulo had tried to stop the killings at the risk of his own life.

If Paulo told his story, that he was told by the *Abu Sayyaf* that they were only trying to destroy the lab and steal antidotes to biological weapons the U.S. was developing, he feared no one would believe him. In fact, the *Abu Sayyaf* told Paulo that the U.S. was providing these weapons to the Israelis to use against Muslims. Paulo did not realize the real goal of the *Abu Sayyaf* was to steal the weapons so they could sell them to Palestinian terrorists.

Abu Sabaya, one of the leaders of the *Abu Sayyaf*, had little interest in Middle Eastern politics and had no concern for the millions that could be killed by these weapons. His only concern was the 100 million dollars he was already being paid to deliver the biological materials to Islamic agents in Oman. With 100 million dollars he could create his own kingdom on Basilan Island and Jolo Island and purchase the submission of the Zamboanga Peninsula for an autonomous Islamic state. Sabaya's passion for power had little to do with religion or ideology.

Unfortunately, Paulo did not learn the truth about Sabaya until it was too late. He had blindly followed Sabaya as a hero, a freedom fighter seeking to overthrow the corrupt Marcos regime and the abuses of the Catholic Church. That was the image crafted carefully by Sabaya, Khadaffy Janjalani, and his Islamic preacher brother Abdurajak when they fought with the MNLF. They manipulated their followers with inspiring rhetoric of religious liberty.

Sabaya said he would be a leader of the people; but it was all a lie. Sabaya was just as power hungry as Marcos and his cronies. He had no more integrity than the Catholic Bishops who abused their privileges by living well off of poor parishioners who lived in shantytowns of corrugated metal.

"Paulo," Niloa said, trying to recapture his attention while they sipped lemonade and crushed ice at a small café on Cebu Island. "Paulo," she said again with more force, placing her hand on Paulo's forearm, "you're daydreaming again."

Paulo finally looked at Niloa. He had done quite a lot of daydreaming, reminiscing during their journey from Samar, reevaluating his life and what he had believed.

"I can't believe how stupid I've been," he confessed to Niloa. "I've given five years of my life to follow a fraud. Now he has enough biological agents to wipe out the city of Manila, and he used me to steal them. What a fool I've been."

"Paulo," Niloa shouted as she glared at him, "you said you weren't part of them! Were you lying?"

"No, I'm not a member of the *Abu Sayyaf* and I didn't know their true intentions. They lied to me! I must put it behind me and do some good."

Niloa remained skeptical. She knew he wasn't disclosing the whole truth about himself.

"We've got to get the biological agents before they use them, Niloa."

"There must be someone, Paulo, whom you trust who could help us find the *Abu Sayyaf*. Once we find them we can contact U.S. authorities and let them handle the situation."

Paulo's eyes brightened for a moment and Niloa noticed the change.

"What?" Niloa asked excitedly, "You have an idea, Paulo? What is it?"

"There is someone, but I would hate to bring him into this mess. I have a very good friend, Stephano, whom I should have listened to a long time ago. We were in the MNLF together. When Abdurajak Janjalani formed the *Abu Sayyaf* in 1990, he asked my friend Stephano to join him and some other MNLF fighters. They wanted Stephano badly because he was a great fighter and organizer. He is such a great leader."

"What'd your friend do?" Niloa asked.

"He quit the MNLF, surrendered his weapons, renounced violence and pledged to support the Aquino government in helping to rebuild Mindanao," explained Paulo. "He would not even consider joining the *Abu Sayyaf*, and warned me of the blind ambition of Abdurajak."

"So you have been helping them anyways as a navigator," Niloa concluded.

"Foolishly, I brushed Stephano aside. I should've listened to him."

"Why did Stephano quit? And what happened to him?"

"After Marcos was deposed by the people's revolution, he felt he had achieved his goal. He never wanted to turn Mindanao into an Islamic state. He was very close to his sister, Lea, a well-known singer, who played a big role in helping him to renounce violence as a political solution.

"Once Stephano made his decision to quit the MNLF, Lea launched a national campaign to support amnesty for all rebel fighters who renounced violence and pledged support for President Aquino. Lea, at the time, was one of the most popular singers in the Philippines. She stirred great support for her brother. Stephano actually appeared with Lea at a large pro-Aquino rally in Manila before he was officially granted clemency. He and his sister had so much respect; no one in the Filipino military had any desire to arrest him."

"Can he help us now?" Niloa wondered aloud.

"Yes. Stephano knows many of the *Abu Sayyaf*," explained Paulo. "He shared with them his deep hatred for Marcos and the government, a hatred that allows them to easily be manipulated by their leaders. Marcos' cronies killed Stephano's father in a bombing."

"Will he even want to help after all he has been through?" Niloa asked.

"I'm sure he will," Paulo responded. "And no one will know how to find the *Abu Sayyaf* like Stephano. He knows the southern islands. Stephano is very smart. You would really like him Niloa. He has the same spirit you have. I'm more cautious. Stephano believes he can do anything. He's afraid of nothin'. We must find him. We'll go to his parents home when we get to Zamboanga City."

"Zamboanga City!" Niloa shouted. "Isn't that a hotbed for terrorists?"

"Yeah–there are some there. But there's many good people there and it's a beautiful place," replied Stephano. "You'll see."

CHAPTER 10
Agana, Guam

Col. Matt Siefer's plane landed in Guam about 20 minutes later than scheduled. He was able to get about five hours of sleep on the long trip from Hawaii. He walked into the Naru Hotel in Guam at 1:20 p.m. The U.S. Air Force base in Guam was not too far from the hotel.

Jarvis had not arrived yet. His trip was not as predictable. Jarvis first had to sail from the island of Gorgona, northeast of Corsica, to Lovorno, a seaport on the western coast of Italy. He then had planned to take a bus to Pisa, where he would catch a train to Rome.

When Jarvis received the phone call from Col. Siefer, he was very close to Corsica. There were no storm warnings in the forecast, but unpredictable storms could arise quickly in the Mediterranean. On Jarvis' recent trip from Gibraltar, he had been caught in a 50-degree temperature differential during a 10-minute period.

A large hot air mass had formed off the coast of Morocco and pushed its way rapidly across the Mediterranean directly into his path. The air mass increased the temperature from 55 degrees Fahrenheit to 105 degrees, causing a freak wind shear that nearly ripped the main sail off Jarvis' yacht. He was able to release the sail just before the full blast of wind came.

Jarvis, an excellent sailor, was in too much of a hurry to deal with any inclement weather on the way to Livorno. His sailing trip went very smoothly this time. He secured his vessel in a yacht harbor he frequented and took a taxi to the bus station.

The bus trip to Pisa took much longer than expected. A road construction project stopped traffic for more than an hour during the construction workers' afternoon break. Instead of taking its breaks in shifts, the whole road crew stopped working, including those directing traffic through the two-kilometer work site. Jarvis missed a train to Rome by ten minutes. He would have had to wait 90 minutes for the next train, which meant he would miss the evening flight out of Rome.

Jarvis wisely called a friend in Milan who owned a private plane and chartered private flights from Milan to various cities in Europe. His friend was available to pick him up in Pisa and fly him to Rome. He arrived there two hours before his Northwest Airlines flight to Tokyo was to depart. After checking in, Jarvis decided to make some calls.

Claudia picked up the phone on her desk. "Buon giorno."

"Hello Claudia, this is Jarvis. *Come esta?*"

"Jarvis! It's good to hear from you. I'm fine. Are you on your yacht?"

"No," Jarvis replied. "I'm at the airport in Rome, on my way to Guam."

"I see. Another South Pacific adventure," Claudia mused. "But did you say you are at the airport? Did you overcome your dislike for flying?"

"Yes, I missed it too much," Jarvis replied with great sarcasm.

Claudia could barely control her laughter. Jarvis hated to fly and avoided it whenever possible.

"How are your boys?" Jarvis asked.

Jarvis had remembered that the boys had turned 20 the previous month. He knew they both had many female suitors and friends, but had wondered if there were any serious relationships that had recently developed.

"Are they still taking out each other's dates?" Jarvis asked, remembering their delight in taking full advantage of being identical twins.

"Only when they're in trouble," Claudia answered, laughing again.

"So, Jarvis, are you taking anyone with you on your South Pacific adventure?"

"I'm actually working on a terrorism case," Jarvis answered soberly.

Jarvis paused and swallowed hard, gaining control of his great sadness.

"Claudia, I'm afraid some bad things have happened. A very close friend is missing after a terrorist attack on his research compound in the Mariana Islands and is feared dead. I thought Dominic might be able to help me. Is he still working with the counter-terrorism task force?"

"I'm so sorry about your friend," replied Claudia. "Dominic is working now. He's still working in counter-terrorism and is currently in Sicily working on a case. Things have been crazy since the Madrid train bombings. He also has been monitoring international drug trafficking. I'll get Dominic's office and cell phone numbers. I know he'll want to help."

Claudia found one of Dominic's business cards and gave Jarvis his phone numbers.

"Thank you, Claudia," Jarvis said. "Tell Dominic I'll try and reach him now, but if I miss him, I'll call him on my return trip."

"Then you must come for dinner next time," Claudia replied.

"Are you still living in the same home? Jarvis asked.

"No, we moved eight months ago to a new home in the hills, about 30 minutes northwest of Rome. We have our own little villa where we grow our own tomatoes and wonderful grapes," Claudia bragged.

"Then I must come and have some of your homemade sauce and wine," Jarvis responded.

Jarvis bid Claudia good-bye and wrote a note to remind himself to schedule a visit soon. He checked his watch—his flight for Tokyo was leaving in 45 minutes. Jarvis noticed the extra security in the Rome airport, not like when he had worked in counter-terrorism during the 1970s and 1980s. During those years Rome was one of the easiest places for terrorists to operate. Only one in one hundred bags were searched in those days. All kinds of contraband came through Rome: narcotics, weapons, plastic explosives, ivory, just about anything illegal and valuable.

Jarvis observed the security procedures. Every bag was being checked and every person was searched. The airports throughout Europe had greatly increased security. Jarvis wondered about the airports in Egypt, Jordan, Syria and Lebanon. *Had they also increased security?* He could not stop thinking about who might be willing to use the biological weapons stolen by the *Abu Sayyaf.* There were many groups in the Middle East who might do such a thing.

"Boarding all business class passengers for Northwest flight 62 for Tokyo," the airline steward said in Italian, French and English. Jarvis did not need to wait for the English version of the announcement before he moved toward the gate. He had learned enough Italian from his parents to travel and converse comfortably anywhere in Italy.

Immediately after sitting down, Jarvis sifted through the pages of computer files he had stored on various terrorist groups. Although he usually traveled business class when he had to fly, which was on rare occasions, he was often the last person on the plane. He hated the confines of airplanes, preferring the open feeling of a yacht gliding across the ocean. There were some exceptions. Jarvis did like the double-winged airplanes of the 1920s, 1930s and 1940s, with open cockpits, the wind in his face, and flying with natural faculties. The automatic piloted commercial aircraft of today had no appeal to him at all.

Before going to sleep, he decided to write out some of his thoughts. The intelligence information he had been given indicated leaders of the *Abu Sayyaf* had fought with other Islamic militants against the Russians in Afghanistan. *They must have known some of the al Qaeda leaders,* Jarvis thought. The U.S. had gathered substantial evidence indicating Osama bin Laden had attempted to develop chemical and biological weapons. Jarvis jotted down an important question: Perhaps the *Abu Sayyaf* would sell weapons to some of these Islamic militants still operating terrorist cells in the Middle East, Europe, or even the U.S.? The most likely targets would be Israel and the U.S.

Jarvis also wrote: How would the *Abu Sayyaf* transport biological weapons to the Middle East or the U.S.? Philippines to Malaysia? Then to Saudi Arabia or Oman? Then to Syria or Lebanon? A heavy sleep enveloped him like a warm blanket on a cold day. He hoped his trip to Guam would yield some answers.

He arrived at the Naru Hotel ten minutes after Col. Siefer had arrived. Siefer greeted him warmly. They had not seen each other in more than four years.

Siefer's face showed deep concern as he ordered two cold Amstel Lights.

"Thanks for coming so quickly, Jarvis. How was your trip?"

"An adventure, as always," Jarvis replied. "It's not easy going from retirement on my yacht, sipping wine and watching sunsets, to chasing terrorists again."

Matt laughed heartily.

"It's good to see you, Matt. I'm glad you have not lost your ability to laugh. I just wish we were here on a more joyous occasion."

"I know," Siefer replied. "I really like this place."

"How are Kathy and the children?"

"Fine, thank you. The girls are four years taller and smarter and Kathy is four years wiser and more beautiful than when you last saw her," Matt responded. "When I told her I had to come on a classified trip to the South Pacific, she was obviously jealous. We have had many happy memories of our time here."

"I'd love to see her," Jarvis replied. "Has it been four years already since your visit to France? Wow, hard to believe."

"I know," Matt concurred. "The girls are growing up so fast. We all need to get together again soon."

"Have you been briefed by Lt. Gen. McGwire?" Matt asked.

"Yes, I talked to her earlier today. Also, while in Rome, I was able to make some phone calls and check in with my Italian counter-terrorist friends. They've been in close contact with the Israelis because of the recent activities of terrorist cells working in Europe and the Middle East. I suppose you've heard the links they've found between *al Qaeda* and a bank in Milan. We've got major problems in Rome too. As you know, Rome has been a central organizing point for many Middle Eastern terrorists. Israeli intelligent agents said that during a recent interrogation of Mazdi Kalaf, a Hamas operative arrested for involvement in several terrorist attacks against Israel, he blurted out in anger, 'You will all be biologically purged before the end of the year.'"

"Does McGwire know about this?" Matt asked in concern.

"No, not yet. I just received this information yesterday because one of Kalaf's close associates flew from Beirut to Rome last night on his way to Germany. The Italian police detained him overnight for questioning but had to release him this morning, since he had not broken any Italian laws. He flew to Frankfurt just before noon, but is being closely watched by German security agents."

"Jarvis, do you think the threat is credible?" Matt asked.

"I asked my Italian friends the same question. They said Kalaf had worked at Baghdad University on biological weapons research. After his father was killed by U.S. troops during Desert Storm, he turned bitter against the U.S. and joined the Islamic Jihad. Recently he joined the *Hamas* to plan and execute terrorist attacks against Israel."

"How could he be linked to the attack on our research laboratories?" Matt wondered aloud.

"The Israelis also told my friends that during the interrogation, Kalaf justified Saddam Hussein's use of biological weapons that he had helped to create. Kalaf said he believed the Jews and Americans were planning biological attacks on the Palestinians. He also said they knew about labs in California and in the Pacific region."

Jarvis took a long slow drink from his mug of Amstel Light.

"Now you know why I'm so concerned, Matt," Jarvis lamented. "That comment greatly alarmed the Israelis, who don't know much about our scientific work on biological research in California or about our U.S. biological research facility in the Pacific. The Israeli intelligence service concluded that Kalaf was fabricating the whole story."

"But you're not so sure?" Matt asked, seeing the deep concern on the face of his old friend.

"No," Jarvis answered. "I'm not convinced that he was just blowing smoke. I think there is a serious possibility that Kalaf in his arrogance let slip some very important information. Perhaps the *Hamas* know much more about our operations than we suspect. We have to find out what kind of contact and possible collaboration they have with the *Abu Sayyaf*."

"Why the *Abu Sayyaf?*" Matt asked.

"Because they are one of the few groups who could pull off the attack in the Mariana Islands," Jarvis answered. "There are many Filipinos working in Guam, Saipan, and the other islands of Micronesia. Someone friendly with the *Abu Sayyaf* might have heard about the research lab. It would not be difficult for a Filipino posing as a fisherman, for example, to scout out the research facilities from a distance with the right kind of surveillance equipment now available."

"Jarvis, I wonder if you have seen too many spy movies?" Matt asked.

"I know it sounds far-fetched, Matt. I probably have seen too many movies, but I also have seen too many spies operating freely in the U.S. I realize that's the price of an open and mobile entrepreneurial society, but it still bothers me."

"I thought these terrorist groups operated independently."

"They did during my days as an intelligence officer," Jarvis explained. "But not anymore. The *Hamas*, the *Hezbollah*, the *al Qaeda* network, and others are all working together now, and they may have linked forces with Indonesian militants and the *Abu Sayyaf* in the Philippines. We need to quickly find out."

"When do we leave for Farallon de Medinilla?" Jarvis asked.

"We have a plane scheduled to take us to Saipan at 1600 hours," replied Matt. We will then take a boat to the island."

Jarvis and Colonel Siefer spent the next hour reviewing the known facts of the attack. The estimated time of attack was between noon on Sunday evening and 7:00 p.m. The normal communication from the lab to an office in California scheduled for 7:00 p.m. that evening was never received. The last email they had received was from the head of security at 12:05 p.m., right on schedule. The message said,

"Afternoon security checks made, no problems. It is a quiet beautiful Sunday afternoon. I'll e-mail again at the 7:00 p.m. security check." At 7:05 p.m. an email sent to the lab was unanswered. Several phone calls that followed were unanswered.

The Marines that had been dispatched to Farallon de Medinilla from Saipan concluded the attackers numbered 8-10 people. The shell casings found indicated they had used AK-47 assault rifles in the attack. The 16 Marines who had been killed all died from gunshot wounds. The bodies of the three scientists found indicated two were executed in their house, obviously taken by surprise, but the third scientist was not as lucky. His body was recovered near his open office in the research lab. His face and back were covered with multiple slashes and cigarette burns, signs of torture before he was killed.

"The Marine commander called me after their initial search last night," Siefer explained.

"He said there was no evidence of any survivors, confirming Niloa Stephenson's report to her parents. However, it was too dark to do a thorough search. They made another sweep of the island this morning."

"What did they find?" Jarvis asked.

"Only some of the personal effects of the missing scientist."

Jarvis leaned forward and listened intensely.

"It's Jack," Siefer said. "Jack is the missing scientist. Then he could possibly be alive!"

Yes, we've identified all the bodies and Jack is not among them."

"What are the chances, Matt?"

"It's possible, but doubtful. The Marine commander said it was an overkill. They made sure that no one survived. Many of the dead were shot in the head at close range. The areas where the lab samples were kept were broken into. Many lab materials seem to have been taken."

"Perhaps that's how they gained access into the high security areas," Jarvis noted. "They probably resorted to executing them in front of one another after torture did not work."

Siefer continued.

"The terrorists seemed to know what they were looking for when they entered the lab. Curiously, they did not touch any of the anthrax samples or antidotes. Anything labeled botulinum was taken, including the weaponized samples that Jack had been testing. The terrorists used battery-powered temperature controlled cases to transport the stolen materials. Siefer and Jarvis discussed their possible means of escape."

"They could have flown out of Guam, Saipan, Tinian or Rota," Jarvis brainstormed, "but they knew the airports would be put on security alert once the attack was discovered."

"Also, how would they have put their samples through security x-ray machines to take them on board the aircraft?" Siefer asked. "The x-rays could damage the samples or their cases could be subject to search. Air travel seems too risky for a way of escape."

"More likely," Jarvis agreed, "they would escape the U.S. territories by boat. It would be difficult to spot a small boat traveling at night in such a large body of open ocean."

"With our sophisticated sonar equipment," Siefer countered, "we could track down boats with powerful engines. They would need to carry large amounts of fuel to travel the more than 1600-mile trek to the Philippines."

"In the Philippines, they would have access to many different islands and hiding places," Jarvis noted. "They could also travel from there on to Indonesia, Thailand, Malaysia, or Burma by boat."

"Yes, in pirates alley," Siefer added.

"There are many open waterways in southeast Asia where pirates have forged a ruthless and lucrative business. Smugglers with many years of experience have distributed all kinds of contraband throughout southeast Asia, moving illegal drugs, jewels, and stolen art from Asia through Arab countries such as Iran, Iraq, and Afghanistan, then through Turkey into Syria, Lebanon or even Europe."

"They could get these weapons all the way to the Middle East, couldn't they?" Jarvis asked Siefer.

"They could."

"I don't like it, Matt. There are a number of Hamas terrorist cells now on the borders of Israel from which they could easily make a strike in a major city like Haifa."

"So, if they are in a boat, we need to track them now," Matt concluded.

"Unless they didn't use a motor boat," Jarvis mused.

"What do you mean?" asked Matt.

"Remember, Matt, I'm a sailor."

"A sailboat would make a quiet entry and escape," Matt reasoned aloud; "and not many people would expect to find a group of terrorists sailing. But aren't they rather slow?"

"Not this time of year," Jarvis explained. "A sailboat could make good time to the Philippines, and sailboats are very rarely checked by Marine security forces."

"If they succeeded in launching a biological attack, Jarvis, do you realize how many people they could kill?"

"I was very knowledgeable about biological warfare ten years ago just before I retired," Jarvis replied, "but I am not up-to-date on the latest biological advances. I do know you can kill the entire population of a city with the contents in a briefcase."

"That's correct," Matt answered. "Let me elaborate."

For the next hour Col. Siefer explained to Jarvis the most recent developments in biological warfare. In order to develop antidotes to current biological agents that could potentially be used against the United States and its allies, American scientists had to create and weaponize these agents and variants in order to develop effective protections against them. Despite the extreme danger involved in working with these agents, scientists had never experienced any fatalities or life-threatening situations. The programs at Stanford and in the Mariana Islands were specifically focusing on airborne botulism toxins and anthrax that spread rapidly and are difficult to contain once released.

Jarvis had heard of the danger of botulism but did not realize the toxins could be spread as easily as bovine spongiform encephalopathy, or BSE for short, otherwise known as Mad Cow's Disease. He remembered that Great Britain had to destroy over five million cattle to stem the tide of the disease, costing the country billions of dollars. Botulism could also be spread through contaminated food and made into weapons. Saddam Hussein had made bombs with similar agents that could be spread airborne and inhaled or ingested.

Siefer explained further, "Food-borne botulism affects about 1000 people a year worldwide through contaminated foods. It creates a paralytic disease caused by neurotoxins such as botulinum, one of the most poisonous substances known to man. Botulinum is found in marine sediments in the Mariana Islands. Trivalent equine botulism antitoxin could handle some strains of the disease, but not the concentrations of more recent variations that may be in the hands of the terrorists. Our lab on Farallon de Medinilla was developing new strains of neurotoxins and their antidotes."

"Matt, it sounds like an airborne biological attack with botulinum in order to contaminate food supplies would be difficult to control. Both Jews and Palestinians would die if such an attack was launched in Israel. Would the Hamas risk killing Palestinians?"

"They are sending their children strapped with explosives on suicide attacks. Why wouldn't they use their children for biological attacks?"

"You're right, Matt. They would sacrifice more of their own. They are desperate. They'll do anything to destroy Israel."

The thought gripped Jarvis in the pit of his stomach. He could see thousands of dead bodies overwhelming the morgues in Haifa, piled on top of one another. An image of the Jonestown mass suicide flashed through his mind. Jarvis was on military assignment in Venezuela when Jim Jones led members of his religious cult in Guyana to drink poison. His commanding officer dispatched him to the compound shortly after news of the suicide reached Washington. He could never forget the piles of dead people, mothers and fathers side by side with their children, infants in their mothers' arms, and sisters still holding hands. In the 22 years of service in the U.S. military and CIA, Jarvis had only lost the ability to control his deep anguish twice. His visit to Jonestown was one of those occasions. He wept for twenty minutes after seeing a deceased family that very much mirrored his own family, with two girls and a boy about the same age as his children. The picture was printed indelibly in his mind.

After finishing their 90-minute meeting, Jarvis and Colonel Siefer left the Naru hotel in Agana and caught their scheduled flight to Saipan. The 120-mile trip was beautiful. Flying over the deepest part of the ocean, the famed Marianas Trench, reminded him of the scuba diving trips he and Kathy used to take when he was stationed at Andersen Air Force base in Guam. The rich coral reefs and blue-green waters held amazing underwater beauty. Except for an occasional shark encounter, the Marianas Trench was an underwater explorer's paradise.

As their plane approached Saipan's airport on the south side of the island, Matt's thoughts flashbacked to one of the hiking and diving trips he had made with Kathy some 16 years ago. The island had gentle beaches on the western and southern coasts, a rugged and rocky eastern coast, and a hilly interior with dramatic cliffs on the northern coast. On the way to their diving location on the north end of the island, Matt recalled how he and Kathy hiked to Banzai Cliff, where thousands of Japanese soldiers leaped to their deaths during World War II rather than be captured by American troops. He had been reminded of the tragic waste of life. Many of the grandchildren of those who died there would come to pay their respects to their grandfathers.

Not far from Bonzai Cliff, Matt and Kathy had decided to dive in the Blue Grotto. It was one of the riskier dives on the island because divers had to swim from a grotto through a 30-foot underwater tunnel out into the open sea just offshore. The similarity of the underground rock formations made it more difficult to find the tunnel in order to return to the grotto. Several divers had drowned in the area after becoming confused and losing their way. The divers that had died had tried to swim to shore around the rock cliffs near Bird Island against very strong currents and surges. They did not have the strength to make it.

Matt and Kathy had wondered if they should have planned a dive in the Grotto or at Naftan Point. The dramatic drop-off and turtles, eagle rays, octopus and schools of butterfly fish they encountered at Naftan Point convinced them to go there. *Looking back,* Matt thought, *I believe we made the right decision.* They had heard later that the Grotto was very rough that day.

The rough landing at Saipan International Airport snapped Matt out of his memories of diving in Saipan. The 25-knot crosswinds had caused a bounce of the wheels off the runway during touchdown.

"The seas will be rough today," Jarvis noted. "I'm glad we passed on the plane food."

"Captain Jarvis," Matt responded with surprised tones, "an experienced sailor like you does not easily become seasick, does he?"

"Only on a stomach full of airplane food," Jarvis answered with a chuckle.

Lieutenant Commander Gregory Calhoun, an affable, experienced military officer from Guam, recognized Jarvis and Colonel Siefer from across the immigration counter. The tall young man introduced himself, "Colonel Siefer and Lieutenant Commander Jarvis, welcome to Saipan. I'm Major Calhoun and will be taking you by boat to Farallon de Medinilla."

"Thank you," Jarvis answered. "I'm retired now, so you can call me Jarvis as do my friends. Only my wife uses my given first name, and that's only when she's mad at me."

Major Calhoun entertained a hearty laugh. "Jarvis, you can call me Greg. Only my wife uses my given first name Gregory, and my middle name Alan, and that's when she's mad at me."

"Greg, I am comfortable with Matt," Colonel Siefer responded. "And I can't tell you what my wife Kathy calls me when she's mad."

"How rough is it out there today?" Jarvis asked.

"Did you eat the tuna salad sandwich on the flight?" asked Greg.

"Aren't you glad, Jarvis, that I warned you to skip the lunch?" Matt interjected.

"Thanks, Matt," Greg replied. "There are three to five footers right now, and we have a 45-mile boat trip. I'm happy to hear you both will not be contributing tuna salad to my boat. I do have some special medicine to ease the stomach."

The three men drove directly from the airport to Obyan Beach where Greg's powerboat was waiting. They departed immediately, traveling around the southern end of the island and turning north along the western coastline. They had a clear site of the majestic Banzai Cliff in Northern Saipan as they headed North East through the choppy seas toward Farallon de Medinilla.

"You seem to know these waters well," Jarvis commented after watching Major Calhoun maneuver his way through the strong currents of Marpi Point in the Philippine Sea.

"Yes, I grew up in Guam and have dived and fished in most of these islands," Greg replied.

"Greg, how did a local boy like you get a good old Kentucky name like Calhoun?" Matt asked. "My father is an American. Born in Indiana," Greg explained. "He might have had some family from Kentucky. My mother is from Guam. They met when my dad was stationed in the service in Guam."

"So, that explains your height," Matt noted.

"Actually my mom is pretty tall too for being from Guam. She's 5'6", but my dad is 6'6" and played two years of basketball at Indiana State University. He became an all American his sophomore year and stayed one until he graduated."

"Did he go on to play professional ball?" Jarvis asked.

"No, this military thing runs in our family. Both his grandfathers were career military, so rather than enter the NBA draft, my father entered the military, became a pilot, and completed two tours in Viet Nam. He flew B-52s and fell in love with Guam, and my mom, of course."

"I didn't think they took pilots that tall," Matt interjected.

"I think you're right," replied Greg. "My dad told me they desperately wanted college educated men; and he spoke fluent French, an asset if he were ever to be shot down in Vietnam. He also said he slouched down as much as he could when they took his height. It was ironic when the Air Force would not admit me into a fighter pilot training program because they said I was too tall at 6'4". But I'm very happy to be in the U.S. Navy. I love the water."

"Are your parents still here?" Jarvis asked.

"No, my dad also spent a lot of time in Thailand. After the war, my parents built a home there just south of Houahin, a popular resort. They live in Thailand about four months of the year and live in Indiana the rest of the time."

"My brother was also stationed in Guam for two years," Greg continued. "He liked it so much that he convinced me to ask for a tour of duty in Guam. They really had a need here in Saipan, so I came here instead. Then I married an American school teacher from Pennsylvania who was teaching in Saipan at a Catholic school."

Both Jarvis and Colonel Siefer had a good laugh. "A typical American," Jarvis replied. "You're a cultural stew, I've only known you for a few hours but I like you already."

Jarvis, Colonel Siefer, and Major Calhoun established a quick bond of mutual trust. The boat trip was not as bad as expected. The choppy seas dissipated about ten miles north of Saipan. The three men enjoyed the 85 $^\circ$F temperature, the blue skies and bright sunshine, and the marine life they observed. They all wished they had fishing lines when they saw two schools of Magi Magi. They also spotted two sea turtles and several sharks.

During the trip they discussed their plan of action while on Farallon de Medinilla. They would each survey a section of the island and study the destruction in the labs. Their primary goal was to ascertain what biological samples were taken, particularly those that were weaponized. Their second goal was to determine how the attack was executed and by whom.

Calhoun easily found the small lagoon on the eastern coast of the small coral island. He had first explored the coral reefs of rich fishing areas around the island when he was a teenager. The island was too small to be of much use to the Chamorro people of the Marianas. Its land area was only a half a square mile and most of that was covered by rocky cliffs, deep caves, wild bushes and savanna grass. There were no good places to build a resort hotel and no beaches big enough to commercially develop. The local people were perplexed that the U.S. military had any use for the island. They understood the military's use of Guam and Tinian to house strategic air bases, but leasing Farallon de Medinilla made no sense, though they did not complain about the income from the U.S. government into the trust territory's economy.

Just offshore, however, marine biologists from the University of Guam had discovered rich deposits of *C botulinum*, a deadly neurotoxin. They had also discovered a thriving population of *Synanceia sp.*, or Stonefish, which use deadly neurotoxins as a defensive weapon. Scientists had wondered how Stonefish living in neurotoxin sediments processed neurotoxin in their bodies. They also wanted to know how they were protected from the toxin's deadly effects.

The U.S. Department of Defense believed that a well-funded research program would lead to the development of more effective antidotes to neurotoxins such as botulinum, toxins that had become plausible biological warfare threats. The only local islanders who knew about the classified research were high-ranking military officers. Major Calhoun was an exception, the lowest-ranking officer with a connection to the islands who knew about the existence of the research laboratories.

Colonel Siefer and Jarvis were prepared to examine the bodies of the 16 dead Marines and four dead scientists. They were especially anxious about the possibility of finding Jack's body. The FBI was arriving soon to process the physical evidence. The Marines had only covered the bodies of the dead and moved them to a temporary morgue.

Donning protective masks, Siefer and Jarvis surveyed the scene, carefully taking notes and recording their thoughts and impressions. By reviewing an inventory list kept they had been given by their sister lab at Stanford, they were able to ascertain the samples that were missing. All strains of botulinum toxin were missing, including the two most recently developed strains and their antidotes. The biological weapons that had been tested were also taken. This was a more serious loss because the weapons could be utilized in a terrorist attack.

They quickly concluded that the most probable groups responsible for the killings were Islamic terrorists from Asia. The shell casings matched the same type of AK-47 assault rifles confiscated from terrorists in the southern Philippines and Malaysia. The size and type of footprints found were consistent with the size and types of boots worn by captured members of the *Abu Sayyaf*. A knife was found with an Arabic inscription. Although there was an outside chance that Japanese terrorists could be responsible, Siefer and Jarvis believed the physical evidence pointed to groups from the Philippines, Indonesia or Malaysia.

Since the arrest and incarceration of the *Aum Shinrikyo* cult members, Japan had virtually shut down biological terrorists in the country. Siefer and Jarvis concluded that the U.S. military and U.S. embassies in those three countries needed to be put on full alert. The U.S. State Department would also need to solicit cooperation from the military and police of the three nations to begin anticipating the possible arrival of terrorists with biological weapons.

Before leaving the island, Jarvis, Siefer, and Calhoun debriefed the Marine commander who had secured the island. Siefer asked the question burning in his mind. "We still have the bodies of only four scientists. Is it possible that the fifth scientist on your list, Dr. Jack Costellona, was actually not an the island during the attack?"

"No, sir," the commander responded. "On a small beach just north of here, we found a knapsack with his wallet, his passport, and some other items belonging to him. We suspect he was killed on the beach and thrown into the ocean. The currents could have taken his body out to sea."

"I heard about finding his belongings," Siefer said. "But there was no blood reported on the beach."

"The tides, sir. Could have been washed away."

Could he have been kidnaped?" Jarvis asked.

"Sir, that is always a possibility," the commander replied. "But we have found no ransom note and it does not make sense that the group who did this would only kidnap one scientist and kill the others. However, that is up to the FBI to determine."

The three men returned to the boat and circled the island, looking for clues. They also visited the beach where Dr. Costellona's possessions had been found. There, they found a sopping wet yellow pad of paper in the sand that had washed ashore. They could see that a page had been ripped from the pad and that an indentation was faintly visible. The FBI would be able to determine what had been written on the sheet that had been removed. They were pretty sure that it was the message that Niloa had found. Colonel Siefer and Jarvis agreed that they needed to go the Philippines as soon as possible.

CHAPTER 11
Shaqra, Lebanon

Imad agreed to meet his friend Arubi at a café they frequented in Beirut. He arrived first and began thinking about the many operations they had carried out. He also began to think about his brother. Imad recalled the day they planned their first operation together many years ago.

Imad and Arubi did not know each other well when they formed a small cell of seven terrorists. Their first meeting was in the basement of an abandoned building in Beirut in March of 1983, where they planned a suicide attack on the U.S. Embassy in Beirut. A month later they successfully carried out the attack, killing 63 people.

Imad was rewarded with a more difficult assignment. Many Lebanese Muslims wanted the U.S. military driven out of their country. Imad's cell was asked to attack the U.S. Marine barracks. He meticulously planned the operation and set the date of attack in October. They would park a truck full of explosives in front of the barracks. The attack was devastating, killing 241 Americans, the bloodiest terrorist attack ever carried out against Americans until the September 11 attacks. A year later Imad's cell carried out the attack of the annex to the U.S. Embassy in Lebanon, killing another 14 people.

In 1985, Imad expanded his terrorist activities. He led the hijacking of TWA Flight 847 in 1985, killing a Navy SEAL on board and terrorizing the crew and passengers. The same year he carried out the kidnaping and murder of William Buckley, the CIA station chief in Beirut. Buckley was a personal friend of George Bush, the Director of the CIA. When Bush later became president, he put a million dollar bounty on Imad's head.

True to his word, Imad continued his rampage of terror, organizing the attacks on the Israeli Embassy in Argentina in 1992, the Jewish Cultural Center in Buenos Aires in 1994, and the U.S. embassies in Kenya and Tanzania in 1998. Imad had distinguished himself as one of the most successful and dangerous terrorists in the world. Yet he did not see himself as a perpetrator of evil, but as a protector of Islam fighting in a holy war against the Israel and the U.S. That was on his good days. On his bad days, Imad was depressed, full of guilt, bitter, and confused. He sought solace from his demons by burying himself in his work, which consisted primarily of planning new terrorist attacks.

"Imad, you thinking again?" Arubi asked after he arrived at the café. "You think too much."

"You're late, my friend."

Arubi noticed the dejected look on his friend. He knew Imad was having a bad day.

"Are you okay?" Arubi asked.

"Yes, just missing my brother. Rafik and I were best friends. Tomorrow is the anniversary of his death."

Although Arubi and Imad had been friends for many years, Arubi had never talked to Imad directly about Imad's brother. Arubi had wanted to know about Rafik, but felt it was such a painful subject for his friend that it was best not to bring it up. This time seemed different to Arubi. He decided to take a chance.

"Tell me about him," Arubi requested. "I've only heard stories from others."

"He was full of courage," Imad recalled. "These Americans and Zionists call us terrorists and cowards. They understand nothing of our sacrifice and courage. They know nothing about total commitment to God. They will soon learn."

Imad spent the next thirty minutes telling Arubi about his brother, explaining how Rafik had been warned by their parents to stay away from the radical Shiite students who had come from Tehran to recruit university students into a Lebanese Islamic Jihad. Rafik was four years older than Imad, and Imad idolized him. Despite their parents' warnings, Rafik joined the Islamic Jihad student association at Beirut Arab University during his second year as a civil engineering student.

The university, established in 1961, had very good academic programs and a good engineering program. Imad's parents had been extremely proud of Rafik's admission into the program and partial scholarship. They feared, however, the radical brand of Islam that was sweeping through university campuses in the Middle East. Their parents were hard-working, honest middle-class Lebanese who were alarmed by the takeover of the American Embassy in Tehran in 1979 by radical students. They feared the growing radicalism in Lebanon, but they couldn't protect their sons from it.

Rafik was lured by the excitement on campus and the religious fervor he grew to respect. He felt his parents were compromising too much with the materialistic lifestyle of the West promoted through Western media and Western culture. He despised the shameless promiscuity, the blatant drug and alcohol abuse, and the godless culture of contemporary American society. He did like some American movies though, especially "First Blood," which was released the same year that Israel invaded Lebanon.

Rafik was a junior in college, deeply involved in helping to form a national terrorist group, which later became known as the Lebanese Hezbollah. Imad was a high school senior. He remembered going to see the movie with his older brother; it was one of the last happy memories he had of his brother. Rafik identified with John Rambo, the reclusive Vietnam veteran who was not respected by those whose freedoms he sought to protect even at the risk of his own life.

During Rafik's junior year, he had taken part in several terrorist activities against Israel. Yet he could not tell his family anything, except for his younger brother Imad. His older brother loved his Western lifestyle and thought Islamic fundamentalism was bizarre and dangerous. His older sister was not as worldly but also feared what she viewed as Shiite extremism. Their family was well respected in the community. Rafik's mother was a schoolteacher and his father worked as a lab technician in a hospital. They believed that a representative government was best for the future of Lebanon, not a religious autocracy like in Iran and Saudi Arabia.

Rafik felt his family could not understand why he was risking his life to fight against Zionists and their Western supporters, particularly the United States. Like Rambo, Rafik was a warrior willing to die for his ideals. He believed the increased secularism in Lebanon would eventually ruin the country and destroy Islam. He felt persecuted by the Lebanese police who tried to follow him and who twice arrested him for simply passing out political leaflets on campus. He felt like a hero without honor in his own family.

Imad, however, was different. He loved Rafik's stories of daring attacks on the Israeli border police. Imad understood very little about geo-politics or how to fight the Zionists. He only knew what he had been told by others. However, rather than blowing up things, Imad's first love was to build things. He had wanted to be an engineer just like his brother after the war with Israel was over.

In the first week of June, 1982, Rafik graduated with a bachelor of science degree in civil engineering. The graduation ceremony scheduled for June 6 was canceled. Israeli tanks had invaded Lebanon two days earlier. Rafik and other members of the Islamic Jihad student organization engaged in open warfare with Israel's best troops. Israeli snipers killed him on the second day of the war, the day of his graduation ceremony.

Imad was inconsolable. He placed his brother's diploma and graduation robe in Rafik's open casket.

On the day his family buried Rafik, he told his family he would avenge his brother's death and uphold the honor of his family and the honor of Islam. On June 10th Imad joined Lebanon's radical Hezbollah Muslim militia. He was only 19 years old. On that day he told his parents, "My life is in God's hands. We have been invaded by evil Zionists. They have stolen Palestine from the Muslim people. They have taken Rafik's life. Now they have invaded our homeland. I will fight to the death for Lebanon. I will fight against all the evil powers that seek to destroy Islam. You will be proud of me."

On the day Rafik was killed his parents buried two of their three sons. Rafik was gone, and Imad had committed himself to a life of terrorism. They tried in vain with many tears to persuade Imad to go to college and fulfill Rafik's dream by becoming an engineer. Even Imad's girlfriend could not convince him that the way of the Hezbollah would only lead to death. But Imad's relationship with Rafik was too strong. He would avenge his brother's death.

"Arubi," Imad told him, "my parents still do not understand fully why Rafik gave his life and don't agree with my involvement in the Islamic Jihad. I don't hold it against them. They are both peaceful people and I know they love me. They just cannot see our enemies the way we do. They do not perceive the threat to Islam."

"My parents are the same way," Arubi had replied. "At least they still send me money and food every month."

"Imad, thanks for telling me about Rafik. I now know how much you loved him. I will fight for his honor, too."

"I need your help, Arubi. The Americans are coming after me. I need to lay low until I can plan the next attack on their soil."

Imad and Arubi worked out a plan over several rounds of coffee and pastries in the small café.

"I need an apartment in a quiet neighborhood, a part-time job, maybe even a girlfriend," Imad stated to his friend.

"I know just the place," Arubi replied. "It is a newly developing suburb called Lailake, south of the city and northeast of the airport. The town is growing. It's diverse too—moderate middle-class Shia's, Sunnis, and Maronites. No one would ever suspect a Hezbollah leader lives in Lailake."

"I need a plastic surgeon, too."

"I know where to go," Arubi replied.

Imad found the recommended surgeon and asked him to change his appearance, fearing there would be too many people tempted to turn against him since the U.S. had put a price on his head. He also arranged to assume the identity of a man who had been killed in a car accident by bribing a Lebanese official. His new name would be Mansur Shukarian.

Arubi then helped Imad to stage his own death and leak the information to Western intelligence agencies. They planned an accidental explosion by paying an informant to reveal to the U.S. the location of a bomb-making facility in Beirut. Arubi illegally purchased corpses from a morgue and placed them in a room. Imad placed many of his personal effects there that would clearly identify him, including a wallet, family pictures, a pair of shoes, and personal clothing. They then set a powerful explosion that destroyed the basement. Immediately after the explosion, Imad paid a paramedic to place blood and hair samples from his body in rubble. The plan worked well.

The word disseminated rapidly through the terrorists in Beirut that Imad had been accidentally killed in an explosion. A Lebanese man contacted a U.S. reporter to claim that he had set the explosion and was entitled to the reward. The U.S. sent an investigation team to work with the Lebanese. Through DNA analysis of the blood and hair samples they found, they determined that Imad was likely killed. The explosion was too powerful to yield many body parts, although they did find some. None matched Imad.

Imad was now believed to be dead. He had a new face and a new name. He also had a new place to live. But he was still a terrorist. He would soon be planning another attack. He and Arubi met the day after the explosion.

"Arubi, you need to call me Mansur from now on. Imad is dead."

"Who's Imad?" Arubi asked playfully.

"So, you have a friend in Lailake?" asked Mansur.

"Yes. I know a young woman there who teaches school and works in her parents' bakery," Arubi recalled excitedly. "Her name is Natacha Haidar. We met at the American University and became good friends. She helped me pass my English course; and I helped her with her basketball. She played forward for the women's team the same year I played for the men's team. She is one of the most beautiful women I have ever met. After we graduated she invited me to come visit her and her parents' bakery; but I never have."

"Too bad you are almost married now," Imad replied. "I would like to meet her."

Suddenly Arubi's countenance fell.

"What's wrong?" Mansur asked.

"I just remembered her parents," Arubi replied. "She told me a little about them. They were born in Lebanon, but her mother's father and her father's mother are both Jewish."

"She is part Jewish?" Imad asked, somewhat perturbed.

"I suppose she is one-half Jewish," Arubi recalled. "Her other grandparents are Greek Orthodox. But she is no Zionist. She is really nice. Even after she learned that I had joined the Hezbollah student association, she never stopped helping me with my English."

"Mansur, sometimes I wish I could forget this war and settle down and marry a woman like Natache. Someone with no prejudices, no political aspirations, no hatred."

"But you are engaged, Arubi. Aren't you happy?"

"Sometimes I am," relied Arubi. "And sometimes I feel trapped in a life with no choices."

"When I begin to feel like that," explained Imad, "I remember my brother and the other friends I have lost. I remember our cause and our duty."

"Mansur," Arubi asked, "please don't be angered. We have been best friends for a long time. Could we be wrong in believing all Jews are evil? Isn't that what Hitler believed when he massacred six million in the gas ovens? Could we ever become as cold-blooded as he was?"

Mansur had never been asked such penetrating questions. They shook him to the core. For the first time since his brother's death he had been confronted with the rightness of his actions. He had killed several hundred Americans and Jews, and was planning to kill thousands more in a new wave of attacks. He had always assumed his cause was righteous. Now, he had hesitated in his response to Arubi as if he wasn't completely sure.

"We don't kill because we like it," Mansur replied quietly.

But the question would not leave Mansur alone. The more he sought to justify the murder of civilians as retaliation for the murder of

Muslims, the more troubled he became. He had to push the feelings of guilt away. He was involved too deeply now. There was no way out, and no turning back.

Chapter 12
Philippine Sea, South Pacific

Paulo fell asleep in the cabin of the *Dawn Teader II* as Niloa sailed through the Philippine Sea. She wondered how much she could trust him. He was dehydrated enough that he could not spend much time on deck during the day. He was also exhausted. Niloa thought she could easily disarm him in his semi-delirious state and cuff him to a steel post inside the cabin below deck, but that would only destroy any potential for building a trust relationship during the trip. Niloa thought of her options carefully. The seas were quiet and the temperature very warm, giving her quality time to meditate. There were many potential dangers that lay ahead in the Philippines: storms, pirates, corrupt military, and then the terrorists themselves. They would need each other. Niloa knew the risk would be great but decided that she had to trust Paulo.

She checked her watch. It might be a good time to call. She carefully retrieved her phone from the cabin where Paulo was still sleeping.

"Hello, Dad," she said quietly.

"Hi, sweetheart. We've been so worried about you. Are you okay?"

"Yes, I'm fine."

"I contacted the U.S. military as soon as we got your message. What did you find when you searched the island?"

"Everyone was killed."

Niloa became emotional again.

"I'm sorry you had to see that Niloa," replied her father, trying to comfort her.

"I never found the man who wrote the note I found in the water bottle."

"You mean from Dr. Jack Costellona?"

"Yes."

"I don't think the military has found him either," Chris added. "Maybe you should come home, honey, instead of going to the Solomons. You've been through so much trauma on this trip."

"No, I'm alright. It was just a terrible scene."

"Well, the military wants to talk with you about what you found.

"Where are you now?"

"About 100 miles west of Saipan. I'm taking a detour due west to the Philippines."

"The Philippines!" exclaimed her father. "What possesses you to sail into the shark infested waters of typhoon alley? I thought you'd be sailing south into the Caroline Islands toward the Solomons."

"I should be," Niloa said.

"You're going through a dangerous area. You remember your Uncle Jarvis warning you about it, don't you? The *Indianapolis* went down there!"

"I remember, Dad. How could I ever forget that story?"

"My reasons for going to the Philippines would take another long story to explain. I don't know how much more time our connection will hold. Can I say hi to Mom?"

"Yes, I'm going to put you on the speaker phone. How much more connection time do we have before you're out of coverage area?"

"I'd don't know on this new system. It covers Saipan and the northern Philippines, but not the southern Philippines."

"Hi, Niloa," her mom chimed in. "Now tell me why you're going to the Philippines."

Niloa realized that she needed to tell her parents what had taken place without alarming them. During the next fifteen minutes she did her best to explain how she had called Jack Costellano's wife and looked for him on Farallon de Medinilla. She explained how she had found the U.S. research laboratory with dead marines both inside and outside the buildings. After spinning the story the best she could in order to put Paulo in a good light, she then described how she found Paulo, the only one alive on the island, and how he had heroically tried to stop an attack from a group of terrorists. She then shared why she was taking Paulo to his home in Mindanao.

Niloa's parents thought they knew her well, but were not prepared for this latest decision. They were shocked that she would agree to sail with an associate of a terrorist organization that the United States was seeking to eradicate. The dismantling of the *al Qaeda* network and reduction of terrorist threats against the U.S. had given most Americans confidence that the war against terrorism was subsiding and the worst was behind them. Since there were virtually no publicized terrorist groups operating in the South Pacific region, Niloa, her parents, and other yachtsmen worried more about storms, sharks, and pirates than they did about possible terrorists. Niloa's parents felt they had failed to protect Niloa by underestimating the threat of terrorism. When Niloa finished her story her parents were speechless.

"Mom and Dad, I know what you're thinking. Don't even go there. There is no way you could have anticipated this. There was no terrorism threat in the South Pacific where I was sailing. We checked with the State Department. I could've walked away from this. I could've left Paulo on that island and simply called the military, but I felt compelled to help. The terrorists sailed to Farallon de Medinella and are sailing back to the Philippines with biological weapons. We are only three or four hours behind them and we know where they're going. Paulo was their primary navigator so they won't be sailing back as efficiently as they sailed here."

"Wait a second, Niloa," her mom interrupted. "Paulo was their navigator? You are sailing with a terrorist?"

"No, Mom; he didn't know they were killers! He tried to stop them." Niloa defended. "He was only a navigator that they hired to sail for them."

Do you and Paulo think you are going to overtake a group of vicious terrorists with biological weapons?" Chris asked incredulously.

"No, Dad, I'm not crazy," Niloa responded with some irritation. "We intend to track them back to their hidden base camp in the southern Philippines and then provide the U.S. military with the necessary information to go in and take them out."

"Niloa," her father responded, "that doesn't make sense to me. Who would sail with biological weapons? Why didn't the terrorists use high-powered speed boats, or a pontoon plane?"

"These guys are very smart, Dad. They know our military's radar, sonar and heat surveillance systems can more easily detect aircraft and powerboats. They make noise and emit heat. By sailing, they can escape quietly and not draw attention. It's a brilliant idea. Can you think of a better cover? Who would ever suspect terrorists to stage an attack and make an escape in a sailboat? It's so ridiculous. No one would expect it."

"But they're slow," her dad retorted.

"Slow but effective. I bet the Marines on Farallon de Medinilla were monitoring powerboats in the area. But sailboats? Probably not. Especially if you make it out like you're deep sea fishing or diving."

"They wouldn't suspect what?" her father asked.

"Dad, Mom, our connection is breaking up," Niloa said loudly.

"Bye, Niloa, we love you. Call again as soon as you can," her parents said quickly.

"Bye, Mom and Dad. I love you too."

Niloa doubted if her parents had heard her last couple of sentences. She could barely hear their good-byes. A heavy weight of apprehension lifted from her shoulders. She knew her parents would immediately take action. They did.

Her father called his good friend again, a Vice Admiral stationed at Pearl Harbor.

"Sam," Stephenson said, "Niloa called again. She's sailing to the Philippines with a man named Paulo. He was the only person she found alive on the island. Niloa said he was a navigator and had tried to stop the massacre. She found him tied to the bottom of the tree exposed to the hot sun."

"Thanks, Chris," Vice Admiral Cardenas replied. "I sent the copy of Niloa's first message to Lt. General Sharon McGwire at the Pentagon. She would like to talk with you directly. I'll also tell her about Paulo."

"That's fine," Chris replied.

Twenty minutes later, the Stephensons received a call at home. Niloa's mother Nanci was closest to the phone. She anxiously picked it up and said hello.

"Hello, may I speak to Chris Stephenson?" A woman's voice was on the line. "This is Lt. General Sharon McGwire calling from the Pentagon."

"Hi, General, this is Nanci Stephenson. We've been expecting your call. I'll go get my husband. He's upstairs on the computer."

"Honey, General McGwire is on the line," Nanci shouted up the stairwell.

Chris grabbed the upstairs phone anxiously.

"Hello, this is Chris Stephenson."

"Mr. Stephenson, Vice Admiral Sam Gardenas called me a short time ago about your daughter Niloa."

Chris interrupted, "General, please call me Chris."

"Chris, I'm sorry your daughter is caught in the middle of this difficult situation. Thanks for providing a copy of Niloa's previous message when she first learned about the attack. We suspect it's the *Abu Sayyaf*. They are extremely dangerous. We've been after them for some time now, but they stay well hidden in small villages in remote areas on large islands. I'll do everything possible to find out about the man Niloa is traveling with who identifies himself as Paulo. He could be dangerous."

"General," Chris asked, "Do you believe he might be a part of the *Abu Sayyaf*? If so, why would they leave him there?"

"I just don't know, Chris. Maybe he's just their navigator and did try and stop them. I think we need to find out before Niloa calls again. When will her satellite phone be in range again?" the general asked.

"Probably not until they reach the Philippines," Chris replied. "She said they were sailing at a brisk 10 to 11 knots and were about 800 nautical miles west of Cebu."

"By then we should have more information," McGwire noted.

"General, Niloa is an extremely capable young woman. She handles herself very well in emergencies. But this pursuit is highly dangerous. I fear for her life."

"I understand, Chris. My 22-year old daughter could have been a Navy Seal had the Navy been willing to train women. My husband is a triathlon athlete and my daughter inherited his genes; but she had no desire to join the military, having grown up in military life all through her childhood. My guess is that your daughter is as bright and tough as mine. She'll be fine."

"Thank you, General, I needed that encouragement," Chris replied.

Sharon McGwire instantly liked the Stephensons. They were not only cooperative, but very bright and insightful. She had worried about needing to deal with emotionally distraught parents, or worse, emotional and irrational parents. McGwire had established a bond of trust with Chris during their 30-minute telephone conversation. They agreed to pass on information to each other and McGwire arranged to have the Stephenson's telephone conversations with Niloa recorded. Chris asked McGwire to arrange to have as few people as possible know about Niloa's involvement. He knew the FBI would want to wiretap their phone line and begin interviewing all of Niloa's friends.

McGwire understood perfectly. She knew the intrusiveness of multiple federal agencies and the complete loss of privacy, especially if the news media were tipped off. Fortunately, the President's new Director of Homeland Security, who answered directly to the President, had streamlined the information management of U.S. law enforcement agencies dealing with terrorism. Since McGwire was in charge of this case, everything would be funneled through her office to the Office of Homeland Security. The Stephensons were especially relieved to learn that the news media would know nothing about Niloa's pursuit of the *Abu Sayyaf*."

Niloa called about 30 hours later. She and Paulo were now 500 miles east of Cebu. They had no knowledge of how far they were behind the terrorists but were picking up a lot of speed by surfing down some large swells.

Niloa checked the data on the current ocean conditions and weather in their area. They were averaging above their maximum hull speed. She sensed that they should sail slightly to the north to avoid a disturbance developing to the southwest of them. If the *Sulu Breeze* sailed into the disturbance on a direct southwest route toward Mindanao, the rough seas could slow them substantially without a highly experienced yachtsman navigating. She and Paulo might be able to close the gap between them even further. Niloa seemed to have it all worked out in her mind when she called her parents again.

"Hi, Dad!" an excited Niloa boomed after Chris Stephenson picked up the phone.

Unfortunately, McGwire had not yet been able to find out more about Paulo. She had contacted the Filipino Government, but the investigation was bogged down in red tape and military authorities were reluctant to reveal sensitive information to the U.S.

"Niloa," Chris interjected early in the conversation after they talked a while, "we are trying to identify Paulo and find out more information about him. I was hoping to know more about him now but I don't. The military is trying to confirm his story about only being a navigator for the *Abu Sayyaf*. What if he is more than a navigator and implicated in their terrorist activities?"

"Dad, I talked with Paulo for a long time about this. He is adamant that he is not a terrorist, but that the *Abu Sayyaf* had hired him as a navigator. I've let him sail a bit. He's definitely good. I believe he is a navigator. He did admit to being a former member of the Moro National Liberation Front, but he had made peace with the government and had been granted amnesty by President Corozine Aquino. He told me how the *Abu Sayyaf* had come into being. They came from a radical faction within the MNLF who would not accept the government's peace offer. That's how the *Abu Sayyaf* knew Paulo since their founding."

"Do you believe him?" Chris asked.

"I believe he's no terrorist. He's not the type. But I still can't figure out why they didn't kill him. That part I don't understand. I would think that they would have executed him if he tried to stop them as he said."

"Didn't they leave him to die?" Chris asked.

"Yes, but why not just shoot him?" Niloa wondered aloud. "It just doesn't add up. Dad, Paulo is waking up. I better go. I'll try and call you tomorrow."

Niloa and her father ended their conversation just as Paulo was climbing up to the deck from the cabin.

"*Kumusta*, Niloa. Talking to your parents again?" Paulo asked, wiping the sleep from his eyes.

"Yeh, that was my father on the phone."

"When ya gonna to start trusting me, Niloa, and stop putting that sleeping stuff in my food?"

Niloa initially tried to respond with surprise, but quickly realized she could not deceive Paulo.

"You needed sleep, Paulo," she replied with no remorse.

"Why do I need sleep an hour or two before you call your parents?" Paulo asked.

"You noticed," Niloa said with acquiescence.

"Like clockwork," Paulo answered. "But I admit I needed the sleep, so I didn't mind. I just want you to be honest. At least respect my intelligence."

"Okay, Paulo, I'll be honest. I don't believe you're a terrorist. I also don't believe you are simply a navigator hired by the *Abu Sayyaf*. They would've shot you with the other Marines and scientists. I think somehow you are connected to them. Now, you tell me the truth."

"It's a long story, Niloa."

"I've nothing better to do," she said seriously. "Go for it."

Paulo decided to share with Niloa some of the details about his life, his involvement with the MNLF, and how he had been trapped in a web of violence and deceit.

"I had convinced myself that I was defending freedom. I demanded political freedom. I argued for religious freedom. When the

MNLF became disillusioned with the gains we had made, it decided to negotiate a peace agreement with the government. I was a respected MNLF leader. I decided for peace. But some leaders did not want to negotiate. They felt we were giving in."

"And now they're the *Abu Sayyaf?*" Niloa asked.

"Yeah. Their founder wanted me and another good friend to join them. My friend, Stephano, refused, and urged me to keep away from them. I didn't join them either, but I didn't keep away. I offered to be a navigator for them."

"According to our President, you're as guilty as they are because you helped them," Niloa replied.

"I was wrong, Niloa, but I never supported their terrorism."

Niloa was still unconvinced that she had learned the whole story about Paulo's involvement with this group.

She commented to Paulo, "That still doesn't explain why they didn't shoot you."

"There are two reasons," Paulo explained. "First, the Filipino Army has been chasing the *Abu Sayyaf* for more than five years. On more than one occasion I had helped their leaders avoid capture. They know I saved their lives. Second, my good friend Stephano, a former MNLF commander, also knows all the *Abu Sayyaf* leaders. They know that if they killed me, Stephano would come after them, and he is much smarter and more capable than I am. He would hunt them down."

"Is this the same friend whom you said would help us once we get to Mindanao?" Niloa asked.

"Yes. Stephano is closer to me than a brother. He just graduated from the University of the Philippines with a bachelor of science degree in agricultural science. He works in Cebu now to be close to his parents. We'll go see him."

Finally, Niloa was convinced that Paulo was not a threat. The more she talked to him, the more comfortable she felt. She was surprised by how much they had in common. Paulo spent a considerable amount of time talking about his friend Stephano. The more she learned, the more Niloa began to like both of them. As they sailed together hour after hour, Paulo began to look less like a terrorist and more like a friend. He was handsome in appearance and in great physical condition despite his severe sunburn. He never spoke of a wife or girlfriend and didn't wear any rings.

Niloa suddenly realized how vulnerable she had been, particularly if Paulo had not turned out to be a gentleman. He had never said an unkind word to her. She was alone on a yacht with a young guy she knew little about. She struggled with her thoughts. Perhaps he was too sunburned to hit on her. Worse thoughts came. *What if he tried to rape her?* There was nowhere to hide. She put her hand on the knife strapped to her leg. She wondered again, *Could she trust him? Who was he, really?*

CHAPTER 13
Lebanon-Israel Border

Arubi checked the timers and detonators for the third time. He spread out a map on the oak table in his small living room and rechecked the target. The synagogue in Haifa would be full on Friday by 6:30 p.m. He was convinced the operation planned was a masterful one. A wedding reception was taking place across town adjacent to a restaurant that was preparing all the food. Arubi and Mansur had worked out every detail to inflict the greatest number of casualties.

At 4:30 p.m., Mansur, disguised as a delivery worker, would pick up a large wedding cake from Desraeli's Bakery. The normal deliveryman would later be found dead in a cardboard box in a warehouse two blocks from the bakery. A large wedding cake would be delivered to the wedding reception held in a grand courtyard at 5:00. Inside the cake a bomb was timed to detonate 45 minutes after delivery.

Anatone's restaurant would receive a large delivery from a bread truck at 5:15. The fresh bread was to provide the needs of the wedding reception. Underneath the bread truck was a powerful bomb, timed to explode at 5:30 p.m.

Fifteen minutes later, a remote production truck for Channel 4 news would pull up in front of the synagogue to record the devastation for the evening news. Two cameramen would exit the truck with cameras on their shoulders and begin filming the scene. Their news media credentials and identification tags would all be in order. Slowly they would walk away from the truck toward the open end of the square, walking backward as they continued videotaping until they disappeared into the streets across the square from the synagogue. Before the Israeli police would realize what was about to take place, the primary target, the Jewish synagogue, would be demolished by a 1000-pound bomb located in the back of the stolen production truck. Everyone in the synagogue would be ripped to shreds or buried in rubble.

The meticulously planned three-pronged attack was intended to provoke a powerful retaliation against the Palestinians by Israel. Mansur hoped to ignite a major conflict and further disrupt the peace process. Arubi would be one of the Channel 4 cameramen. He knew Israeli police would likely kill him. He still had 24 hours to think through the attack. Mansur told Arubi he could easily have someone else drive the truck if he was not prepared to die, but Arubi was more than eager to sacrifice his life. He had grown weary of his life of terrorism. He had already spilled much blood. He wanted to die. However, he also wanted to see Natacha, his college friend in southern Lebanon, one last time.

The bells chimed on the back of the door as Arubi entered Bershokof's Bakery in Saida. A joyful heavy-set gentleman in his 60s greeted Arubi warmly in Arabic.

"Is this your first time to our bakery?" the gentleman asked.

"Yes," Arubi replied. "I've wanted to come for a long time."

"Please, have a seat," the gentleman insisted, pulling a chair out at one of the two tables adjacent to the storefront window.

"Natasha," he yelled toward the back room, "we have a guest. Please come out with a cup our very best Turkish coffee, and bring some of today's fresh pastries."

Good. She's here, Arubi thought. He had not been honored with such warm hospitality in many years. He thought of his grandparents and the general store they used to have in Bartroun, also on the

Mediterranean Coast. They also were lavish with their hospitality to strangers.

"You are very kind," Arubi said to the old man, "like my grandparents were when they owned a general store."

Natasha came from the back room with a steaming cup of Turkish coffee.

Arubi had a puzzled look on his face.

"I was hoping to see Natacha. Is she your daughter?" Arubi asked as she placed coffee and fresh pastries in front of Arubi.

"Yes she is," Natasha replied. "She inherited my name, but she spells it with a c – Natacha, to avoid confusion. I also go by Samita, my middle name, because we both work together and our customers get confused. My husband still prefers Natasha.

"This pastry is delicious," Arubi replied, still chewing on the fresh breakfast Danish. "Did she inherit your baking abilities as well?"

"As a matter of fact, I did," Natacha said as she walked into the room from the stairway that went to the second floor.

Arubi stood up and froze as Natache walked toward him.

"You finally came, Arubi," she said with a big smile. "Welcome to our bakery."

Arubi was nearly speechless. Natacha was even more beautiful than she had been when they had gone to college together.

"So, Natache, are you going to formally introduce us to Arubi?" her father asked.

"You know my name?" Arubi inquired with great surprise.

"I recognized your picture," he answered. "You've been a regular part of our family prayers for two years. Come, I'll show you."

Mr. Bershokof and his wife took Arubi up the stairs and into the living room to a large framed corkboard filled with photographs. Natacha followed them. Arubi saw a maze of photographs.

Shen then put her right hand on the board.

"This is our memory board filled with people we ask God to bless and watch over," she explained.

Arubi looked through the pictures and quickly found the section of college photos. Amidst those pictures, he spotted a 3 inch by 5 inch photo of he and Natacha on the campus of the American University of Beirut. On another part of the wall was a board with newspaper photographs of children.

"Who are these children?" Arubi asked.

"These are the children of Lebanon, the children for whom God's heart aches. They are Muslims, Christians, and Jews, who have been killed in acts of terrorism and violence. I put them here so we remember to pray for their families and to pray for peace," Samita explained.

"We're a Christian family, Arubi, but we also love Muslims and Jews," said Natacha.

Her father then added, "They are our friends and neighbors. We are called by God to be peacemakers. We hate this endless war of terror."

Samita turned to Arubi and said with a compassionate voice, "Arubi, I know you have suffered. Natacha told me about some of your suffering when you befriended her in college. We are sorry you lost so much. We have prayed that you might come to know peace in your life by believing in the prince of peace, Yeshua Hamashea."

"Mrs. Bershokof, you are very kind and very religious. You are a different type of Christian than I've known. I think you really live your faith. But as long as there is injustice in this world, there will be no peace."

"We never lose hope," Mr. Bershokof said. "Someday things will change."

"We'd better give you two some time together," Samita said. "I'll get you some more coffee."

For the next three hours Arubi and Natacha drank coffee, ate pastries, and reminisced about their days at the American University in Beirut. They also talked about their families, their dreams, their disappointments, and their hopes for the future. They laughed much, especially when explaining why they both thought they were still single.

"If you were Muslim instead of Christian," Arubi said, "I would have asked your parents for your hand in marriage two years ago."

Natacha looked deep into Arubi's dark brown eyes and replied, "And if you were Christian instead of Muslim, I would have told my parents to give their blessing."

"Arubi," she continued, "I can see the inner demons that you wrestle with. I can feel your bitterness and rage. Evil can never be overcome by more evil. The death of others will never overcome the bitter taste of having lost those you love. Jesus said you can only overcome evil with good."

Tears welled up in Arubi's eyes. He knew if he started to weep it would be difficult to stop. His heart was broken inside. He had to leave.

"Natacha," Arubi said softly, "I have to go now. I will be going away for a long time, but I will never forget this day. I will always remember the kindness you and your family have shown to me. Perhaps we can meet again in another time, or in another life. Please keep praying for me."

"Arubi, remember all I told you," Natacha replied. "I will never stop praying for you, but you must pray, too. Ask and believe. You'll hear His voice and you'll know His peace."

Arubi gave Natacha a long embrace and kiss on each cheek. He also said warm good-byes to Natacha's parents. After he left the bakery, he could no longer hold back his tears. He went to a quiet place outside of town and wept. He wept for his parents, knowing what he had become. He wept for himself, knowing his life was over. He then prayed that he might find God's forgiveness, and wept bitterly that it was too late to stop what was already set in motion.

Mansur delivered the wedding cake on schedule, just a few minutes past five o'clock. It was placed on a long table covered with a velvet white tablecloth, which was in the middle of a courtyard adjacent to Anatone's Restaurant. The courtyard was large enough to hold several hundred people.

Arubi pulled up in front of the restaurant in the bread truck not long after Mansur left the area. After delivering the pastries for the wedding reception, he inconspicuously exited in the back of the bakery, leaving the truck parked out front. Although the reception had not yet begun, the restaurant and courtyard were both filled with people.

Nicoli, the restaurant owner, noticed that the truck had been there for what seemed a long time. He looked around for the driver but could not find him. Suspicious, he went outside and looked at the delivery truck. He had a strong premonition of danger but did not see anything unusual about the truck.

A news reporter approached him while he was looking around the truck, waiting for the driver. The reporter asked to speak to the organizers of the reception immediately. Nicoli quickly found the father of the bride and the head of security. The reporter handed them a note and quickly left the area. The note simply said: *Bomb under bread truck is diffused. Bomb in cake must be diffused before 5:45. Evacuate immediately.*

The reporter, not waiting for the note to be read, quickly left the reception. Within minutes sirens were screaming as Israeli police and a bomb squad descended on the wedding reception. People panicked and ran in all directions away from the area. The bomb squad had less than 10 minutes to diffuse the bomb.

Mansur checked his watch. He felt something was not right. There were sirens going on as police vehicles raced through the streets, and Arubi was uncharacteristically late. He should have been there by 5:30. Eight minutes later he arrived.

"I had to avoid all the security forces," Arubi said when he arrived.

"Look at your watch, Imad," Arubi said.

"Why are you calling me Imad? I'm Mansur."

"Not to me," Arubi replied; "you'll always be Imad to me."

The two waited in silence until 5:45 p.m. There were no explosions.

"What's going on, Arubi?" Mansur asked. "Why are there no explosions?"

"It's over. Imad," Arubi said in a solemn voice.

"What do you mean, *it's over*?"

Arubi pointed his semi-automatic pistol into the window of the news production truck where he was sitting.

"It's over," Arubi repeated. "No more killing of innocent civilians. The bombs have been diffused. I'll give you 24 hours to leave Lebanon. You are my friend, Imad, but I'm not going to let you kill people here anymore. You changed your name and identity, but you haven't changed. You have a chance to start again. To become Mansur, a new person. If you don't leave Lebanon, I'm going to come after you."

"You would turn on your brother?" Mansur shouted in astonishment. "How could you do such a thing?"

"Because I'm tired of killing," Arubi shouted back in anguish. "Our hands are covered with the blood of the innocent. Imad, how can we go on like this?" Arubi was now weeping.

"At first it was just military targets; and then, paramilitary. Then we decided to go after sympathizers. Now we are killing a bride and groom, along with innocent children; and we are going to bomb those worshiping God? Don't you see what has happened to us?"

"Drop your weapon," shouted the Israeli police who had spotted Arubi with his gun fixed on Mansur. From their vantage point, they had mistakenly concluded that Arubi was attempting to hijack the news production truck. The police could not see Mansur very well.

Arubi turned around slowly to face the two policemen and carefully placed his semi-automatic handgun and assault rifle on the ground. A burst of gunfire then rang out. Arubi crumpled to the ground as blood began oozing from the exit wounds of the four bullets that had pierced his back, exiting through his chest. Three bullets had missed vital organs but one bullet had ripped through his left aorta.

Before the policeman could discern what was happening, Mansur was firing at them. He drove the truck away from them as he raked them with gunfire. Both policemen were hit with multiple bullets, but one of the officers was able to return fire into the back of the production truck. He could not stop Mansur. Mansur checked his watch: 5:55. There was now no diversion set up and the bomb would detonate in five minutes. He didn't have enough time to reach the synagogue. He quickly decided on a secondary target— another popular restaurant nearby.

He parked the news truck in front of Michaela's Restaurant at 5:58 p.m., and hastily exited the truck with his news camera. He then ran as fast as he could down the street with the camera as if to film an event, and suddenly turned around and pointed the camera at the truck. The few people who saw Mansur were totally confused by his behavior.

A patron in the restaurant walked outside, saw the truck and then spotted Mansur down the street. With horror he ran back in the restaurant and shouted, "Get out! Get out! A bomb is ..!"

He was never able to finish the sentence. A deafening roar pierced the air as the truck exploded. Glass, metal, concrete, smoke and body parts of men, women, and children were blown into the air. Mansur had the camera on but had lost his hearing as the shock wave of the blast impacted his eardrums. He could barely believe what he saw through the lens. He put the camera down and saw the most grisly site he had ever seen, a site he would never be able to flush from his memory. Arms, legs, heads, torsos and pieces of flesh were strewn across the street.

Mansur slipped into the building behind him in shock. He had never seen the results of his terror up close. He emerged from the back of the building a few minutes later in an Israeli military uniform with a military ID and military issued weapon. The uniform had been taken from an Israeli soldier kidnaped and killed that afternoon. Mansur walked through the outer security perimeter that the police were forming as they streamed into the area. He passed two policemen; tears were running down his face. Mansur was a gifted actor, but his tears were genuine. He regretted killing his friend, Arubi. For the first time, he also regretted using explosives to kill. He had condemned the Israelis for gruesome deeds but realized Arubi was right. He had also committed gruesome acts.

On his return trip to Lebanon, Mansur determined in his heart never again to use explosives as a weapon of terrorism. He needed to change. He wrestled with what to do. *The war was a just cause*, he reasoned within himself, *and innocent people die in wars*. He believed the Israelis were killing innocent people.

The next day, Mansur learned the results of his attack. Twenty-seven people were confirmed dead and 112 were wounded. In a small café in Zahle, east of Beirut, Mansur met with his men. He told them how the Israeli police had killed Arubi in the attack. No one but Mansur would ever know what had really happened. All three Israeli policemen shot by Mansur had died. In a back room of the café, Mansur showed his men the footage he had shot of the restaurant attack. His men recoiled when they saw the graphic images of body parts landing on the pavement. Mansur then told his men he would have nightmares about that blast and wanted no more involvement in blowing up people. He questioned why he had killed like that.

One of his men spoke up, "Well, they kill like that, too!"

"That's the problem," Mansur shouted. "We cannot be like them. We must be superior to them!"

Mansur's men were again shocked, this time by his statement. They wondered if he was going to stop his terrorist activities. He was a leader of terrorism. There was a long period of silence. Al-Shiatun, the second in command, gathered enough courage to ask Mansur what he was thinking.

"We must kill humanely," Mansur replied.

"What do you mean? asked another one of his men.

"I mean, think of how the Americans carry out capital punishment," Mansur replied.

"The electric chair," another man proclaimed.

"Lethal injection," Al-Shiatun added. "And poison gas."

"Exactly," Mansur said with a gleam in his eye. "Most choose poison gas. It is relatively painless. It is the most humane means of punishment, like going to sleep and not waking up. We need to acquire a powerful poison, either chemical or biological."

It never occurred to Mansur's fellow terrorists that the Germans had used poison gas to kill millions of Jews in the holocaust, and the world had condemned their actions as one of the greatest horrors in man's history. Even Mansur had put Arubi's mentioning of Hitler's atrocities out of his mind.

"I will not carry out another bombing," Mansur declared. "We will learn to destroy our enemies humanely. We do not like killing, but it is a necessary evil of war."

Everyone agreed with Mansur's argument. They thought it was a good idea. Mansur gave part of the credit for the idea to Arubi. Mansur's men esteemed Arubi and Mansur even more. They were both heroes.

Mansur rationalized his killing again. He put the murder of his best friend out of his mind. *That was the deed of Imad*, he reasoned. *Imad was now dead*. Mansur was becoming schizophrenic. He had no idea how quickly he would be able to acquire biological weapons to use against Israel, but he would pursue them diligently.

CHAPTER 14
Mindanao, Philippines

Niloa was the first to see the Philippines archipelago. Paulo was again sleeping at the time she sighted Leyte. Turning the *Dawn Treader II* south, Niloa knew she needed to sail along the coast between Cebu and Mindanao and then follow the northern coast of Mindanao until she could turn south following the western coast toward Zamboanga City. She had been unable to contact her parents for two days and was anxious to hear more information about Paulo. At 6:00 p.m. she tried her cell phone again. She still could not get through.

Paulo came on deck. He asked Niloa with a genuine interest, "Did you call your parents?"

"No," Niloa answered. "I'm still trying. I haven't been able to reach them in two days now."

Paulo scanned the horizon and noticed that two powerboats off in the distance seemed to be heading toward them. He went into the cabin and grabbed a pair of binoculars.

"I think we have company, Niloa," he said as he tracked the boats through the lenses. "It's not good, Niloa. They look like pirates."

Paulo was clearly agitated and concerned. Niloa put the *Dawn Treader II* on autopilot and retrieved her assault rifle.

"Under the bench on the starboard side," Niloa shouted to Paulo, pointing to a secured locker. "The combination in 17-26-05. You'll find some firepower in there."

Niloa was now very concerned as she saw the boats closing in with men on board carrying what looked like weapons; automatic assault riffles.

Paulo opened the locker and pulled out a rocket propelled grenade launcher. One of the gunmen began shooting at the *Dawn Treader II* with an automatic weapon, hoping to frighten Niloa and Paulo into submission. Fortunately, the boat was still too far away and out of range. Niloa returned fire with her Heckler & Koch MP5-N submachine gun, shattering the cabin window. She managed to maneuver the boat away from the attacker. Just as the second boat pulled along the starboard side, Paulo fired a grenade into the stern, blowing a hole in the support structure for the two powerful outboard engines. Both engines fell backward into the water, immobilizing the boat. The attackers scrambled to find a life raft as the *Dawn Treader II* sailed away from them.

Paulo quickly reloaded the grenade launcher. The second attack boat, realizing they were overpowered, backed off.

"Paulo, you shot that like a pro," Niloa shouted. "Have you used that before?"

"I've used something like it," Paulo replied. "But this one is much lighter and more powerful.."

"What is a yacht racer like you doing with a weapon like this?" Paulo asked.

"My Uncle Jarvis got it for me," Niloa replied, "and showed me how to use it too."

"Have you used it?" Paulo asked.

"Never had to, thank God. I did practice several times when my uncle was training me. I haven't had the chance to fire it in about a year, but I always keep it loaded and ready."

"Does the *Abu Sayyaf* have these?" Niloa asked.

"I'm afraid so," Paulo answered. "They have all kinds of weapons. Osama bin Laden's *al Qaeda* organization has supplied them with money to purchase sophisticated weapons, including a couple of stinger missiles."

"Paulo, I don't know who you work for," Niloa said, "but I'm convinced you're not a terrorist. Still, you're certainly more than a navigator."

"Yeah, well you're more than a sailboat racer," Paulo retorted.

"I'm going to try calling my parents again," said Niloa. "We are close enough to the coast of Cebu. I should be able to get through. Take the helm, Paulo."

Niloa went back below deck, found her satellite phone and called home. This time she reached her father, although the connection was not a good one. Niloa's father reassured her that she was safe with Paulo. Colonel Siefer had called him from the Pentagon. Paulo worked for the National Security Office of the Philippines. Niloa confirmed that Paulo was a former MNLF leader recruited by the *Abu Sayyaf.*

After he refused to join, the Philippine government granted him amnesty and asked him to become an intelligence officer in order to penetrate the *Abu Sayyaf.* He agreed, and posing as a navigator, began to monitor the group's activities. The Philippine government gave Paulo permission to sail them to other islands so they could locate all their bases of operation.

They then told Paulo they were going to scout out some places in the Caroline Islands. The *Abu Sayyaf* had become suspicious of Paulo, so they lied to him about their true destination until they were hundreds of miles at sea. U.S. authorities were on alert in the Carolines to ready to arrest them. They redirected Paulo to sail to the Marianas for a scouting trip, concealing from him their true intentions to attack the research lab.

"Niloa," her father said, "Paulo could not tell you he is working as an intelligence officer for the government without compromising his cover."

Paulo looked at Niloa's facial expressions as she talked, but could not really discern the conversation.

"Thanks, Dad," Niloa finally responded after she listened for a long time. "I'll tell Paulo your tip for healing sunburn."

She partially succeeded in misdirecting Paulo as to the nature of their conversation.

Before ending the conversation, Niloa's father asked her to call her Uncle Jarvis at a new phone number she did not have in her possession.

"So, what's your dad's tip for sunburn?" Paulo inquired after Niloa ended the conversation.

"Mix fresh lemon and lime juice with Aloe Vera cream, and stay below deck as you have been," Niloa answered. "We have all those ingredients in the galley."

"I'll go mix some up now," Paulo said eagerly as he headed into the cabin.

Niloa picked up her satellite phone again and called her Uncle Jarvis.

"Hi, Niloa," Jarvis said warmly. "It's been a while. How are you?"

"I'm fine, thanks to the firepower you stocked on this boat," Niloa answered with equal enthusiasm. She then went on to explain the pirate attack and how Paulo had fought off the attackers with a well-placed grenade.

"I told you to watch out for pirates," Jarvis reminded after hearing the story. "Did the grenade launcher work OK?"

"Just like in practice," Niloa replied.

"Niloa, you and Paulo need to be extremely careful. You are in way over your head. The *Abu Sayyaf* is ruthless. Soldiers train for years to do this sort of work. You are a peaceful, fun-loving sailor. We have enough family members involved in military service who have placed their lives at risk. Your parents and I are sorry this has happened to you."

"Uncle Jarvis, I'm fine," Niloa assured him. "Maybe I can finally help someone with my skills. By the way, where are you now?"

"I'm in Manila," Jarvis replied. "I just flew in from Guam after a trip to Saipan and visit to Farallon de Medinilla."

"Did they find the missing scientist, Jack?" Niloa inquired.

"I'm sorry, Niloa," Jarvis explained. "Pieces of his blood-stained clothing washed up on shore a couple of days ago. It appears that sharks devoured him. I doubt if his body will ever be found."

Niloa paused and swallowed hard. Tears welled up in her eyes as she thought of Jack's last words and the conversation with his wife, and the love they had expressed for each other. She gathered her composure, commenting, "He was a good man, Uncle Jarvis. He was a very good man."

"He was indeed. He was also Dennis' good friend. Dennis is pretty upset."

"I didn't know you knew him."

"Jack and Dennis worked together for a time," Jarvis explained.

"Uncle Jarvis, are you coming to Mindanao?"

"Yes. I'll see you in Zamboanga City. How far do you think you're behind them?"

"It's hard to say, but probably less than an hour or two, maybe even less. We don't know if they'll sail directly to Basilan or stop first in Zamboanga City."

Just after Niloa and Jarvis ended their conversation, Paulo spotted a sailboat through his binoculars, but the twilight made it too difficult to see if it was the *Sulu Breeze*. They were now only 8-10 nautical miles behind them. They seemed to be heading toward Zamboanga City. The U.S. government already had special forces in the city working with the Filipino Army against the terrorists.

Niloa was now pushing the *Dawn Treader II* as hard as she could, staying out of the current along the coastline, seeking to close the distance even more.

"I don't know what we'll do if we catch up," Niloa said to no one in particular.

She then turned to Paulo and said, "Paulo, if I catch up with them, you figure out what we're going to do."

When the *Dawn Treader II* sailed to within a few miles of the *Sulu Breeze*, Paulo confirmed their identity. They sailed to within two miles of the *Sulu Breeze*, within sight of the terrorists, when they realized it had stopped just outside of Zamboanga Harbor. Two speedboats immediately converged on the sailboat. There were no military patrols in sight.

"They've been paid off," Paulo said disgustedly.

"What do you mean?" Niloa asked.

"This place has operated on bribes and threats for centuries," Paulo explained. "That's why there are no police or military patrols around."

"Are those speedboats the *Abu Sayyaf?*" Niloa asked.

"That's the way it looks to me," Paulo replied, looking through the binoculars and showing his disdain for the corrupt system that allowed terrorism to have a stronghold in the south.

"They're unloading materials from the *Sulu Breeze* onto two speedboats."

"Probably from the lab," Niloa added.

"They must be splitting up the stolen samples," Paulo guessed.

"We can't follow two speedboats, Paulo."

"We might have to wait until the sailboat heads toward Basilan," Paulo concluded.

Niloa was happy that Paulo was becoming more decisive and taking more leadership. During the voyage from the Marianas to the Philippines, Niloa had made almost all of the decisions. She had felt very unsure of herself in the Philippines.

The Filipino military patrol boats did not visit the *Sulu Breeze* until ten minutes after the two speedboats left her port side. The crew had expeditiously unloaded all of the cargo, except for a few cases of wine and liquor, which they had stolen from the U.S. military base. These items, along with generous cash payments, provided the patrols with sufficient motivation to leave them alone, despite the government's crackdown on accepting bribes. So, as not to arouse suspicion, the Filipino crews searched the *Sulu Breeze* as they would any other ship, but found nothing amiss. The *Abu Sayyaf* had removed all the biological samples and weapons on board. Two crew members were thoroughly washing the boat with formaldehyde. After the inspection and cleaning they sailed into the harbor and anchored the boat.

During the time the cargo was unloaded, Niloa and Paulo had kept the *Dawn Treader II* at a safe distance from the *Sulu Breeze* but kept some distance. They wanted to follow one of the speedboats south toward Basilan. However, they could not keep up with a fast speedboat in the dark, so they kept their attention on the *Sulu Breeze*.

Paulo knew that they didn't keep the *Sulu Breeze* anchored in Zamboanga Harbor, so he and Niloa decided to wait until she sailed again. They noted that the second speedboat turned east, probably heading toward Davao on the southeast coastline facing the Davao Gulf.

Paulo and Niloa sailed the *Dawn Treader II* into Zamboanga City Harbor and anchored the boat there. They then waded ashore. Jarvis and Colonel Siefer were waiting for them on shore at an outdoor café. Siefer and Jarvis spotted the *Sulu Breeze* not far from where they anchored the *Dawn Treader II*.

"There they are," Jarvis said excitedly, pointing out into the bay. "Let's go greet them." Jarvis and Siefer left their seats in the café and walked toward the water. Niloa spotted her uncle first and began running through the knee deep ocean water. She met Jarvis in ankle-deep water and leaped into his arms.

"Uncle Jarvis, you don't know how happy I am to see you!"

"It's mutual. Now introduce me to your gallant friend and I'll introduce you to Colonel Siefer."

After Jarvis made the introductions, the four of them returned to a private area in the café and ordered some Singapore fried rice, fish and Coca-Colas. Jarvis thought Niloa had done enough, and that she should continue her trip to the Solomon Islands and let the U.S. troops and Filipino Army pursue the *Abu Sayyaf*. Despite the fact that the terrorists were outnumbered, Paulo felt the Filipino Army and American military advisors would still have difficulty finding the *Abu Sayyaf* on Basilan. He also feared they may escape to another island, and that sailing in may be one of the few ways to get close to them without raising suspicion.

Paulo also believed the *Abu Sayyaf* would make contact with al Qaeda through either Indonesia or Malaysia. The second group of Abu Sayyaf members that headed southeast toward Davao in one of the speedboats could more easily be tracked by the Filipino military. Colonel Siefer agreed that it would be easier and more important to first intercept the group traveling toward Davao. Davao had a large airport and they could have arranged to take the biological weapons out of the country and sell them. There was no use for them on a small island. Niloa argued that she and Paulo should sail to Basilan, posing as a couple on a fishing and diving trip.

In the heat of the discussion, a tall Eurasian man and a high-ranking Filipino army officer approached their table.

"Stephano!" Paulo shouted, jumping out of his seat. He then ran over and gave the young man a bear hug.

"Kumusta ka?"

"*Mabuit naman, ikaw?*" Stephano answered.

"*Mabait!* In fact, very good!" Paulo replied.

"Stephano, you look great. We were planning to come to your home in Cabu to ask for your help."

Niloa observed the reunion with great interest. Paulo had told her all about his friend Stephano, who he described as a local hero. *He did not exaggerate when he described his appearance*, Niloa thought. Stephano stood six foot one with a lean muscular body. His face looked younger than his age 33, which is what Paulo had told her. His hands were weathered and his olive skin sported a deep tan. His eyes were brown and his long hair a sandy brown. He did not look Filipino, although he had some Filipino features like a flat nose. He did not look Caucasian either, although his height, body size, and jaw made him look more European. Paulo never did mention his nationality.

In what sounded like perfect English without a local accent, Stephano said, "It's good to see you Paulo. Please let me reintroduce General Ramos to you and then you can introduce us to your friend."

"General Ramos, you remember Paulo Servantes. We are as close as brothers."

"How could I forget Paulo," Ramos replied after giving Paulo a warm handshake. "We've been in many conflicts together. I'm so glad we're on the same side now."

General Ramos had spent many months trying to capture Paulo when he was an MNLF leader. When President Aquino offered amnesty to the MNLF members, as a sign of respect, Paulo and Stephano walked into General Ramos' military headquarters and surrendered their weapons.

"That day Stephano and Paulo walked into my barracks," Ramos explained to the others, "was one of the happiest days of my life."

Paulo then introduced General Ramos to Colonel Siefer, Jarvis and Niloa. They all shook hands warmly. Niloa noticed that Stephano gave her a little longer eye contact than usual upon a first greeting.

"Paulo," General Ramos said, "Colonel Siefer is a bioterrorism expert from the National Security Council in Washington; and Mr. Jarvis is a retired special operations officer who worked in counter-terrorism for the U.S. military."

"This beautiful young woman," Paulo replied as he looked into Niloa's eyes, "is the best sailor I've ever known and an excellent fisherman, I might add."

"She's also my niece," Jarvis interjected.

"I'm happy to meet you, General Ramos," Niloa said warmly.

Then turning to Stephano she said, "And you too Stephano. I feel as if I already know you. Paulo has told me so much about you."

"Whatever he has told you, Niloa, I hope you only remember the good parts. I doubt if I could live up to Paulo's stories. He knows way too much."

Paulo and Stephano laughed generously. Niloa noticed his infectious smile and beautiful white teeth. Contrasted with his olive skin, his countenance was striking. He spoke with a kind, but strong voice. Niloa was instantly attracted to him, a reaction Paulo had predicted.

Turning to Niloa, Paulo said, "Stephano knows Basilan Island like you know the island of Kauai. If he can come with us, we will find their camp."

"Also," General Ramos added, "the *Abu Sayyaf* respect Stephano. They even tried to recruit him at one time."

"I do know most of their hiding places," Stephano admitted, "but they are very clever. I haven't seen their new leaders, so they might even kill me now. If they hear or see any patrol boat approach, they will hide, kill you, or take you captive, depending upon the size of the force."

"What about a sailboat?" Niloa asked. "They are quiet; and if they saw one, would they be suspicious?"

"Probably not," Stephano answered. "There are people who sail throughout these islands and the *Abu Sayyaf* use sailboats themselves."

"You've done enough already," Jarvis said to Niloa. "Although I do think it is a great idea. They wouldn't suspect you, Niloa, of being part of the military or any kind of threat."

"Probably not," Stephano concluded. "If you could hide Paulo and me on board, I think we could find them."

"I think the idea has merit," Colonel Siefer chimed in.

"The problem is that they would recognize me if they saw me," Paulo reminded everyone.

"That's right," Niloa said. "Paulo, it would be too dangerous for you. They would kill you this time."

"Then I can sail in with Niloa," Jarvis concluded. "We can pose as a father-daughter pair enjoying the sea life and ocean reefs, sailing innocently through the islands. We can then hide Stephano on board in the cabin."

"There is a viewing monitor in the cabin connected to a camera on the mast," Niloa explained to Stephano. "My dad set it up so that the cabin can be secured from the outside elements during a storm, but you can still see the outside."

"After this one last trip," Jarvis said to Niloa with a fatherly consternation, "you are going to take the *Dawn Treader II* down to the Solomon Islands."

"Uncle Jarvis," Niloa responded with amusement, "that was excellent. You are picking up the role well. You sounded just like my father." They all laughed heartily.

General Ramos put the Davao International Airport on high alert. He also notified the port authorities in Cotabato. Extra troops were sent to guard all aircraft and to patrol the major port areas in Mindanao, especially in the Davao Gulf. Intelligence officers were sent to the airport to increase check-in security.

Colonel Siefer would meet with the U.S. Special Forces in Zamboanga City who were working with the Filipino military. The military would dispatch Black Hawk helicopters with satellite navigation and infrared nighttime capabilities to hunt down the *Abu Sayyaf* once their location was pinpointed. They had to be careful not to disrupt any of the biological samples.

Five hours later six musicians boarded Philippine Airlines Flight 810 from Davao City to Manila, with continued service to Narita, Japan. Security was extremely tight, but as customary, the musicians were allowed their clarinets, saxophones, and electric guitars on board. Their cases all fit into the overhead compartments.

Forty minutes into the flight, one by one, the six musicians began using the bathrooms. No one noticed since drinks had been served and a few others were also using the bathrooms. However, they did seem to be in the bathrooms for a long time. A fine invisible mist began to fill the cabin of the plane. Unknown to any passengers, each musician had placed a round cylinder inside their plastic cups filled with water, and left them on their tray table. Deadly botulinum poison, a colorless and odorless toxin, was filling the air. Within 20 minutes everyone on board was dead or incapacitated except the six terrorists posing as musicians. The terrorists emerged from the bathrooms donning gas masks.

The air filtration system circulated the toxin to the pilot's cabin. They had put the plane on autopilot, as expected. The pilots were nearly dead when they pulled them out of the cockpit. Two trained *Abu Sayyaf* pilots began flying the 737-400 jet. They had enough fuel to reach northern Indonesia. The plane had a range of 2370 miles, so they needed to stop several times to reach their final destination.

They first touched down in Medan, Sumatra, where they refueled but did not exit the aircraft. The Islamic authorities at the airport decided not to pay attention to the warnings about a high-jacked jet by Islamic terrorists. The Indonesian military was ordered to leave the plane alone and let it leave Medan.

Their second stop was in the Maldives, an island chain one hundred miles southwest of India.

"We need more food and water," the terrorists told authorities.

There several of the terrorists existed the plane for a short time and two additional terrorists joined them. *Al Qaeda* had effectively infiltrated the infrastructure of the small island chain, now in control by radical Muslims sympathetic to their cause. The plane was refueled and then flew to Yemen.

The terrorists' third stop was in northern Yemen. Again, authorities refused to stop the flight although they knew the plane was hijacked. The plane was refueled and proceeded on to Syria, landing at a private airport in Dummar, just outside of Damascus. There, the musical instruments and much of the baggage was unloaded and placed in several four-wheel drive vehicles and pick-up trucks. All the terrorists exited the aircraft except two new pilots who had boarded in the Maldives. The plane was then be flown into Israeli airspace where it was initially mistaken for a commercial airliner simply off course.

Once the Israeli authorities realized it was PR flight 810, hijacked from Davao, they tried to contact the plane. The terrorists flying the plane would not respond. Fearing another suicide attack, Israeli jets scrambled and shot the plane down as it neared Jerusalem. The plane disintegrated over a populated area on the outskirts of the city, injuring 37 civilians, including eight Palestinians, three Americans, and a married couple from France, on the ground. In addition to the 54 adults and 19 children that were killed on board by botulinum poisoning, including the pilots, both new pilots died on the suicide mission.

The next day, four SUV's were driven across the Syrian border. Inside the cases holding the musical instruments, were carefully packed vials of biological samples and deployable botulinum weapons, the same ones used on PR flight 810. The toxin had worked very efficiently on the aircraft.

The Lebanese Hamas were waiting for the delivery. Soon Imad Al-Ferradi, the alias Mansur, one of the most dangerous terrorists in the world, would have in his possession deployable biological weapons and the will to use them.

CHAPTER 15
Sulu Sea, Philippines

Niloa, her uncle Jarvis, and Stephano loaded the *Dawn Treader II* with supplies for their trip to Basilan Island, including new communication equipment provided by the U.S. military. General Ramos asked if he could receive regular updates from them to keep him abreast of their progress. The goal of their trip was to sail around the island and pinpoint the area where the *Abu Sayyaf* were shipping their supplies onto the island. From there Stephano would follow their trail and find the location of their training camp. He would then relay this information to General Ramos, Colonel Siefer, and Major Joshua Ryan, the U.S. Special Forces commander on assignment in the Philippines.

Colonel Siefer and Jarvis first met Major Ryan in Manila. They then traveled together to Mindanao. Major Ryan was in charge of training the Filipino troops who were pursuing the *Abu Sayyaf*. He commanded 100 Filipino Rangers and a small Delta Force counter-terrorism team of six men. Ryan had a keen interest in the well being of Paulo and Stephano, who were allies in the war against the *Abu Sayyaf*. Ryan also had a keen interest in Niloa, whom he had heard much about from Colonel Siefer.

While preparing the *Dawn Treader II* to be ready to sail, Niloa noticed some activity aboard the deck of the *Sulu Breeze*. The sailboat had taken on new supplies from the port and new crew members had arrived to join the two already on board. Niloa informed her Uncle Jarvis and Stephano, who suggested they wait and see where the *Sulu Breeze* sailed next. If by chance it sailed to Basilan Island, they could follow it to the area of the island where the *Abu Sayyaf* picked up its supplies.

The *Sulu Breeze* sailed out of Zamboanga Harbor under the cover of darkness. Fortunately, the waning moon was three-quarters from full, providing good visibility on the seas.

The Sulu Sea was unusually calm. Niloa had no difficulty navigating her way to Basilan Island, the stronghold of the *Abu Sayyaf*.

"I don't see how they can miss seeing us in this moonlight," Jarvis voiced to no one in particular.

"Maybe they haven't," Stephano replied.

"At least there are several other vessels out here at night," Niloa observed.

"I still think they might know that we are following them," Stephano quipped. "Niloa, we better keep our distance."

Shortly after the *Dawn Treader II* began to approach the southern tip of Basilan, they noticed the *Sulu Breeze* continued on a southerly course.

"They're not going to Basilan," Stephano said with concern in his voice. "They seem to be heading toward Jolo Island."

"Do you think it's because they know they are being followed?" Jarvis asked.

"I don't know," Stephano said, "but we need to decide what to do. All the intelligence information indicates the *Abu Sayyaf* is still hiding on Basilan. However, the U.S.-trained Filipino Scout Rangers have killed and captured many of the *Abu Sayyaf* guerrillas, including some of their top leaders. There is a possibility that new guerillas have joined them from Islamic countries. The remaining force has moved deep into the jungle. At least that is what our scouts believe."

"Could they have moved from the island?" Jarvis asked Stephano.

"It's possible, but a security perimeter patrol has been put around the island. The leaders of *Abu Sayyaf* are very clever though."

"Then I suggest we continue following the *Sulu Breeze*," Jarvis offered.

"I agree," Stephano responded.

"They'll probably see us following," Niloa said, "but I will try to stay far enough behind."

After about an hour of sailing, the *Sulu Breeze* began to turn on a course slightly west. Stephano had also spent a considerable amount of time on Jolo Island. During one intense period when the Filipino government was hunting down MNLF leaders, Stephano had escaped to Jolo Island for three months. He continued to stay below deck so as not to be spotted by the *Abu Sayyaf* who undoubtedly kept an eye on the deck of the *Dawn Treader II* through binoculars.

What they would have seen most the time was Niloa at the helm and her Uncle Jarvis deep-sea fishing with a thick 10-foot rod. The Sulu Sea was full of excellent fish and it was not unusual to see foreign sport fisherman sailing and fishing in the area. Jarvis and Niloa acted like a father and daughter to the best of their ability, which came naturally to them, since Niloa's father and Jarvis were close, and Niloa felt close to her great uncle.

Shortly after the *Dawn Treader II* approached the northwest corner of Jolo Island, the *Sulu Breeze* disappeared from their sight, having rounded a point on the northern tip of the western side of the island. Niloa was able to round the tip of the island quickly, bringing the *Dawn Treader II* closer to the coast. The *Sulu Breeze* was still not in sight. There did not seem to be any natural bay or inlet in the area, but there were several small islands just off the coast, which could obscure their line of sight to the *Sulu Breeze*.

Stephano viewed the coastline from below deck on the television monitor. One of the advantages of the camera on the mast was that it had the ability to zoom in on a particular piece of land.

"I see them!" Stephano shouted from below through the open cabin door. "There is a small strip of land curled in the shape of a sickle, protecting a small bay."

The *Sulu Breeze* sailed around a small island, then turned south, sailing along a narrow cape. It then sailed north again into the harbor.

Niloa closed distance carefully but kept well off shore. It was difficult to see in the dark. They decided to wait till early morning before approaching the harbor.

Jarvis fell asleep quickly, but Niloa and Stephano stayed up to talk and navigate. The more Stephano listened to Niloa, the more he realized how much he liked her. Niloa was also fascinated by Stephano's life and fight for freedom. He thought deeply about the ideals he cherished.

After talking for two hours, Niloa fell asleep in Stephano's lap. He let her sleep for a few minutes before waking her with a gentle kiss. She reciprocated, and grabbed the back of his neck, drawing him toward herself. They kissed passionately for the next ten minutes. Stephano cuffed his hands around her face and began talking softly to her, gently stroking her beautiful skin. He didn't want to ruin their relationship by becoming too physical too fast. They had a big day tomorrow and needed sleep.

"If we get through this, Niloa, I'm ready to talk seriously about us. I want to get to know you intimately. I know we just met, but we both share the same ideals and have the same spirit. I have a dream for the Philippines and you can be a part of that dream. At least think about it."

"I've been doing that," Niloa replied. "I'll be thinking seriously."

After taking turns at night watch, all three were awake by daybreak and sailed the *Dawn Treader II* toward the place where the *Sulu Breeze* had gone the previous night. Before they reached the elbow of the cape, a speedboat approached them. Whoever was in the speedboat was likely guarding the harbor. Jarvis thought their base camp must be close by, but Stephano was not sure. He knew it was extremely difficult to travel on the island. They could see four armed men were on board the boat.

"Stay cool," Stephano said before climbing into a hidden locker below deck. "We can't start a fire fight here."

"They're coming on board, Niloa," Jarvis warned. "Just stay calm."

Jarvis greeted the armed men as they climbed on board the *Dawn*

Treader II. He had a pipe in his mouth and a fishing rod in his hand. The Filipino men looked angry and offered no greetings. They were obviously very upset. Jarvis did have several large fish on ice to verify that he had been fishing.

"Who are you and what are you doing here?" one of the leaders asked with a harsh tone.

"My name is Jarvis and this is my daughter Niloa. We are on an extended sailing expedition and wanted to spend some time fishing in these islands."

"Why did you come to Jolo Island?" the leader asked, almost yelling now. "Don't you know how dangerous it is here? There are many pirates who would kill you just to steal your boat!"

"Sir," Jarvis answered respectfully, "we were only warned that there is occasional fighting between the Filipino troops and Muslim freedom fighters. After the end of the hostage crisis on Basilan Island, we heard that things had calmed down. Also, our friends told us that the people here are very hospitable to foreigners, and not to worry. We saw another sailboat in the area and thought it might be a good harbor to anchor in and get some sleep."

Jarvis' answer seemed to calm the guerrillas. He was very complimentary toward them. Jarvis concluded that they were members of the *Abu Sayyaf*. They had made a tactical error in not recognizing the harbor would be guarded. Jarvis knew they were in danger of being kidnaped.

The leader shouted commands to the other three guerrillas who began searching the *Dawn Treader II*. They all had automatic weapons and long knives. If Stephano was discovered hiding, they all would be killed. After the search turned up nothing, the leader spotted the locker on deck on the starboard side of the yacht.

"What's in there?" he asked.

"Just some life jackets," Jarvis replied.

"Open it!" he demanded.

Jarvis leaned over and opened the combination lock. Signaling with his automatic weapon, the leader of the group asked Jarvis to move away. Another one of the guerrillas checked the locker. It was filled with life jackets. Jarvis was wise to have moved the grenade launcher to the locker where Stephano was hiding below deck.

The leader seemed to be satisfied. He then turned to Jarvis and said, "We'll let you live, old man."

He then said to Niloa, "You, come with us."

Jarvis had a decision to make. He was not in a position to fight them. If he objected fiercely, he could be killed. On the other hand, if he failed to object fiercely, they might think he wasn't Niloa's father, and that he'd been lying to them.

"You're not taking my daughter anywhere without my permission," Jarvis said calmly. "But since our lives are in your hand, I will allow her to go with you only if you promise to bring her back safely."

The *Abu Sayyaf* leader was shocked by Jarvis' bold reaction, convinced that he indeed was the father. However, he wondered why Jarvis was curiously calm. It made him think that perhaps Jarvis had a military background.

"You'll get her back, old man, and long as you pay up. You need to go get $100,000 in U.S. currency and then return here. If you tell the police or military authorities, we'll kill her. We'll give you one week to bring these funds, and you better return alone."

Niloa was taken on the motorboat, which headed toward the shore. Immediately Stephano emerged from his hiding place. He had heard the entire conversation and was not convinced the Abu Sayyaf would keep their agreement.

"I can swim ashore from here," he said quietly. "I need to get to shore as soon as I can to track them to their camp."

"The risk factor is extremely high," Jarvis replied. "The camp perimeter will be well guarded. Make sure you take the new radio equipment."

"I can do it!" Stephano said confidently. "I know this island well and Colonel Siefer gave us night vision equipment. My geo-sat locator will indicate my exact location at all times. I hope to be back in the morning with the exact location of Niloa and the camp."

Stephano quietly slipped off the *Dawn Treader II* with a buoyant airtight plastic bag filled with his equipment. The patrol boat, having gone to shore, did not see him.

Jarvis sailed the *Dawn Treader II* out to sea away from the harbor. He could not leave the boat in full view, but had to be seen sailing north as if he was returning to Mindanao. Then he had to find a good hiding place so he could wait for Stephano's return at night.

Shortly after Jarvis had left the harbor, he realized one of the *Abu Sayyaf* patrol boats was following him. They might have planned to escort him all the way back to Zamboanga City. Jarvis realized he could not lose them. He had to turn and fight.

He sailed out to sea away from the coastline of Basilan Island. After sailing a couple of hours, he went into the cabin, retrieved the grenade launcher and two M-10 assault rifles, and slung the combination assault rifle grenade launcher onto his right shoulder and one of the M-10 rifles onto his left shoulder. Jarvis had been trained to carry two weapons at a time some 30 years ago when he was in Ranger School; but he had not been in a live combat situation in more than 12 years. Jarvis, perspiring heavily now, nervously placed the back-up weapon on the deck to the right of him.

The terrorists sprayed the water with machine gun bullets as they approached the *Dawn Treader II* to frighten Jarvis into submission. Jarvis would soon be within range. He laid down on the deck, picked up the loaded grenade launcher, and took aim over the side, elevating himself slightly on his knees. He really liked the weapon; it was lighter than what he had used in Ranger School and had a longer range. When the attacking boat reached within 100 yards of his position, he fired a grenade. The cabin of the boat exploded, sending debris within a thirty-yard radius. All the men on board were killed or wounded, but the boat continued to move toward him and he could not discern how many were still alive on board.

Jarvis heard machine gun fire pierce the side of the *Dawn Treader II* just below him. He reached for a second grenade and reloaded just as a bullet passed through the outside of his left shoulder. At least one guerrilla was still alive. The second grenade punched a hole in the hull and killed the wounded man, starting a fire and igniting leaking fuel. The speedboat's gas tank suddenly exploded in a ball of flames, knocking Jarvis on his back.

The intense heat was a danger to the *Dawn Treader II*. Jarvis ran to the helm and maneuvered the yacht away from the burning boat. A sharp pain seized his left shoulder where he had been wounded as blood oozed from the wound through his shirt. It was more than a nick, but thank God, not an incapacitating wound. His mantra of "*I'm OK, I'm OK,*" did not seem to lessen the pain. Jarvis found the first aid kit in the cabin, soaked his shirt with some bourbon he found in a cabinet, applied gauze in the area where the shirt had been torn by the bullet, and taped his shoulder under his armpit to hold the gauze in place and apply pressure to the damaged tissue.

"Damn that stings!" he complained under his breath as the alcohol found its way to the exposed tissue. He guessed that the bullet just missed damaging any bone. His main concern was first, to stop the bleeding; and second, to leave the area. He could later ask Stephano to dress the wound more properly.

Jarvis turned the *Dawn Treader II* back toward Jolo Island. He decided to stop sailing until a couple hours before daybreak, far enough to be away from land until daybreak, the time he had arranged to pick up Stephano. At 4:00 a.m. he began sailing back toward the bay to rendezvous with Stephano. The *Dawn Treader II* approached the end of the cape just before daylight. Shortly after Jarvis cleared the cape and began to enter the small bay, he noticed a small boat off shore. He could not discern who might be in the boat. Jarvis reloaded the grenade launcher just in case. His M-10 assault rifle was on the deck next to him.

Stephano began rowing a small fishing boat in the early morning light, hoping that no one would see him in the bay. He had been waiting more than 30 minutes for the *Dawn Treader II* to enter the bay. Stephano wondered if another patrol boat for the Abu Sayyaf was in the area. He was not sure if Jarvis had spotted him, and contemplated shooting a flare toward the *Dawn Treader II*. He decided against it.

Jarvis sensed movement in the water and raised his weapon as he sat on the floor of the cockpit. Looking through the binoculars, he saw a man rowing steadily toward him and recognized that it was Stephano. Jarvis rose from his defensive position on deck, scanned the harbor, and took the helm, directing the *Dawn Treader II* toward Stephano. The two boats approached each other just before the dawn fully broke.

While Jarvis was pulling Stephano up onto the deck, machine gun fire rang out from the shore. Several *Abu Sayyaf* soldiers had spotted them but did not have a boat to pursue them in. Bullets pierced the hull of the fishing boat Stephano had used. He climbed quickly on board and laid on the deck. Jarvis sailed the *Dawn Treader II* out of range and headed toward the open sea.

"We need to get her out of there," Stephano said to Jarvis, "she looks OK, but I'm worried about her. The *Abu Sayyaf* may take her out of here to sell her for a ransom if they conclude Jarvis isn't coming back with the money they demanded."

"You saw the camp then!" Jarvis concluded with hope in his heart.

"Yes, I know exactly where they are. It is heavily guarded, but I think there is a way I can free Niloa. I've got to try."

"Stephano, you need to first give a detailed report of the camp to Colonel Siefer and General Ramos," Jarvis instructed.

"I don't know if I can do that," Stephano replied. "What if they try to go in there and do something stupid? Niloa could be easily killed. Jarvis, I trust you, but I don't completely trust the judgment of the Filipino military. And I don't know the U.S. Special Forces well enough to trust them."

"Stephano, Niloa is like my own daughter. I will go in there with you," he said emphatically.

"You're wounded and shouldn't be going into a combat situation."

"It's only a minor wound," Jarvis replied.

Stephano was relieved to know Jarvis was well enough to join him.

"Just in case we're not successful," Jarvis continued, "we need to give Colonel Siefer the camp coordinates. I trust him, Stephano. We have been friends for many years. He'll give us time to extract Niloa before attacking the camp."

Stephano looked down and closed his eyes for a moment. He

realized that if they were killed and the camp location remained unknown, Niloa would not be rescued. The only logical thing to do was to give Colonel Siefer the information and to trust his judgment.

Stephano looked up at Jarvis. "You're right, Jarvis. Let's ask Colonel Siefer to give us until tomorrow morning. We cannot rescue her in broad daylight."

"I agree," Jarvis responded.

Jarvis then contacted Colonel Siefer by cell phone and they agreed on a rescue plan. The camp would not be attacked until 6:00 the following morning. Jarvis and Stephano would break into the camp in the early morning hours, take Niloa out of there, and return to the *Dawn Treader II*. In the morning Filipino Scout Rangers and a small Delta Force unit from the U.S. headed by Major Ryan would obliterate the camp.

Jarvis and Stephano hid the *Dawn Treader II* on the ocean side of the sickle-shaped cape just after midnight, hoping the trees would hide the mast, and followed the Cape inland by foot, moving quickly along the shoreline. At 4:00 a.m. they came upon the outskirts of the camp. Stephano led Jarvis through an opening in the secured perimeter that he had previously found in between two of the posted guards. The two had to cross 40 yards of swamp area to reach the eastern edge of the compound. Stephano led Jarvis to the makeshift cabin structure were he had seen Niloa. He had actually been close enough when he first found her to be able to pin a transmitter on her pants through the thatched wall while she slept.

With night vision equipment, Stephano scanned the structure.

"Something's wrong," he whispered to Jarvis. "There are no guards posted outside the thatched hut. Last night there were two guards posted outside the front door."

"Perhaps they moved her," Jarvis replied. "Keep looking and see if guards are posted in front of any of the other structures."

Stephano scanned the area. There were no guards in sight. They decided to approach the back of the structure, which had a small window area. Stephano peered through the window with his night vision glasses. The structure seemed to be empty. Jarvis and Stephano moved around to the front and unlocked the triggers on their semiautomatic handguns, both of which had silencers affixed to them. The door was not locked. They quickly entered, peering into the room with their night goggles. It was empty. They could see that this was the place Niloa had been held. Jarvis recognized a piece of her shirt on the floor.

Stephano and Jarvis then checked the other two makeshift cabins. There were still *Abu Sayyaf* soldiers at the base but no sign of Niloa. They decided to go to the bay to see if the guerillas might be attempting to move her. She could still be somewhere on the compound. They just did not know. Their inclination was correct but they were too late. They heard the engines of a plane just as they approached the bay. They arrived on the beach just as four *Abu Sayyaf* guerrillas and Niloa were boarding a turboprop seaplane. Jarvis and Stephano were powerless to help her and watched the plane take off in great frustration.

Two guerrillas began returning to shore in the transport boat they had used.

"We need to capture one of these two alive and find out where they are going," Stephano blurted.

Jarvis and Stephano executed an ambush. The two guerrillas were both shot in the legs, disarmed, and interrogated by Stephano in Cebuano, a language spoken in Mindanao. They told Stephano that Niloa was being taken out of the country, but they did not know the destination.

They discovered the plane had a range of nearly 1000 miles before it needed to refuel. The guerrillas did not hold back this information because they knew there was nothing that Stephano and Jarvis could do to stop them. They also told them they now had acquired weapons of mass destruction and were part of a larger Islamic network that would fight for the just cause of all Muslim people. Jarvis and Stephano realized that the biological weapons the *Abu Sayyaf* had taken out to the island were now being taken out of the country. The men bragged that soon the southern Philippines would have an independent Islamic state. The guerrillas refused to divulge how many guerrillas remained in the camp. Knowing what would soon be coming upon the camp, Stephano and Jarvis stripped the men and let them go.

They then took the 20-foot motorboat the guerrillas had used and headed back toward the *Dawn Treader II*. Before they had reached the tip of the cape, Jarvis contacted Colonel Siefer and told him the bad news. It was 5:30 a.m. Satisfied that Niloa was out of the camp, Siefer green-lighted the attack.

Thirty minutes later, elite Filipino Rangers and Major Ryan's small Delta Force team descended upon the hidden Abu Sayyaf camp on Jolo Island. The 40 guerrillas left in the camp put up a fierce fight for an hour before being overwhelmed by 120 highly trained Special Forces. Helicopter gunships landed in the compound. Ryan and his men captured two *Abu Sayyaf* guerrillas alive.

One of the *Abu Sayyaf* survivors was a leader. He was taken to a secure location in Luzon to a military base south of Manila. After two days of interrogation by the Filipino Intelligence Agency, he finally cracked. He indicated that Niloa and two other woman hostages, one French and one German, were being taken to the Middle East to be exchanged for a large sum of money. The *Abu Sayyaf* had been promised $180 million from the Hamas for three hostages and the biological weapons.

With that much money, the Abu Sayyaf would have enough funds to bribe government officials into separating part of Mindanao and the chain of islands to the southwest, including Basilan and Jolo islands, from the rest of the Philippines and form a new Islamic state. Several influential senators were already predisposed to grant the separation, tired of the decades of bloodshed. The current Vice President was also sympathetic to the Islamic cause. The Abu Sayyaf targeted the President in a planned attack. The Vice President, who did not know about the planned attack, knew the President was a target of the terrorists. He was prepared to trade territory for peace. The Abu Sayyaf believed that the U.S.'s preoccupation with homeland security and the growing Middle East crisis would deflect attention away from the planned break-away.

After the successful attack on Jolo Island, Jarvis and Stephano sailed the *Dawn Treader II* to a safe birth in Zamboanga Harbor and traveled to Batangas in an M6-520 military helicopter. It was there that they conferred with U.S. and Filipino intelligence officers and developed a broader picture of what was being planned. The government of the Philippines concluded that the *Abu Sayyaf* never had any intentions of using biological weapons in the Philippines. They simply wanted millions of dollars so they could buy more political influence and military firepower.

The Hamas had been searching for biological weapons on the open market. They had already recruited Islamic militants who would use them in attacks against Israel. Through the *al Qaeda* network, the *Abu Sayyaf* was actually contracted by the Hamas to attack to U.S. biological research lab in the Mariana Islands.

"What happened to the guerrillas who headed toward Davao?" Stephano asked the Filipino intelligence officers. An officer looked down in disgust.

"We never caught up with them. On the way to the airport, rebels ambushed two groups of our counter-terrorism forces. They didn't seem to be *Abu Sayyaf* guerillas. They could have been a group of MNLF fighters who were violating our cease-fire agreement, but there also seemed to be foreign Arab fighters among them. There was a fierce firefight. Your friend Paulo was wounded in the attack. He was hit but several bullets but is in stable condition in the hospital. By the time we reached the airport, they had already slipped aboard a Philippine Airlines flight disguised as musicians and took control of the plane in flight."

Stephano was visibly shaken. He realized they now had taken a much larger group of hostages and could use the plane as a weapon.

After the debriefing was completed, Jarvis and Stephano recognized they needed to go different directions.

"Jarvis," Stephano said, "we have become good friends. You know I risked my life to save Niloa. I want to go the Middle East and help rescue her, but I also have a commitment to Paulo and my family in Mindanao. Paulo is closer than a brother to me. I need to help him recover."

"Stephano, you have done everything you can. I did not expect you to come to the Middle East and you have no legal authority there."

Colonel Siefer then added, "It would be very difficult if not impossible to authorize your involvement."

Jarvis then said, "Stephano, you have helped us immensely. Go back to Mindanao and help Paulo recover. The U.S. Special Forces will find Niloa, just like they found the missionaries held by the Taliban in Kabul. When she is freed, we'll come back to the Philippines to see you and will pick up the *Dawn Treader II* at that time. Please take care of her until we return, and take her out whenever you want."

"You take care of that shoulder," Stephano replied, "and find Niloa quickly."

Stephano reluctantly returned to Mindanao, knowing that he could not follow his heart, which wanted to free Niloa from terrorists in the Middle East. He wondered about the last conversation they had on board the *Dawn Treader II*. *How serious was she?* He thought they had shared their honest emotions. He savored the memory of their passionate kisses. Now he wondered, *Would he see her again?*

Niloa landed in a small airport in Syria. She was blindfolded, handcuffed, and depressed, not sure if anyone knew where she was being taken. At least there were two other women who were kidnaped with her.

As she thought back to waving good-bye to her family on the shores of Oahu, she wondered if she would ever see them again. She also realized how far she was from home and from the *Dawn Treader II*. Her dream of sailing to the Solomon Islands had turned into a nightmare.

CHAPTER 16
Chicago, Illinois

Daniel Patrick Ryan picked up the picture on his desk of his son and wondered where in the world he might be deployed now. He chuckled to himself and thought, *You couldn't be content with police work like your dad, you had to go and join the Special Forces.* Ryan did not rise to the level of the number three cop in Chicago through political alliances as other high-ranking officers had in the illustrious history of America's third largest city. He was constantly harassed by those jealous of him. Some of the lesser minds on the force thought he only received the promotion because of his famous name.

In truth, being a relative of a famous native son of Chicago for which a freeway was named, the Dan Ryan expressway, gave him no serious advantages over other officers with affluent family connections. Ryan, after all, had only moved to Chicago after his oldest son graduated from college and returned home to run their family farm in central Indiana. Ryan had managed the farm the entire 24 years he served as a police officer for the city of Indianapolis, including eight years as Chief of Police. Ryan and his wife Rebecca loved their home and traditional farmhouse 25 miles northeast of the city.

When Chicago's mayor contacted Ryan through a mutual friend, he was flabbergasted to be asked to apply for the head of counter-terrorism for the city of Chicago. The position carried the title of Deputy Superintendent, third from the top under the Superintendent of Police and First Deputy Superintendent.

The mayor wanted an educated man who understood some of the risks of chemical and biological weapons. Ryan had earned a bachelor of science degree in environmental science from Purdue University and a master's degree in chemistry from Indiana University-Purdue University in Indianapolis. Working on his farm and with several biology labs, Ryan had a broad understanding of chemical and biological agents.

Rebecca thought about the job offer for six weeks before she decided it was a good opportunity for both of them. Their oldest son could manage the farm and they could give the next ten years of their lives to the people of Chicago. Rebecca's cake decorating business had succeeded in Indianapolis. She could easily launch a new business in Chicago and give her present business to her daughter-in-law, who was already working with her in the business.

The Ryan's youngest son, Joshua, had become an Army Ranger and then a member of the Delta Force's counter-terrorism unit. Recently advanced in rank from Captain to Major, he had fought against the *al Qaeda* terrorist network in Afghanistan and Pakistan and commanded a small Special Forces deployment in the Philippines. Joshua, or "Josh," was the only child among three sons and two daughters who wanted any kind of career in law enforcement or the military. Neither of Josh's other two brothers or two sisters even liked to hunt.

Ryan put down the picture of Joshua and placed it into the corner of his desk.

A knock at the door broke his thoughts about Josh's safety. His secretary Diane opened the door slowly.

"Mr. Ryan, you have a call from Chief Summers on line one."

"Thanks, Diana," Ryan responded with a smile. "Put him through. I was just day-dreaming."

"Hi, Danny," a cheerful voice said.

"Hi, Bobby. How are things going in home security?"

"Not good," Bobby responded with a somber voice. "Did you hear what happened in the Philippines?"

"No," Ryan responded. "What's going on? My son Joshua is there now."

"Turn on CNN," Summers said.

"First, your son Joshua is now on his way back to Washington," Summers explained. "They have put him on the kidnaping case."

"What kidnaping case?"

"Did you get the news yet?"

Ryan grabbed the remote control to his television and turned on the news. The station was tuned to Fox News and was reporting that a biological attack had taken place in the Presidential Palace in Manila. The President of the Philippines had been exposed to a deadly toxin called botulinum, and was now fighting for her life in the hospital. They also reported that a Philippines Airline passenger jet, believed to have been highjacked by terrorists, was shot down outside of Jerusalem by the Israelis, who feared it was on a suicide mission.

"Oh no!" Ryan exclaimed. "This has to be stopped. Where did they get it, Bobby?"

"They stole it from a U.S. military lab," Summers replied.

Fox News also reported that the European intelligence community was worried that Middle Eastern terrorists also had access to these biological agents. They are expecting an attack on Israel and wonder if the Philippines Airline jet was part of a coordinated biolgical attack. They are testing the crash site for biological agents.

"I don't like it," Summers said. "All the focus is on Manila and Jerusalem overseas, and on New York and Los Angeles here. We are forgetting about other cities."

Ryan had learned over the years to trust Bobby Summers' instincts. A tough cop from Philadelphia, Summers was working with a former colleague in the Office for Homeland Security.

"What are you thinking, Bobby?" Ryan asked.

"I'm thinking Chicago is a prime target," he said without hesitation. "I don't have any evidence, only a hunch. We lost some guy last week who took a fishing trip down the St. Lawrence River and then mysteriously disappeared near the beaches of northern New York, while his boat captain slept."

"That's not so unusual," Ryan replied.

"The captain said he was drugged, and we think the man was traveling with a false identity. He could have been from the Middle East," Summers explained.

"I've been trying to contact your son Josh to find out if he knows any more than we do about U.S. threats," Summers said. "We are supposed to be sharing information but it is still hard to get a straight answer from the NSC on where the biological agents came from that were used in Manila. I hope I won't get him in trouble by pressing for this information. I did leave a message to have Josh call you too."

"No, it's fine," Ryan answered. "Josh has already obtained clearance from his commander, Colonel Matt Siefer, to pass on any credible threats to specific cities directly to city police chiefs as well as to your office. Josh called me just before he left for Manila and said they believed some of the stolen biological agents have made their way into the Middle East, but there were no threats on the U.S."

"My office has so much information flowing in and out, Dan, and the new National Intelligence Director is still getting his people organized. Half the time I feel we don't know what's going on," Summers replied. "Just keep me informed, Dan, and keep your forces in a state of preparedness. I have a very uneasy feeling."

Ryan put down the phone and wondered if Joshua had received the message from Chief Summers. Ryan thought that Joshua was probably in the middle of trying to figure out what happened on Jolo Island and where the hostages were taken.

Diane knocked on Ryan's door again. He invited her in.

"Your son Joshua is on line one, Mr. Ryan."

Ryan eagerly picked up the phone.

"Hi, Dad!" Joshua said enthusiastically. He then changed has tone dramatically.

"I did receive your message and a message from Chief Summers. Dad, we are in a dangerous situation. Some of what I am going to tell you hasn't been cleared yet by the National Intelligence Director, so please be careful with this information. I heard a rumor (which Ryan recognized was Josh's code word for reliable information) that the biological agents used in Manila were stolen from a U.S. military research lab, and that some of these weapons have been sold to the *Hamas* through the *al Qaeda* terrorist network. We did not recover any of these agents on Jolo Island."

"That's quite a big rumor," Ryan replied.

"Dad," he continued, "there is no credible evidence that anything is planned against the U.S. Our intelligence sources indicate that the *Hamas* have mapped out intended targets inside Israel. The *Hamas* have never been interested in attacking the United States."

"But you're not convinced, are you?" Dan discerned by the tone of his son's voice.

"No, Dad, I'm not. *Hamas* is working with *al Qaeda*. They could easily recruit martyrs to attack the U.S. Despite our increased patrols, our border with Canada is still relatively easy to penetrate. This is particularly true in the Great Lakes region. It just takes one fishing boat to cross the water to sneak in enough biological or chemical weapons to create a catastrophic event."

"I feel the same way, Josh. I just talked with Bobby Summers in the Office for Homeland Security. Last week a man illegally entered the U.S. by drugging a boat captain and is believed to have come ashore in New York, just as you described. He is believed to be of Middle-eastern decent and was guardedly carrying a large backpack."

"Hopefully, he's just another illegal immigrant here to make it rich," Josh said sarcastically, with a special foreign accent on the word *rich* that made his father laugh.

"Dad, you're in the third largest city in the U.S., at the center of America's heartland. I think Chicago is a logical target."

"Why not Detroit?" Dan asked, playing the devil's advocate. "There is a large Islamic population in southeastern Michigan. Aren't they an important center of support for Islamic terrorists?"

"We know there are support cells in the area," Josh responded. "But Detroit is too close to the Islamic community living in Michigan to be a target for Islamic terrorists."

"I agree that our waterways are vulnerable," Dan concluded.

"You'll need heavy security in your large buildings and in transportation centers," Joshua thought out loud, feeling a little stupid since he knew his father was much more of the security expert then he was and knew what to do with his resources. "I hope you have enough help, Dad. If you ever learn that terrorists are in the city, I can ask my commander to send a unit immediately."

Dan thanked his son Joshua for the input and ended their discussion in even greater concern for the city.

Shortly after this conversation, Josh received a call from Colonel Siefer, his commanding officer. Siefer indicated they had located the three women kidnaped by the *Abu Sayyaf*. They were now in the hands of the *Hamas* is Lebanon. A hostage rescue team was needed to extract the three women from Lebanon.

"Are we sure Colonel the *Hamas* have the same three women held by the *Abu Sayyaf*?" Josh asked.

"Yes," Siefer answered. "We have positive ID. The three women and biological agents were traded to the Hamas for a large sum of money. The Mousad had discovered their location by intercepting some cell phone messages. They then found the building where they are being held."

"Why don't they go in and get them?" Josh asked.

"Two reasons," Siefer replied. "First, all three are Westerners. They don't want to be responsible for their lives. Second, they are being held in Beirut. They are desperately trying to salvage the shattered peace process and don't want to intensify military conflict between their government and the Palestinian Authority. Also, things are too hot in Lebanon with the recent assassination of the former prime minister. The Syrians are on edge and they don't want to increase the tension"

"I'd be honored to be involved in the rescue, Colonel."

"I knew you would, Major. I want you to lead a small extraction team. You need five of your best men. I think Captain Brent Reynolds should be with you as your second in command."

"I wholeheartedly agree," Joshua responded. "I need Sergeant Mike McKinnen too. What about language?"

"I'll give you Corporal Jermanos Tarabay," Siefer replied. "He's working counter-terrorism in Israel. He speaks fluent Lebanese. He's a good man. He'll help you get through the check points. Pick two more and then develop a plan together. I'd like to review it with you in 24 hours."

Within two days of being assigned to lead the hostage rescue team, Joshua found himself on the way to the Mediterranean region off the coast of Lebanon. Under the cover of darkness, the rescue team was dispatched from an army helicopter not far from southern Lebanon. The six-member team inflated a rubber raft and paddled onto shore near a secluded private beach in Antil. Awaiting them was a four-wheel drive Toyota land cruiser in a parking lot on shore. The keys were attached to the front bumper with a magnet on the passenger side of the car. Joshua found the keys and opened the driver's side door.

Two team members stayed near the beach in a private residence, guarding their escape route. The other three team members and Joshua put their gear inside the Toyota. Joshua took out a well-marked map from his protective vest and began driving.

The target was only a 90-minute drive away from the coast. Only four Hamas guards were present when Joshua cut through the metal door of the two-story stucco home where the women were held. At the same time, his first lieutenant cut the glass out of the back window. The two other team members erected a portable ladder that reached the second-floor window. It was almost 3:00 a.m.

The two guards stationed outside the door to the room where the three women were sleeping were not awake. The men who had come through the upstairs window shot both with silencers. One of the guards downstairs awoke when Joshua entered the front door. He was killed from behind by one of the men who had come through the upstairs window. The fourth guard, also stationed downstairs, awoke and tried to turn on the light. Joshua shot and killed him just as he was reaching for the light switch. All four Hamas guards were killed in less than two minutes after the team had entered the two-story home.

One of the major concerns of Joshua and his men was awakening the women suddenly. They were already terrified and would not know what was taking place. By now they might have been awakened by the sound of the bodies hitting the floor. Any loud screams would jeopardize their mission.

Joshua pushed a typed sheet of paper under the door of the bedroom where the women were chained and shined his flashlight under the door. Fortunately none of them were awake yet. Niloa, a light sleeper, awoke first and saw the light and note it illuminated. She read the words in the diffused light from the flashlight.

PLEASE BE QUIET. WE ARE AN AMERICAN RESCUE TEAM. KEEP LIGHTS OFF. WE WILL CUT OPEN YOUR DOOR. PLEASE STAND BACK. SLIDE NOTE BACK IF OK.

Niloa peered at her roommates through the darkness. The light from the flashlight was just enough to enable her to see that they were both still sleeping. She grabbed a pen off the desk near her and wrote on the other side of the white piece of paper, *Wait a minute. Roommates sleeping. I'll wake them. Guards rotate at 4:00 a.m.* She then shoved the paper under the door.

Josh read the message and thought, *I can't believe how calm and levelheaded this woman is. Most people would be freaking out.* He looked at his watch. It was 3:40 a.m. They had very little time. He wrote on the paper, "It's 3:40. Knock twice when ready then clear the door."

Niloa woke her two friends quietly and whispered, "We're getting rescued now. Quickly and quietly get your things together. We have to move fast."

She then knocked twice on the door and moved away from it. With a propane blowtorch, a member of Joshua's team cut around the metal lock.

Joshua opened the door and shined his flashlight on Niloa's face. His first thought was, *God she's beautiful,* followed by, *Please get us out of here.* Niloa saw the slight hesitation in Joshua's actions as he looked at her. Niloa's first thought was, *He looks like one of the terrorists.*

Joshua and his three men were all sporting facial hair and Palestinian clothing.

"I'm commander Joshua Ryan of the U.S. Special Forces," he whispered to Niloa and the other two women. "I have three other men with me. Please follow me as quietly as possible."

"Glad to meet you Joshua. I'm Niloa. This is Daphne and Bridgett."

"We know all about you," Joshua whispered. "So do millions of people that are praying for your release."

Joshua looked at his watch; it was 3:45 a.m. The other guards would be arriving soon.

The four men helped the three women climb through the window of the house to avoid the front door and into the Toyota van. The three women were aghast by the foul smell of the van. They were told to lie face down in the back storage area on a 3-inch piece of foam and were completely covered by heavy blankets. Joshua then gave them each a package of chewing gum and pulled a gray storage compartment cover over them.

"Chew quietly when we are moving and not at all when we stop," he cautioned. The women were puzzled why Joshua had given them gum.

Then the men put fishing poles, nets, and other supplies, including jars of bait that they had taken out of the Toyota, on top of the plastic cover. The whole van was filled with the aroma of a fishing boat.

Niloa knew the smell well. She immediately put a stick of gum in her mouth and urged Daphne and Bridgett to do the same to keep them from getting nauseated.

"We have a two and a half hour drive to the coast," Joshua said, "and two major check points."

On their way out of town they passed another vehicle with four men. It was the replacement guards. They would discover their dead comrades but would not be able to dispatch Hamas guerrillas to try to prevent their escape until an hour later. By that time Jermanos had already driven them safely through the two check points.

When they reached the shores of the Mediterranean near daybreak, there was already armed militia patrolling the area. They were going to need to go to plan B. Joshua made a cell phone call and

Jermanos parked their van in the designated spot in front of a small grocery store. The men exited the van, took out their fishing gear, and gave the three women Arab scarves to cover their heads. The seven of them walked onto the beach.

Joshua spotted a jeep full of Hamas militia heading toward them. He then saw the other two members of his team who had secured the area for their escape crouched behind a wall, hidden from the militia. They fired on the jeep just as soon as it stopped. The jeep drove out of range.

Two Israeli helicopters then appeared on the horizon. One hovered a few hundred feet above the beach providing protection, and the second one landed. Joshua and his men helped Niloa, Daphne, and Bridgett into the helicopter and then climbed aboard. The Hamas that had exited the jeep opened fire on the helicopter from behind a small stonewall, just as it was lifting off the ground. A burst of gunfire from the second chopper obliterated the wall, killing the guerrillas behind it.

"Is everyone OK?" Joshua asked, shouting loudly above the noise of the rotating blades as the chopper moved out over the water away from danger.

"I'm hit in the left arm," Michael McKinnen replied as he began wrapping his left forearm with medical tape he had in his pocket. "I do need some help wrapping this."

An Israeli medical officer on board went to his aid.

Everyone else seemed to be OK but there was no response from Daphne.

"Oh no!" Bridgett shouted. "Daphne is bleeding."

Daphne could not talk. Two bullets that passed through the helicopter had struck her. One pierced through her right shoulder and one went through her left foot and shattered her ankle. Blood was flowing from two wounds in her foot and from both sides of her shoulder. Daphne had gone into shock. A second medic on board quickly stopped the bleeding and administered some painkillers to make her more comfortable. Her wounds were not life threatening.

The helicopters landed safely inside Israel. Daphne and Jermanos were taken to a military hospital for further treatment and Niloa and

Bridgett were taken to a secure military site. Joshua and his men were commissioned to escort the women to a U.S. military base in Italy for debriefing before they would each be returned to their home countries of Germany, France, and the United States.

Niloa went to sleep that evening in a well-guarded military base in Israel, thankful that she had been rescued but anxious to learn the fate of Stephano, Paulo, and her Uncle Jarvis. She hoped that the U.S. military could provide her with some information about the situation in the Philippines. Although rescued, Niloa was still in great emotional turmoil. She went to sleep wondering if her friends were still alive, and if she would ever see her Uncle Jarvis again.

CHAPTER 17
Nablus, West Bank, Israel

Taban Abaza was glad when he learned he did not need to strap plastic explosives to his body and sacrifice his life in order to achieve his goal of striking a blow against Israel. He had been fully prepared to die. His younger brother had already been killed by Israeli troops in the massacre in Jenin and had been declared a hero by the community. Taban was fortunate to have escaped the Israeli blockade to find shelter in Nablus. If he had been found with his brother's friends, known terrorists, he would certainly have been arrested or even killed by the Israeli Defense Force. Fortunately, no one suspected his involvement in any terrorist activities.

Although he was eager to fight, he was not eager to die. He wanted to help create a Palestinian state where he could pursue his passion—playing basketball. At six feet nine inches, Taban was among the tallest Palestinians in Israel. He was the star of his high school basketball and football teams and practiced for one year with the Israel Olympic basketball team while still in high school.

No one had a greater chance of escaping the depressing fate of most Palestinians than did Taban. His dream was to play college basketball in Europe or in the U.S. and eventually to play for a professional team. He followed the European league, the NBA and the NCAA closely. Now his dream was on hold because of the war in Israel. He could not leave his family in Nablus to their hopeless fate.

"You alright?" Mansur asked as he walked into the basement room where Taban was hiding.

"Yeah, I was just thinking about my chances of surviving this war," he replied. "I'm no better than bin Laden at trying to hide. I've got two inches on him. They'll eventually find me."

"I thought you were ready to die," Mansur said.

"There's a difference, Imad—I mean Mansur, between being ready to die and wanting to die. I want a future Palestinian state. I want to survive. I've never felt that suicide bombing was an effective strategy. We can't blow them all up. And those who die as suicide bombers cannot fight another day."

"That's why we're going to use biological weapons," Mansur explained. "We will live to fight another day and we will achieve our goal once they realize they cannot prevent biological attacks."

"How am I going to disguise myself? I can't hide my height."

"I've already taken care of that," Mansur replied. "In the van outside is your new wheelchair. Actually, it's a used one. But it will do. You will not be seen as a big threat in the wheelchair and you'll not need to carry any guns or explosives – only shaving cream cans."

Mansur had made all the arrangements for Taban and three other men that he had trained to carry out biological attacks against Israel. Each of the attackers would be in wheelchairs and would check into four of the best hotels in Haifa. Taban had reservations at the Holiday Inn Bayview Hotel located atop Mount Carmel. The three other Hamas operatives had reservations at the Haifa Tower Hotel, the Mount Carmel Hotel, and the Nof Hotel. All four men were given three canisters filled with botulinum toxin. The meticulous plan called for a synchronized attack on a Sunday evening.

On Saturday afternoon, Taban checked into the Holiday Inn Haifa Bayview. He rolled into the lobby in his wheelchair and paid a bell boy to escort him to his room on the seventh floor, overlooking beautiful Haifa Bay. He was pleased to be placed in a luxurious room on a floor where no smoking was allowed. After finding an NBA game on cable television, he was even more pleased. This was the life he wanted. He was not a devout Muslim and did not shun a Western lifestyle

Not long after the game ended and after enjoying Chateau Briand and a bottle of Pinot Noir through room service, Taban tried to sleep. He had great difficulty resting his thoughts. His mind seemed to be racing with so many simultaneous thoughts. The tension within was building. He wondered when the Israeli security force would come through the door to arrest him or kill him. He knew that fate could overtake him at any time. He had only been a member of the Hamas for three months. He wrestled with the idea that perhaps his connection with them was not yet known, and there was an opportunity to leave them before he got too involved in terrorism.

Taban thought about his parents. They had so badly wanted him and his brother to go to college. Now his brother was dead. At least his older sister, Fahmida, had made it out of their horrible existence. She immigrated to London after meeting a British reporter who was on assignment in the West Bank. Fahmida lived up to her name. She was both intelligent and wise. She was also very beautiful and the most charming tour guide in the West Bank. Her husband was completely captivated by her.

At least she fulfilled her dream, Taban thought as he finally succumbed to near exhaustion.

Taban awoke suddenly to loud pounding on the door. Before he could even find the lamp switch near his bed he heard the door being opened. He knew he had been found and that the hotel management had given the Mousad the electronic key to his room. He reached beside his bed and found one of the three 9-ounce canisters. Just as the lights came on, he pressed the release valve. Then he entered another realm.

He could see his blood spattering across the clean sheets but could not hear the semi-automatic hand guns nor could he feel the bullets enter his body. He began to rise above the bed, as if floating upward while also peering downward at the whole scene. He saw the Israeli agents shoot the canister out of his hand as the fine toxin formed an unseen cloud above his bed, a mist he could somehow see. He then saw them back up and frantically search for their gas masks attached to the left side of their belts.

He saw at least a dozen bullet holes in his body. He then drifted higher, above the 15-story hotel. He could see everything clearly, as if it was noon, although it was only 4:00 a.m. The entire bay was illuminated and he seemed to be surrounded by light. He then saw his sister off in the distance. She was surrounded by such bright light; it was difficult to look upon her face. He tried to move toward her but could not.

He realized that he was moving away from her and away from the light. He felt himself shiver as the temperature began to decrease rapidly. He drifted farther and farther away from the light that surrounded his sister. He was moving backwards and could not see where he was going. He turned his head around and saw a thick mass of blackness ahead of him. He was being sucked into an abyss. He knew that once he entered the black mass he would no longer be able to see his sister. He tried to call out to her but could not speak. He then screamed in terror, but no sound came out of his mouth. Taban felt lost forever and totally forgotten.

He then awoke. His sheets were drenched from his perspiration. He turned on the light. Fear was all around him. It was so real and overwhelming he could feel its tangible presence, like an incarnate evil. He looked at the alarm clock on his night stand. It was 4:00 a.m., the same time in his dream that he was attacked and killed. Taban was almost completely paralyzed by fear. He managed to find his address book in his briefcase and immediately dialed his sister in London. He hoped that she was still awake. She was. He shared his deep feelings with her for the first time. Hearing her voice caused his fear to subside.

"Fahmida, they murdered our brother. They must be punished!" he pleaded, longing for her support.

"Then let God judge them," she pleaded back. "Vengeance does not belong to you."

"I already promised, Fahmida, the Hamas will kill me if I back out now."

"And you'll be killed if you don't back out."

They talked for more than an hour. He told her everything on his mind, including details of their planned biological attacks and then his vivid nightmare. They argued back and forth about his involvement with the Hamas. His sister couldn't hold back her words any longer.

"Taban, I fear not only for your life, but for your eternity. There is only everlasting darkness for those who die as murderers. Your friends have lied to you. You will not be a hero. You will be one who killed innocent people. You must stop these attacks. Please let me help you."

"I can't Fahmida," he replied, "I know they'll kill me. And if I turn myself in, the Israelis will kill me."

"Why can't you give the police all the information and then get out of the country?"

"How can I get out so quickly?"

"Swim to Cyprus if you have to. Just notify the authorities and get out as quickly as possible. If you can get into Europe you can get to London. There are all open borders now. We'll take care of you here."

Taban was finally convinced he had a possible way out. He took out the hotel writing pad and looked at the clock. It was 5:10 a.m. He printed the details of the planned attacks the next day. He then checked out of the hotel at 5:30, leaving the note for the hotel's manager who was scheduled to arrive at work at 8:00 a.m. He left in a wheelchair, as he had come in, and caught a taxi ride to the Avis car rental office at the airport in Haifa and ditched his wheelchair.

He then drove his car rental to Nahariyya, just south of the border, and purchased a small fishing vessel from a local fisherman with the advanced funds he has been given by the Hamas. He packed his supplies in the boat and headed north toward the southern coast of Turkey. Fortunately, he did not encounter any patrol boats on the open water. One of the benefits of being a member of the Hamas was the false identity he had been given. Taban carried a false Greek passport and false driver's license from Greece, although he had never set foot in the country.

The manager of the Holiday Inn Bayview arrived on time that morning. The night clerk gave him the letter Taban had written. He opened it and read the detailed information. His face turned ashen. He had difficulty standing and needed to sit down immediately. He summoned his assistant to call the police and let them know they have received a detailed terrorist threat for four hotels, including their own.

The police arrived with military counter-terrorism units within ten minutes. They searched Tabas' room and found the three canisters on the bed with another note that said, "These cans contain a deadly botulinum toxin. They are on a timer scheduled to detonate at 6:00 p.m. I could not turn off the timer."

At 8:15 a.m. the manager received a cell phone call.

"Hello, this is Rafael Kantor, can I help you."

"Yes, Mr. Kantor, did you receive a letter this morning?"

Kantor felt weak again, almost as if he would faint. He realized he could be talking to one of the terrorists.

"Yes, I did."

"Did you call the police?"

"Yes,." Kantor answered

"Good. You have saved many lives."

The caller then hung up.

The Israeli police moved quickly to arrest the other terrorists. Taban had provided enough detailed information to enable the Israelis to prevent all of the planned attacks. Within two hours of finding Taban's note, the police found his car rental in the small town of Nahhariya. The Israelis also found the person who had sold him a boat and some fishing gear. Although Taban had used a false name, the Israeli police were able to identify him.

They decided not to go after him. He had prevented the attacks and they realized he had been pressured into joining the terrorists. They knew he was a good man who had turned bitter through the death of his brother. TheIsraelis kept the Hamas from ever finding out what really happened by staging Taban's arrest and execution on charges of terrorism. Taban was now free. His former identity as a Hamas terrorist was destroyed. In two months he would be with his sister, beginning a new life and preparing a new home for his mother, who waited in Nablas for his return. A post card from Greece let her know that he was alive.

Chapter 18
Livorno, Italy

Niloa awoke to a gentle knock on the door. She had been taking an afternoon nap, recovering physically from the incredible ordeal she had just experienced with religious zealots who would not hesitate to slit her throat. While her physical recovery would take only a week or two, her emotional recovery would take many months. She still was emotionally raw but feeling much more secure.

"Come in," she said with a cheery voice, wiping the sleep from her eyes with a Kleenex on the oak night stand to the left of her bed. She liked the old wooden furniture in the guest quarters at Camp Darby. It was very rustic and Italian.

Major Joshua Ryan opened the door slowly while Niloa sat up in bed.

"I'm sorry to disturb you, Miss Stephenson, I'm so sorry. I didn't know you were still in bed."

"It's OK, Major," Niloa countered, somewhat amused. "Can I help you?"

"I was wondering if you would be interested in a bit of sightseeing and dinner in Florence? You missed lunch at the camp's officers' club," Ryan explained, recovering from his initial embarrassment.

"I can't believe I slept right through lunch," Niloa replied. "I just meant to take a 30-minute nap. I usually have no trouble taking short naps."

"You didn't miss much," Miss Stephenson. "After what you've been through, I'm sure you needed the extra sleep. I know that three and a half hour debriefing this morning must have been exhausting."

Niloa thought about the morning meeting that had begun at 8:00 a.m. In her first debriefing on the previous day, she had explained how she'd been blown off course in the Pacific, how she'd found the bottle with the note in it while sailing in the Mariana Islands, how she had found Paulo tied to a tree on Farallon de Medinilla, and how she had teamed up with Paulo's friend Stephano and her Uncle Jarvis to locate the *Abu Sayyaf* and the biological weapons they had stolen.

This morning she had detailed how she had been kidnaped by the *Abu Sayyaf*, taken to Syria and then Lebanon, and handed to the *Hamas*. The military intelligence officers asked many more questions this time, helping Niloa to remember as many details as she could about the *Abu Sayyaf* and *Hamas* guerrillas who had held her as a hostage.

Niloa slowly realized what Major Ryan had just said.

"Did you say Florence?" she asked with excitement. "I'd love to go to Firenze again! How far is it?"

"Just a short taxi ride to the train station in Livorno, then a beautiful 80-minute train trip," Ryan answered.

Niloa did not realize that it took considerable persuasion on his part before Major Parkhill, his immediate commanding officer, and Lieutenant Colonel McPherson, Parkhill's commanding officer, would even allow him to ask Lieutenant Colonel Matt Frederick, Camp Darby's base commander, to take Niloa off the base.

Joshua remembered how delighted he was when Frederick responded to his request with, "If you clear it with Major Chandler, commander of the medical clinic who examined Niloa yesterday, you can take her into town." Since Niloa had a clean bill of health, permission was granted.

"Major Ryan," Niloa finally replied after a long pause, "I would enjoy going to Firenze with you for some sightseeing and dinner, under one condition."

"Yes, Miss Stephenson?" Joshua asked eagerly.

"Please call me Niloa, Major."

"Of course, Niloa. I didn't want to assume familiarity. Please call me Josh. My friends all call me Josh."

Joshua and Niloa left Camp Darby at 1:35 by taxi to Livorno Centrale, where they caught the 2:00 p.m. train into Firenze.

Niloa was captivated by the sites on the 80 km Firenze-Pisa-Livorna railroad trek, the oldest one in Toscana dating back to 1843. They passed Mt. Verruca with a medieval fortress accessible in its head, the old S. Miniato station between Firenze and Pisa, and the historic bell tower of Badia a Settimo. In between Niloa's many questions and Joshua's answers about the historic landscape and architecture they passed on the way, Niloa learned how Joshua had become involved in special operations for the military. Joshua, in turn, learned how Niloa had become deeply involved in professional yacht racing. They arrived in Firenze at Tutte Le Stazioni at 3:20 on a beautiful balmy Saturday afternoon.

"I'm so glad they brought me to Italy," Niloa told Joshua as they walked through the station in Firenze. "I guessed that I would be taken to Germany."

"We did discuss a briefing in Germany," Joshua answered. "But they have an excellent media facilities here to provide further treatment for Daphne and Lieutenant McKinnen, and we have been working closely with the European counter-terrorism task force operating out of Rome. The intelligence officers who interviewed you today and yesterday will be passing on relevant information to our allies in Rome."

"I just love this city," Niloa insisted.

"How many times have you been here?" Joshua asked.

"Twice," Niloa replied. "The last time was in 1998 when my family came for vacation with my uncle Jarvis, who now lives in southern France."

"You mean your uncle who was with you in Mindanao?" Joshua asked.

"Yes. I know he and Stephano would have found me if they had not taken me out of there. My uncle has as much courage as you, Joshua, and is extremely intelligent. He worked as a terrorism expert for the U.S. intelligence community for many years."

Niloa did not realize that Major Ryan had first planned to rescue her in Mindanao.

"I've met your Uncle Jarvis twice," Joshua replied. "First in Ft. Bragg when he taught our class in an all-day seminar on chemical and biological threats of terrorism. That was when I was in Army Ranger School. Then, I met him again in the Philippines during our briefing after our failed rescue attempt. You are right about him. He is an incredibly gifted person and a great teacher. We all remember him at Ft. Bragg."

"Wait. You know my uncle? And what rescue attempt are you talking about – the one on Jolo Island?"

"Yes. Do you remember meeting Colonel Matt Siefer with your uncle and General Ramos in Zamboanga City?"

"Yes, I remember well," Niloa replied. "That's when we decided that Stephano, Uncle Jarvis, and I should sail to Basilan Island."

"Well I was under Colonel Siefer's command conducting training exercises on Mindanao. After you were kidnapped, Stephano gave us the exact coordinates of the *Abu Sayyaf* base. Stephano and your Uncle Jarvis had tried to get you out of there. They found the thatched shelter where you were kept captive. You were asleep and chained to a guard, so they could not free you at that time. Our Special Forces deployed my hostage rescue team the next morning to assist Stephano and Jarvis in getting you out of there before the raid on the camp. We just missed rescuing you. By the time we reached the place where you were, you were gone."

Niloa was overwhelmed with gratitude when she realized how many people had risked their lives to rescue her. Joshua realized she was about to cry.

"Let's forget about that for now, Niloa, and explore this beautiful city."

Niloa regained her composure.

"Gladly," she replied.

During the next four hours Joshua and Niloa were able to visit the Affix Museum, the Cuomo, one of Italy's most famous cathedrals, the Ponte Vecchio Bridge, where Niloa bought a garnet ring (two rings she had worn were stolen by the *Abu Sayyaf*), and the Piazza della Signoria, the fabulous open-air museum and square filled with famous statues and surrounded by breath-taking architectural landmarks. Niloa had not had such an enjoyable day out in a long, long time. She loved the narrow streets of Firenze, the red-tiled roofs that covered the city like a royal blanket, and the art and culture that exuded from every building and home.

Major Ryan treated her like a royal subject. He was incredibly polite and formal, almost like a bodyguard. This was definitely an unusual date, if it was a date at all. Niloa simply could not read him. He had an uncanny wit and humor and was personable, yet he kept his distance emotionally. He was very different from most other single men she had spent time with who were more interested in a physical relationship than building a true friendship.

Ryan had made reservations at the Da Pennello restaurant near Dante's House in the Cuomo area. There they dined on *gorgonzola* cheese, fresh tomatoes and *proscuito*, crusty Italian bread dipped in light virgin olive oil, and red wine made in a local vineyard to the south. They topped off their meal with cappuccinos and freshly made *gelato*.

During the three-hour feast, Joshua and Niloa explored each other's family backgrounds, experiences, values, beliefs, and passions in life. They discovered they both shared deeply religious beliefs that resided in their families. Joshua grew up on a farm in central Indiana in what he called "Larry Bird country." Basketball was his passion from an early age, although he had also played baseball and football in junior high and high school. Ironically, it was Joshua's baseball team that had made it to the state finals during his years in high school. He had been an outstanding shooting guard on his high school basketball team, but two powerhouses in their league had outmatched his team.

Joshua told Niloa how he had played third base on the baseball team and batted a respectable .328 his senior year, with 16 home runs and 40 RBI's in a 45-game season.

"I know I probably boring you, Niloa, but these numbers have stuck in my head all these years because it was such a great season. That year we played for the state championship, narrowing losing 3-

2 in a great pitching dual. I hit a two-run homer in the top of the eight inning to tie the game, but our opponents from Terre Haute High School scored on a perfect bunt play with a man on third base in the bottom of the ninth inning to win in dramatic fashion."

"You obviously love sports. Why did you join the army, Josh, instead of trying to get an athletic scholarship to college?"

"It's rather complicated, Niloa. I actually was offered a baseball scholarship by Indiana University. Deep down I think I wanted to be like my dad. He was in the army and then went into law enforcement after he left the military."

"But I thought you grew up on a farm," Niloa responded.

"We did. Farming was my dad's first job, and mine and my brothers, too. Even my mother and two sisters worked on the farm. We split up the chores and hired a couple other people so we would never have to give up the farm. It has belonged to my father's family since 1860. My parents still own the farm jointly with my older brother, even though they now live in Chicago. My brother leases some of the land and farms some of it. That farm is a part of me. I really miss it."

"Is there anyone at home who you are especially missing?" Niloa asked.

Joshua was taken back for a moment. It seemed like a very personal question. He didn't know if she was referring to family members or perhaps a girlfriend.

Niloa saw an awkward expression come across Joshua's face. As soon as she asked the question she regretted it. It was too late to take the words back.

"Other than my family and a few close friends at church, I have been somewhat out of touch," Joshua answered, breaking his eye contact and looking downward.

Niloa detected sadness in his voice.

"Was there someone special at one time?" she asked, digging further since she had already ventured into deep waters.

Joshua contemplated for a moment and thought, man this is personal. She really wants to know me.

"I'm sorry Josh, you don't have to answer that if this is something you would rather not talk about," Niloa said with compassion before Joshua could answer.

How does she know? I really like this Niloa. She is not afraid to take chances and be honest.

"No, I can tell you, Niloa. It's still a little painful," he said softly. "Right before I left for training at Fort Bragg, I became engaged to a close friend I had known since we were freshmen in high school. We went to the senior prom together and we strongly supported each other's athletic endeavors. Her name is Keli Sims. She is an incredible athlete, a great swimmer and diver, and a wonderful person. I loved her. We decided to wait to get married until after she finished college at Indiana University where she was competing on the swimming team and training for the Olympics. We were still young—engaged at age 20. I never imagined I could be with anyone but Keli."

"What happened?' Niloa asked.

"The swim team at Indiana is a very tight-knit group. It spends a lot of time traveling together and competing in high stress situations. Keli needed emotional support and became very close to her coach her senior year. She began to develop strong feelings for him and he was single. I was away at Army Ranger School and probably didn't call as much as I should have, although I wrote letters at least once a week. By the time she graduated, she had fallen deeply in love with her coach, and he adored her. She decided to break off our engagement. Two years ago they were married. They now have an 18-month old boy and another child on the way and live in Chicago. My parents see them now and then and are still close to her."

"And have you talked to her since her marriage?" Niloa asked, probing further.

"No, not since the wedding reception; but we've sent Christmas cards to each other. She will always be a friend I will love, although I initially felt deeply hurt and betrayed. In retrospect, I don't think she would've been happy in the military life I have chosen. I'm always traveling and my work is dangerous. Life is a constant adventure in the military, and Keli needed stability. Now, I'm very happy for her and the way things worked out."

Niloa was impressed by the mature way Joshua had handled this great disappointment.

"Niloa, your *gelato* is melting," Joshua said with a false alarm in his voice. "Is my life really so interesting that it would keep you from *gelato*?"

"How did you know I was a gelato lover?" Niloa replied. "I'll just order another one. You're paying, right?"

Niloa was surprised by how quickly she had grown to like Joshua. Naturally, she was physically attracted to him the day he rescued her in Beirut. His 6'1" 180-lb body was in great condition. But she had been around a lot of guys in great physical shape who were so full of themselves they were absolute jerks. She was not expecting that Joshua would be a sensitive and caring person.

Joshua did not reveal any personal feelings that he might have had for Niloa, but she sensed that he had a romantic interest in her. She was relieved that Joshua did not initiate any physical contact with her as did most of the men whom she had gone out with over the years. He would have liked to kiss her after they had caught the train back and ended the evening, but was not sure if that was appropriate. Instead, after he had walked her to the guest quarters on base, he gave Niloa a sweet smile, grabbed her right hand gently, looked directly into her eyes with a sincere gaze that communicated genuine care and said good night. Niloa paused for a few seconds, mesmerized by his big brown eyes. She wanted to savor the moment. A rush of emotion swept across her body. She wanted to do this again.

"Good night, Josh," she reciprocated warmly.

Niloa had difficulty getting to sleep. She had too many conflicting emotions. She still had very strong feelings for Stephano and thought back to their passionate encounter on the *Dawn Treader* II in the southern Philippines. She could have easily made love to him that night had she not used all her will power to exercise self-control, as did Stephano. He had risked his life to save her. He had entered the well-protected *Abu Sayyaf* compound at night, and had found the makeshift shelter were she was being kept. If she had not been chained to the guards, Stephano would have been able to help her escape. At least he had been able to pin an electronic sensor under her long pants leg that enabled the U.S. government to pinpoint her exact location by satellite. This proved to be critical to her eventual rescue by Joshua's rescue team.

Now she was developing a strong attraction to Joshua. He had a very different personality than Stephano. Josh was quiet and contemplative, whereas Stephano would tell you exactly what he was thinking and how he felt. Josh seemed like a person who had to have his thoughts and feelings drawn out over time. That is why it was difficult for Niloa to discern how he felt about her. His actions, taking her sightseeing and to dinner in Florence, indicated that he was interested in her. But his emotions did not reveal his heart. Yet, somehow she knew that he liked her. She just didn't know how interested he was in her.

The choice on which man to pursue would be difficult.

Perhaps I should pursue neither one. No, she reasoned, *that would be wasting opportunities. I have never met two wonderful guys like this. In fact, I've never met even one. I can't believe the odds of meeting both at the same time. Two men of courage and kindness, two men of moral character and commitment to help others.* She concluded she needed to make a decision soon.

Niloa awoke at 7:00 a.m. to the alarm clock in her room. She looked at the clock, turned it off, and went back to sleep. At 8:15 a.m. she woke up again to a knock on the door.

"Who is it? she asked.

"It's Linda West, the assistant manager. I have a message for you."

Niloa jumped out of bed, put on a robe, and went to the door and opened it.

"Good morning," Niloa said.

"Miss Stephenson, Major Ryan would like you to know that your table is ready."

"Oh, no!" Niloa exclaimed, "I completely forgot about our breakfast meeting. Please tell Major Ryan sorry for the delay and I'll be down in 20 minutes."

Niloa prided herself that she didn't need an hour to shower, choose her clothes, which wasn't much of a choice, and put on make-up like most of her friends. She thought she was looking pretty good in 20 minutes, except for the clothes. *It's just breakfast. I shouldn't be so caught up in every nuance of my appearance. At least I am much thinner after that terrible food I had while in captivity.* Niloa decided that like the other day in Firenze, she would not try to impress Joshua, but just be genuine.

"Hi, Niloa," Joshua said as Niloa walked up to their table. "I hope I didn't wake you. I have a plane to catch at 10 this morning, so Linda volunteered to check on you."

"No, that's fine," Niloa replied. "For some strange reason when my alarm woke me at 7, I turned it off and went back to sleep. I used to do that in high school but not since then. I'm sorry to keep you waiting."

Niloa sported a rose-colored blouse with black cotton pants. Her long auburn hair fell across her shoulders six inches below the collar of her blouse. Her slightly Hawaiian complexion gave her the appearance of a moderate even tan, but her skin was surprisingly soft, despite her many years in the sun. She wore strapped sandals with a modest one-inch heel, adding slightly to her 5'8" frame. She was very fit and trimmed down during her captivity, although she had lost some muscle tone. Joshua found her to be extremely attractive that morning. Why she seemed more attractive than the previous day in which he had spent a lot of time with her, he wasn't exactly sure. He was careful not to reveal this perception.

After devouring an omelet with spinach, onions, and bell peppers, some bacon, toast, and a cup of coffee over casual conversation, Joshua's facial expression turned serious.

"Niloa," Joshua began in somber voice, "I have a serious question to ask you."

Niloa sat nervously in her chair. *What could be so serious*; they had just met.

"When our Israeli friends interrogated one of the terrorists they had caught in the Middle East last month," Joshua continued, "he boasted about two biological attacks that were in the making: one in Israel and one in the U.S. The attacks in Israel were miraculously thwarted because of some vital intelligence information from one of the terrorists who had remorse, but we know very little about the threat to the U.S. We haven't intercepted any more information about the U.S. threat, but are worried about our three largest metro areas: New York, Los Angeles, and Chicago.

"My father is the head of the terrorism task force for the city of Chicago. We suspect some of the same terrorists who might have been involved with your captivity in Lebanon might be involved in planning this attack against the U.S. My father asked me if you would be willing to join his task force for the next 4 to 6 weeks until this state of highest threat is over. If there is an attack, we expect it to occur during or just after Ramadan."

"I don't understand Josh. How could I be of help?"

"Chicago has many tall buildings that could be prime targets, including landmarks like the Sears Tower. These buildings have television monitors that are connected to a central surveillance center in the Chicago Police Headquarters Building. We need a person in our headquarters who could recognize the faces of any of these terrorists if they came to Chicago and attempted to enter one of these buildings or other public places. We do have sophisticated surveillance technology, but the equipment is new and is not one hundred percent accurate. You know the terrorists who held you captive were planning a U.S. attack. We are monitoring the tallest buildings and other key public places like the two airports and the United Center the best we can. If they come there, you would be a tremendous asset in helping us to prevent an attack."

Niloa felt overwhelmed again. She never dreamed she would be helping to fight terrorists. It was a fight she did not want. She desperately wanted to get back to the *Dawn Treader II*.

"Niloa," Josh continued, "you may be able to recognize the voice of someone we intercept, or the face of a terrorist who was with you in Lebanon but who might not be in our data base. I know you are probably anxious to return home, but your parents will be here tomorrow and will be able to spend several days with you. I told my dad I would ask you to think about it."

Now I understand the breakfast, Niloa thought. *Perhaps all the time he spent with me was about helping his father, not about getting to know me. I shouldn't have been so self-centered thinking it was about me.*

Niloa tried to conceal any hint of disappointment. She had hoped Joshua was going to ask her about keeping in touch and developing an ongoing friendship.

She responded, "Of course, Josh, I would like to help. But honestly, I'm very anxious to get back to the *Dawn Treader II* in the Philippines."

Niloa's comment confirmed what Joshua had thought, that Niloa had a serious relationship with Stephano and wanted to return to the Philippines to see him. He could not tell her how much he really liked her and had enjoyed his time with her.

"It would just be through the Thanksgiving holiday," Joshua explained. "And my parents would like to have you and your parents to come over to their house for Thanksgiving. Our intelligence officers think the imminent threat will be during late October and the month of November."

"I suppose I could be delayed for another month," Niloa replied. "If you think I could be of help, Josh, I will go to Chicago. Just let me talk it over with my parents tomorrow."

"Niloa, thank you so much. I have to go to Israel, but I plan to go to Chicago in four days and hope to see you there."

"That would be great," Niloa replied, again hiding her feelings of disappointment.

I guess I have my answer, Niloa thought. *God must want me to pursue my friendship with Stephano.*

Joshua gave Niloa an air ticket to Chicago and a description of who would meet her at the O'Hare Airport.

"If your parents approve, Niloa, I've arranged for you to take a military flight to Munich and a commercial flight to Chicago. I've got to run, but hope to see you soon."

INTO THE WINDS OF FEAR

This time he gave Niloa a warm hug as he said goodbye and left hastily to catch his plane. *Too bad,* she thought. *He gives good hugs.*

Joshua left so quickly Niloa didn't really have any time to ask any questions. She wanted to say, "Wait a second, how come you knew I would say yes?" He had already arranged her entire trip.

Niloa's parents arrived the next day on schedule. It was a wonderful reunion. Her parents felt very good about her returning to the U.S., given the recent terrorism activity in the world. They were very concerned about the threat in Chicago but agreed that she should help if she could. If there was a way she could play a role in preventing a catastrophe, it was worth the risk. Her parents knew it would be selfish to hold her back just to keep her out of danger.

They decided to meet her in Chicago instead of returning to Hawaii, but Niloa did not know of their plan.

"Wait till she sees us again at the gate in O'Hare," Chris said to his wife Nanci.

But before then, Chris would call Dan Ryan and find out the nature of this terrorist threat and determine how safe of a place she would be working in.

Niloa watched her parents leave Italy after three great days together. She wondered what her next adventure might be in Chicago. She also wondered when she would hear again from Stephano. *Was he still thinking about getting engaged? If so, when would he ask her?* She needed to hear from him soon.

CHAPTER 19
Rome, Italy

Mansur calmly caught the escalator downstairs and walked toward the baggage claim area in the Rome airport. Everything was going according to plan. He had no problem obtaining the visitor's visa he needed to stay in Italy two days. Hidden in his luggage were uncut blue diamonds that were smuggled out of Tanzania. A cursory inspection of his suitcase by a customs officer did not reveal the hidden lining in his case containing two-dozen gems that would be worth $240,000 in U.S. currency.

Mansur took a taxi to his hotel in Rome. After checking in, he turned on CNN News, plopping down on his comfortable bed at the Ritz Carlton. There were no follow-up stories about the three women hostages freed in Lebanon. The previous day's report had only indicated that the hostages had been released after being held for three days in the Philippines and for five days in Lebanon. CNN had no information on the U.S. Special Forces military operation that led to their freedom. It simply read the statement released by the Hamas that said, "As a good will gesture, the *Hamas* had negotiated the release of three Americans detained by the *Abu Sayyaf*." It would be embarrassing for the *Hamas* to admit that the U.S. had rescued people being detained by its elite guards. The U.S. military also did not want publicity regarding how they had rescued the three women. They had enough challenges trying to prevent the news media from compromising the secrecy of its Special Forces operations.

Mansur turned off the television. He worried that the American woman kidnapped could identify him, and even considered changing his appearance again. He decided against it, having already spent considerable effort to forge a new identity. His plastic surgery and the staging of his death had given him another life. Besides, he liked his new name Mansur, which meant "divinely aided and victorious." He did not at all look like one of the most hunted international terrorists in history, and most terrorist experts believed Imad was dead. He did not want to attract scrutiny by appearing very different from the photo in his new passport. He felt a little better when he learned that none of the three women kidnapped lived anywhere near Chicago.

Mansur noticed a light flashing on the telephone. He was not familiar with American hotels. He picked up the phone and dialed a "0."

"Front desk, Mr. Shukarian, can I help you?"

"Yes," Mansur answered, "There is a light flashing on my phone."

"That's the automatic message system," replied Charlene, the woman at the front desk. "Would you like me to retrieve the message for you, or explain to you how to do it?"

"Please retrieve it. Thank you," replied Mansur.

"One moment, please," replied Charlene.

The message was in Arabic.

Imad, this is Raja. We have a new meeting place tomorrow. Please meet me at 8:00 am in the coffee shop of the Fontiana Hotel. I have already contacted Sudani. He will be there. Make sure you are not followed.

Mansur became angry. I told him to use my new name Mansur, not Imad! He then pondered, Why would I be followed? No one knows I'm here.

Mansur fell asleep with many concerns. He did not sleep well. He awoke at 5:00 a.m. and waited for daylight before getting out of bed. He meticulously packed his briefcase before leaving for the Fontiana Hotel by taxi. In the briefcase were the detailed plans for a biological attack on the third largest city in the U.S.

Raja and Sudani were waiting when Mansur arrived. They were both relaxed but Mansur could see the intensity in their eyes. They spoke in good English, although it was a second language for all of them. They were very careful not to draw attention to themselves in public. Sudani told his two colleagues that he feared that someone might be following him, so they had to be careful.

They discussed in vague terms the business deal they were working on. Sudani indicated that one of their associates had already successfully traveled to the U.S. to make arrangements for the entrance of their product into the market. Mansur would soon be traveling to Chicago to set up a customer distribution plan under his new identity, Mansur Shukarian. He reminded his friends quietly but fiercely in Arabic never to use his old name Imad. Mansur's business expertise was the efficient distribution of the new product line and expansion of existing customer bases.

To anyone listening in on their conversation, the three men sounded like they could have been distributing a new line of office chairs or a new phone system, or a new type of fluorescent ceiling lights. They spoke of how many product units they needed to service some of the large office buildings. No one would have suspected they were actually discussing how to efficiently disperse botulinum toxin through the filtration systems of Chicago's tallest high-rise buildings. No one was listening, but they were being watched carefully.

Not far from the three terrorists sat Dominic Arone, inconspicuously drinking a cup of cappuccino and reading the morning paper. Dominic had been conducting surveillance on Sudani Zalmai for three months. Sudani lived about six months of the year in Avignon, France, and the other six months he split between Rome and Istanbul. He also made frequent trips to Montreal. Sudani first came under suspicion when his company, Persian Interiors, Ltd., headquartered in France, turned up as a company that did frequent business with Al Barakaat. U.S. and French intelligence agents had identified Al Barakaat, which operated businesses in 40 different countries, as a major supplier of funds to the *al Qaeda* terrorist network. The U.S., western nations, and those supporting the U.S.'s war against *al Qaeda* had frozen most of Al Barakaat's assets. Sudani had made several trips to Al Barakaat's office in Columbus, Ohio, which was shut down by the U.S. government along with their offices in Seattle, Minneapolis, and Boston.

Dominic, who worked on Rome's drug intervention task force, had suspected that Sudani was smuggling drugs in shipments of Persian carpets from Istanbul to Rome. He always stayed in the nicest hotels, dressed immaculately, and ate in expensive restaurants, a lifestyle that seemed well above that of an importer of fine rugs and wall hangings. Afghanistan was the number one grower of poppy plants in the world and many Afghans thrived on the drug trade. When Dominic began his surveillance work, he was not sure what Sudani's connection might be to *al Qaeda* or to other Islam terrorists groups.

However, after his wife Claudia had told him about her conversation with Jarvis, Dominic contacted a good friend in the Israeli Intelligence Service to discuss the possible connections between Sudani and the funding of Islamic terrorists. The Moussad had Sudani's name on a list of suspected financial supporters of the *Hamas* in Israel. Regarding the people Sudani was meeting in the Fontiana Hotel coffee shop, neither the Israelis nor the Italian police had any information on Raja Osmani or Mansur Shukarian. Since Dominic was also a part of Rome's counter-terrorism task force, he continued to follow Sudani as a possible terrorist suspect and drug smuggler.

Dominic's small camera hidden in the saltshaker on his table was able to take digital pictures of the three men. The distance was too far to record their conversation electronically with the hidden microphone, which appeared to be a tiepin without recording all the other conversations between them. Dominic assumed they would not risk speaking openly about any illegal activities in a public setting and they kept their voices low. The pictures Dominic obtained were not of sufficient quality to be useful to the electronic data base they had been developing in Europe and the U.S. of terrorist suspects.

After about an hour together, Mansur and Raja left the hotel and departed in separate taxis. Dominic knew that Sudani was staying in the Fontiana Hotel another night, so he decided to follow Mansur to see if he could find out more information about his travel plans. Sudani returned to his room in the hotel. Dominic followed Mansur back to his hotel and found out he was checking out in the early afternoon. Dominic knew the manager personally, who had given Mansur permission to check out 30 minutes past the standard 1:00 p.m. checkout time. The manager arranged for their hotel limousine to take Mansur to the airport at 2:00 p.m. to catch his flight to Chicago. Ironically, it was the same flight that Niloa had taken two evenings before. Mansur would be totally shocked if he knew how close he had come to being on the same flight with one of the few people in the world who could identify him as a terrorist.

Dominic was surprised when Raja arrived at Mansur's hotel at 1:45 p.m. with a medium-sized suitcase. He met Mansur in the hotel lobby and gave the suitcase to him. Mansur took the suitcase to the airport as one of his two check-in bags. Dominic wondered if he was smuggling illegal drugs or something else. He had a nagging dread in the back of his mind that it might be something far worse than illegal drugs. He knew he had to take action immediately.

Jarvis picked up his cell phone. A familiar Italian voice greeted him. Dominic Arone was on the line. He told Jarvis about the man he had been tracking in Rome and the two other men he had met with at the Fontiana Hotel. Jarvis was very concerned about what Mansur might be bringing into the U.S. Dominic also gave Jarvis the names of Raja Osmani and Sudani Zalmai, indicating he had no information on Mansur but he had been tracking Sudani for three months. Dominic indicated he had found nothing illegal in Sudani's business dealings yet, but suspected that he was a drug smuggler. As for Raja, Dominic was told by a Jordanian intelligence agent that he was an accomplished scientist from Pakistan who had developed a number of biological agents to fight plant diseases. There were some allegations that he was sympathetic to bin Laden, but no hard evidence that they were linked in any meaningful way. He definitely needed to be watched closely.

After the conversation with his friend Dominic, Jarvis contacted Colonel Siefer, who had returned to Washington. U.S. intelligence officers worked quickly with the digital photos Dominic had emailed to Colonel Siefer's office at Jarvis' request. They were able to confirm that Raja was a Pakistani who had worked on various agricultural projects for the Pakistani government. His expertise was on the use of biochemical agents in fighting plant diseases, including work on the means of delivering such agents to plants through an aerosol spray system. Raja had developed an advanced technology to remove the electrostatic charge from biological and chemical agents. This was a key technology to delivering the agents in the form of a fine powder that could cover hundreds of square kilometers of cropland. Even more impressive was Raja's innovative method to reduce particle sizes of the agents he used to 2.5 microns, making it easy for plants to absorb them.

Mansur Shukarian was the mystery man whom Dominic had no information on. He traveled as a businessman who imported leather shoes to Europe and the U.S. from Romania and Turkey. Because of his legitimate business, he had no problems traveling back and forth between Europe and North America, which he did quite often. No one even imagined that he might be Imad Sahadi, a munitions and explosives expert and one of the most dangerous terrorists in the world.

Colonel Siefer and his colleagues feared that Raja could provide the means to disperse biological agents. He could have given Mansur a suitcase that was rigged to be some kind of biological weapon. They immediately alerted customs agents in New York to make sure that Mansur's luggage was thoroughly searched upon his arrival at Kennedy Airport.

Mansur's flight departed Rome on time. He did not look at all like a suspicious passenger, and certainly not a terrorist. He was very friendly to the flight attendants and engaged in casual conversation with two other business class passengers. Mansur rehearsed the plan in his head that they had devised in Beirut and reaffirmed in Rome. He believed it would not be difficult to implement. He fell asleep already thinking ahead to his one-year sabbatical in Penang, Malaysia. He would be glad when all of this would be over.

CHAPTER 20
Montreal, Canada

Sudani Zalmai passed through immigration at the Montreal Dorval Airport without any difficulties. He was granted a 30-day tourist visa after providing his local address as the Montreal Le Ragence Hyatt Hotel. He listed his home address on his immigration form as Avignon, France, and he carried a French passport. Canadian authorities could see that he was of Middle Eastern descent but didn't know that his true nationality was Afghani.

Sudani was bitter against the U.S. after the Americans toppled the Taliban regime. Although he was not a Taliban, his two uncles were both killed in a misguided U.S. bombing raid. They were in a caravan on their way to greet the new Afghani President and were mistaken for a fleeing group of Taliban soldiers. A younger brother who was recruited by the Taliban, was also killed by American troops using cluster bombs outside the city of Kandahar.

Sudani was in France, running his business, when he heard about the deaths of his uncles from a family member. By the time he received the news, he could not enter the country. He later heard about his brother's death while on a business trip in Pakistan. Sudani had been supporting his family in Kandahar with his import business of Afghan rugs and embroidered wall hangings.

Although his mother and two sisters had survived the war, Sudani felt as though he had no future. His father and an older brother had been killed by Soviet troops in 1982. Now the Americans had killed his father's brothers who were helping to support his family financially, and his last brother. Sudani was the only son left. He felt it was his duty to avenge their deaths. Biological warfare was a logical choice.

Sudani was not a chemist, but he was extremely bright and had obtained an MBA degree from the University of Lyon. He spoke fluent French, Arabic, English and Pushtun, his native tongue. He also traveled extensively and made many friends because of his gregarious personality. Very few people would have guessed the depth of emptiness and brokenness he felt inside. Sudani was one of the most unlikely persons to suspect as being a terrorist. This made him the most dangerous kind of terrorist. Only his fellow terrorists understood the degree of his bitterness and hopelessness.

Sudani was Muslim, but not a devout one, although he strongly sympathized with *al Qaeda* and other Muslims who felt mistreated and dishonored by the West. Ironically, Sudani developed his strong hatred of the U.S. and England while studying in France. Several of his professors were openly Marxists and highly critical of Americans and Britons. He became convinced that Afghanistan and Iraq were simply used as pawns of infidel empires: the Greeks, the British, the Russians, and now the Americans.

When Islamic terrorists attacked the U.S. on September 11th, Sudani felt a vicarious excitement. He was not elated by the loss of life, but by the crumbling symbol of American capitalism and hegemony. He felt like a child enraptured by the majesty of a violent storm, excited by the destruction but not wishing that any would die from it. After a couple of weeks he rationalized the loss of innocent life, believing that the U.S. had killed innocent people in the Islamic world through its political and military policies and activities, especially through its support of Israel.

Sudani's primary concern in the aftermath of his intended strike against America was the ongoing welfare of his mother and two sisters. He did have more than 50,000 in Euro dollars saved in a bank account in Avignon, but that was not enough for his family to live on for the next twenty years. He had opened another account in Lausanne with 10,000 Euros, also with his mother and sisters as the beneficiaries. The Hamas promised to put 150,000 Euros into his account the day after the successful completion of his mission if he lived, and 250,000 Euros if he was killed. That would give his mother and sisters 310,000 Euro dollars to live on after his expected death, enough money to live comfortably in France with his uncle; or, if they so desired, to live like the wealthy in Afghanistan.

The *Hamas* gave Sudani enough botulinum toxin to kill 100,000 people. Instead of risking a search through the sophisticated airport security systems, Sudani did what many terrorism experts had not anticipated. He walked into a DHL office in Lyon and air freighted Afghan wall hangings and Styrofoam packages filled with vials of botulinum toxin to a friend's house in Montreal. When his flight from Lyon arrived in Montreal, the packages were already waiting for him.

"How was your flight?" Victor asked his friend at the Montreal airport.

"Tres bien merci," he replied. "Comment ca va?"

"I'm fine," he answered, preferring English over *Quebet Qu*a, the local French dialect.

"Did a package of my samples arrive?" Sudani asked.

"*Oui*, I received four DHL packages for you yesterday," Victor replied.

Victor Haddad, Sudani's Lebanese friend, had no idea that the packages that arrived had enough biological toxin to kill the entire population of a small city. Victor did not detect anything unusual about his friend's behavior. Sudani was very nonchalant about the packages. He even showed Victor some of the wall hangings in the packages.

While in Montreal, Sudani arranged for a private fishing boat to take him on a fishing expedition down the St. Lawrence River and into Lake Ontario. On a previous visit, Sudani had taken two sightseeing tours, one on Lake Ontario and one on Lake Superior. He had taken note of the lax security on the long U.S.-Canadian border through the Great Lakes region. There were many miles of small inlets and coves where a small boat could slip onto U.S. shores. Although the U.S. Coast Guard had vastly increased its patrols in recent months, it still did not have enough manpower to guard hundreds of miles of shoreline adequately, especially during periods of low-lying fog.

Sudani had planned well. In the town of Chateauguay, just south of Montreal, he found an experienced old sea captain by the name of Sebastian Croker. Croker had been taking visitors up and down the St. Lawrence River and through the Great Lakes on fishing expeditions for more than 30 years. Croker knew the best fishing areas in the lakes, especially on Lake Ontario where he had spent most of his time. The Great Lakes were experiencing a warmer winter, perfect for producing heavy fog. Sudani arranged for a five-day 600-mile trip to Lake Ontario and then back to Montreal. Croker piloted a 32-foot fishing vessel that slept up to six people in a cozy cabin.

On the third morning of the expedition, a heavy fog hugged Lake Erie's New York shoreline. Croker, a rough no-nonsense veteran of the Canadian Navy, had begun to like Sudani, whom he knew as Mihai. Sudani never revealed his true Afghani name. He had told Captain Croker that he was a Romanian immigrant to France and that he loved fishing. Croker knew right away that he was not a seasoned fisherman but had some deep-water experience. Not suspecting that this young French immigrant posed any potential threat, Croker was a little too trusting of Mihai. After drinking his morning two cups of coffee, Croker found himself struggling to keep awake. Despite having had a good night's rest, he became so sleepy by mid-morning he had to lie down.

"Mihai," he said wearily, "How would you like take the helm for a while? Just keep going due west. I'm going to lie down for a few minutes to rest my eyes."

When he was a young boy, Croker worked long hours helping his father on their family farm. He learned how take short naps. He could fall fast asleep and wake up five minutes later without an alarm clock, feeling completely refreshed and ready to work another 4-6 hours. When he began working on boats in the Navy, he continued to take short naps so he could stay alert during long watches. This day Croker did not wake up. Sudani had laced his coffee with a powerful sleep-inducing drug.

After steering on a southwesterly course, Sudani piloted the fishing vessel into U.S. territory northwest of Oswego. He used Croker's on board electronic equipment to calculate his position at about 20 miles from the coast. Visibility was still poor at 10:30 a.m. and a light snow began falling as he motored closer to the New York shoreline. Sudani's goal was to come on land close to Sodus Point and then get a ride to Alton, where he could take a bus to Rochester. Finally, Sudani spotted the shore. He anchored the boat about half a mile offshore and inflated the small rubber dingy kept on board. Before leaving the fishing boat, he took the remaining Canadian money he had, about $400, and put it in the pocket of Captain Croker along with a short note.

Sudani had grown to like the old man during the two and a half days they had been together, fishing and telling stories. Sebastian Croker reminded Sudani of his Lebanese grandfather, Bashir, his mother's father, who often fished in the Mediterranean when he was a young man before he moved to Afghanistan. Because Afghanistan is landlocked, Sudani had very few opportunities to fish. But one summer his grandfather had enough money to take Sudani on a fishing trip to the southern Caspian Sea region of Iran. It was during that trip that Sudani grew to love his grandfather and think about leaving Afghanistan. Afghanistan's civil war had decimated its few universities and learning centers, so Sudani longed for a chance to receive an education in the West.

Sudani marveled that though he and Captain Croker were from very distant cultural worlds, they had much in common. Sebastian Croker loved the seas and loved fishing. He was very proud of his close family and deeply respectful of his parents. He was also generous and hospitable. These were all the same character attributes Sudani had admired in his father and grandfather, who were both very fine tailors. Sudani highly respected those who kept their father's trade, something he had been unable to do.

Sudani carefully put the raft in the water and climbed in with his backpack, two fishing rods, a tackle box, and two wooden paddles.

Although there were a few fishing boats out, no one saw him as he pulled his small dingy up on shore just north of Alton. He easily found the paved road that led from Sodus Point to Alton. There was hardly any traffic. He decided to walk and only take a ride if someone offered, still carrying some of his fishing gear. About two miles from town a bread truck driver gave him a ride into town. Within an hour he was able to arrange a bus trip to Rochester, while Captain Croker still slept soundly.

Captain Croker awoke totally disoriented. He looked through the cabin glass, but it was already dusk and getting difficult to see. He estimated that he was about a mile offshore, adrift along the U.S. coastline of Lake Ontario. He wondered how long he had slept and what had happened to his Romanian passenger, who was nowhere in sight. As his grogginess cleared, Croker descended into a state of panic.

"Mihai! Mihai!" he shouted as he looked into the waters around the boat and along the shore. He could not believe Mihai was not on board. Croker ran back into his cabin, as if somehow Mihai might be there lying on the bed and he just had not seen him. He even looked into the cabinets under the bed. Mihai was gone. Croker put his hand on his forehead in anguish. He had never lost a passenger in more than 30 years of taking people on long fishing expeditions. *Where could Mihai be? Could he have fallen overboard?* He feared the worst.

"The life raft!" he shouted out loud.

Croker went on deck to where the life raft was stored. It was missing. He then ran back into the cabin and called for assistance on an emergency radio frequency. He reached the U.S. Coast Guard and reported a passenger missing.

"We should be there in 10-12 minutes," an officer said.

Captain Croker noticed that his coat was neatly hanging on a doorknob in his cabin.

I never hang up my coat, he thought.

He grabbed the coat and instinctively began searching the pockets. In the right bottom pocket he found a neatly rolled wad of Canadian bills wrapped around a white piece of paper. He unrolled the money and discovered the white paper contained a note, written in French. The note said:

Dear Sabastian. Thank you for being so kind to me. I like your stories. The fish stories are the best. I only needed a ride this far. The money is for you. It pays for the rubber dingy I took. Take the rest and make the improvements to the Samantha that you told to me. If any money is left, get your grandchildren presents. When you think of me, remember the eagle in the story you told me. I am like that eagle. I'll be flying to heaven soon. Don't worry about me. Your friend, Mihai.

Sebastian sat there for several minutes in emotional shock. Mihai was such a nice young man. He counted the money: $403.00. *Why would he have to die like the eagle? Where was he going? What was he planning to do?* Sad thoughts overwhelmed his mind, thoughts of Mihai ending his life.

While in deep turmoil, Sebastian overheard a loud speaker through the early morning mist.

"This is the U.S. Coast Guard responding to your call for assistance."

Just as Sebastian climbed down to the deck, the Coast Guard vessel came into view.

"Captain Croker?" an officer asked.

"Yes, thank you for coming," Sebastian replied.

"I'm Lieutenant Charles Reston. You said one of your passengers is missing?"

"Yes," Sebastian replied. "We were on the third day of a fishing expedition yesterday. I was feeling incredibly sleepy by mid-morning so I asked my passenger, Mihai, to take the wheel for a while. I only planned on taking a five minute nap. When I awoke, my passenger was gone."

"How long were you asleep Captain?"

"Since ten this morning," he replied. "It's still hard for me to believe."

"Seven hours? Are you sure you slept for seven hours?"

"Yes, sir, but I don't know how this happened," Sebastian replied incredulously. "I have never slept that long during the day unless I was sick."

"Captain," Reston instructed, "please describe this passenger to me."

"He told me his name was Mihai Carnea, and that he was Romanian but now lived in France. I really liked him. He paid me $1000 cash up front for a five-day fishing trip. Then he left me another $403 dollars along with a note before he left."

"He left a note for you and cash?" Reston asked.

"Yes. I didn't find the note until after I called you. Here it is," Sabastian said, handing Lt. Reston a white piece of paper.

"Captain, I don't read French. Can you read it to me?" Reston asked.

Sebastian translated the note in English as he read it out loud. Reston studied the piece of paper carefully, in deep contemplation. After what seemed to be a long time to Sebastian, he finally asked,

"You said his name was Mihai. Did he show you his ID?"

"Yes," Sebastian answered. "It was a Canadian driver's license issued in Quebec."

"Did you look at it closely?"

"No, but I did notice that in the picture on the license he looked much heavier. He said he had lost a lot of weight."

"Are you sure he was from Romania?' Reston queried further.

"No, he said he was Romanian but now living in France. He travels back and forth from Toulouse to Montreal for his business. He speaks very good French; not like the *Quebet Qua* we speak in Montreal."

"What does he mean in the note when he said he is like the eagle in the story, and he is going to heaven?"

"It's a long story," Sebastian replied. "I mean, it's actually a short story that I told him that my father used to tell me. He really liked it, too!"

For the next ten minutes, Captain Croker explained to Lt. Reston the story of the eagle. Even Lt. Reston was moved by the captivating story. When Sebastian revealed the climax of the story, Reston became visibly agitated; concern swept across his face.

"So the eagle sacrifices himself in the end by attacking the pack of coyotes?"

"Yes."

"Did this Mihai look Romanian?" Reston asked.

"Well, he had a dark olive skin like some Romanians and Italians I know," Sebastian explained, "but his accent was different, more guttural."

"Different from the other Romanians you know?" Reston asked.

"There are only two Romanians I have met besides Mihai. And I met them years ago. But I know Mihai is a Romanian name."

"Could he have been Middle Eastern or Arab?" Reston asked.

"You don't mean an Islamic terrorist, do you? I know you are concerned about terrorists. But not this guy. He's polite, a gentleman, a man who loves his family. Like I said, I didn't look at his license closely. Maybe he was not Romanian. But he is not the kind of person who kills people. If he was, he could have easily killed me."

"Captain, I need to take this note and examine it for fingerprints," Reston explained. "I also would like to take your fingerprints right now, which will also be on the note. That way we can isolate Mihai's fingerprints. Then you are free to return to Canada."

Lt. Reston thanked Captain Croker for his assistance. The Captain sincerely hoped that Mihai could be found before he sacrificed his life. Reston immediately contacted his commanding officer in Rochester. He explained the whole situation regarding Mihai and his theory on what had happened. Reston believed that Mihai, who was likely traveling under a fictitious name with a forged or stolen Canadian driver's license, likely drugged Captain Croker. He also explained how Mihai had taken a dingy from the boat to come ashore; entering illegally into the U.S. Reston anticipated that Mihai was carrying a large amount of cash. More importantly, he carried a large blue backpack that was filled to capacity.

Reston's commander faxed this information to the Office for Homeland Security in Washington. The fax was one of nearly 200 received that day from all over the U.S. and from 14 nations overseas.

Paul Richfield was the senior analyst in the Office for Homeland Security. He reviewed more than 500 security threats each day sent by letter, phone, fax, or email. After quickly scanning the report sent by Bill Westford, Lt. Reston's commanding officer in the Coast Guard, he picked up the phone and made a call.

"Hi, Terry, this is Paul. I just received a fax from the Coast Guard Commander in Rochester, Bill Westford. You need to look at this."

"A problem in the harbor?" Terry asked.

"No, from a patrol boat on the lake near Sodus Point. They have an illegal border crossing."

"So what's new, Paul?"

"Just come on over. I'll beat you in horse this time."

Five minutes later Paul Hirschwiler, all 6'5" of him, walked into Terry Swindol's office. Without saying a word, he closed the door, grabbed the Nerf ball on Terry's coffee table, and made a perfect hook shot, lofting the ball through the center of the plastic hoop mounted to the back of Terry's door. Terry picked up the Nerf ball and tried to replicate the shot, but came up short.

"Close," Paul said.

"At 45 you still haven't lost your shot, Paul," Terry offered with a chuckle.

"Sweet 16 in 83'," Paul replied. Paul would never forget the marvelous season he had at Boston College. They were just two baskets away from going to the final eight teams, but Virginia beat them out by three points. Virginia only lost to the NCAA champion North Carolina State by one point. Paul also held that had they beaten Virginia, he knew they could have beaten N.C. State.

"We just matched up well against them," he would always say.

"BC is going to the final four this year," Paul quipped. "Boston is now the center for championships: Red Sox, Patriots, and Boston College!"

Terry chuckled as he handed Paul the fax from Commander Westford.

"We've got some serious threats Paul – look at this."

After reading the fax and asking Terry a few questions, Paul picked up the phone and called Westford. He then made a call to Lt. Reston.

He wanted to interview Captain Croker.

"Did you take his blood sample?" Paul asked Reston.

Reston explained why it was too late to determine if Croker had been given barbiturates to make him sleep. Also, Croker was now traveling by boat back to Montreal. He would not be back home until two days, but Reston had his home telephone number.

"Two days is too long," Paul replied. "Doesn't this guy have a cell phone on board?"

"No," Reston replied, "Only an emergency radio transmitter. He is an old-fashioned fisherman."

"Commander, could you please dispatch a boat and track Captain Croker down?" Paul asked.

"Sir, Captain Croker left this area two hours ago. Lake Ontario is very big. But I will alert the other two boats immediately and we'll begin a search."

"You only have three boats total?" Paul asked incredulously.

"Yes, three boats to patrol the entire northern New York coastline, which is about 200 miles along Lake Ontario and another 100 miles along the St. Lawrence River. And I am glad to have three! Before the extra monies appropriated by the President, we only had two boats."

"Just do your best to find him as soon as you can," Paul urged.

Paul then gave Lt. Reston his private number.

"Sir, is there something I should know?" Reston asked.

"We have nothing solid, Lieutenant, just some speculation about a planned biological attack on a major U.S. city. We are concerned about Detroit and Chicago. The border with Canada is easy to permeate. This fellow who disappeared is potentially a serious security risk."

"We'll be on the highest alert," Ruston replied.

Paul hung up the phone and grabbed the Nerf ball, taking a fadeaway jumper that again found its mark in the center of the basket.

"What are you thinking, Paul?" Terry asked with great inquisitiveness.

"I'm thinking we are going to get a terrorist in our back yard," Paul replied without hesitation. He then looked at his friend.

"I just don't know," he replied in exasperation. We receive so many reports. There's probably another hundred on my desk. An Iranian man is lost on a hunting expedition near the Idaho border. A suspicious canoe party is spotted in Lake of the Woods heading toward Minnesota — they look Middle Eastern. A low-lying plane is spotted crossing Lake Michigan into U.S. territory. If someone wants to get from Canada to the U.S., there are a thousand ways to do it. Do all these hundreds of reports ever amount to anything? Hardly ever. Is our national security really in danger by these illegal entries? I doubt it. It's just the one time that a threat may be legitimate, and we miss it, that I worry about. So, we have to take them all seriously, and this one report from Captain Croker makes me very nervous."

"How so?" Terry asked.

"It seems like Croker was drugged. A healthy man just doesn't go to sleep for seven hours in mid-morning. I want to know more about this Mihai Carnea. I doubt that's his real name, and I doubt that he is Romanian. A Romanian would have fished in the Black Sea, not in the Mediterranean. I want to know what was in this guy's backpack. I also want to hear Captain Croker's story about the eagle. I just don't feel good about this one, Terry."

"We'll get on it right away, Paul."

"I'm going to brief the Director," Paul concluded.

"Bobby is really concerned, too," Terry noted, "about this biological attack in the Philippines. "He told me he thinks we'll get hit soon."

Colonel Siefer picked up the phone again. He had just made phone calls to the police chiefs in New York, Detroit and Los Angeles. He began dialing Dan Ryan in Chicago when his assistant walked into his office.

"Colonel Siefer, Lieutenant Charles Reston from the Coast Guard station in Rochester is on the line. He is with a fishing boat captain on the St. Lawrence River."

"Thanks, Tim, please put him through."

"Lieutenant Reston, this is Colonel Matt Siefer. You called just at the right time. I was just calling various police chiefs to be on alert. We have received information from our friends in Europe and the Middle

East that another major attack is planned against the U.S., so I'm investigating every border incident seriously. Did you have a hard time finding Captain Croker?"

"Colonel, it's rather miraculous that I did find him. We are in the midst of heavy snow squalls, so visibility is less than a mile."

"Well, thank you, Lieutenant, and thank God. Is Captain Sebastian Croker ready to speak to me?"

"Yes, sir. I'll put him on."

For the next 20 minutes Colonel Siefer conducted a detailed interview with Captain Croker. He learned that Croker's passenger, Mihai Carnea, was carrying a large backpack that he seemed to overprotect. He would not let Captain Croker touch it. He also suspected that Mihai's true identity might not be Romanian but Middle Eastern. Captain Croker only noticed one inconsistency that made him think twice about Mihai's identity. During a conversation about fishing, Mihai said his father had retired in the town he worked all his life in Afghanistan. Earlier he had said he grew up in Romania. He later corrected himself and said his father moved from Afghanistan to Romania to retire after his mother died.

"Is there anything else you can think of that might be important?" Siefer asked Captain Croker.

"Now that I think of it, there is something odd about his signature on the note he wrote to me," Croker explained. You can see it if you look closely. He began signing his name with what looked like an 'S' and then wrote a capital 'M' over it."

"I noticed that too. We're going to have a hand-writing expert analyze it," Siefer replied.

"Colonel," Captain Croker said, "I don't know what this fellow is doing in the U.S., but I was taken totally by surprise that he left my boat. He is a nice young man. I could see that he was in turmoil. If he is planning any kind of trouble, I think he could be talked out of it."

"Thank you, Captain," Siefer said, "I'll keep that in mind."

Dan Ryan received a phone call from his friend Matt Siefer, who was calling from Washington. Ryan's worst fears were confirmed.

Siefer indicated that an unidentified man traveling under the name Mihai Cornea and claiming to be Romanian, illegally crossed into the U.S. near Sodus Point on Lake Erie. He was believed to have taken a bus into Rochester from the town of Alton. The names of passengers are not registered on that small bus route unless they pay by credit card. The man is likely traveling under a false identity and could be from the Middle East.

"We are checking with our European friends to see if it might be any of the suspected terrorists they have been tracking, particularly in Rome," Siefer explained.

"Anything else?"

"Yes, there is another suspect, Mansur Shukarian, traveling from Rome to Chicago via New York City. He may be a drug smuggler who is funding source for *al Qaeda*. He could be a terrorist. We just don't know, Dan. Chicago might be a target."

"Matt," Ryan concluded somberly, "I think its time to put the city on alert."

"One more thing you should know about Dan. I found out through my sources in the National Intelligence Office that Israeli intelligence confirms a planned biological attack was thwarted by their security forces, and that they suspect the biological agent used was the same toxin as used in the Philippines. It's called botulinum. They also suspect the agent was on the Philippine Airlines flight that was shot down, but in a much more concentrated form since they believed it killed the passengers in less than an hour. They're doing final testing now of the agent. We are trying to get details of the planned attack but we've received no further information. We don't know if the hold-up is our National Intelligence Office or the Israelis.

"You mean we don't know how the agent was to be released or anything about the method of dispersement?" Ryan asked in frustration.

"Sorry Dan; we don't even know if they planned to put the toxin in food or in crop dusting equipment or in pipe bombs. We only know they planned to attack with what they believe is botulinum. I've been digging and there are rumors that the arrests were made at hotels and that several Israeli agents are in the hospital after being exposed to the toxin, but that's all I can find out and that information is unconfirmed. The news media are also in the dark but they're digging for the real story. If I hear something more I'll let you know. Right now, you need to get your city ready, Dan."

"We're ready Matt. I just want to catch these bastards before they can kill."

CHAPTER 21
Rochester, New York

Sudani walked up to the Amtrak station in Rochester and purchased a one-way ticket to Chicago. He noticed the heavy security inside the station. The state of New York was still on alert from a recent terrorist threat in New York City. After boarding his train, he quietly took his seat and read the *USA Today* he had picked up at the station. The headlines on page three captured his attention: "U.S. Office of Homeland Security Warns of Terrorist Attack During or After Ramadan."

The article explained how recent activities had led U. S. authorities to believe terrorists might try to strike during the next four to six weeks, or at the end of Ramadan, the Muslim holy season, which began on October 4 this year in the U.S. and ended on November 3. The article did not mention a specific threat from stolen biological agents, but did say that biological attacks were a real concern. The news media had still not learned about the attack in the Mariana Islands. The article did indicate that police departments in major cities were on high alert.

Sudani shook his head slightly. *They just don't get it*, he thought. *Increased security cannot stop us as long as we are free to travel and associate with whomever we want.* Sudani's train arrived in Chicago at 8:14 p.m. He took a taxi to the Renaissance Hotel. Mansur was scheduled to arrive the next day.

Niloa walked into her morning briefing with Dan Ryan wondering if she was being of any help. She had been working in Chicago's counter-terrorism office for three days, scouring faces on videotape sent electronically over the internet from various office buildings, airports, and train stations. The first day she had viewed 112 pictures.

After three days she had viewed 351 faces, recognizing none of them. The electronic system seemed to be working well, but none of those screened had matched any of the known or suspected terrorists in the data base they had available. Ryan, the Deputy Superintendent, and the Chicago police would later be accused of profiling Middle Easterners, but they were willing to take the heat in order to prevent a terrorist attack. All the suspects they were looking for were from the Middle East.

Whenever building security encountered Middle Eastern men they deemed suspicious, a digital picture of the person would immediately be sent electronically to a surveillance room in the basement of police headquarters in downtown Chicago. The security personnel would then hold the person's ID until Niloa and the others working with her would clear him. There were some 32 buildings and public places networked into the system, including the major train and bus stations, United Center, Soldier's Field, the Museum of Science, and the two major airports.

The system also contained an electronic database of digital photographs of known terrorists. A powerful computer software program quickly compared the facial features of people in different photographs and determined if they matched each other. The U.S. INS was outfitting all immigration stations with digital cameras that would access the same database, thus preventing known terrorists from entering the country through the nation's international airports. The Chicago Police Department had recently installed a multimodal biometrics surveillance system manufactured by Identix, a leading biometrics technology company headquartered in Minnetonka, Minnesota. The company fuses data on skin texture with fingerprint and facial data, increasing its recognition accuracy to more than 90 percent.

Unfortunately, the digital pictures taken by Dominic Arone in Rome were not of high enough quality to develop a skin print of the three suspects he was watching. When their pictures were run against the data base of known terrorists, none of them matched. Due to these limitations, a person like Niloa who could identify voices as well as faces would be invaluable.

At Kennedy Airport, the customs agents carefully scanned the luggage delivery area for a Middle-Eastern man, 5'9" in height, wearing a dark blue business suit and a long beige wool coat. They knew Mansur's flight had arrived from Rome. Susan Caine, a 12-year veteran of the customs service, was first to spot Mansur. He had no difficulties passing through immigration since he had a valid French passport, a valid import-export business, and no known criminal record. Mansur was standing by the conveyor belt of luggage carrier 2, waiting for his check-in bags to be unloaded, when he was spotted by immigration officials. Mansur, however, knew that only one of his two check-in bags would be sent through on the luggage carrier.

Susan Caine and her colleague, Mark McClendon, watched Mansur as he picked up his bag and placed it on a cart with his hand carry-on bag and briefcase. He then walked directly toward them. Mark discerned immediately that something was wrong. Mansur was missing one bag. He joined the line that Susan was processing and noticed Mark walked over and said something to her discreetly. When he reached the counter, before Susan could address him, Mansur said, "Ms. Caine, can you please help me? I had two check-in bags, but only one came through. I checked the luggage carrier but it is missing. What do I need to do?"

Mansur's politeness and excellent English surprised Susan. He communicated clearly and considerately.

"After I check your bags," Susan replied, "you need to see an American Airlines agent back inside off to my left in the back. The agent will help you find your missing bag."

"Thank you so much," replied Mansur. "All my rug samples are in that bag. It is very important for my sales contacts."

"Sir, could you please open your suitcase for me?" asked Susan.

Mansur opened his suitcase. It was unusually neat. All his clothes looked pressed and were neatly folded. Nothing was out of order. His suitcase, which looked new, could have been used for a luggage sales commercial. It was an expensive piece of designer luggage from Gucci. Mansur's handbag and briefcase were also meticulously packed and organized. He presented himself as a classy professional businessman. Susan knew she would not find any contraband in Mansur's belongings.

She also searched his briefcase but found nothing unusual.

Mansur passed out of customs, went to the American Airlines agent, and dutifully reported his lost bag. The agent explained to him that after the bag was found, possibly arriving on another flight, it would be sent on to Chicago and held there in customs until he went to pick it up. Mansur's bag was found 45 minutes later; it apparently had been placed by mistake on the wrong luggage wagon. The bag was placed on Mansur's plane to Chicago with a custom's hold on it. An American Airlines agent at his gate indicated he could claim the bag at the custom's office at O'Hare Airport after he arrived in Chicago.

Mansur realized that while his bag was at Kennedy airport, it had likely been x-rayed by agents and inspected by a trained bomb-sniffing dog. He knew they would find no evidence of any illegal materials or substances in his suitcase, but only the Afghan rugs.

Mansur arrived at O'Hare's custom's office promptly after his flight. The custom agent there already knew there would be no illegal materials in his suitcase. Mansur unlocked the suitcase with a key, unlocking each of the two metal snaps. He then turned the 3-digit center combination lock to 127, and opened the case. Inside were neatly stacked samples of Persian rugs from the Middle East. The agent inspected the suitcase thoroughly. There were no hidden compartments on the sides. It was clean.

Colonel Siefer took two calls from the head INS agents at O'Hare and Kennedy International Airports. Mansur had brought in no unusual possessions. However, his bag had been missing for 45 minutes. Siefer realized they might have been outwitted. Forty-five minutes was plenty of time to remove contents from the bag. The bag could have been lost on purpose. He asked the FBI to immediately detain the airline workers who unloaded the American Airlines flight from Rome and to hold them for questioning.

The crew was scheduled to work until 8 p.m. They were asked by FBI agents to stop loading a plane that had arrived at 7:10 p.m. It was too late. Two of the crew members had never returned from their 7 p.m. coffee break. The FBI agents interrogated the crew. None of them saw the two crew members tamper with any bags on the Rome flight, but the two had been alone with some of the luggage from that flight.

The two crew members were not well known by the other workers, but had worked for American Airlines for two years. They both lived in New Jersey and were of a minority ethnic background, but both were American citizens. Colonel Siefer developed a sick feeling when he learned this information. He was now sure that Mansur had smuggled into the U.S. some kind of illegal materials, and possibly biological or chemical agents that could be used in a terrorist attack.

In the morning, Mansur went down to the front desk of his hotel in Chicago. Calvin Hess, a 20-year veteran police detective, was across the street in an unmarked car, watching the hotel. He arrived at about the same time a Federal Express truck was leaving the area.

"Yes, Mr. Shukarian," the concierge said to Mansur, "your Federal Express package arrived just a few minutes ago. Will you need help with this?" he asked.

"No, I'll be fine," Mansur answered as he took the small package from the concierge.

On the outside of the package was a return address to Summit, New Jersey. Mansur quickly opened it and removed the disassembled canisters, placing them on one of the double beds in his room. He counted the canisters and their parts: 4 in total, all of equal size, about the size of a 12-ounce can of liquid gel shaving cream. He inspected them closely to make sure these were the same four cans he had packed in his suitcase, the one that was missing for 45 minutes. They were.

Mansur emptied his briefcase and placed the cans at the bottom. His case was just big enough to hold the canisters and a molded cardboard structure to keep the cans from touching each other. On top of the hard foam cover was enough room to keep a notebook and some papers. He had measured everything very carefully.

Mansur picked up the phone and called the front desk.

"Yes, Mr. Shakarian, can I help you?"

"Yes, can you tell me where I can find an internet café nearby?" Mansur asked.

"Yes," said Jan at the front desk. "There is one on 1137 Belmont Street called *The Interactive Bean*, a short taxi ride from here."

"Can you call a taxi for me?" Mansur asked.

"I'd be happy to."

"Thank you so much," Mansur replied.

Calvin Hess followed Mansur's taxi, keeping his car well behind him. He watched him go into the internet café. Mansur accessed the website set up for the Chicago project. On it a message was waiting for him from Sudani. He had arrived safely in Chicago. They were to meet in the NMR lab of the Tech Building at Northwestern University at 9:00 p.m. that evening. Mansur decided not to return to his hotel. It was already 6 p.m. He would take his time traveling to Northwestern by subway and taxi, Hess parked his car hastily in the street and managed to follow him on foot, almost losing him twice on the subways and a third time while Mansur visited a large shopping complex to kill some time.

Sudani, who had arrived by train from Rochester, and Raja, who had flown to Toronto, driven to Buffalo, and then flown to Midway Airport in Chicago, were both in the lab when Mansur arrived. A lab student sent there to assist them led them to a small room attached to the lab. He unlocked the door and let them in.

"The campus security will check this building at 11 p.m.," he said to Sudani. "They will check every room. You must be out of here by 10:45 at the latest."

"Thank you, Sergi. We should be finished by 10:30 p.m. We'll turn the lights out and lock up just as you have told us. And stay out of the city tomorrow. It will not be a good day for walking around, especially if it's windy," Mansur warned.

Sudani could see the anger in Sergi's eyes. He didn't like being used in this way.

"Sergi," Sudani continued, grasping Sergi's shoulders gently and looking into his eyes, "your parents will be well-cared for in Lebanon. Your sister and her husband will also be protected. Thank you for your assistance."

Sergi left the premises still angry. He knew they were planning some sort of attack, but felt blackmailed. If he double-crossed them they would kill his family. Mansur carefully took the biological agents from the Styrofoam cases in his backpack. Sudani took the seven cans out of his backpack and Raja took out the four can he had brought with him using the same strategy as Mansur. Raja worked quickly to set the detonation devices on the canisters and to prepare the aerosol mechanisms to emit the particles in a steady flow. By 9:45 p.m. they were finished.

They now had 15 canisters with enough botulinum powder to kill most of the people in more than half a dozen large buildings and public gathering places in the city. The aerosol cans could be easily placed in ventilation systems. Once airborne within the circulation systems of large buildings, they would be nearly impossible to contain. They calculated that they could kill 50,000 to 100,000 people in one day.

They also knew that the emergency centers in the city would not be equipped to treat so many people at once. It would take time for the hospital epidemiologists to identify the agent, and when they finally identified the botulinum, they would realize the limited supplies of antitoxin resided at the Centers for Disease Control in Atlanta.

Although the hospitals were prepared for anthrax and smallpox, they were not prepared for the botulism toxin. Raja, Mansur and Sudani each took the canisters they had brought with them.

"Tomorrow," Raja boasted, "Allah will give us a great victory."

Hess did not see the other terrorists enter the building and did not risk going inside. He thought he saw three men leave the building, but it was dark and he did not get a good look at them. He followed Mansur back to the hotel and informed Deputy Ryan before retiring.

After learning that a small research lab was inside the campus building, Ryan interpreted Mansur's visit to Northwestern as an ominous sign. In the morning he would direct his detectives to interview those who worked in the NMR lab and to search the lab for explosive residues. He would learn that multiple lab teams use the lab in the evenings, and no one saw or heard anything unusual during the previous evening. Even before the interviews, Ryan thought he could not wait any longer. He had to take a chance that he might be wrong and search Mansur's hotel room.

Ryan arranged for a search warrant and called one of his task force members and contacted the hotel where Mansur was staying. Calvin Hess was still there outside the hotel in his car. He went to the hotel lobby to determine which room Mansur was in. Ryan then called the SWAT team to get ready for an arrest. Calvin called Ryan. It was about 11:30 p.m.

"He's gone," Calvin said.

"What do you mean?" Ryan asked.

"He paid his bill immediately upon his return, and left the hotel through a side door at 11:00 p.m. His car was already packed Dan. This was all planned."

CHAPTER 22
Mishawaka, Indiana

Dan Ryan hated to be away from the city, even for a few hours, but his 90-year-old mother was sick with pneumonia and he needed to go see her in the hospital where she lived in Mishawaka, Indiana. At least he could drive with his cell phone attached to his visor and equipped with an earphone to give his security team and his family easy access to him.

When he entered his mother's room she was sitting up in bed watching the game. "They're up by 7 over Purdue," she said excitedly after she and Dan exchanged warm greetings and hugs. "I should have known, Mom," Dan responded, "Notre Dame football. I hope you're not here just to use the cable to see the game."

Dan's mother thought cable was too expensive, so she found other ways to see the games.

"Dan, Josh called me five minutes ago. You were on the line, so he's going to call again. He said it is very urgent that he talk with you."

"Thanks, Mom. I'm glad you're feeling well and that Notre Dame is winning, for your good health."

"Well, you know those Boilermakers, they always come back, especially against Notre Dame. At least none of my grandsons are playing for them now."

Two of Dan's sons, Jason and Kevin, had played football for Purdue. Dan and his older brother Ben had played football for Notre

Dame. Dan's mother learned to sing the fighting Irish victory song, even though she did root for Purdue when they were not playing each other. She began humming it quietly as she drifted off to sleep.

Dan left the bedside and retreated to the corner of the room so as not to disturb his mother, but before he could call Joshua, his cell phone rang.

"Hi, Josh?" Dan asked.

"Hi, Dan, this is Matt Siefer calling from Washington."

"Sorry Colonel, my son is urgently trying to reach me."

"Dan, there is a high probability that terrorists may be planning an attack in Chicago. When Joshua calls he'll provide you with new information. I'm sending his team to assist you. Are your people ready?"

"We're ready to stop an attack if we can get some specific information."

"And if you can't stop them?" Matt asked. "Are you ready to treat casualties?"

"I think we are as prepared as any other city, Matt"

"OK, Dan, keep me posted."

Dan's phone rang again. This time it was Joshua.

"Dad, we have confirmed that there are suspected terrorists in the city. We think they're planning a biological attack with a toxic agent they acquired from an attack on a U.S. research laboratory. Our best guess is they'll use botulinum, the same agent terrorists used in Manila and on the airline they hijacked in the Philippines. We also suspect the terrorists are some of the same ones who held Niloa and the other two women as hostages in Lebanon."

"Thanks, Josh. Colonel Siefer just called me from Washington and gave me a similar warning. He said you're coming to help."

"I'm at the airport now with my team. I'm getting the last flight out of Boston. The Secretary of Defense has lent our commando unit to the Office of Homeland Security. Colonel Siefer did not hesitate to send us to Chicago. I'm looking forward to being there."

"It will be great to be with you, Josh," Dan replied. "I just wish the circumstances were different."

"Dad, I'll enjoy seeing you, too. But I was particularly thinking of Niloa. How is she?"

"Right now, she's a bit weary. When she first arrived she was completely surprised when her parents met her at the airport. Instead of returning to Hawaii they came here to welcome her. They met me and the other police officers she has been working with at the station. Her parents wanted to make sure she was not in another dangerous situation. They are wonderful people and are relieved she is working with me closely in a secure area."

"I'd like to meet them someday," Josh replied.

"I didn't realize you were seriously interested in her Josh."

"Neither did I, Dad. I've been reluctant to get hurt again."

Dan ended his conversation with Joshua just as his mother started dozing off. "How's my dearest grandson?" Lois asked, surprising Dan.

"I thought you were sleeping, mother," Dan answered.

"Moms never sleep when their children are awake, my son. They just rest quietly."

"Joshua is fine, Mom. He's coming to Chicago to help me. He'll come see you as son as we finish our work. The doctor said you'll be going home in a couple of days. Cheryl will take you home."

"I know son. I'll be fine. Chicago needs you now. I may be old but I watch the news. You need to protect the people, Dan."

Lois Ryan knew her son was in a critical situation in Chicago. She had seen news reports about the terrorist threats and understood Dan was in charge of the city's counter-terrorism task force. She did her best to take the stress of worrying about her off his list of concerns.

"I need a cup of coffee," Jackson said to his young assistant. "Do you want some, Niloa?"

"How about a hot chocolate with marshmallows?" Niloa asked.

"No problem," Kevin replied.

"Niloa, I don't know how you can look at these hundreds of faces day after day and hour after hour without going crazy," Jackson commented.

"Jackson, if you had sat day after day watching the same ocean flow beneath your boat and the same clouds swirl above while in the doldrums like I have, this, in comparison, would seem exciting," Niloa answered.

Dan Ryan arrived back in his office at 6:00 a.m. He took out his Bible from his front desk, opened it up to Isaiah, Chapter 54, and read verse 17 aloud. That's all he had to hang onto for the day—the hope of Divine intervention. He had spent his morning commute praying for intervention, believing somehow that God would not allow the terrorists to succeed. Despite all the manpower, all the technology, all the sophistication of the U.S. intelligence agencies and their outstanding police department in Chicago, Ryan felt helpless to stop them.

He looked at the calendar on his desk. It was Tuesday, November 1st, a day or two before the end of Ramadan in the U.S., depending upon which official Muslim calendar you followed.

They first had expected another September 11th strike. It never came. They then speculated other dates, but such speculation did not help. *Had the terrorists purposefully waited until the end of Ramadan to launch a biological attack, or would they wait for Thanksgiving weekend?* No one really knew but the terrorists. The office buildings would be opening in an hour or two.

The stores would be opening by mid-morning, and they had very little defense in place to stop a biological attack at a shopping mall or large department store. They were open for anyone to walk in and out. A suicide bomber could walk into a crowded mall, or onto a subway train, or into a bus station and blow himself up. Such attacks were commonplace in Israel. But if a suicide bomber packed himself with anthrax, or live cultures of the Ebola virus, or radioactive materials instead of nails and metal shards, the result could be much more devastating. This was Ryan's dread.

Niloa arrived at 7:00 a.m. for another day of surveillance. She was now used to working with everyone on the surveillance team. Today two new people would be added. The police had installed some new high-resolution thermal imaging cameras in the Sears Tower and several other buildings. The researchers at the Mayo Clinic had been testing the cameras in detecting those who lie. The heat-sensing cameras could map facial imaging with different colors to indicate when a person was not telling the truth.

When suspicious people would be questioned whom Niloa or other security staff could monitor, the thermal imaging could prove to be extremely helpful. A simple direct question like, "Are you carrying anything that could be harmful to people?" could be asked. The surveillance team decided to use this question as a follow-up question. First, they would ask, "What is your purpose for being in this building?" A second follow-up question that they knew would really catch people by surprise was, "Do you love Americans?" Those with deep hatred toward Americans would have great difficulty hiding their deception from the thermal imaging system. If a terrorist answered the question truthfully with a "No" then they would be asked, "Are you planning to harm Americans in any way?" Such a line of direct questions would likely catch any would-be terrorists off guard.

Dan Ryan, Niloa, and the terrorist surveillance team were in place at 7:15 a.m. Ryan briefed the team on the latest developments. He had received a call from Calvin Hess who had followed one of the suspected terrorists to Northwestern University. The building search yielded nothing out of order and no explosive residues were found.

At 7:30 a.m., the first pictures began to arrive on the electronic surveillance network. Mansur Shukarian walked into the Sears Tower at 8:05 a.m. Calvin Hess was close behind. Mansur was wearing a dark gray business suit, a cap he had bought in Italy, and a long black wool coat he had purchased at half price at Filenes basement in Boston.

He looked more Southern European than Middle Eastern. He was also carrying a black leather briefcase. Security was not even going to send his picture to police headquarters but decided to do so as a precaution, since he was a foreigner. However, Niloa did not get to take a good look at him because she was glued to another monitor from another building checking out a suspicious character. This was a big mistake.

Mansur gladly submitted himself to x-rays and a search. His briefcase contained only carpet samples and a shaving kit. He was allowed entrance into the building. Hess continued to follow him. Mansur's identification indicated he lived in France and he described himself as a businessman. As Mansur had stated, a call to the 45th floor confirmed his 8:45 a.m. appointment with a marketing firm.

Calvin Hess passed through security shortly after Mansur and tipped off the front security officers that Mansur was a suspected terrorist. After Hess had lost Mansur when he had checked out of his hotel the night before, he worked all night calling hotels before he found the new one Mansur had checked into near the Midway Airport. Hess found out at the hotel that Mansur had taken a taxi to the Sears Tower. He had already contacted Dan Ryan, who would send Joshua and his team as soon as they arrived at the station.

At 8:35 a.m. Hess called Dan again to tell him he had lost Mansur. They went to the 45th floor on the same elevator, but Hess stepped off the elevator first after he saw Mansur press the button for the 45th floor. Mansur acted as if he were getting off too but stepped back onto the elevator and quickly closed the door.

He then proceeded to the 50th floor, got off, and entered a large conference room at the end of the hall. He removed a ceiling tile, quickly climbed up into the ceiling, and found an opening through the ventilation system. He took out a shaving cream can, set the timer and set the can in the ventilation system.

He then proceeded to the 5th floor and entered a ballroom. He placed a second shaving cream canister in another air vent and then proceeded immediately to the 45th floor for his appointment. He arrived at 8:50 am. He asked the secretary to forgive him for being five minutes late for his meeting, but said he needed a quick shave.

Hess had called the office where Mansur had his appointment and told them to contact him when Mansur arrived. Hess received the call at 8:52 a.m. when Mansur went into his meeting. The secretary told Hess the apology Mansur had given as to why he was late. Hess called Ryan and relayed the story.

Dan had seen Mansur on the monitor.

"He looked clean shaven when he came in," Dan said to Hess. "Keep a close watch on him. Joshua is on his way with a small team to assist you. We need to place him under arrest and take him in for questioning."

"Suddenly Niloa's ears perked up. Did you say a suspicious person entering the building said he was shaving?" she asked with great concern.

"There is one businessman from France we have been trailing. He was a few minutes late for a sales meeting in the Sears Tower because he said he wanted to have a quick shave. Didn't you take a look at him, Niloa?" asked Dan.

Niloa actually never had a chance to study Mansur's picture. The surveillance operators began searching back through the pictures of people who had entered the Sears Tower to find the picture of Mansur. When they found it, Niloa felt that she might have seen him before. Niloa asked for the voice recording. When the audio of his conversation with the security guards was sent, she knew he had been in the house where she had been held hostage in Beirut. Niloa told Deputy Ryan, who then warned Joshua and the security officers at the entrance of the building.

"What's this about shaving?" Niloa asked again. "Did he bring shaving cream?"

"Yes, he had a toiletry kit in his briefcase along with his carpet samples," Dan replied.

"That's it!" Niloa shouted. "When I was kidnapped I remember seeing a man bring in a box of shaving cream. The terrorists mocked us by asking us if we needed some for our legs, since many women do not shave in their culture. I thought it was odd that they had that much shaving cream since most of them had beards. Those canisters could hold biological agents!"

Dan Ryan immediately picked up the phone and called Hess on the 45th floor.

"Hess, please stall Mansur. We are going to place him under arrest in the office. We can't risk letting him loose in the building. He may have already planted biological agents during the 10 minutes that you lost sight of him. After we arrest him we need to evacuate the building immediately."

Dan Ryan picked up his cell phone and looked at the incoming number. It was Joshua.

"Reporting for duty, Dad. My team is five blocks from the station."

"Josh, proceed to the Sears Tower immediately. I need your team to arrest a terrorist suspect who may have placed one or more biological weapons in the building. We need to evacuate the building immediately. One of my detectives, Calvin Hess, is with the man now on the 45th floor. I must stay here to monitor further threats. You are now in charge in that building. I'll let my officers know."

"Mr. Ryan," Niloa said excitedly, "I recognize that man."

Niloa was looking at a picture sent on their computer network from the Chicago Mercantile Exchange building.

"Hold him up," Ryan communicated by computer to the security officer at the security desk on the ground floor of the building.

Niloa and Ryan were staring at a picture of Raja Osmani on one of their 27-inch computer monitors. The man wore a dark olive green suit, burgundy wing tips, and a light green shirt and tie. He looked like a businessman from Florida, with his dark-tanned skin and pleasant disposition. He carried a leather-covered burgundy colored briefcase and wore stylist thin-rimmed gold-tinted glasses.

"Where did you see him, Niloa?" Ryan asked.

"He looks like another one of the terrorists I saw in Beirut when I had a chance to look under my blindfold; but I can't be sure until I hear his voice."

"Ask him some test questions and send us the audio feed," Ryan instructed on the instant messenger system they were using.

"Mr. Osmani, what is your purpose for being in this building?" one of the two security officers sitting at the desk asked.

"I am a trader," Raja answered calmly. "More specifically," Raja continued, "I came to purchase some commodities for my clients."

The thermal camera indicated that Raja was telling the truth.

"Mr. Osmani, is that your only purpose today?"

"No," Raja answered, "There are other things I will probably do today, like eat lunch here, talk to some friends, write memos, and make some calls."

"This guy is too good," Ryan mumbled to Niloa and the other staff members in the surveillance center. "He is trained to handle interrogation."

The thermal camera did pick up some heat when he mentioned eating lunch, one of the monitors noted.

"Mr. Osmani, do you love Americans?" the security person asked.

"What kind of question is that?" Raja responded in anger. "Are you trying to insult me because of my nationality?"

Ryan and Niloa sat up intensely at the reaction.

"His lofty persuasive baritone voice sounds just like one of the terrorists I heard in Beirut," Niloa said.

"I apologize, Mr. Osmani. I did not intend to insult you. We are simply being extra careful because of the current threat by terrorists who hate America."

Search his briefcase. Don't let him leave. Ryan wrote back to the officer.

"Mr. Osmani, please put your briefcase through the x-ray machine and you will be able to enter."

Raja thought he had won the battle.

"I'm sorry I became upset," Raja replied. "I am very appreciative of this great country and the opportunity to do business here."

The monitor showed colors around his face indicating he was lying.

"Can you open your briefcase Mr. Osmani?" the security officer asked.

Inside the officer found a set of samples of Persian carpet material samples and a toiletry kit with two cans of shaving cream.

"We must arrest this man," Ryan wrote to the security officer. "Stay calm, but keep the shaving cream away from him. It could be a biological weapon. A team of officers is coming to assist you."

Raja saw the change in the facial expressions of the security officer when he read on his monitor that the man in front of him might have biological weapons. At first he did not know why the officer was typing on the computer. He then noticed the camera pointed at him and figured out that there was some kind of surveillance system in place. *They must have identified me*, he concluded.

Raja looked at his open briefcase on the table three feet from him. The second security officer who was operating the x-ray machine was about to close the briefcase when Raja suddenly lunged forward and grabbed one of the shaving cream cans in the case. He then pulled off the top off in an attempt to activate the pressurized spray nozzle that would emit the contents of the can. Several people waiting in line at the security desk ran for help.

Two Chicago police officers entered the lobby and ran toward the security desk to assist the two officers. Raja, with his briefcase pinned under him, freed his left hand and found a small bottom on the left inside panel of his case. He pressed hard on a hidden button on under the leather exterior. A tremendous explosion blew him and the two security guards off the table, dismembering their bodies and spattering body parts throughout the lobby. Four police officers were killed with Raja, and more than two-dozen other people in the lobby were on the floor injured.

The C-4 plastic explosives hidden in the panel of Raja's briefcase was powerful enough to be heard on several of the trading floors above them and to blow out two of the plate glass windows in the lobby. The two cans in Raja's briefcase were also punctured by the metal parts of the case and sent careening off two of the walls and granite floor of the lobby, spewing deadly botulinum toxin throughout the room. Fine botulinum particles mixed with dust from the explosion were sucked into the building's ventilation system and began to infiltrate the 10-story trading floors of the Mercantile Exchange above them.

The more than 2,400 people in the building tried not to panic after they heard the explosion, but it was difficult to stay calm. Dozens twisted their ankles running down the stairwells. The gruesome scene overwhelmed those who encountered the lobby. Body parts were strewn across the floor and blood was splattered on the walls and pillars.

Those who heard the explosion and who saw the carnage in the lobby believed that terrorists had struck with a bomb. No one but the police realized that the real attack was from the botulinum toxin that had been released. Before the building could be evacuated, more than 1000 people were exposed to the toxin and some 450 would become sick during the week with nausea, vomiting, gastrointestinal distress, and blurred vision. Most of those who checked themselves into hospitals had difficulty speaking, seeing, and/or swallowing. Among those patients, 12 of them suffered severe muscle paralysis and died from lung and heart failure.

Another 35 people were seriously injured in the mad rush to exit the building. Many of those running down the stairwells remembered the World Trade Center collapse and panicked in an effort to escape. Very few people took the elevators down, although they were perfectly safe. Fortunately, Raja never made it to the trading floors where he had intended to plant the weapons with timer devices. If he had, the fatalities could have numbered into the thousands.

Joshua Ryan and the other five men on his commando team entered the ground floor of the Sears Tower dressed in street clothes but equipped with concealed automatic weapons to prevent panic. Two of the men stayed in the lobby to cover the stairwells. They felt it was unlikely that Mansur would try to run down 45 flights of stairs. They could not possibly cover the 103 elevators in the building, but focused on six elevators that went to the 45th floor. They put four of the elevators out of service and then traveled in pairs in the remaining two elevators up to the 45th floor. Calvin Hess knew they were coming, and Mansur's appointment was almost over.

When Joshua and three of his men reached the 45th floor, Mansur was just emerging from his sales appointment. He noticed that Calvin Hess was waiting for him. Mansur smiled at Hess, and said "Good Morning" with a loud voice, simultaneously uncovering a tiny spray nozzle from the side of his briefcase. Hess pulled his handgun from inside his holster hidden by his suit coat but it was too late. Mansur had swung the briefcase forward, toward his face, and had sprayed a chemical agent that struck him in both eyes. The secretary screamed as she saw Hess crumpled to the floor in intense pain. Mansur stepped around him and ran out of the office toward the elevator.

Joshua stepped off the elevator first and saw Mansur heading toward them. He commanded Mansur to stop and lay down. Mansur kept coming. Josh's father had told him on the way about the bomb in the Chicago Mercantile Exchange. Joshua and his men immediately hit the floor as Joshua fired his handgun twice. Mansur fell backward as one bullet pierced his left arm and a second bullet pierced his left shoulder. The wound to his arm caused him to drop his briefcase. Joshua knew that Mansur might have had powerful plastic explosives in his briefcase, but at the same time he did not want to kill him since he had information about other possible terrorist attacks in progress.

Joshua's decision proved to be the right one. Had he waited another second, Mansur would have been close enough to kill Joshua and the other three men with him with the C-4 he was about to detonate in his case. He was unable to reach the detonation trigger.

Joshua immediately gave the order to evacuate the 110-story building, beginning with the top floors and working their way down. It was an enormous task. It would be nearly impossible to find where Mansur might have hidden canisters of toxin before they were set to detonate, or how many canisters, if any, he might have set.

The building was completely evacuated before noon. The two canisters of botulinum that Mansur had planted began emitting their contents on the 50th and 5th floors at 11:30 a.m. Only 46 people received enough exposure to become sick, and none of these died, although four did suffer severe muscle paralysis and impaired vision. Niloa's identification of Mansur had saved the lives of thousands of people in that building. It could have been as disastrous as the World Trade Center attack had no one known about the botulinum released in the building. Office workers would have been exposed to the botulinum toxin throughout the day. The average incubation period of the toxin is 12 to 72 hours after ingestion, and up to eight days for some people. Thus no one would have known until it would have been too late for hundreds or perhaps thousands of people. The long incubation period is one reason why this toxin, the single most poisonous substance known, is such a deadly biological weapon that Dr. Jack Castellona had feared.

Ryan and his counter-terrorism task force, with Niloa's help and Joshua's experienced terrorism commando team, had foiled two disastrous attacks. Deputy Police Superintendent Ryan and the Chicago Police Departmentdid not know how many more attacks were still planned, how many more terrorist were in the city, and how many more biological weapons existed.

Chapter 23
Chicago, Illinois

Colonel Siefer received a call from Dan Ryan at 10:45 a.m.

"We're under siege, Matt," Ryan said, distraught yet not panicked. Ryan explained how they had evacuated the Sears Tower in the first attack and about the explosion that had taken place at the Chicago Mercantile Exchange Building.

"I've been watching it on CNN and Fox," Siefer replied.

"We haven't identified what it is yet," Ryan continued. "We're testing for botulinum based on the information you provided from Israel. Whatever it is, it can kill you."

Siefer asked Ryan if he had contacted the CDC in Atlanta yet. He had. They were sending two scientists on the next available flight to Chicago and asked some of their research scientists in the Chicago area to provide immediate assistance. The CDC scientists were due in at 2:45 p.m.

The public health officials and scientists at the University of Chicago also suspected botulinum based on the symptoms of those who were heavily exposed to the substance. Specially trained police in protective gear were dispatched to collect air samples from the lobby of the both buildings, which would then be taken to a lab for analysis, a process that could take many hours.

"So, one terrorist is dead and one was wounded and is in custody?" Siefer asked.

"Yes," Ryan confirmed. "I've contacted the FBI and asked it to come and handle the interrogation."

"That's fine, Dan. I'm glad you're following the procedures outlined by the Office of Homeland Security. Please ask the FBI interrogator to call me before he begins the interrogation. We've got to find out if any more attacks are planned."

"Dan, I heard back from Rome. Two of the terrorists, Mansur Shukarian, who you have in custody, and Raja Osmani, who was killed, were seen meeting with a third man in Rome whom we believe is also in Chicago. We know he is called Sudani by his friends, but don't know much about him. We don't have a good picture of him but have already sent what we have by email to your office. Assume he is there and that he is also planning attacks. We think he may be the man who illegally entered the country in Sodus Point, New York."

"I'll let you know, Matt, as soon as we catch him," replied Ryan.

Colonial Siefer immediately contacted Bobby Summers in the Homeland Security Office.

"Bobby, let me update you on the two terrorists who launched these attacks in Chicago."

"I've been watching CNN, Matt. They say one is dead and you have one in custody?"

"That's correct. The leader of the TRRT (Terrorism Rapid Response Team) that I sent to Chicago to assist Deputy Superintendent Ryan wounded one terrorist in the Sears Tower before he could blow himself up. The FBI office in Chicago is sending interrogators. Dan Ryan, the Deputy Superintendent of the Chicago Police Department overseeing the city's counter-terrorism force, wants the FBI to have approval to use every legal method of interrogation at its disposal, including sodium penathol, if necessary. There may be thousands of lives at risk, Bobby."

"Is he an American citizen?" Summers asked.

"He claims he is an Italian citizen and carries an Italian passport," Siefer replied.

"I'd better ask the President and obtain some legal advice," Summers concluded. "Tell Ryan and the FBI I'll get back to them on this question as soon as I can, Matt."

"Thank you, Senator," Matt replied.

"Thank you, Colonel," the Head of Homeland Security responded.

Bobby Summer's administrative assistant walked into his office.

"Sir, Silvia Spencer of the FBI is on hold on line two. She's been holding for three minutes and said it's urgent."

"Thank you, Janice, put her through."

Senator Summers greeted Spencer warmly and immediately asked about the terrorist in custody.

"Have you begun talking to him?" Summers asked.

"Yes, his wounds were not as serious as first thought. One bullet broke a bone in his left forearm and a second bullet pieced through his left shoulder. Neither one damaged any main arteries. We took him to the Cook County hospital, set his arm in a cast, and bandaged his shoulder. We're still at the hospital, using one of its observation rooms. Agent Wes Babbington has been talking with him for six or seven minutes now. I'm in the observation room, which is why I am talking very softly. He is not telling us much. He indentifies himself as Mansur Shukarian, which also matches his ID. He said he is a businessman from Italy and sells Persian rugs and wall hangings. He regularly travels to and from Turkey and London from his home in Italy. Apparently he had a sales appointment in the Sears Tower, which we confirmed. He adamantly denies having any knowledge about the release of toxins in the Sears Tower."

"Do we have any hard evidence he is a terrorist?" Summers asked.

"He nearly blinded one of our detectives who was trailing him with a chemical agent?' Spencer exclaimed. "We can arrest him on assault; but we do not have hard evidence that he is a terrorist unless we can physically connect him to the toxin. And we still haven't even found the source of the toxin in the building."

"How are you planning to interrogate him?"

"Sir, Niloa Stephenson, one of the women held hostage by the Hamas in Beirut, is working surveillance with Ryan and his team here. She said she believes she saw Mansur in Beirut, although she was blindfolded and only had a partial look at him; but she did hear him speak and remembers hearing his name. She also recalls seeing a box of shaving cream canisters arriving at the house where she was held. They were the same type of canisters that released the toxin in the Chicago Mercantile Exchangethat were seen in Raja Osmani's briefcase before he blew himself up. I believe her, Colonel."

"At the cost of your career if you are wrong?" Summers asked. "You know the Islamic community has had enough of false arrests without hard evidence. They are angry and they will sue the next time it happens."

Spencer paused; an awkward few seconds of silence passed. "I trust her judgment, Colonel," she finally replied.

"OK, I'll find out from the President what you can do," Summers replied, encouraging her to keep up the psychological pressure.

Five minutes passed. Agents Babbington and Spencer learned Mansur had a family in Lebanon. Mansur said his parents and an older brother didn't like him traveling to the U.S. after September 11 because of the mistreatment of Middle Easterners. Spencer doubted his truthfulness. She guessed that his family disapproved of his terrorist activities. He was not going to say anything about any other planned attacks. Valuable time was slipping by. Both Babbington and Spencer were getting frustrated. They needed to know if more botulinum canisters were in the city; and if so, they had to know where they were planted.

Sudani traveled west on I-290 heading out of the city toward O'Hare Airport. Before the airport, however, he had an important stop to make. He exited the freeway onto the East-West toll way toward Aurora, and got off at Cermak Road. Oakbrook Center was easy to find. The mall was already crowded by 11:00 a.m. Another busy shopping day was getting started during the fall shopping season.

He parked in the central parking area and proceeded to the center mall opening. He immediately noticed all the colorful Halloween decorations strung from the ceiling, which they were replacing with Christmas decorations. A small group of girls came into view as they were greeting customers with boxes of leftover Halloween candy they were selling at the entrance for a local fundraiser. He passed several people, including a young mother with two small children holding candy canes, a group of teenage girls walking arm and arm giggling, a grandfather with his tired grandson on his shoulders, draping his hands and arms over his grandfather's head.

Everyone Sudani passed seemed to be happy. Very few of them had heard about the attacks at the Sears Tower and the Chicago Mercantile Exchange. He walked into the food court after traveling up the escalator to the second floor. It was half full but bustling with activity. Sudani saw about a dozen mothers with their young children.

I can't do this, he thought.

He then verbalized to himself, "I cannot do this."

He struggled to visualize the women and children killed by Israelis commandos whom he had seen on the training films while at camp. He tried to convince himself that innocent Muslims die in the Middle East every day.

Perhaps, he thought, *but not by my hand. I will not target women and young children.*

Everyone was counting on him to carry out his assignment. The food court in the mall was a perfect target. There were many people in the area. Sudani simply could not justify the target initially selected. He walked up to the Taco Bell counter and ordered a burrito and medium Dr. Pepper. This was one American establishment Sudani appreciated—Taco Bell. He liked the fast food, although his favorite was authentic Mexican cuisine, which he would definitely miss.

Sudani was precise in everything he did. He checked his Landjager Rural-Policeman Swiss-made watch as he sat down at a table. It was now 12:05—he had to make a decision soon. It then occurred to him – a perfect place—why didn't he think about it before? The mall had a Loews Cineplex with eight screens. He left his table quickly and walked to the end of the mall where the theater was. He checked the shows and times and ratings.

"Good," he said out loud.

Sudani saw that two R-rated films were playing, one beginning at 4:15, and the second beginning at 4:30. He knew there would be no children allowed at those showings. Another PG-13 film was playing at 4:40 p.m. All three were the first film showings of the day. Sudani walked up to the ticket office. It was closed. The tickets did not go on sale until 3 p.m. That was too late. He needed to be at O'Hare by then.

Sudani spotted a janitor—a high school teenager who had just started his noon shift. His name Dason was on his uniform.

"Excuse me, young man," Sudani said, walking up to the teenage. "I'm wondering if you can help me?"

Dason looked up and smiled. Sudani looked like a sharp businessman.

"Last night," Sudani continued, "my wife lost a large diamond in her wedding ring. We don't know for sure, but we think she might have lost it in the movie theatre. I realize the theaters are cleaned after every movie, but a stone might not get swept up. If I find it I will surely reward you."

"Go ahead and look." Dason replied. "The theaters are open and I'll turn the lights on for you. Which theater were you in?"

"I'm not sure, but I think either theater 5 or 7," Sudani replied.

Sudani entered theater 5 and carefully placed a canister underneath the seat in the center of the theater. He then placed another canister in the same location in theater 7. Dason was waiting for him outside theater 7.

"Any luck?" Dason asked.

"No, I'm afraid not." Sudani replied.

"Were these same films that are playing today also playing in these same theaters last night?" Sudani asked Jason.

"I think so" Dason replied. "What did you see?"

"I don't remember the title, but it was a PG-13 rated film. Let me go check the title again." Sudani said as he walked toward the corridor entrance and back toward the box office.

Sudani scanned the movie titles. The Hunted was playing in theater 4.

"We saw The Hunted in theatre 4," Sudani recalled. "See, it's PG-13."

Dason paused a moment. He thought it was odd that Sudani could not remember the name of the film. It was one of the most popular films of the season with a memorable cast.

"Let's go look," Dason said.

"I don't want to trouble you, young man, by asking you to scrounge around the isles with me. If you can just get the lights, I'll go have a look," Sudani said.

Sudani was able to plant the third canister without Dason's notice. Dason saw Sudani put his wallet back into his back pocket.

"No diamond?" Dason asked.

"No diamond," Sudani responded. "But I did find this," he said as he revealed a $20 bill folded in his hands.

Mansur handed the bill to Dason, saying, "It's yours, son. Thanks for letting me look."

Sudani smiled and said, "Maybe it fell out in the car somewhere. We'll find it someday."

"I hope you do," the teen replied. "So you like Tommy Lee Jones?"

"Who is that?" Sudani asked.

"The star of The Hunted," Dason replied.

"Yes, of course," Sudani said sheepishly.

It was obvious to Dason that Sudani either did not see the film or was drunk or asleep when he did.

He then unexpectedly asked Sudani, "And if someone finds the diamond later, how can we contact you?"

Sudani took out a business card from the inside pocket and gave it to Dason.

"I travel a lot," Sudani said, "So you can best reach me by email." Sudani smiled nervously and proceeded to the central exit doors. He felt good about the decision he had made, but hoped Dason was not still on his shift when the canisters were timed to discharge. Sudani found his way back on the Interstate. It was now 2:00 p.m. He had one more target before leaving the country.

Silvia Spencer finally received the call she was waiting for from Colonel Siefer, who had heard from the Office for Homeland Security.

"The President has authorized the use of sodium penathol," but no physical abuse," Siefer instructed. "Remember the prison scandal in Iraq, and remember the heat we are taking at Guantanamo Bay."

"You can use lights, sleep depravation, harsh words, nonverbal gestures, and one or two shots of sodium penathol, but that's all. Most importantly, you need to formally place him under arrest for suspected terrorism."

"Yes, Colonel," Spencer responded. "I clearly understand your guidelines, we did arrest him and read him his rights. The sodium penathol should be all we need. Thank you, sir, and thank the senator for going to bat for us."

"One more thing, Spencer."

"Yes, sir..."

"Pray to God that this man is the terrorist who planted those canisters. If we have the wrong man, we both are in deep ...."

"You don't have to say it, Colonel," Spencer interrupted. "I understand the gravity of the situation. I believe we'll have a confession during the interrogation."

"It won't be usable in a court of law," Siefer replied.

"I know," Spencer responded, "But it'll cover us and demonstrate we took the proper course of action."

After the brief conversation, Wes Babbington returned to the interrogation room with a nurse.

"We're going to give you a shot to calm your nerves," he said to Mansur. "It will help you relax. We don't want to keep you here longer than is necessary. There's been a terrible tragedy and we just want to find out what you know about it. A few more detailed questions should clear this up."

Mansur took a deep breath and tried to relax. He realized he could not lose his composure. He still had to travel to Midway Airport. The realization that one way or another, it would all be over soon, comforted him. They would find out he had planted the botulinum, or they would hold him long enough to find his car rental, trace it back to Midway, and link him to the attack at the Midway Airport.

He was glad that he had decided to plant his other two canisters at Midway earlier in the morning. They were set to go off at 6:00 p.m., 1 hour, 10 minutes after Raja's 4:50 p.m. scheduled flight from O'Hare and 50 minutes after his flight out of Midway. Mansur had not yet heard that Raja had died at the Chicago Mercantile Exchange. By 6:00 p.m., Mansur had hoped that Sudani would be driving to Michigan on I-94, heading toward a small town where he had a boat waiting to take him to Canada.

Mansur encouraged himself with the thought that they might release him due to insufficient evidence. He was glad to see that detective Hess, who had also come to the interrogation, suffered no permanent damage to his eyes. He had to keep calm and continue to play the role of a businessman who was mistaken for a terrorist due to his ethnicity.

Mansur felt complete peace as the drug began to take effect, almost as if he had entered another world. He thought about his parents, his older brother who couldn't understand him, his former girlfriend who would not marry a man who would commit violence against innocent people.

Agent Babbington began the questioning again.

"Tell me about your day, Mansur. Start from the beginning, in your hotel room this morning."

"Tell you again?" he asked.

"Yes, I just want to make sure I understand," Babbington replied.

"I woke up at 7:00 a.m. and checked out of my hotel," Mansur began. Then I drove to the Midway Airport nearby.

Spencer whispered into Babbington's earphone, "Wes, he stayed at a hotel near O'Hare, not Midway."

"Mansur, didn't you check into the Holiday Inn near O'Hare Airport last night?"

"Yes, I did."

"And when did you check out?"

At 1:00 a.m."

"Then what did you do?"

"Then I drove to the Holiday Inn Hotel at Midway Airport and checked into the Holiday Inn."

"Do you remember what time you arrived there?"

"Yes, I arrived at about 1:45 a.m." Mansur replied.

"Why did you change hotels, Mansur?"

"That was part of the plan."

"And what did you do when you checked out of the second hotel?" Babbington asked.

"I checked out at about 7:15 a.m."

"Then what did you do?"

"Then I took the hotel shuttle to the airport."

"What did you do at the Midway Airport?"

"I had some things to drop off," Mansur said.

"Do you mean canisters, Mansur?" Babbington asked with great concern.

"No on can know but me," Mansur answered.

"You can talk to yourself Mansur. It is OK. It will still be a secret. Where did you put the canisters?" Babbington asked. "In the airport," Mansur said, "But they are safe."

Spencer realized that Babbington needed to change tact. Mansur was communicating true statements but was still not volunteering all the information. She gave Babbington a new line of questions.

"Mansur, are there any canisters on the 1st floor?" Babbington asked.

"No," Mansur said.

"Are both canisters on the 2nd floor?"

"Yes," he responded again.

"So there are only two canisters at Midway?"

"Yes," he answered softly.

"Are the canisters on the floor or in the ceiling?"

"No," he answered.

"Are they in the walls?"

"No, not in the walls."

"Are they on posts," Babbington said, growing in frustration.

"No, not on posts."

"Mansur, would you like some cold water?" Babbington asked.

"Yes, I would."

Spencer had some ice water brought in. She realized Mansur was trained to evade questions and not volunteer information. The relaxation produced by the sodium penathol helped him to answer openly, but did not cause him to give the detailed information they needed.

Babbington felt like he was playing the game "20 questions," which his family played on cross-country car trips when he was a boy. "Is it bigger than a bread box?" his mom would ask. "Is it a person?" his sister would ask, and so forth. Babbington was trying to think in those question patterns.

"Mansur, are both of the canisters inside the airport on the second floor where the people go to board their planes?"

"Yes," Mansur confirmed.

"Are the canisters somewhere in the hallways where people are walking?" Babbington asked.

"Yes," Mansur confirmed.

"Are the canisters attached to structures that don't move?"

"No," Mansur answered.

"Did you put the canisters on things that move?"

"Yes," Mansur continued.

"Brilliant," Spencer whispered. "These guys are very bright."

"Ask him about the carts," Spencer nearly shouted into Babbington's earphone in excitement.

"Mansur, did you attach the canisters to the carts that are driven to carry people through the airport."

"Yes," Mansur said. "They are safely on the carts."

"Are all the canisters on the carts?"

"Yes," he confirmed a second time. Mansur was becoming much more cooperative.

"How did you attach them?" Babbington asked.

"With adhesive," answered Mansur.

"Mansur, what is in the canisters?"

"Toxin."

"What kind of toxin, Mansur?"

"Deadly toxin," he replied.

"Is it botulinum?"

"Yes, but don't tell," he whispered as if telling a secret.

Ryan and his staff, who were also monitoring the interrogation from their surveillance center, realized the speculation of the CDC scientists was correct. Health officials and the CDC were already preparing treatments for botulinum poisoning.

"What time will the canisters begin emitting the toxin?"

"At 6:00 p.m.," he answered.

Spencer looked at her watch. It was almost 3:00 p.m. They had been interrogating Mansur for nearly three hours. Mansur's answers came much more slowly. He was growing weary. Spencer knew they had to find out about all the targets as quickly as possible.

"Ask for the targets," she told Babbington.

"Are there other targets besides the Sears Tower, the Chicago Mercantile Exchange, and Midway airport?" Babbington asked.

"Yes," Mansur said.

"Where are the other targets?"

"I don't know," he answered.

"Mansur, are you sure you don't know the other targets?"

"Yes," he said.

Babbington changed strategies again. They needed precise detail. Spencer felt it was now time to tell him about Raja. She asked Babbington to zero in on the total number of cans and the targets he knew while mixing in the news of Raja's death.

"Mansur, how many canisters are there in total?"

"There are many cans."

"How many?"

"I don't remember," Mansur said faintly.

"More than 10?"

"Yes."

"More than 15?"

"15, yes, 15."

"How many canisters did you have?" Babington pressed on.

"I had four."

"Your friend Raja – how many canisters did he have?"

"Raja only had four, too," Mansur offered.

"Who had the other 7 Mansur? Please try to remember."

"Sudani has the rest. I'm too tired – I have to sleep now."

"We're losing him," said Spencer. "Perk him up. We've got to get the locations."

"Mansur, I am sorry to tell you that your friend Raja died in the Chicago Mercantile Exchange."

"Raja is dead?" Mansur asked. The question gave him a boost of energy.

"Yes, we are sorry. He set off an explosive device in his briefcase before we could save him," Babbington explained. "Do you know where he placed his other two canisters of botulinum?"

"I didn't know his other target. He said something about wanting to see some of the players before he left. He was a good friend."

"Did Raja like basketball?" Babbington inquired.

"He loves basketball," Mansur replied.

Ryan and his staff immediately called the United Center to have the arena evacuated.

"What are the other targets, Mansur?"

"I just know my targets," he answered. "I don't know all the others."

"Are there other people working with you besides Raja?" Babbington asked.

"Only Sudani," Mansur said. "You will never catch Sudani. He is too smart; too smart."

"How many canisters does Sudani have?"

"He has the rest of them," he responded.

"So, you had four, Raja had four, and Sudani has seven?"

"Yes," Mansur replied.

"So, you and Raja were placing two canisters of botulinum in each place?" Babbington asked.

"Yes," Mansur confirmed.

"And your other friend, Sudani, has seven cans?"

"I don't know. He has the rest."

"Where was Sudani placing his cans Mansur?"

"I don't know his targets."

"Is he flying out?" Babbington asked.

"Yes, this evening."

"Which airport, Mansur?"
"O'Hare."
"Is O'Hare a target?"
"I don't know."
"Are all the attacks planned for today?"
"Yes," Mansur replied sleepily. He was nearly dosing off now. The stress of the interrogation and effects of the sodium penathol were putting him to sleep.
"One last question Mansur. What times were all these canisters set to release the toxin?"
"After 6:00."
"All of them after 6 tonight?"
"Yes."
"Why are they all set for after 6?"
"We were all leaving by 6:00," he barely responded. "The others will go off after we leave. I need to leave now," Mansur said with his eyes closed, forgetting where he was. "I must go home now."

Babbington took a deep breath and exhaled deeply as he closed his own eyes. They had recovered two canisters at the Sears Tower and two canisters exploded at the Chicago Mercantile Exchange. Two cans were on the moving carts at Midway. The United Center and O'Hare airport were probably two more likely targets. That left one more unknown target and 11 more canisters to recover before the end of the day.

Ryan and Niloa were listening intently to the interview. They guessed that two more canisters where designated for O'Hare Airport. They had no idea where the remaining four canisters were placed. Raja must have hid two other canisters, possibly in a sports arena like the United Center.

"Perhaps he did not set them up yet," Ryan thought.

"Or," Josh reasoned, "he could have set them early before he went to the Chicago Mercantile Exchange."

Joshua had to talk with Niloa immediately. She might remember some details that would help them find the last terrorist.

CHAPTER 24
Cebu City, Philippines

Stephano put his pen down again. He tried hard not to cry, but tears dripped onto the letter he struggled to write. In a very short time he had grown to love Niloa. He dreamed about marrying her, leaving the Philippines, and beginning a new life in Hawaii. He looked up at the coconut palms swaying in the evening breeze from the front lanai of his parents' home. The sun was setting across the island, reflecting off the clouds that stretched across the Cebu Sea toward Bohol. Stephano believed it would be difficult to find a place more beautiful than the southern Philippines; and he sensed there were no people warmer or more hospitable to be found anywhere in the world.

He knew Hawaii would be beautiful, but feared American culture would be overpowering, cluttered, and harsh at times. He would hate to leave the simplicity of life he could finally enjoy here.

Stephano was torn. His friend Paulo had risked his life for him many times. He was now wounded and his family needed help. It was Paulo who had told Niloa numerous stories about him. Without Paulo, Niloa would never had even met Stephano or become interested in him as much as she had. Although Paulo also had been attracted to Niloa, he remained faithful to his bride to be, even before they were officially engaged. He could have no better friend than Paulo. They talked about running a business together, raising their children together, and watching their grandchildren grow up in peace. They both carried a new vision for the Philippines in their hearts. He would ask himself over and over, how could he leave his friend and that vision?

Talking to his parents had helped him to make this difficult choice. He knew what was right, but he didn't know how to tell Niloa without hurting her. Stephano looked down at the first sentence. "Dear Niloa, I am looking out across the Cebu Sea right now, at my parents' house, missing you terribly and making the most painful decision in my life." He picked up his pen and began writing again. "Tears are streaming down my face because of the call I must answer, a call I must answer alone right now."

Two hours and ten minutes later Stephano finished the letter and sealed it in an envelope. He had poured out his heart to Niloa, holding nothing back. He would mail it to her at her parents' address the next morning, via Federal Express, after making a copy for himself. He knew Niloa had been safely rescued, but he had no idea she was in the midst of another battle. Had he known, he would have waited to send the letter.

Joshua Ryan called his father and asked to speak to Niloa.

"I'll put you on speaker phone, Josh, so we can all hear you in the command center."

"Thanks, Dad, that'll be good. I was in the observation room with Silvia Spencer. So I saw the whole interrogation of Mansur."

"Niloa," Joshua said. "Did you hear the whole interview with Mansur?"

"Yes," Niloa replied.

"Then you heard the shaving cream canisters you saw in Beirut have been filled with a deadly botulism toxin. Mansur said there were 15 cans, but he could have been lying."

"Isn't the sodium penathol supposed to make him tell the truth?" Niloa asked.

"Actually Niloa," detective Martin chimed in before Joshua could tactfully answer, "sodium penathol does not cause people to tell the truth. It just helps people to relax and talk openly so the truth is more likely to come out. There is a common myth that it is a 'truth serum,' but it really cannot prevent people from lying."

Joshua was grateful. He did not want to embarrass Niloa and Martin had the heart of a teacher.

"I'm beginning to like this police work," Niloa replied. "I'm learning there's a big difference between the reality of what you do and the Hollywood ideas that have created this fantasy in my mind."

"Niloa," Josh continued, "can you think of any conversations that you overheard in Beirut, anything at all, that might give us a clue as to what might be some other targets?"

"They usually spoke Arabic, Joshua, when they didn't want us to understand," Niloa said.

"Is there anything about America they talked about in English? Anything at all, Niloa?"

"Joshua, I need a few minutes of solitude to think. I'll call you right back in a couple of minutes."

Time was running out. It was now 3:20 p.m. Niloa went into a quiet room on the floor above the command center and closed her eyes. She tried desperately to remember. Most of the time the men ridiculed them in English. She visualized them talking. Then she saw the picture: one of the terrorists with a Michael Jordan T-shirt and another with an Arnold Schwarzenegger T-shirt. Niloa left the room abruptly and called Joshua.

"Joshua, I remember something that stuck out to me. Two of the terrorists asked us lots of questions about American lifestyles, like what Americans like to do for fun and what big cities they like to visit. They did ask us about Chicago and about Michael Jordan, although they realized that he now helps run the front office for the Washington Wizards. I remember I was amazed by how much they seemed to hate America but like some of its popular culture. They occasionally wore American T-shirts. I remember two in particular: Michael Jordan and Arnold Schwarzenegger. The terrorists like American basketball and American films."

"Sports complexes and theaters," Joshua replied. "That confirms Mansur's hint that they planned to attack a basketball arena, probably the United Center."

"The United Center makes sense," said Niloa. "But there must be hundreds of movie theaters in the Chicago area."

"We must go to the news media again," Joshua replied. "Niloa, you might have just saved thousands of lives."

"We shouldn't rule out shopping malls either," Niloa added. "The terrorists despise American materialism. They think we are opulent and wasteful."

Dan Ryan immediately set up a news conference to be simulcast on all network stations and cable networks. He sent Joshua and his team to O'Hare airport, one SWAT team to the United Center, and a second SWAT team to Midway airport. They had only found four of the 15 canisters of botulism toxin in the city, if, indeed, there were only 15. Based on the information provided by Mansur, they believed that two were planted at Midway, two at the United Center, and two at O'Hare. That left five more canisters that they had no idea where to find, except in theaters or maybe shopping malls. But the Chicago subway system was also an inviting target.

Ryan arranged his second news conference of the day to begin at 4 p.m., giving media outlets just 40 minutes to get their camera crews to the steps of the police station.

"Ladies and gentlemen," Ryan shared soberly after some preliminary remarks, "I want to provide you an update from my news conference before lunch. We have credible information that there may be more biological terrorist assaults planned in the city. We strongly suspect that movie theaters and transportation hubs are likely targets. The underground subway system must be considered as being vulnerable to attack. We also must consider the safety of our shopping malls."

Ryan hated making that statement, knowing that it could cost merchants millions of dollars of lost revenues.

"We have captured one terrorist and another is dead. However, we believe at least one terrorist is still at large, and maybe more. We ask you to calmly consider vacating public areas until the threat is abated."

Ryan had asked the mayor to consider closing the two airports and the United Center, but even the mayor had no mechanism for closing down all the theaters in town. The city government also did not have the authority to mandate the closing of shopping areas. Mall owners were particularly reluctant to close, since it was one of the profitable shopping days of the year. There also were no credible threats against the malls. The mayor decided against closing down all public buildings without specific threats, but immediately put a group together to decide what should be shut down.

Oakbrook Center, one of the most popular malls in the state, was one of the public shopping centers caught in the middle. The manager thought about closing the theaters but decided to keep them open, since many parents shopped while their children watched movies.

Dason McKonkey walked into the kitchen just as he noticed his mother fixated on the news conference on television.

"What's up, Mom?" Dason asked.

"Didn't you hear about the terrorist attacks this morning?" Cherrie asked. "Now they think there's another target. The police just gave a news conference. They said that the airports, subways, sports arenas, and movie theaters may be possible targets.

"Movie theaters?" Dason asked.

"Yes, I'm glad you're off work. I don't want you near a movie theater."

Dason walked into the living room and began watching. It was 4:15 p.m.

"Oh, my God, Mom!" Dason said, panicking as he looked at the sketches on television of eight possible terrorists that may be in the area. "I saw a Middle Eastern man who looked similar to one of those sketches in the theater. It was just after lunch. He said his wife had lost a diamond in her ring, so I let him in three of the eight theaters to look for it," he explained.

"We need to call the police immediately," Cherrie exclaimed.

Ryan took the call from Cherrie at 4:20 p.m. The first movie of the afternoon would be beginning in ten minutes. Police units began converging on the large mall five minutes later. They immediately proceeded to the Loews Cineplex and began evacuating the eight movie viewing rooms.

The first canister in theater five began quietly releasing botulism toxin at 4:45 p.m. Fortunately, almost everyone had been evacuated, but two teenagers went back inside to retrieve their coats that they had left in haste. Within an hour, they were both in the hospital fighting for their lives.

The canister in theater seven was found by special police units in protective masks about five minutes later. It had not yet detonated. The can was attached with a magnet to the metal support structures of one of the seats in the middle of the theater. Theater 5 was filled with the deadly toxin when the police entered. The canister was still releasing toxin when they found it, also attached to the metal seat support. Both canisters were placed in solid metal cases with the double-sided rubber rings that made them airtight. The box was given to officials from the CDC for analysis.

Cherrie drove Dason to police headquarters so he could meet with Ryan and the terrorism task force. Dason provided a police artist with a description of the terrorist. Niloa looked at the drawing carefully. She did not recognize Sudani.

"Did he have a French accent?" Niloa asked Jason.

"He did sound European, but I don't know if he was French or not," Dason answered.

"It could be 'the captain,'" Niloa said. "The captain must be Sudani. I never heard the name Sudani spoken out loud in Lebanon, but I think they talked about him as *the Captain*."

"Well, whoever he is," Joshua noted, "he is heading for another target and has at least two more canisters of botulinum."

Fans were already pouring into United Center to watch the Chicago Bulls play the Washington Bullets when a specially trained police unit arrived to check the arena. More than 20,000 fans were expected to turn out for the game, most to see Michael Jordan honored in the arena where he had won six NBA championships. A few minutes after the teams arrived, the call came to evacuate the stadium after Ryan informed the mayor of the magnitude of the potential catastrophe. There was simply no practical way to find two seven-ounce canisters that could be hidden under any two of 21,711 seats in the arena.

The mayor made the right decision. Before attacking the Chicago Mercantile Exchange, Raja had entered the United Center on the previous evening. At the end of the Bulls game he had duct taped the two canisters to the bottoms of two seats close to the playing floor. The canisters were timed to begin emitting botulism at 7 p.m. By 5:45 p.m. there were already six to eight thousand people in the building. Police officer Mike Flannigan found one of the canisters at 6:25 p.m. in section 101 near center court.

The second canister in section 3 was on the opposite side of the court. Fireman Jamal Strahan found that canister 20 minutes later, just 15 minutes before it would begin releasing toxin into the arena. Strahan had a specialized gas mask that protected him from the toxin. He pulled the can off one of one of the seats, wrapped its top in duct tape to prevent any release of gas, and placed it in an upright plastic container. Thousands of fans and two sports teams were saved from botulism poisoning because of the decisive action of Ryan and the mayor.

Sudani drove north on I-294 after leaving the mall and entered O'Hare Airport. Joshua and his team arrived with Niloa shortly after he did. Sudani did not realize that authorities were already expecting him to try to place canisters on the airport passenger transport carts. They did not know, however, which terminal Sudani would target. Joshua placed two of his men in terminal one, two in terminal two, and he and Niloa went to terminal three. His father placed six plain-clothed detectives in each terminal to drive the electric passenger carts.

Sudani limped into terminal three with a briefcase and one carry-on bag. He was scheduled to depart to Detroit on an American Airlines flight where he had reservations on an international flight to London. Because he had no check-in bags and an electronic ticket, he planned to get his boarding pass at the gate.

None of the terrorism task force security team saw him enter the terminal. Although Ryan had placed one of his detectives at each security checkpoint with the sketch that was created from his sighting at the Oakbrook Mall Cinemas, he was not recognizable at the checkpoint. No one at the time realized that Sudani was wearing two-inch heels on his boots, a fake mustache, a wig, and make-up at the mall, making him look taller and younger. Sudani was actually partially bald and clean-shaven, like the picture in his passport.

Niloa and Joshua acted as passengers waiting on the passenger carts. Niloa's driver took her up and down the L and K gates and Joshua's driver took him up and down the H and G gates. Niloa received a call on her two-way airport communication system from Joshua.

"Niloa, I spotted a Middle Eastern man at the entrance of the K and H gates. He is between gate K2 and H3. He is standing there and might be looking for a cart. Can you pick him up?" Joshua asked.

"Yes, I'm at gate L2 and will be there in a minute," Niloa answered.

Niloa directed her driver to Sudani, who hobbled onto the passenger cart.

"Thank you," Sudani said to the driver, who was actually Chicago police detective Victor Majkowski. "I hurt my leg in the gym the other day—pulled my hamstring."

"You're welcome," Majkowski replied. "What is your gate number?"

"H18," Sudani responded.

Niloa immediately struck up a conversation with Sudani. He did not look familiar and Sudani gave no indication that he recognized Niloa. In fact, Niloa was sure she had never seen him. But there were times she was blindfolded and interrogated by various terrorists. Sudani's voice sounded very familiar, but she had not heard Sudani in Beirut. Finally, she remembered.

"Sir," Niloa asked, "you sound very familiar to me. Have you ever been in Syria?"

Sudani thought it was just a coincidence that Niloa looked like one of the women whom they had taken custody of in Syria. He was stunned by the question.

This couldn't possibly be the same person, he thought. *What are the chances of that occurring?*

"Yes, I've been in Syria," Sudani replied. "Have you been there, too?"

"Well, I just passed through, "Niloa responded. "I didn't actually get to see the place," she said, referring to her blindfolded condition.

"Too bad," Sudani responded. "It's a beautiful country." He's dismissed the idea that Niloa might have seen him before.

Once they arrived at the gate, Sudani got off the cart with his briefcase. While slowly climbing down he placed a canister on the side of the cart, attached by a strong magnet. His work was so smooth and the view of the others on the cart was blocked, so that no one realized what Sudani had done.

"Good-bye now," he said to Niloa.

Quickly, Niloa and detective Majkowski searched the cart after they had pulled away from the gate area. Majkowski found the canister affixed to the side of the cart.

Niloa immediately called Joshua.

"He's our man." Niloa said.

Joshua ordered his men into position. "I'm coming to pick him up," Joshua said.

Just as Deputy Ryan was beginning to doubt that they could catch the suspect before he launched another attack, he received a call from Colonel Siefer from Washington.

"Dan, our Italian friends confirm that the suspect you are chasing is a terrorist from Afghanistan by the name of Sudani Zalmai. Niloa's memory of his nickname, *the Captain*, is correct. They confirmed that he was the one who had met with Mansur Shukarian and Raja Osmani in Rome. He is a very intelligent man who knows quickly how to change his appearance."

"Major Ryan's team is closing in on him at the airport," Dan responded.

"Keep me posted, Dan. The President is tracking this closely."

Ryan immediately called Joshua and his team, confirming to them that the suspect they were chasing was Sudani Zalmai, an Afghani national.

Sudani was already standing in the corridor in front of gates 17 and

18, looking for another cart. He still was looking for a second cart to place a canister on.

Joshua arrived on a cart with another police detective posing as a driver. Sudani immediately grew suspicious. He looked like no ordinary passenger, even in plain clothes. Joshua also struck up a conversation with Sudani. Sudani knew he was caught, but kept his cool and determination to place and activate the weapons. He had to get rid of the remaining canisters and exit the airport.

Calmly, Sudani asked his driver to take him to the men's room up ahead. Wisely, Joshua said he needed to make a stop there as well. Joshua was carrying a single crutch and bent his leg slightly. His crutch also doubled as a weapon. While climbing down from the cart, Sudani discreetly attached one of the canisters underneath the cart. Neither Major Ryan nor Detective Strahan could see what he had done.

Sudani entered the handicapped bathroom stall, immediately changed, and attached the canister to the ceiling near an air duct with duct tape. He then put on a full disguise and slipped into the empty stall beside him through the bottom opening. He then vacated that stall and walked past Ryan who was washing his hands and keeping his eye on the door of the handicapped stall.

Sudani said with a perfect British accent, "Sir, there is a man in the stall beside me going up into the ceiling. Should I call security?"

"I'm a security officer," Major Ryan replied. "I'll take care of it."

Sudani exited the bathroom, unrecognizable to Joshua, Niloa and detective Strahan. Joshua went to the stall that Sudani had entered. It was still locked. He knocked on the door and asked if he was all right. There was no response. Joshua looked under the door and saw that the stall was empty. He then kicked the door in, climbed up toward the ceiling and spotted the canister of botulism toxin attached to the air duct. It had already been activated. Joshua held his breathe after he heard the faint sound of the aerosol emitting tiny particles into the air in the bathroom.

Joshua pulled the canister off the vent with his right hand and threw it into the toilet. He then took off his jacket and draped it across the top of the toilet bowl, placed the seat cover on top of his jacket to keep it in place. He then scrambled as fast as he could to get out of the bathroom. It was already too late. He had breathed numerous deadly particles of botulinum. Joshua immediately evacuated both bathrooms and ran to the cart where detective Strahan was waiting.

"Evacuate this terminal immediately," Joshua instructed. "I've breathed some toxin. Get me to the hospital."

Strahan took out their emergency medical kit and gave Joshua a shot just as Niloa arrived in the other cart. Strahan then called the paramedics standing by to take him to the hospital.

"Where's Sudani?" Niloa asked.

"He's escaped somehow," Joshua replied.

"He must have slipped into another stall and disguised himself. We may have lost him. Right now, we need to evacuate terminals," Joshua instructed. "We also need to get that canister in the toilet and stop the toxin emission. Then we need to look for Sudani."

The specially trained firemen were on the scene in five minutes and retrieved the second canister, stopping the city's fifth biological attack that day. Joshua was taken to the hospital to receive emergency treatment for botulinum poisoning. Niloa accompanied him to the hospital. Although the Chicago police were detaining and questioning all Middle Easterners leaving the airport, Sudani slipped out of the terminal, caught a taxi to the Greyhound station in Chicago and purchased a bus to Lansing, Michigan. Once again, he believed he had divine help to escape. Major Ryan was looking for divine help to stay alive.

CHAPTER 25
Chicago, Illinois

Joshua Ryan opened his eyes. It took almost a minute for him to get his bearings. He saw his father in the corner of the room talking quietly to Niloa. Both of their heads were down. Joshua felt the tubes down his throat and thrust into his nostrils. An IV was implanted in his right arm. Various electronic monitors were connected to his chest by electrodes taped to his skin. His first impulse was a strong desire to rip the tubes out of his mouth and nose, but he gained control of the temporary claustrophobia that had gripped him. He could not speak because of the tubes and an incredibly weak diaphragm.

His thinking ability, however, was intact.

He tried to remember why he was in the hospital. He had no recollection of how he had gotten there. He could feel all his limbs and there were no obvious wounds to his body; but his breathing was more deliberate, not effortless as it should be. Then he remembered seeing the green canister that reminded him of the can of Edge shaving cream in his toiletry kit. He remembered wondering, *What a brilliant idea – to hide a weapon in a can of shaving cream.* Then he recalled hearing the small particles emanate from the top of the can with a quiet, eerie, sound. Immediately he sensed death in the midst, and remembered he had thrown the canister into the toilet before had scrambled to get away from it as fast as he could. But he couldn't scramble fast enough.

Joshua tried to slide his body toward the top of the hospital bed so he could elevate his head on the pillow. The hospital room was unusually large. He focused his eyes on Niloa and his father. They were still talking with their heads down. He could see now that Niloa was crying softly and his father was trying not to cry. *They must think I'm near death,* he thought. They still had not realized that he was conscious, but he had not realized that he was nearly comatose when he was first brought in to the hospital. Joshua again wanted to pull the tubes out of his mouth and nose and shout, *Hey, stop crying you two, I'll be fine!* But he wasn't fine. In fact, he had been one or two inhalations from death.

Beside his desk on his left side Joshua saw a clipboard with a pen attached. He reached out with his left hand and knocked the clipboard on the floor. His father and Niloa jumped up and ran to his bedside.

"Joshua, you're awake!" Niloa shouted.

Yeah, and I hope I'm not dreaming, Joshua thought. Niloa looked very good to him; almost as if he were meeting her for the first time.

Tears welled up in their eyes again as they saw that Joshua was conscious. Joshua reached out his left hand toward the clipboard, and Niloa picked it up and handed it to him. He tried to move his right arm to signal for a pen but it was strapped onto the bed in an immobile position for the IV. He then signaled with his left hand that he wanted to write, and his father handed him a pen and turned over the white medical form so he could write on the blank side of the paper.

In barely legible printing, Joshua wrote, *Thanks. Will be OK. Want out. When?*

Joshua was surprised by how long it took him to write left-handed. Fortunately, he was somewhat ambidextrous. He could throw a football and shoot a basketball fairly accurately with either hand. As he wrote, he felt some strength coming back. Perhaps it was just the psychological euphoria of being able to communicate again.

"He can't talk," Deputy Superintendent Ryan said to Niloa, "but he hasn't lost his strong fighting spirit."

"Joshua," Ryan said slowly, "You have been fighting the effects of Clostridium botulinum, the bacterium you inhaled from the canister in the airport men's room. The neurotoxin paralyzed your respiratory system and nearly killed you. The paramedics injected you with an antitoxin in time to save your life. There have also been many people praying for you, including your grandmother. So death had no chance to win this battle."

"Thanks, Dad," Joshua wrote. "Close, eh?"

Dr. Giovanni entered the room. "I see our patient is finally awake," he said with a booming voice and unmistakable Italian accent. Giovanni checked the various machines monitoring Joshua's heart rate and breathing.

"Looking good!" Major Ryan. "We'll be able to take those tubes out tomorrow if you regain sufficient strength. Right now you ought to get some more rest."

"Son, I need to return to work," his father interjected. "We have one more terrorist to catch. You need to get some rest. I'm going to take Niloa out for breakfast and then I'll be back in the surveillance center."

Joshua picked up the pen and clipboard and wrote, "Not fair! I want breakfast with Niloa!"

Niloa, refusing to be embarrassed as the object of attention, said to his father, "I never realized the full extent of his humor."

"Keep up those spirits," Dr. Giovanni added. "A merry heart doeth good like a medicine."

Niloa then turned to Joshua and said, "Get better Josh, I'll be back."

"I'll wait then," Joshua wrote.

Ryan and Niloa left the hospital room. Dr. Giovanni picked up the clipboard off of Joshua's lab, turned the paper over, and recorded Joshua's vital signs. He then gave Joshua a mild sedative to help him sleep.

"I'll be back too, Major," he said, giving Joshua a look of assurance. "You're going to be fine."

The doctor turned out the light and left the room.

Joshua had a little time to think before the drug took effect. He was puzzled by Niloa's behavior. He had assumed she was not interested in him because of her impending engagement to Stephano. *Perhaps her sympathies were taking over because of my brush with death,* he thought. Joshua didn't want to get involved with someone who was engaged or nearly engaged. He had been on the wrong end of that equation before, and it was not a pleasant experience. After his fiancé had fallen in love with her swimming coach in college while he has off trying to stay alive in Mogadishu, he vowed to himself never to do that to anyone else. It took tremendous self-discipline for Joshua to hide his serious interest in Niloa during their trip to Firenze. He related to Niloa like a sister he had not seen in a long time. *I would like to continue the friendship,* he thought, *even if she does marry Stephano.*

As Joshua drifted into sleep, he remembered how fulfilled he had felt after rescuing Niloa and the other two women who had been held by the Hamas. *She will always remember I saved her life,* he mouthed slowly with his lips. He then fell into a deep sleep.

Ryan took Niloa to an IHOP near the hospital. She had not eaten a solid meal in a couple of days. After they both ordered the international passport: three eggs, three pancakes, three sausages, orange juice and coffee, they resumed their conversation about Joshua.

"He nearly died when he was born," Ryan explained. "The cord was wrapped around his neck three times, cutting off his oxygen."

Ryan explained how his son had grown up as a natural athlete, but how he had wanted to join the military since he was in junior high so he could see the world. He worked his way through the army, becoming a Ranger and then a member of the elite Delta Force. In high school he developed a love for languages, and learned how to speak French and German fluently. He later learned Russian in the army.

When Joshua was 20, he became engaged to a 20-year-old friend in college. His fiancée was a junior in college and training for the Olympic swim team. Ryan explained to Niloa how she had fallen in love with her swimming coach while Joshua had been deployed to Somalia.

"He told me about Keli when we were in Italy," Niloa responded.

"He deeply loved her," Ryan recalled. "He was writing to her every week. Then the fire fight happened."

"Fire fight?" Niloa asked. "He didn't tell me that part."

"Two helicopters were shot down during his mission in Mogadishu, Somalia. One of his friends wrote a book about it and a movie version was made."

"Yeah, *Black Hawk Down*. I remember hearing about it but never saw the movie."

"Several of his close friends were killed, Niloa. When he returned to the U.S., he learned he had also lost his fiancée to another man. The combination of tragic events took a big toll on Joshua. He never expected to lose so many people close to him at once."

"That must have been awful to have lived through that hell in Somalia only to come back and face another loss. How did he handle it?"

"Not very good at first," Ryan answered. "He was deeply depressed for a couple of months. He went through that phase where he wished he had been killed instead of some of his friends. I'd never seen him more down. He finally pursued pastoral counseling, which turned the tide on his depression. He began to actually laugh again. When he began to come out of the hurt of his breakup with Keli, he vowed that he would never get involved in a romantic relationship with a woman who had a competing romantic interest. That's why he wouldn't ever tell you directly how much he cares about you."

"Why wouldn't he tell me?" Niloa asked.

"Because of your close friendship with Stephano. Aren't you getting engaged soon?" Ryan asked.

"No, not at all" Niloa replied. "Stephano and I became very close and we did talk about marriage, but he had a close friend he needed to see whom he had known for many years. Her name is Olivia Pirroco. She had moved to Honolulu to attend the University of Hawaii in Manoa to pursue a nursing degree and an MBA. Her dream was to build several orphanages in the southern Philippines with corporate sponsorships. They were very close friends."

"Did he go and visit her?" Ryan asked.

"Actually, she came home to visit her parents in the Philippines and he spent some time with her in Manila. He then went to his parent's home in Cebu City to talk with them. He wrote me a nine-page letter, a very beautiful letter, from his parents' home. It was the most precious letter I have ever received," Niloa recalled with tears in her eyes.

"He felt he needed to stay in Mindanao and take care of Paulo and his family until Paulo was back on his feet. He also felt he needed to follow the vision he had for rebuilding the island of Mindanao. I was greatly saddened," Niloa said, explaining how she had reacted to the letter. "But I respect him so much for following his vision. I just feel called to more of the world than the southern Philippines."

"Does Joshua know this?" Ryan asked.

"No," Niloa responded, "I never told him. But I don't even understand how he knew about our close friendship in the first place."

Ryan could see that Niloa was perplexed.

"That was not hard to figure out, Niloa," he answered. "When Joshua was in the Philippines he had access to classified information. Stephano was working closely as an operative with the government. The intelligence officers probably knew of his close friendship with you and provided that information to Joshua."

"That explains his behavior!" Niloa reasoned aloud.

"Do you think he has any interest in me?" Niloa asked.

"Niloa, if Joshua knew you weren't about to get engaged, he'd try to get up out of that hospital bed and take you out to dinner tonight," Ryan answered.

"I totally misread him," Niloa responded. "He must think I'm really insensitive and arrogant."

"Quite the opposite, Niloa. Joshua told me you are one of the most caring and self-sacrificing women he has ever known. He said he has met many women adventurers and athletes, and a few women heroines, but most have been self-absorbed and materialistic. Then he even got poetic, saying that your life 'provided a delightful new fragrance.'"

"A new fragrance. He actually said that?"

"I know," Ryan concurred, "Joshua doesn't easily share his feelings, especially in words. And rarely has he uttered anything close to poetic."

"Thanks, Mr. Ryan," Niloa said as they both begin to laugh.

"Niloa, you can call me Mr. Dan. That's what most young people call me, even my nieces and nephews, although I'm their uncle. It's a term of endearment."

"Mr. Dan, you just changed my world. I had no idea Josh was romantically interested in me."

Ryan returned with Niloa to the surveillance room. A statewide hunt was in full progress to capture Sudani, whose picture had been televised throughout the U.S. and Canada. No one believed he was able to leave Chicago by air, since the airport was closed for three hours after his escape from the men's bathroom in terminal 3.

Sudani shivered as the cold winds whipped up the snow flurries in the air as he walked out of the Greyhound bus station. He felt good about outwitting America's best security forces by making them think that he planned on flying out of O'hare. *My diversion worked perfectly*, he proudly thought. He marveled at how easy it was to place his last canister or botulinum on the back of a large metal trash can in the middle of the terminal.

He carefully stepped onto the bus that was taking him to Lansing, Michigan. Wrapped in a heavy winter scarf, a black three-quarter-length wool coat, and a Russian hat, it was difficult to discern Sudani's nationality. He certainly did not look like a terrorist.

CHAPTER 26
Northern Indiana

The bus driver explained that the lake effect snow would only slow them down but would not prevent them from making a safe trip to Lansing. The bus departed the station on time at 8:00 p.m. Sudani looked out the window. Big fluffy snowflakes melted as they struck the window. He was desperately homesick as the bus finally left the city limits of Chicago. Sudani breathed a big sigh of relief. His escape from the airport was nothing short of miraculous. The canister was set to detonate at 9:00 p.m. *Surely God is with me*, he thought, *No one even recognized me at the bus station.*

Ryan received a transferred call at the surveillance center from Christine, who worked at the information hotline.

"Deputy Superintendent Ryan," Christine said. "I have Janice Dolman on the line. She works at the Greyhound bus station downtown. She said she thinks she might have sold a one-way bus ticket to a man who could have been Sudani."

"Put her through," Ryan responded.

"Deputy Ryan, this is Janice Dolman from Greyhound. I just watched a news report and saw a picture of this terrorist named Sudani Zalmai. He looked familiar but I could not place him. Then I remembered a man who came up to the counter at about 7:15 p.m. to buy a ticket to Lansing. I could not tell his nationality, but he did have darker skin and curly hair. He had a mustache that did not look real to me. He could have been southern European, or Latin American, or from the Middle East. He spoke with kind of a French accent. He was very much a gentleman though. I would not have thought twice about him, but I wondered why such a sharply dressed man—he was dressed like an executive—would be taking the Greyhound bus. Then I noticed his mustache looked fake. My brother-in-law sells wigs, false sideburns and false mustaches. It just seemed like one that my brother-in-law sells. Then when I saw the man named Sudani on television; his eyes looked the same."

"You said he purchased a ticket for Lansing, Michigan?"

"That's correct," Janice replied. "The bus left our station at 8:00 p.m. It's about a four hour trip but the snow may slow them down a little bit.

"Just to be clear," Janice stressed again. "I'm not saying I sold a ticket to the terrorist I saw on the news. I am just saying it could have been him except he had a mustache. It could be the two guys looked similar, and that's it."

"What did he say his name was?" Ryan asked.

"I don't know," Janice replied. "There were 46 people on that bus and I sold tickets to every one of them. I'll give you the list; but I don't know who it was."

"Did he use a credit card?" Ryan asked.

"No, he paid cash," Janice responded.

"The first thing you need to do right now, Janice, is to call security and help them to evacuate the bus terminal. Get everyone out of there immediately but try not to create panic. This man may have planted a biological weapon in the terminal. I'll order police units there right after I get off the phone with you."

"Second, we need to track this man down," Ryan continued. "Do you take the names of passengers?"

"We do now. Just started doing it last month—new security procedures."

"Then go through your records in a safe location," Ryan explained, "and mark off all the names of men who paid for their tickets by check or credit card. Then we'll be left with a small group who paid by cash. Look for the name of Mihai Carnea; I doubt that he would use his real name."

"Ok – I'm moving everyone out now," Janice responded. "I'll have that information for you in 30 minutes."

Ryan called Joshua's second in command and arranged for them to fly to Lansing so they could be waiting for the bus at the Lansing station. He then asked Niloa to join them, since she had seen Sudani close up while talking to him in the airport transit cart in O'Hare. Ryan, Niloa, and three men from Joshua's terrorism response team, along with another detective from Ryan's office, arrived at the Lansing Greyhound station 35 minutes before the bus was due to arrive. They each positioned themselves at strategic locations for intercepting Sudani as soon as Niloa identified him coming off the bus.

Four miles before the Greyhound bus reached the Lansing station, Sudani rose from his seat and courteously asked the driver if he could let him off at the next stoplight.

"You would be doing me a great favor," Sudani said. "Since my car rental company is at the next light."

Sudani slipped the driver a $20 bill. The driver was happy to comply with the request.

By the time the bus reached the downtown Lansing station, Sudani was getting his keys from the rental attendant as an Avis Club member.

Joshua's team waited in great anticipation for the sign from Niloa that Sudani was stepping off the bus. With each new male passenger exiting the bus, they became more anxious to move in. The sign never came. Niloa did not recognize any of the men. When the last man exited the bus, Ryan knew they had been fooled again.

He asked the driver if he had dropped off any passengers on the trip from Chicago.

"Just one," the driver answered. "A businessman asked to be dropped off at the Avis car rental place."

"In Lansing?" Ryan asked.

"Yes, it's about four miles away."

Ryan called the Avis rental office. He was eight minutes too late. A man matching the description of the suspect had rented a Buick using the name Dan Isu. His exact route was difficult to determine, but Ryan believed he was heading to Canada. Ryan then received a call from Janice at the Greyhound ticket office. None of the four men who paid cash for their tickets had a Middle Eastern surname. Janice read their names to Ryan: Jerry Tarkinton, Robert Braddac, Tim Redstone, and Dan Isu. There is no one by the name of Mihai Carnea and no Sudani on the record. Ryan realized that the suspect had taken the letters of his first name to create a new alias. He contacted the border patrol police in Detroit, Port Huron, and Sault St. Marie and put them on alert to be on the lookout for Middle Eastern man by the name of Dan Isu.

It would be difficult to locate Sudani now. He had probably already changed the license plate of the rental car. If he tried to go to Detroit, he would likely take I-69 East. Or he could head north along Highway 27. An alternate route would be to take I-69 East to Flint and then take I-75 North to Canada. The best strategy seemed to be to wait at the borders and to guard the airports closely. Ryan and his team considered all these possibilities and deliberated at length about how to split up and travel to the various border crossings.

Then Niloa complicated the matter even more by interjecting, "What if this guy doesn't intend to cross into Canada by car?"

"We'll get him at the airport then," one of Joshua's men replied.

"What if he doesn't leave by either car or plane? What if he plans to leave Michigan by boat?" Niloa asked.

Everyone froze in silence for half a minute. They all realized it would be very difficult to stop Sudani by boat. There were too many miles of Lake Huron and Lake Superior to monitor.

"Didn't you say, Niloa, he might have been nicknamed 'the captain?'" Ryan asked.

"Perhaps that refers to 'boat captain.' If he escapes by boat it would brilliant."

"That's what I'd do," Niloa added. "Remember that the attack on Farallon de Medinilla was by boat."

"And Sudani likely came in by boat through Canada," Ryan noted.

"Mr. Dan," Niloa suggested, "we should try to call up the major boat harbors along the coastline to see what boats are going out tonight and tomorrow."

Ryan and his team raced to the Lansing police station to organize a phone blitz to alert the major boat harbors. Ryan also contacted the U.S. Coast Guard after discussing the situation with Colonel Siefer. Siefer agreed that an escape by boat would be the most difficult escape to stop.

Ryan was able to acquire a list of all boat harbors and corresponding office numbers from the Michigan Department of Natural Resources. He then asked for a large map of the state from the police department. The Director for Homeland Security gave Ryan jurisdiction over the local city and county police forces in Michigan to lead Michigan's city and state police forces during this crisis.

"Niloa," Ryan asked, looking out over the map with this team, "If you were Sudani and planned to escape to Canada by boat, where would you leave from?"

Niloa studied the map carefully. She then answered, "I would leave somewhere along the coast from Alpena to Cheboygan along the northeastern shore. Or, I would cross the Mackinaw Bridge and leave from somewhere near Drummond Island or west of Sault St. Marie near Whitefish Point. That would take much longer though."

Ryan agreed. The Canadian border was not far from the northeastern shore of Michigan and only about 10 miles from Whitefish Point and just off of Drummond Island. After 30 minutes on the telephones, Ryan and his team had put every major harbor on alert from Bay City to Sault St. Marie on the eastern shores, and then continuing west to Whitefish Point on the northern peninsula. They also called some of the major harbors from Mackinaw City south to Traverse City and then up to Northport on Lake Michigan.

At 1:30 a.m. a call came from George Chesterfield, a harbormaster in Rogers City. Ryan took the call. Chesterfield indicated that three days ago a man had arranged to lease a boat for the day. He planned to pick up the boat at 5:00 that morning for a fishing expedition.

Chesterfield arranged for the man to pick up the boat keys from him at the harbor.

"The thing that seemed unusual, Deputy Ryan, is that the man didn't sound like a fisherman. He did send me the money in advance by Federal Express, including a $5,000 security deposit for the boat."

"Anything else you remember?" Ryan asked.

"He had a foreign accent, "Chesterfield answered." But he sounded more European. He didn't sound like he could be one of those terrorists you are looking for, but Sheriff Meehan thought you ought to know."

"Do you know when he is arriving in town?" Ryan asked.

"No, he didn't say when he was getting here. I'm assuming he arrived earlier tonight. The harbor office opens at 5:00 a.m." Chesterfield replied.

Chesterfield gave Ryan directions to a local hotel where the man could be staying and directions to the boat harbor. Chesterfield agreed not to give the man his boat if they were not there by 5:00 a.m., but to delay him somehow without raising suspicion.

"We should be there by 4:00 to 4:30 a.m.," Ryan assured him.

Ryan and Niloa arrived in Rogers City at 4:30 a.m. It took them 10 minuets to find the boat harbor. Two other cars carried Joshua and his team. One group went to the hotel to find that a man had already checked out. They all met at the harbor Ryan and Niloa pulled in the parking lot first. Only a few cars were parked there. One was a white Buick; the plates did not match the car rented from Avis in Lansing, but the description of the rental did.

Sudani was already out of the car, walking around the shore looking at the various boats in the bay.

Ryan and Niloa walked up to Sudani with fishing poles and tackle boxes they had borrowed from the sheriff.

"Good morning," Niloa said to Sudani. "Going fishing?"

"Yes," he replied, "I hope to get an early start."

"We're fishing, too," Niloa replied. "We plan to catch a big one."

That was the sign Niloa, Deputy Ryan, and Joshua's team had agreed on if she confirmed that the man was Sudani. Niloa was wearing a hidden microphone that was being monitored by Ryan.

Ryan pulled out his weapon.

"You're under arrest for conspiracy to commit murder. Place your hands into the air and kneel down on the ground."

Sudani closed his eyes. He expected to be executed. He didn't understand U.S. law, that there actually would be a trial and chance to defend himself. The bullet never came.

He opened his eyes and looked at Niloa closely. He recognized her face but could not remember where he first met her. He then realized she had been on the cart and reminded him of one of the women hostages in Syria that he had seen and traveled with into Lebanon.

"Sudani," Niloa said to him. "You can relax now. Your journey is over."

Sudani saw Joshua's men surround him with automatic weapons in their hands. He knew it was futile to resist, and unlike his comrades, he had no intention of killing himself. He had hidden away much money and could still help his family while in prison.

"And what about you?" Sudani asked Niloa. "Was that you on the airport cart?"

"Yeh, that was me?"

"And we met somewhere else, didn't we?"

"It wasn't exactly a meeting," Niloa responded. "Our paths crossed in Syria, but I was blind-folded at the time. Too bad, I heard it's a beautiful country."

Sudani was astounded. Indeed, he was now caught by one of the women that he had ordered held for ransom.

"What are you going to do now?" Sudani asked.

"I'm going sailing, Captain," Niloa replied. "In some nice warm weather."

I just have one more friend to visit, she thought.

CHAPTER 27
Downers Grove, Illinois

Deputy Ryan and Niloa pulled up to a two-story brick home in Downers Grove, exhausted from their trip.

"Thanks so much, Mr. Dan, for letting me stay with you," she whispered, still half asleep. They had talked all the way from Roger's City back to Chicago.

"Niloa, we wouldn't have caught him without you."

Niloa did not even remember arriving at Ryan's home and retiring to the guest bedroom. Completely exhausted, she fell asleep, never really comprehending the truth of what Ryan had said. She had been too busy trying to do a good job and had no time to think about the critical role she'd filled and the many lives she had saved.

The next morning Niloa arose and looked out the second story bedroom window. Joshua was chopping wood in the back yard. Light snow was falling. It appeared that Joshua had completely recovered from his toxic poisoning. Niloa watched him for a while. She then put on some jeans and a wool shirt and opened the bedroom window and storm window. With a loud voice, she yelled, "I see you're back to your old self."

Joshua looked up and said with a smile, "Hey, I'm not that old. I can still chop wood with a dull ax."

Ten minutes later Niloa was outside in the snow with him.

"Care for a horseback ride?" Joshua asked.

"You've got horses?" Niloa asked with great excitement.

"No, my neighbor does. And he'll let us ride."

Twenty minutes later Joshua and Niloa were riding horses in a grove of pine trees amidst a moderate snowfall. It was so quiet and beautiful. Joshua did his best to hide his passionate desire for Niloa. She was the kind of woman he could give his life to and share his life with.

They came to a low hanging tree branch and stopped the horses. Joshua dismounted first and then helped Niloa off so they could walk their horses through the trees.

Joshua kept his hands on Niloa's sides as she put her feet on the ground. She slowly turned around and looked Joshua in his eyes, placing her hands on his shoulders. He leaned forward and kissed Niloa for the first time. She then grabbed his sides and pulled Joshua on top of her as they both fell into the powdery snow. They kissed again, this time for a much longer time. Joshua rolled over on his back in the snow and pulled Niloa on top of him. They continued to kiss passionately. Then Niloa sat up and said, "I never knew you felt that way about me, Joshua."

"I thought you and Stephano were getting engaged," Joshua said. "Remember, I'd been burned once already."

"I know," Niloa said. "Your father told me about it."

"No, I told you about it in Firenze."

"Yeah, but your dad told me about the emotional scar—why you keep yourself emotionally distant."

"Joshua," Niloa continued, "I really do love Stephano. We have a very close friendship. He cares for me a great deal. We did consider getting married, but we each decided to think about it carefully. He went home and did that, and then wrote me a nine-page letter. My parents sent it to me last week. Stephano realized that his future was in the Philippines, not in the U.S. He has a great vision for helping his community and others in Mindanao. He could not in good conscience commit his life to me. We have different callings in life."

"And what is your calling, Niloa?" Joshua asked.

"I want to make a difference in the world," Niloa said. "I want to help people, but I want to do it in more than one place. I want to help many people."

"And are you willing, Niloa, to follow a man around the world moving from place to place every three to four years?"

"It depends on who that man is," Niloa replied. "He must be able to keep up with me!"

Throwing some snow in Joshua's face, she leaped off of Joshua, jumped on her horse, and started riding at a gallop. Joshua caught up to her quickly.

"I can keep up," Joshua said confidently.

"Then the answer is yes?" Niloa said with a smile.

Niloa and Joshua returned from their ride. Ryan was standing on the front porch waiting for them. He had seen them horseback riding and guessed what might be happening.

When they got out of Joshua's pickup truck, they were both soaked and still had some unmelted snow on their clothing.

"I hope you didn't fall too hard," he said chuckling as he looked at Joshua, who understood the not so subtle pun. "Your mother has cooked up a great breakfast."

Niloa greatly enjoyed waffles, fresh fruit, scrambled eggs and blueberry muffins. "You're making me homesick, Mrs. Ryan. You cook as well as my mom, and she is a fabulous cook." "Niloa, you are welcome in my house anytime!" Becky Ryan replied, "And please call me Becky."

"Mom," Joshua said, "We definitely need to invite Niloa back. But personally, I wish she never had to leave."

"Well congratulations, Niloa, that's the first time I've heard Joshua give a compliment like that. I take it you two have developed a close friendship. Is there something else I should know?"

"Just that I need to meet Niloa's parents," Joshua said.

"I very much enjoyed meeting your parents," Ryan said.

"I think we should all take a trip to Oahu," Niloa said. "How about in late December? It's a beautiful time in Hawaii."

"Especially if you live in Chicago," Ryan added.

Becky rose from the table and gave Niloa a big warm embrace.

"Niloa, I have a big surprise for you," Ryan said with a twinkle in his eye. "I received a call from Colonel Siefer early this morning. You know the President authorized up to a maximum five million dollar award for citizens who provided information leading the arrest of Sudani, Raja, and Mansur."

"I really didn't know much about that," Niloa replied.

"As law enforcement, our job was to catch these terrorists. But you are just an ordinary citizen. There were many people who helped catch these men, but you played a big role. It turns out Mansur Shukarian is actually Imad Sahadi, the vicious terrorist who has been on our most wanted list since he orchestrated the 1983 attacks on the U.S. embassy and U.S. Marine barracks in Beirut. Because you played a big role, the President has authorized a $2.5 million dollar award to be given to you, Niloa — $1.5 million for Sahadi and half a million dollars for each of the other two."

Niloa sat there in shock. She could not comprehend what she had just heard. That was more than 50 times the most amount of money she had ever won in a yachting race. Although she had never imagined she would one day have that much money, she knew exactly what she wanted to do.

The Stephensons and the Ryans stood along the railing and waved good-bye as Joshua and Niloa sailed out of the Waimea Boat Club in the *Dawn Treader III*.

"Are we crazy letting them sail to the Solomon Islands for their honeymoon?" Becky asked Niloa's parents and her husband Dan.

Chris and Nanci looked at each other and laughed. Dan and Becky then started laughing too.

"I think we'll be asking that same question again," Dan said.

Joshua and Niloa put the sails up and turned the *Dawn Treader III* on a south- westerly course. He then opened a bottle of champagne, poured two classes, and proposed a toast.

"To a peaceful romantic voyage to the Solomon's with the most beautiful sailor in the world."

Then Niloa added," And to no storms, no sharks, no terrorists, no pirates and no diversions!"

"Amen," Joshua replied.

"One more toast," Niloa said. "To our friends Paulo and Stephano, to Paulo's quick recovery and to Stephano's foundation to help orphans."

"And to each orphanage they establish with your generous gift," Joshua added.

They then gently brought their glasses together, drank their champagne, and kissed each other warmly.

"I'm so proud of you, Niloa, giving that million dollars to Stephano to build a foundation to fund orphanages and educational programs for orphans in Mindanao."

"I told you I wanted to make a difference," Niloa replied. "It also gave me great joy to give Paulo the *Dawn Treader II*. We need to go to visit them soon."

"Maybe after our honeymoon," Joshua replied. "The military has given me two whole months off."

"I'm sure we'll find lots to do," Niloa said, smiling at Joshua.

"I'll toast to that, too," he replied.

Joshua and Niloa tipped their glasses one more time. They then watched a beautiful Hawaiian sunset unfold as they sailed for the Solomon Islands.

THE END

Printed in the United States
34697LVS00003B/403-417